# DEEP DESIRE

Libby gave a half sob, half laugh and wrapped her arms around Gabe's neck, bringing her lips up hungrily to meet his. They stood there together, not moving, arms wrapped tightly around each other, lips locked together, for what seemed like an eternity. Then, reluctantly, they broke apart.

"That kiss will certainly last me a lifetime, Mrs. Hugh Grenville," Gabe said shakily.

That night Libby lay awake, looking up at the stars through the filigree of leaves and branches. Her body ached with longing. To be kissed and held in such strong arms, to be desired so intensely, was almost more than she could bear.

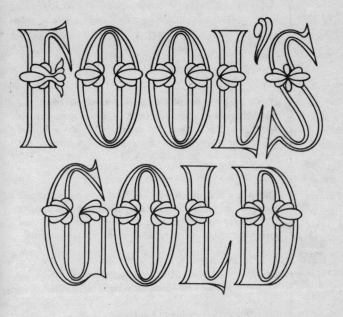

# FOOL'S GOLD

# Janet Quin-Harkin

HarperPaperbacks
*A Division of HarperCollinsPublishers*

This is a work of fiction. The characters, incidents, and dialogues are products of the author's imagination and are not to be construed as real. Any resemblance to actual events or persons, living or dead, is entirely coincidental.

HarperPaperbacks    *A Division of* HarperCollins*Publishers*
10 East 53rd Street, New York, N.Y. 10022

Cover illustration by Diane Sivavec

First printing: June 1991

Printed in the United States of America

HarperPaperbacks and colophon are trademarks of
HarperCollins*Publishers*

10  9  8  7  6  5  4  3  2  1

## CHAPTER
# 1

ON THURSDAY, 18TH April, 1849, Hugh Grenville ran away from home. Put like that it sounds more the act of a little boy than a husband, but those were the words Libby Grenville wrote in her diary that evening: *Today Hugh ran away.*

Libby had known as soon as the letter arrived that something was wrong. She had been sitting at her vanity mirror, in her third-floor bedroom at her parents' Boston brownstone, trying to coax a stubborn curl around her finger when she saw her husband come into the room with a letter in his hand. In her mirror she watched him glance at the writing on the envelope, tear it open, read it silently, grimace, and then stuff it hurriedly into his pocket.

"Who's it from?" she asked.

"It doesn't matter," Hugh said, glancing toward the half-open door. "It's not important."

"It obviously is," Libby insisted. "A mistress you don't want me to know about?"

"Hardly," Hugh said, flushing again as Libby

1

laughed. "It's from my brother if you really must know."

"In England?"

"In England."

"But you never hear from your family in England."

"I just have," Hugh said.

"And?"

"I'll tell you about it later, Libby."

"You're being annoying!" Libby said, getting up and coming over to him. "Why can't you tell me?"

"Because one can never finish a sentence in this house without . . ."

"Cooee, children!" Libby's mother's voice floated up the stairs ahead of her heavy footsteps.

Hugh looked at Libby triumphantly. "See, what did I tell you?" he whispered. "She missed her calling. She'd have been the best news hound in Boston if she'd gone to work for the *Globe*."

"Hugh!" Libby warned, putting her finger to her lips as the feet reached the doorway.

"Are you there, children?" the high voice called and Libby's mother, Harriet Parsons, came in without waiting for an answer. Earlier in life she might have looked like Libby. She still had the same delicate cream complexion and traces of the same stunning red in her graying hair, but she had become chubby with years of too much sitting and too many cream cakes and she held onto the doorframe, gasping for breath.

"Since you saw us go up after breakfast and the only exit is down the fire escape, you must have known the answer," Hugh said with a grin at Libby.

Libby's mother looked around the room, as if checking whether any piece of furniture had been moved during the night, then focussed her gaze on Hugh and Libby. "Oh look at you, you're not even ready," she said in exasperation.

"For what?" Hugh asked.

"I reminded you at dinner last night that we were to be lunching with the Robertsons. I've already sent for the carriage and you don't have your bonnet on, Libby."

"Oh, tragedy. Libby Grenville has been spotted running around bonnetless!" Hugh exclaimed dramatically. Libby gave him a warning look. "Just coming, Mother," she said.

"If you'll excuse me, Mother Parsons, I think I'll pass up the Robertsons," Hugh said. "I'm not in the mood for festive gatherings."

"Katherine Robertson will be devastated." Libby looked up at him with a grin as she tied her bonnet over her auburn curls, then followed her mother out the door, the letter already forgotten.

"I do wish you could do something about Hugh," Libby's mother commented as the carriage set off, clattering over the cobblestones. "He can't just keep turning down invitations like this. And the Robertsons too. So useful, seeing that Mr. Robertson's cousin runs that magazine . . . what's it called?"

"Mother, it's a penny dreadful. You're not suggesting Hugh could write for that?"

"At least it pays good money," Mrs. Parsons said, smoothing her dress over her large stomach. "I wouldn't have thought Hugh wanted to depend on us forever."

"He doesn't," Libby said, frowning out at the dark Boston buildings, "but he's a poet, not a hack writer. Poets often take time to become well-known."

"Then maybe the time has come for him to think of some other form of employment as well, as your father suggested. Your father has come up with some excellent suggestions and, of course, he has many connections in the business world. . . ."

"Mother, can you see Hugh in the business world?" Libby exclaimed, half laughing. "He'd forget which office he worked in, or he'd see a rainbow and stare at it for hours while the work piled up on his desk. He wasn't made for business, Mother. He's not like Father and he never will be."

"That has become painfully obvious, I'm afraid. Your father despairs of him."

"If I remember correctly, Father was pretty impressed with him at the beginning, just like the rest of us."

"Everyone said in those days that he showed promise," Mrs. Parsons snapped. "How were we to know? Your father doesn't know one end of a sonnet from another."

"Maybe he'd still show promise if he had a little more freedom," Libby said. "It's not easy living in another person's house, you know."

"If you didn't live with us, you'd starve," Mrs. Parsons said shortly. "I don't need to remind you of that, do I?"

"You remind me of it constantly, Mother," Libby said angrily. She stared out across the park, her face turned away from her mother's.

"Libby, darling child, I didn't mean to upset you," Mrs. Parsons placed her pudgy hand over her daughter's. "I just want my little girl to be happy!"

"I'm happy enough, Mother," Libby said, taking her hand away, "or I would be if you'd realize that

I'm twenty-five years old and I'm not your little girl anymore."

"Don't be angry with me, Libby," her mother said, putting her lace handkerchief up to her face as if she were about to start crying. "It's only because you mean more than the whole world to us that we want the best for you. We want to see you successfully set up in your own household with a good future for our grandchildren, but it doesn't seem that Hugh's even trying. . . ."

"I know, Mother," Libby said, patting her mother's hand idly. "But it's hard for him. It will all work out, I expect. He realizes he can't go on trying to succeed as a poet forever."

The tall brownstones were left behind as the carriage moved towards a more spacious part of town where brick mansions stood back from the streets among manicured gardens. Libby's mother sighed again. "If only you'd married Roger Kemp instead. He worshipped you, you know, and now look where he is." She waved at one of the mansions. "Or Edward Knotts. The Knotts are so proud of him. His law practice is really thriving, they say."

"They were both boring, Mother," Libby said.

"You always were so stubborn, Libby. You always thought you knew best. Remember what Miss Danford used to say about you?"

"She said I'd come to a bad end," Libby said with a laugh. Miss Danford had been her first governess, very strict and humorless. She had been hired to shape Libby into a future queen of Boston society. Libby had refused to be shaped. In the battle of wills that had lasted two years, Libby emerged the winner and Miss Danford left, a broken woman.

Libby smiled to herself at the memory of Miss Danford, peering at her through pince-nez and wagging a finger. "Mark my words young woman, you'll come to a bad end," she said. On that occasion Libby had insisted on crossing a stream via a dead branch. The branch had tipped Libby into the swift current and she had to be dragged to safety.

"And you still haven't learned, have you?" her mother asked sadly.

"I don't suppose I ever will, Mother," Libby said.

The carriage turned into a gravel driveway and soon everyone was embracing on the terrace.

"Libby, I must say you're looking wonderful," Mrs. Robertson gushed. "So youthful. One would never imagine you were a mother of two little girls. I know Katherine envies your figure. She's had such a hard time getting hers back after Oswald was born."

Libby grinned to herself. "Poor dear Katherine," she said.

Mrs. Robertson took her arm and steered her through to the conservatory where lunch tables had been set up amid the plants.

"Of course, Oswald was such a big baby," she went on. "Over ten pounds they say. Katherine and Roger are so delighted to have a son. I expect Hugh would like your next one to be a boy, since he has such an aristocratic English name to carry on. Where is dear Hugh?"

"He's working on a new poem. He sends his apologies," Libby's mother said quickly.

"So creative," Mrs. Robertson said. "You must tell us where we can buy his poems. I'd love to impress my guests by showing them that I actually know a living poet. Everyone seems to think they are all dead."

Libby laughed dutifully, but she looked around the room, feeling trapped by Mrs. Robertson's clawlike hand on her arm. How was it that Hugh always managed to get out of these boring things and she was stuck with them? she wondered resentfully. Because she felt it was her duty to go, and because it was better than staying home.

She glanced out through the long windows to the smooth green lawns beyond. This can't be all there is to life, she thought. There has to be more. This is all so petty, so boring.

Katherine entered at that moment, carrying baby Oswald, who was duly admired and cooed over.

"Where's Hugh?" she asked as Libby kissed somewhere near her cheek.

"Working," Libby said. "He sends apologies."

Katherine handed over the baby to an elderly aunt and slipped her arm through Libby's. "Let's take a stroll through the gardens before lunch, shall we?" she asked. "We hardly get to see each other these days with all these domestic things to worry about. It's hard to remember how carefree we used to be."

Libby allowed herself to be led, out through the French doors and down the neat flagstone path between beds of spring flowers. Lilacs were blooming and horse-chestnut candles decorated the big shade trees, wafting sweet scents across the garden. It was very pleasant and civilized. Libby smiled at Katherine. It always used to amuse her that both sets of parents assumed they were best friends. They had never been; they had been best rivals at best, best archenemies at worst, but in the polite society they moved in, their duels always had to be carefully veiled as conversations.

"Look at you with your tiny little waist," Katherine said. "I'm having such a time getting my figure back after Oswald. Of course, he was such a big baby. I can't wait to get pregnant again, can you? At least then one has a perfect excuse for not wearing those horrid corsets."

"I'd rather wear corsets," Libby said. "I was horribly sick last time."

"But that was four years ago now, Libby," Katherine said in horror. "I don't know how you manage to avoid it for so long."

"Hugh says he doesn't want me old before my time with childbearing," Libby said. "He says we are not animals."

"Then Roger must be an animal," Katherine said with a laugh. "He couldn't wait to get his hands on me again after Oswald. But then I expect poets are different. Hugh always did have that distant quality about him—like something out of a book. I know he'll be devastated to have missed me," she added. "He was longing to see Oswald."

"I'm sure he was," Libby said, trying not to smile. She still felt a sense of triumph when she remembered how much Katherine had wanted Hugh. Katherine's family had brought Hugh to a literary evening at Libby's home, Libby's father going through a phase for culture at the time.

"Here's a brilliant young poet, newly arrived from England," Katherine's father had announced. Libby had been entranced. Hugh's manners had been perfect as he bowed and kissed her hand. When he read some of his works his voice was so smooth and rich and elegant that she wanted to go on listening all night. She watched him, his mop of boyish dark curls falling across his forehead as he read from the paper, his eyes dark and haunted, and decided then and there that he was the man she was going to marry. The fact that Katherine was also in love with him helped her to make that decision. She was just seventeen and sure that she knew everything there was to know about life.

Now, eight years and two children later, she hated to admit to herself that she had been wrong. She suspected that Hugh would never be another Longfellow. He was more dreamer than poet, a charming little boy who would probably never grow up, unworldly and very endearing. It was hard to be angry with Hugh when he acted irresponsibly.

"But Libby," he'd say, his large dark eyes looking at her like a spaniel puppy she'd once owned, "green is so absolutely your color. It makes that red hair of yours into a crowning glory. I just had to buy this shawl for you."

It didn't matter to him that they didn't have the money for a cashmere shawl. He left Libby with two choices, to take the shawl back without his knowledge or to grovel to her parents for more money. This she hated doing. She had inherited not only her father's strong will, but also his pride.

As they came back into the house she heard her mother talking to Mrs. Robertson. "The poor child. Of course we do all we can," she heard her saying and was surprised to realize that she was talking about her. "But you know what she's like. She'd never listen, would she? Her father tries to advise her."

He never stops, Libby thought ruefully.

"Listen to your father," was her mother's favorite saying. This was not hard to do, because her father loved to lecture and instruct on almost any topic from the correct nutrition of little children to the correct way to wear a bonnet. Libby's mother, who adored her husband and thought he was the wisest man in the world, was prepared to listen for hours. Libby was not born with her mother's docile and submissive nature and often had to leave the room rather than explode with anger.

Mrs. Robertson summoned them all to table and Libby found herself seated between Katherine Robertson, now Kemp, and Colonel Hardwick, her mouth giving polite answers while her thoughts strayed. They were talking about handwriting when she remembered the letter. Why hadn't Hugh wanted to share it with her? In all their eight years together, she could not remember his receiving any communication from his family. He had stormed out after an argument, so he told her, and broken off all ties with them. Libby kicked off her tight shoes under the table and wriggled her toes in impatience.

The luncheon party stretched on to late afternoon and when they arrived home, she found that Hugh had gone out for a walk. So it was not until they were in their own bedroom, preparing for the night, that she was able to tackle him about it.

"So what was in the letter?" she asked. "Bad news?"

"On the contrary. Good. My father has just died."

"That's bad, surely."

"I loathed my father. He loathed me. His last words to me as I left for America were to come back a man or not come back at all. I wasn't his sort of man, you see. I didn't like killing small animals for sport or any of the other things English gentlemen are supposed to like." He laughed, a light, brittle laugh.

There was a silence while Libby waited for him to say more. Through the closed door she could hear the grandfather clock in the hallway outside, its deep *tick tock* like the heartbeat of the house.

"But he forgave you on his deathbed?" Libby asked when she could stand the silence no longer.

"Not that I know of," Hugh said. "I expect he died thinking I was a hopeless failure."

"So what was the good news?" Libby demanded, her patience exhausted.

"My brother William has inherited," Hugh said evenly. "He feels badly about the way I've been treated. He wants to make amends. He's offering me a property. . . ."

"A property? What sort of property?"

"Quite an attractive property," Hugh said. "Crockham Hall in Wiltshire. A nice, large, elegant house. The kind English gentlemen live in and Americans copy. You'd like it."

"But that's wonderful," Libby burst out. "A big house of our own, away from my parents. Peace and quiet for you to write your poetry in the country. Hugh, isn't that what you've wanted? Aren't you happy? If it had been me, I'd have been bouncing up and down on the bedsprings like a little child with joy."

"I dare say," Hugh said dryly.

"But don't you want to go home? I thought you'd dreamed of it."

"But not like this," Hugh said with a sigh. "How can I go home like this, Libby? A total failure, completely dependent on my father-in-law for my bread and butter and a roof over my head."

"Father knows that poets don't become famous

overnight. He understands that," Libby said. "All great literary figures had patrons, even Shakespeare."

"Yes, but they did manage to publish a few pieces occasionally to prove that they weren't taking their food under false pretenses," Hugh said hopelessly. "What do I have to show for my entire time in America, except for a couple of minor verses in very minor magazines?"

"You have me and the children," Libby said. "I should say we are accomplishments of the highest order."

She had thought Hugh would laugh at this, or ruffle her hair and tell her that he prized her above gold, but he turned his face away from her, staring at the bedroom wall. "One goes to America to make one's fortune, Libby," he said. "If I return home with nothing, how can I ever hold up my head? They'll whisper about me, saying there goes the man who would have let his wife and children starve if it hadn't been for his father-in-law."

"You've done your best, Hugh," Libby said quietly. "You weren't meant for an ordinary job, I understood that. And one day you'll show them all. You'll write the great poem you have inside you and they'll all claim that they never doubted you for a moment."

"Sometimes I wonder," Hugh said quietly. "Sometimes I wonder if I am deceiving myself. Maybe I'm not the great creative genius that I've always thought myself to be. But I do know one thing. I'm not going crawling back to my brother's charity."

"So you're turning down his offer?" Libby demanded. "Our one chance for a home of our own and you're turning it down?"

"Don't raise your voice, Libby," Hugh warned, putting his finger to his lips. "We don't want them to hear this, do we?"

Libby sighed and sank back against the pillows.

"I'm not going home a pauper," Hugh said. "If I could think of any way that I could face my brother as an equal, with my head held high, then I would take us on the first boat out of here. But I can't, short of writing another *Paradise Lost* overnight."

"But Hugh," Libby began.

"I really don't wish to discuss this any further," Hugh said and rolled over, away from her.

Libby lay awake staring at the pattern of shadow branches on the ceiling, dancing in the night wind. How differently it had all turned out from the way she thought it would.

She turned over cautiously in bed and looked at Hugh, who was giving a good imitation of being asleep. His breath was slow and rhythmic and one long, white hand was draped over the coverlet.

Oh, Hugh, she thought, what am I going to do with you? and then, surprising even herself, how much longer can this go on?

She slid across to him and wrapped her arm over his body. The fact that he did not stir convinced her that he was either sound asleep or wanted her to think that he was. He was very good at pretending to be asleep. Libby remembered her conversation with Katherine that day. She had not told Katherine the truth. Hugh's concern for her youthful figure veiled his lack of enthusiasm for the act of making love. After Eden, their first child, was born, he confessed that he was "more a creature of the spirit than of the flesh." Libby, unfortunately, discovered that she was very much a creature of the flesh. Night after night she would lie awake yearning for fulfillment as he slept beside her.

Libby tightened her arm around him and moved her body closer but got no reaction. He probably was asleep, she thought. Hugh had a remarkable ability for shutting out anything unpleasant. They could have an argument, be faced with creditors or a sick child and two minutes later Hugh would be sleeping while Libby lay awake worrying for both of them. One of us has to be the realist, she knew, although for once it seemed that their roles were reversed. She was the one eager to take their chance at a new life and Hugh was the one suddenly squeamish about their financial failure. She had not realized before how much the break with his family had wounded him.

Our own country house, she thought wistfully. It would be square and gray with a fireplace big enough to roast an ox and there would be a long dining table where they would entertain, good company, laughter, drinking toasts in the firelight. Libby smiled to herself at such an impractical dream as she drifted off to sleep.

When she woke in the morning, Hugh had gone.

# CHAPTER 2

AT FIRST LIBBY was not too worried by Hugh's disappearance. She suspected that he wanted to get away to think. He had done this before, wandering for hours along the Charles River when he was grappling with a poem that would not come to him or when her father had just given him another of his make-something-of-yourself lectures. She made an excuse for him at breakfast and lunch. When he had not appeared by the time the sun was setting, she began to feel concerned and instinctively checked his closet. Some of his clothes were gone—not enough to suggest that he had left for good, but enough for more than a night or two.

"Where's Papa?" seven-year-old Eden asked as Libby went to kiss the girls good night.

"He'll be back shortly," Libby said, tucking in the covers tightly the way Eden liked them.

"I don't want to go to sleep until Papa kisses me," four-year-old Bliss declared. She was headstrong like Libby and used to getting her own way. "I shall stay

15

awake all night until he comes."

"Don't be silly," Libby said shortly. "Papa might not be back for a few days. His business might keep him away from home for a while. You don't want to stay awake for a week, do you?"

"I don't mind," Bliss said. "I like staying awake."

"Where's he gone, Mama?" Eden demanded. "He didn't say goodbye. He always says goodbye when he is going away. I hope nothing bad has happened to him."

"Nothing bad has happened. Go to sleep," Libby said, patting her hand firmly. If Bliss had inherited her mother's spirit, then Eden had inherited her tendency to worry. Even at seven the child was developing two frown lines between the eyes. Overheard quarrels about money would make her physically sick and when her little sister had chickenpox, Eden ended up being by far the sicker of the two, having sat by her sister's bedside for three nights.

Libby stood in the doorway, looking down tenderly at the children. She thought them both quite perfect and was amazed that her body could have produced two such miracles. Eden, dark and wide-eyed like her father and Bliss not, thank goodness, red-headed like her mother, but a picture-perfect blond like a china doll. "Don't worry," Libby said. "Everything will be just fine."

She managed to conceal her own worry from her parents as they went in to dinner that night. Her parents entertained often and there was a lively party around the dinner table. The party should have been of twelve, but there was an empty place across from Libby, for which she apologized.

"Hugh might have business to attend to," she mentioned to her father as they waited for the guests to arrive.

"Business? What sort of business?" her father asked skeptically. "He's been here eight years without showing the least modicum of interest in business."

"He's just received news from England," Libby said. "It appears he might have inherited a property."

"A property, where?" her mother asked eagerly.

"We'll know when he comes back," Libby said, "which probably won't be tonight."

"How inconvenient not to have known this earlier," her mother twittered. "Then I could have invited Mr. Bellows to make the numbers even."

"Mr. Bellows is a bore, Mother. We're better off without him," Libby said smoothly.

The party went on late and Libby's mouth felt as if it were fixed into a false smile. Every time she heard footsteps across the marble hallway she looked up, half expecting to see Hugh creeping in. A young lawyer friend of the family, Edward Percival Knotts, was telling her a long and involved story about a Harvard prank he had witnessed. "And then they hitched the dogs to the carriage," he went on, laughing in anticipation, "and away it went. Can you imagine how he felt when he woke up, in full evening dress, in the middle of a cabbage patch?"

Libby smiled politely.

Edward rose to his feet. "Would you care to take a stroll in the garden, Mrs. Grenville? It is uncommonly mild for April and I can smell the jasmine from in here."

Libby could hardly refuse the offered arm. She walked beside Edward down the narrow path between flowering shrubs.

"Now," he said when they were sufficiently far from the house. "Would you like to tell me what's wrong?"

"Wrong?" Libby asked. "What should be wrong?"

Edward smiled. He had a fair, boyish face, even though he now parted his hair severely in the middle, as was befitting a a lawyer. "Libby, I've known you since you whipped me with seaweed on the beach at Cape Cod. I've watched you grow up. Your face is composed, but your eyes give you away. You're as jumpy as a kitten, and you haven't listened to a word I've been saying."

"I'm sorry, Edward. I apologize," Libby said. "I've been poor company tonight."

"Please don't apologize," he said. "I wondered if I could be of help in your dilemma. A worry shared is a worry halved, so they say."

Libby smiled and shook her head. "In this case I don't think . . ." she began.

"It's a marital tiff then, that I should stay well away from," Edward said, smiling.

"There was no tiff, as you put it," Libby said shortly. "It's just that Hugh's. . . ." Her voice trailed off.

"Yes, where is old Hugh, by the way?" he asked.

"I wish I knew," Libby admitted with a sigh. She laid her hand lightly on Edward's arm. "Edward, I am worried about him. He was gone this morning without any message, and he's taken some of his clothes."

Edward raised an eyebrow. "Any indication where he was headed?" he asked. "No, er, other lady in the picture?"

"Nothing like that," Libby said. "He was very despondent last night over a letter from England."

"You think he's gone to England?"

Libby shook her head. "I think not," she said. "His

brother has asked him to come home, but he refused
to consider it at the moment. He talked about his family and how he couldn't face them as a failure. Edward,
I worry that he could have decided to end it all."

Edward patted the hand that still clasped his arm. "I
don't think you have to worry about that," he said. "If
he had wanted to end it all, would he have bothered
to select and pack some clothing?"

"Well, no," Libby said hesitantly, "unless he wanted
us to think he was going away. . . ."

"But he worships you," Edward said grudgingly.
"He would surely have left you a parting note. He
is, after all, an English gentleman. He'd be correct
to the last."

Libby thought this over and nodded. "I believe
you're right. Hugh is always correct, which makes
this so troubling."

"Have courage, my dear," Edward said, still patting
her hand. "It's my belief that Hugh has decided to
do something you would not approve of. He therefore wants to get it finished before he presents it to
you. What it is, I can't surmise, but I'm sure, before
the week's out, that he'll be back on your doorstep,
grinning like a little boy who played truant and is now
back home."

"I hope you're right," Libby said. "Thank you,
Edward. You're a good friend."

She started to walk back toward the house.

"I'll always be here when you need me, Libby.
Remember that," Edward called after her.

No news came for two weeks and each day Libby
half expected to hear that Hugh's body had been
found in the river. She said nothing to her parents but

they both speculated wildly about where he was. Her
mother's main theme was that Hugh had gone back
to England without Libby, where he would probably
claim to be a bachelor and marry the daughter of some
earl or duke. Her father thought that he was probably
engaged in a shady business deal that had gone sour
and didn't dare show his face again in Boston for a
while. Libby was amused by both of these specula-
tions, which she knew to be very unlike Hugh, but
she could come up with no better answer.

   Then on May sixth, she received a letter from him.
Luckily, she was just crossing the hall when the mail
arrived and was able to remove her letter from the
silver tray which the maid was about to carry through
to her parents in the morning room. She ran straight
upstairs with it and shut herself in the bathroom,
which had a solid lock on the door.

   My dearest wife, my dearest children, Hugh had written, Can you ever forgive me for the worry and heart-
ache I have certainly caused you? When you hear what
I am embarked upon, I hope you will find it in your
hearts to forgive and understand. Once I made up my
mind to try my luck I knew that I had to leave without
telling you, as you or your parents, possibly both, would
have certainly tried to dissuade me. And you know my
weakness, Libby. I should probably have allowed myself
to be dissuaded.

   You will no doubt be amazed when you hear that
your good-for-nothing husband has gone to make his
fortune. Libby, I am off to be a Forty-Niner, to make
my fortune in the gold fields of California. You have
not been around the Boston waterfront much of late,
but I can assure you that all the talk there is of great

wealth in California gold, lying at the feet, waiting to be picked up by those who get there first. There was no time to be lost, Libby. I am afraid I took out what little money we had in the bank to buy my ticket to the Wild West, but it will be repaid many times over.

Think about it, my darling girl. Men are making fortunes in weeks, real fortunes of thousands and thousands of dollars. When I return we can take the children to England and live in that house as country gentlefolk should with enough for fine horses and lavish entertaining and ballgowns to make you and my lovely daughters the most talked-of women in England.

So be patient, my darling. I promise I will return as soon as I have made my "pile" as they so crudely put it here. I am at present in Independence, Missouri, which is the setting off point for the great adventure and I fear we have left civilization behind us already. It is a world of men and of crudity. I feel like a fish out of water, but cannot let them see that I am lily-livered, as they would put it. Of course I am afraid, but I am driven by the desire and opportunity to succeed for the first time in my miserable life.

Think of me, my darling. Kiss those adorable pink faces for me and remind them often of their papa. I am consoled by the fact that you will be well looked after by your parents. Many of the men have left their wives to manage farms alone, with precious little cash, so I feel myself fortunate that I do not have that additional worry about your future.

I will try to return in the fall, my knapsack bulging with gold. What a celebration we'll have then, won't we?

Your devoted husband,
    Hugh Grenville.

Libby stood looking at the letter.

"Oh, Hugh, you idiot!" she said out loud, not knowing whether to laugh or cry. "How do you think you can ever survive in the wilds of California!" She gazed up at the black and white tiled walls and the black and white shapes swam in her unfocussed gaze. "We'll have to send someone after him before it's too late. He'll need rescuing by now. He'll probably head out in the wrong direction for California or something." She laughed before she remembered how serious it all was. The question was whom could she send. If she had had brothers or cousins, it would have been the sort of job she could entrust to one of them. But she had no brothers and her only relatives were elderly aunts and uncles. Family friends like Edward Knotts crossed her mind, but she dismissed them instantly. "I can't send someone to bring him home in disgrace, like a little child," she said. "That would be utter humiliation for him. He doesn't deserve that. It's very brave of him to attempt such a crazy undertaking—just the sort of mad, foolish thing he would do. Poor Hugh, he really must have felt desperate."

She felt guilty as if she had been responsible for driving him to this. In a way she was. If she hadn't persuaded him to marry her, he'd never have been stuck here in Boston with two children to support. He wasn't the sort of man who was meant to be tied down.

With a sigh, Libby unlocked the bathroom door and tiptoed across to her own bedroom. The windows were open and lacy curtains were fluttering in a gentle April breeze. The bed was piled high with white lacy quilts and pillows. From the window she could glimpse distant green countryside over the rooftops. Libby had always loved that view, and the way you could see a tiny piece of the Charles River between rooftops, if you leaned right out. Now, as she stood taking in all that was familiar and dear to her, a disturbing thought crept into her mind. Hugh could not possibly survive alone among the rigors and dangers of the Wild West. She could ask nobody to rescue him; therefore she would have to go to him herself.

Having made up her mind, she wasted no time and went downstairs.

Her parents were sitting together in the morning room, her father reading the paper as he usually did after breakfast. Her mother was going through the day's mail, seated on the red velvet chaise by the window, while her husband always sat in the leather armchair by the fireplace, even though there was no fire alight in it. It always amused Libby that they both carried on independent commentaries on what they were reading, to which the other paid no attention. She could hear them as she crossed the entrance hall and pushed open the door.

"Oh, how nice, Sophie's having a new dress made for the ball. Dark green velvet . . ."

"Fools in Washington. Why can't they get their ideas straight? It's no good giving in to these southerners . . ."

"Rather a harsh color with her fair hair, wouldn't you think?"

"Show them who's boss, that's what they should do."

Libby glanced around the room with affection. It was cluttered with furniture, potted plants, draperies, pictures and ornaments according to her mother's taste, but it represented home and security.

She took a deep breath and closed the door behind her.

"I've finally heard from Hugh," she said casually.

Two faces looked up expectantly.

"And?" her father demanded.

"He's gone to California, to join the gold rush," Libby said.

"Damn fool," her father muttered, loud enough for his wife to hear and say, "Language, Henry" in a shocked voice.

Libby's father put down the newspaper he had been reading. "Well, I suppose that's that then. What was I just saying, my dear?" He addressed his wife. "I remarked to you only yesterday that I thought it would all turn out for the best. I'll get onto young Knotts to start dissolution proceedings right away."

Libby looked at him as if he was speaking a foreign language that she didn't understand. "What are you saying, Father?" she asked.

"I'm saying we'll be able to do what I've been itching to do for years. We'll get the marriage dissolved. Desertion—that's good solid legal grounds. Give you a chance to start again while you're still young enough. Plenty of fine young fellows in Boston for you and you've still got your looks and figure."

"I have no intention of getting divorced," Libby interrupted, not knowing whether to be amused or angry. "I married Hugh for better or worse and this just happens to be a temporary worse."

"But dearest child, he could be away for years. You could grow to be an old woman waiting for him. He might never return," her mother said soothingly. "Why take that chance?"

"I quite agree with you, Mama," Libby said. "I have

no intention of waiting around and growing old. A wife's place is with her husband. I came to tell you that I'll be leaving for California to join him as soon as possible."

She thought her father might explode at any moment. His face had turned beet red and his eyes bulged. "Follow him to California? Are you out of your mind, child?"

"I'm not a child, I'm a married woman," Libby said, "and I'm perfectly sane."

"I always knew the fellow was a scoundrel and a weakling," her father blustered, "but I never thought he'd sink low enough to ask you to undertake that worst of journeys. The man has no pride and no conscience."

"He did not ask me, Papa," Libby said. "All he asked of me was forgiveness for leaving me alone. I made up my own mind to join him. I don't think he is the type to survive alone for long on the frontier."

"And you are?" her mother demanded, her voice quivering on the verge of tears. "Do you think that we've brought you up to be a lady, given you the finest education so that you can become a frontier drudge? You can have no conception of what life is like for women out there, none at all."

"Neither do you, Mother so that makes two of us," Libby said.

"Don't be rude to your mother, young woman," her father interrupted.

"Father, I'm not a little girl, so please don't speak to me like one," Libby said. "I've made up my mind and there's nothing you can do to stop me."

"Oh, isn't there? We'll see about that," Mr. Parsons blustered. "It takes money to get to California and I'm holding up any further allowance for you as of now. I doubt your husband left you a bank account healthy enough to pay for such an undertaking."

"And the children," her mother interjected. "How could you think of leaving those little angels for what might be years?"

"I'm not," Libby said. "I'm taking them with me."

"Now you've convinced me that you really have taken leave of your senses," her father shouted. "You're insane. You're no mother taking innocent babes to hardship and suffering."

"You can't be serious about this, Libby," her mother said, getting up and coming to put an arm around her daughter. "She's distraught, Henry. The shock has unhinged her mind. We'll take her to the Cape for the summer. I know the good ocean air will make her strong again."

Libby shook herself free. "I'm perfectly well, thank you, Mother. I know this whole thing has been a shock to you and father, but I want you to understand that I am a grown-up, married woman. I'm no longer your precious little girl who has to be spoon-fed and coddled."

"You're right about that, miss," her father said shortly. "If you go through with this foolish, harebrained scheme, you are no longer our little girl. Leave this house and you can expect no further help from us. Furthermore, do not think that we will sit by and let our grandchildren be taken away. I'm off to consult our lawyers instantly. I'll have you certified as an unfit mother. I'll have you certified as insane if I have to. I might not be able to stop you from going, but you're not taking the children with you."

He stormed out of the room, knocking the fringed lamp on the table beside the door to the carpet.

"Oh dear, now you've upset him," Libby's mother said, rushing to pick up the lamp as if that was the most important thing to do. "But don't worry," she added as she righted it and straightened its fringe. "When he's calmed down we'll be able to talk about it. We'll find a way to get the whole thing straightened out . . . a nice summer at the Cape, as I was saying. That's what we all need."

Libby left her talking as she walked silently from the room. She ran upstairs, all the way up to the third floor, and looked in at the nursery. It was empty. Lace curtains, like those in her own room, were flapping in the breeze. Schoolbooks lay open and there was a doll on the floor, but no sign of the children. Irrational panic overtook Libby. Her father had somehow known what she had in mind and had spirited the children away to a safe place. She knew that this was completely illogical, but nevertheless, she ran down the stairs until she saw Mrs. O'Rourke, the housekeeper, coming out of one of the bedrooms on the floor below.

"Mrs. O'Rourke, do you know where the children might have gone?" Libby asked.

Mrs. O'Rourke looked up the staircase, surprise showing on her round, placid face. "Why, out for their morning walk with their governess, Mrs. Grenville, same as they always do at this time," she said. "Is something wrong?"

"No, nothing, what could be wrong?" Libby said, gaining control of herself. Control was essential at this moment, she decided. She must think everything through carefully, not give herself away:

"Miss Hammersham still takes them to the park, I suppose," she tried to say carelessly as she turned back up the stairs.

"I'm sure she does, Mrs. Grenville," Mrs. O'Rourke said.

Libby nodded. "Oh, and Mrs. O'Rourke," she called after the woman, "please tell my mother that I have a luncheon appointment today. I have a headache and I'm going to rest until it's time to go out."

She turned away, back up the stairs. Her heart was hammering, but she managed to give the impression of a normal conversation with a servant. Glancing around to make sure that the maids were occupied downstairs, she darted into her childrens' bedroom, and started taking articles of clothing from drawers and stuffing them into a leather travel bag. A complete feeling of unreality overtook her. All she wanted to do was get away quickly, before her father could stop her. It was only when the bag was full and she fought to close the clasp that she began to come to her senses again. What am I doing? she asked herself. Can I possibly go through with this?

# CHAPTER

# 3

AROUND MIDNIGHT LIBBY finally admitted that sleep was not going to come. She had lain sweating under her sheet in the small, stifling ship's cabin, her mind racing through all the events of the past days until she heard a nearby church clock chime twelve. Silently, she slipped from her narrow bunk and pulled on her cotton wrap. In the top bunk Bliss moaned in her sleep. "It's all right, darling, Mama's here," Libby whispered, stroking the child's sweating face until she felt the small body relax.

Going over to the shutters she opened them in the hope of letting in more air. But the night air outside was heavy with the smell of the river. The slightest of breezes which came from the unseen land was not cooling but carried with it other odors; rotting vegetation mixed with spicy cooking and the heady, sickly scent of unseen flowers. Mosquitoes whined around her face. Libby sighed and leaned against the window frame, looking out across the black waters of the mighty Mississippi to the few dots of light glimmering on the opposite shore.

It was their first night out of New Orleans on the *Mississippi Belle*. The stern-wheeler had put into a little town before dark because the river was running low and too dangerous to navigate at night. Libby resented being held up like this. Now that she had started on her journey, she felt she had to get on and finish it as soon as possible. The blackness outside the cabin was full of strange noises; the plop and gurgle of the river waters as they flowed past the moored boat, the croak of frogs and the screech of millions of insects along the banks, the whine of the ever-present mosquitoes. Libby brushed back a damp curl from her face and idly slapped at a mosquito.

What am I doing here? she thought. How can I have embarked on such a senseless, dangerous journey?

It had seemed so simple when she rushed from the house in Boston some three weeks earlier. She would take the boat to New Orleans, go upstream to Missouri, then head out with one of the wagon trains to California. There she would find Hugh, help him make a fortune, return to Boston to see her parents' faces, then sail to England triumphant.

How naive I was then, she thought, smiling at her own stupidity.

Those three weeks had made Boston seem a lifetime away. She was already amazed at how little thought she had given to such a huge undertaking. She realized now that if her father had not forbidden her so strongly, she probably would never have left. They could have talked it over like sane people and then hired someone like a private investigator to go after Hugh. It was her father's bluster that had clinched

everything. Her concern that her father would stop
her before she could take the children had made her
rush through a decision which should not have been
taken lightly.

She had not paused for a second as she packed
hastily, pawned all her available jewelry for the pal-
try sum of three hundred and twenty dollars, and
snatched the children from their surprised governess
in the park. She had then taken the first ship sailing
from Boston Harbor. It was only when she unpacked
in the ship's cabin that she had a chance to examine the
items she had packed for such a long journey. Many of
them were unsuitable for travel—white muslins which
creased, and no iron, three pairs of pantaloons for Bliss
and none for Eden, and glaring omissions which would
have to be purchased later with her precious cash. But
all things considered, she was not unhappy as the ship
sailed from Boston and put her out of her father's
grasp. She was still fired with the elation of having
dared to do something so unthinkable and having got
away with it. She almost believed that the hardest part
was behind her.

The first voyage on the *S.S. Venture* had been smooth
and simple. They had sailed with all speed southward,
calling in at Charleston, South Carolina and then at
St. Augustine, Florida before reaching New Orleans.
She had spent her time sitting in the sun on deck
while the children played beside her, had dined at
the captain's table with pleasant southern gentlemen
who had fought to sit next to her and charmed her
with their flattery. By the time she came ashore at
New Orleans, she was convinced that the hardships of
the journey were vastly exaggerated and that the next
stage would be just as smooth sailing as the first.

She had enquired at the dockside and found that a paddle steamer would be sailing up river the next day. Unfortunately, every berth was already taken.

"But if you care to stick around," the pleasant, soft-spoken young clerk informed her, "we might be able to squeeze y'all in a little bitty corner someplace." He smiled encouragingly. "And cabins do open up," he said, still smiling. "There's plenty of travellers who never make it to the boat."

"How come?" Libby asked naively.

The smile did not falter. "They get themselves in fights or they get themselves robbed or they get themselves in card games or they get themselves the cholera," he said. "There's a whole lot of cholera on the river this year. Comes with all these Yankees passing through on their way to the gold."

"I'm sure the Yankees don't bring cholera with them," Libby said indignantly. "Our northern cities are very clean."

"For sure, ma'am," the clerk drawled pleasantly, "but wherever you gets a whole mess of people crowded in one place there's sure enough going to be the cholera there with them."

"I'll be back in the morning, then," Libby said stiffly and left the office.

"Come, children," she said, picking up the bags, which seemed to have increased in weight since she set out. "Hold onto the handles and stay close to me. We're going to find a hotel."

"A hotel, Mama? I never went to a hotel," Bliss sang excitedly.

They set off from the dockside, dodging loaded carts and barrows, taking in the unfamiliar sights and smells of the city. The odor of roasting coffee mingled

with the heady sweet scent of unknown flowers and
less pleasant smells rising from the open ditches and
drains. In the first narrow side street washing hung
from ironwork balconies and a black maid appeared,
yelling down to a black man passing below in a language Libby could not understand. The man looked
up and yelled back, showing big white teeth in a smile.
The maid called something else, then threw down a
bucket of waste water, splashing near Libby as it hit
and ran into the open drain.

"It smells bad here, Mama," Eden commented.

Bliss wrinkled her button of a nose. "It smells disgusting," she said, making Libby laugh.

"I know," she said. "Don't worry, we'll see a hotel
soon. I don't want to go too far from the harbor in
case we lose our chance at a cabin on that boat."

"Will we see Papa soon?" Bliss asked, tugging at the
straps of the carryall.

"Not yet," Libby said. "We must be patient."

"I've been patient a long while," Bliss said, stomping in a puddle.

"Bliss, don't do that, you're making your petticoat
dirty and Mama can't get it washed for you," Eden
scolded.

At a crossroad Libby halted. To her right was a
broad street of elegant homes, a glimpse of an open
square with a statue and gardens in it, reminding her
painfully of Boston and civilization. If only there was
someone she knew in this strange city, someone of
her own social class she could go to with an introduction and spend a comfortable night. But there
wasn't, and she didn't want her parents to find out
where she was.

"This way," she said, steering the children away

from that square, down another narrow street.

"It's going to rain, Mama," Eden said. "I felt a drop on my face."

At that moment there was an ominous rumble of thunder and the skies opened. A solid sheet of rain fell, big fat drops bouncing off the cobbles and thundering on iron porch roofs. Libby dragged the girls under an overhanging balcony. In no time at all the water covered the whole street and the foul-smelling contents of the drains began to overflow to meet the flood water. Remembering what the clerk had said about cholera, Libby looked up and down the street. Two doors down, a small sign advertised Hotel St. Pierre. They ran across to it, getting drenched in the few yard's sprint.

"I'd like a room for the night," Libby told the large, sleepy-eyed woman who appeared when she rang the bell.

"A room? You?" the woman asked.

Libby wondered if the woman maybe didn't understand English well.

"Yes, me, and my little girls. A room. *Une chambre*. You have one?"

The woman shook her head. "I don't know," she said, as if undecided.

"This is a hotel?" Libby demanded, angry now.

"Oh, yes, but not for people like you," the woman said. "They go to the St. Louis."

"I don't have the money for the St. Louis," Libby said shortly, "and my little girls are very wet from this storm. They'll catch cold if I don't get them into dry clothes."

The woman shrugged. "Very well, if you insist," she said in a very French manner. "Follow me, please."

She led the way up the stairs to a little room at the back, looking onto a small courtyard. "I put you out of the way," she said. "It can get a little noisy at night. That will be one dollar."

"I don't suppose you could send up some tea and maybe some bread and butter for the children?" Libby asked.

She saw amusement flicker in the woman's eyes. "Down the street. Dubois Coffee House," she said. She noticed Libby glance out at the rain. "Don't worry. It will stop. This is afternoon rain," she said. She waddled to the door, then thought to look back. "The door locks," she said. "Turn the key."

By the time Libby had changed the girls' clothing and spread the wet things to dry over chairs, the rain had indeed stopped. They went down the stairs without meeting anybody and had soup with crusty bread at the coffeehouse.

Later that evening both girls slept soundly in the big double bed while Libby paced up and down by the window. From the street outside came the sound of shouts and laughter, a piano being played, voices joining in a song. She felt very alone and cut off from life. Carefully locking the door and taking the key with her, she made her way down the stairs. This time she passed two other guests, a man and a young woman, coming up.

To her "Good evening," she got a muffled grunt from the man and a giggle from the girl.

The streets were still wet and littered with debris as Libby picked her way daintily across the puddles. The piano music was spilling out from a lighted room farther down the block and dark figures were going in and out. A lady's voice started singing in French

and soon male voices joined it. Libby was almost level
with the lights when three men turned toward her.

"Hello, *chérie*," one of them said. "Are you free
for a little entertainment?" He leered at her, blowing
drunken breath into her face.

"Certainly not," Libby said in her most haughty
Boston manner.

Another of the men grabbed her arm. "Whats-
amatter, ain't we good enough for you?" he asked
belligerently. "We've got money, good as the next
man. We're just back from three weeks at sea. We'll
show you a good time."

"Get your hand off me," Libby demanded, trying
to shake herself free.

"Don't act so high-class with us," the first man
threatened. "We saw you come out of the St. Pierre.
You're not going to do better than us tonight. We've
just been paid off. Come on, *chérie*, what do you
say?"

He pulled her close to him and tried to plant a kiss
on her cheek. Libby recoiled in horror. The other man
came up from behind and wrapped his arms around
her waist. "I love 'em when they play hard to get," he
said. "Feisty little baggage, ain't she? But we'll knock
the stuffing out of her. Come on, doll, quit fooling
around with us. We haven't got all night."

"Will you let go before I call for help!" Libby
shouted, wriggling desperately as the man lifted her
off the ground with enormous strength. Fear was
beginning to replace her anger. The arms around her
waist were almost crushing her while a big hand felt
upward for her breast. She struggled helplessly, wondering if anyone would even come if she screamed.
Perhaps scenes like this were a normal occurrence in

the back streets of New Orleans and nobody would even care.

"Please," she begged, trying now to appeal to their decency. "Please let me go. I'm not the girl you want. Please, you're hurting me."

"Leave her alone, boys," said a quiet, smooth voice, and an elegantly dressed man stepped from the doorway. "Can't you see you've made a mistake?"

"But she came out of the St. Pierre, I saw her," the first man insisted.

"Take a look at her," the smooth voice continued. "Look at the way she's dressed. She's not one of Yvette's girls. She's a lady. She's not what you're looking for. Go ask Yvette. She's got plenty of them."

Slowly, Libby felt the giant arms loosen around her waist. The men stumbled off, one of them murmuring, "Sorry, ma'am. No offense?"

Libby tried to straighten her dress and turned to face her rescuer. He was tall, made even taller by the black top hat he was wearing. He was dressed in a fashionable tailed jacket and she could see the glint of gold from his watch chain. There was a neat line of moustache on his upper lip but he was otherwise cleanshaven. In his hand he carried a cane topped with either gold or silver that sparkled in the light spilling from the window.

"Thank you very much, sir," she stammered. "You saved me from a very difficult and unpleasant situation. I was just walking past when these men attacked me."

The tall man smiled, bowing slightly. "My pleasure, ma'am," he said. "I'm always glad to be able to help a lady in distress. Although you really were asking for trouble, you know."

"I?" she said. "I certainly did not. I was out for an evening stroll, minding my own business."

She saw a smile spread across his face. "Hardly the place for an evening stroll," he said. "You should have kept to the Rue Royale."

"I'm staying across the street at that hotel," she said. "When I booked the room during the day I had no idea this was a dangerous part of town."

The man's smile was now even broader. "You're staying at the St. Pierre?" he asked.

"Yes," she said, annoyed by the amused eyes on her. "Is something wrong with that?"

"Ma'am, that hotel just happens to be a place that the, er, ladies of the night take their, er, escorts," he said with a chuckling cough.

Libby's face flushed bright scarlet as she digested this. She was very glad of the darkness of the street so that he could not see her embarrassment. "You mean, those men thought I was . . . ?" she asked.

He nodded. "They said they saw you come out of the St. Pierre. What else were they to think?"

Libby's hand flew to her mouth in horror. "My children," she gasped. "I've left them sleeping in that place."

"You have children?" the stranger asked. "You don't look old enough, if you'll pardon the impertinence."

"I have two little girls," Libby said stiffly, "aged four and seven and I'm older than I look."

The man chuckled. "I'd say your children were quite safe," he said. "It's big girls the men are looking for. But if I were you, I'd go back to your room and lock the door before there's any more unpleasantness. I'll escort you, if you'll allow."

"I'd be most grateful, Mr., er?" Libby said.

"Gabriel Foster at your service, ma'am," he said.

"I'm Elizabeth Grenville," she said. "Mrs. Hugh Grenville." He took the hand she offered, bowing slightly over it.

"Well, Mrs. Hugh Grenville," Gabriel Foster said evenly, "if I might be so bold as to make a suggestion, I would recommend that you change your place of abode in the morning for a safer part of town."

"That won't be necessary, thank you, Mr. Foster," she said, "because I intend to leave this place in the morning, heading up the river."

"Ah," he said. "You're sailing on the *Mississippi Belle?*"

"If I can get a cabin," she said. "I hear they are all taken."

"Tell the captain that Gabe Foster says to find you a cabin and I think you'll have no problem," he said, smiling at her.

This time she smiled back. "Why thank you, Mr. Foster. You really seem to be my guardian angel tonight. You must have great influence in this city if even the steamboat captains obey you."

Gabe's smile broadened. "Let us say that there are many doors that are open to Gabriel Foster."

They stopped at the doorway to the hotel. "I would come up with you, but it would not be seemly," he said. "I trust you can make one flight of steps without mishap."

"I'm sure I can, now that I'm aware of the situation," she said. "Thank you once again. I was indeed lucky that there was one true gentleman passing through this part of town."

He took her hand. "Good luck on your journey,

wherever it takes you, Mrs. Hugh Grenville. Or may I presume to say Elizabeth?"

"Thank you for your good wishes, Mr. Foster," she said, "and I'm usually known as Libby."

"Libby," he said as if considering it. "It suits you. Good night, Libby Grenville."

"Good night, Mr. Foster."

"Gabe."

"I hardly think we need to be on first-name terms when we will not be meeting again."

He nodded seriously. "The world is much smaller than you think, Mrs. Hugh Grenville." He raised his hat to her with the slightest of bows and went on his way. Libby turned to watch him go, then made her way cautiously up the stairs, strangely disturbed by the encounter.

The little girls were still sleeping just as she had left them, lying close together like two puppies in a litter. Libby smiled as she looked down on them. Before going to bed she wrote in her diary: *May 28, 1849. Tonight I had an unpleasant encounter and I met a most fascinating man.*

# CHAPTER 4

THE REST OF the night in the dubious hotel passed without incident and in the morning Libby found that there was indeed space for her on the *Mississippi Belle*. As the big stern-wheeler drew away from its berth and started to churn northward against the current of the river, Libby began to relax again, glad to be getting on with the next stage of her journey. She had learned a lesson last night and would know how to be more careful in the future, she decided, watching the traffic along the levee grow smaller and smaller as they pulled into midstream. She felt free and very alive, as if she had woken, like Rip van Winkle, after many years of sleep. For the first time she considered the possibility that her desire to undertake this journey was as much the desire to escape from the restrictive life of her parents as it was to find Hugh.

Eden and Bliss were delighted with the river, first watching the giant wheel thrash through the muddy water and then, when they tired of that, leaning at the railings to watch the countryside slip past, waving to slaves in the cotton fields and delighting when they waved back. The scene was a peaceful one; large trees festooned in spanish moss along the banks, half concealing low white mansions surrounded by magnolias in bloom.

"Look, Mama, the trees are so old they have beards," Bliss shouted delightedly.

"I like those houses, Mama," Eden commented. "I'd like to live in a house like that one day."

"Maybe we will, darling one," Libby said.

"Really?" Eden asked excitedly. "Really truly?"

"When we find Daddy we might all go and live in a big house just as grand as that," Libby said.

"Did you hear that, Bliss?" Eden asked, grabbing her little sister. "Mama says we're all going to live in a big house like that one."

"And I'm going to have my own pony, right Mama?" Bliss asked.

"What a charming family group," said a smooth, deep voice behind them. Libby spun around to see Gabriel Foster leaning against the railing farther down, watching them. "You have very beautiful children, ma'am. Although I see that neither has inherited Mama's delightful red hair."

"Who is that man, Mama?" Bliss demanded.

Libby's cheeks had flushed bright red. For a moment she had thought that she was imagining things and that the man was not her rescuer from the night before. But there was no mistaking the even drawl or the smile.

"But perhaps you don't recognize me in daylight," Gabe Foster went on, seeming to enjoy her confusion. "We met last night in considerably less pleasant circumstances. Gabriel Foster at your service again, ma'am."

"But why didn't you tell me you were also to be a passenger on the ship today?" Libby stammered, fighting to regain her composure.

"I hadn't intended to be, until last night," he said, leaning back against the railing as if to survey her better.

"I sincerely hope you did not decide to take a trip up the river just to act as my guardian angel for a few more days," Libby said, having regained her Bostonian frostiness. "In which case it will be a very wasted journey. I am usually perfectly able to take care of myself and, in any case, I'm going to join my husband."

Instead of embarrassing Gabe Foster, this outburst made him look even more amused. Libby noticed that there were laugh lines around his eyes when he smiled, which he seemed to do most of the time. She found them disturbingly attractive. She also noticed in daylight that there were small streaks of gray at the sides of his dark hair. Maybe in his thirties, she found herself thinking.

"Pray don't concern yourself about my wasted journey, Mrs. Hugh Grenville," Gabe Foster said. "I had been intending to take the trip for some time. Your being a travelling companion was enough to spur me into action."

"But I understood the ship was full."

His smile broadened. "As I said, the captain can always find a corner for Gabe Foster. Would you care to take a stroll around the deck?"

"I'm afraid I can't leave the children," Libby said politely.

"Then they can stroll too," Gabe said. He bent down to them. "Would you young ladies care to take a stroll around the deck?" he asked. "It's the thing done when on board ship."

The two little girls looked at each other and giggled.

"Oh, forgive me," Gabe said seriously. "I forgot that in polite society a lady cannot walk with a gentleman until they have been formally introduced." He held out his hand to Eden. "My name is Foster, ma'am. Gabriel Foster. And yours?"

"Eden Grenville," Eden said.

Gabe looked up enquiringly at Libby. "Eden?" he asked. "Is that a nickname?"

"It's my proper name. My daddy chose it. He's a poet," Eden said, as if that explained everything.

"And I'm Bliss," Bliss said, pushing in front of her sister. "And I'm four years old." She held up four fingers.

"Are you indeed—that old?" Gabe asked. Bliss giggled.

"Well, now that we're over the formalities, what about that stroll?" Gabe asked. He held out a big hand to Bliss, who took it instantly.

The matter having been settled, Libby could hardly refuse to fall into step beside him.

"You have business in St. Louis, Mr. Foster?" Libby asked him.

"Possibly," he answered. "Couldn't we dispense with the Mr. Foster if we're to be companions for at least ten days?"

"I hardly need to remind you that I'm a married woman, Mr. Foster," Libby said. "And since you are not a friend of the family, I think it would be wiser to remain on formal terms."

"How do you know I'm not a friend of the family?" he asked.

"Your business takes you often to Boston?"

"Boston? Know it well," he said. "In fact I could swear that I've seen you before, when I dined at your parents' house and you were a little bitty thing. Great big brick house, it was close to the park, or was it the river, and you had on the prettiest muslin dress, or was it white silk? And a black ribbon in your hair. Remind me what your parents' name is again?"

Libby had to laugh. "Mr. Foster, are you sure you are not Irish? They say in Boston that the Irish have the gift of the blarney and you most certainly share it."

He laughed too. "But I made you laugh, didn't I?" he asked, "and you were looking so serious before, as if you carried a big burden on those young shoulders."

"A journey like this is a serious undertaking, alone and with two such small children," she said. "Every now and then I am overcome with concern for them."

"But you will soon be meeting your husband and all your worries will fade at journey's end?" he asked.

"Not that soon," Libby said.

"He's not going to be waiting on the dock in St. Louis?"

"He's in California, Mr. Foster. I'm taking the children to join him."

"Holy Mother," Gabe Foster mumbled, taken off guard for the first time since they had met. "That's certainly an undertaking for a woman alone. I tip my hat to you, Mrs. Grenville. You are indeed a woman of courage." He solemnly lifted his hat.

"This husband of yours," he went on as they resumed their walk, "He has already made his fortune in gold and is sending for you to share it?"

"I doubt it," Libby said. "He only left a month before me. I'm going because he was not born to be a backwoodsman. I don't think he can survive the rigors of the outdoor life alone."

"He's a lucky man," Gabe said softly. "You must love him very much."

"It's not a question of love. It's a question of duty," Libby said. "A wife's place is with her husband. I married him for better or worse."

"I do not think you would undertake such a journey for duty alone," Gabe said, "not to join an overweight, bad-tempered, middle-aged bully, for example. Therefore I still suggest that it is love that drives you."

"Love, duty, what's the difference?" Libby asked.

He gave her a long, even stare. "If you have known love, I'm surprised you need to ask that question."

"Of course I love my husband," Libby said curtly, "and I am not used to discussing the affairs of my heart with a stranger."

He touched his hat again. "Forgive me. We southern gentlemen are known for our boldness," he said. "The hot climate brings out the passion, so they say."

"Then I beg you to make an effort to restrain it in the presence of a very northern lady," Libby said with a smile, making Gabe throw back his head and laugh loudly.

"Libby Grenville, I think you can match me, wit for wit," he said. "I like that in a woman."

"Mama, I've had enough walking," Bliss interrupted, tugging at her skirts. "And I'm too hot. Can we sit down now?"

Libby bent to scoop her up into her arms. "Of course, darling," she said. "If you'll please excuse us, Mr. Foster."

"Naturally, ma'am," he said with that slight nod of the head he used as a bow. "Might I request the honor of your presence at dinner tonight?"

"I'll . . . consider it," Libby said.

"Please do," he said, looking at her long and hard. "I have all the time in the world, Libby Grenville."

After he had gone, Libby gathered her little girls to her. "Shall we go down to the cabin, children?" she asked. "I could read you a story."

"You could read us a story here on deck," Eden said. "Do you like Mr. Foster, Mama?"

"Do you?" Libby countered.

"He's very handsome," Eden said.

"But not as handsome as Papa," Bliss said loyally.

"Not nearly as handsome as Papa," Libby said, as if trying to convince herself of that fact.

That evening she had almost made up her mind to join Gabe Foster at dinner. She had reasoned with herself that she would attract less attention in the dining room when escorted by a man, than as a woman alone. Having tucked in her little girls for the night, she went out on deck for a stroll, hoping to run into him. The deck was bustling with activity as the passengers made the most of the cool evening breeze that had sprung up. In the twilight she could see a small town up ahead and some passengers stood patiently at the rail, bundles and bags in hand, waiting to disembark. There was much ringing of bells as the pilot brought the craft closer to the bank, and a deep voice called out the soundings. Then ropes were thrown ashore and the ship bumped gently against the dock as she was secured for the night.

Some passengers chose to go ashore and local trades people pushed to come on board. Not wanting to get caught up in the crush, Libby walked around to the other side of the boat and went up to the top deck. As she passed the upstairs saloon, she caught sight of a silk top hat, planted on a chair beside the window. She looked in and saw the back of Gabe Foster's head. He was seated at a table with four men, playing cards. Standing in the shadows, unseen, she watched him shuffle and deal. The cards seemed to fly from his hands with such fluid grace that she was fascinated. Money was put into the middle of the table, cards were turned over.

"Pair of tens," exclaimed a young, freckle-faced man across the table from Gabe.

"Sorry about that, pair of queens," Gabe said and drew the pile of money toward him.

Libby stepped back from the window as if burned. Of course, it all made sense now, the fact that he had been walking through a bad part of town late at night, that he was known to the riverboat captain who always had a cabin available for him. She still could hardly believe what she had just seen. She had seen Gabe's hand as he held his cards up toward the window, and she could have sworn that one of his cards was not a queen. The queen had come with lightning speed, from his sleeve, when all eyes were turned to the young man and his tens. Libby turned and stalked away. She went through to the dining table and seated herself deliberately between an elderly colonel and a large woman going to visit her married daughter in Illinois. When Gabe came in later, she noticed his eyes scanning the room and she concentrated on her food, pretending she had not seen him.

After dinner she refused the colonel's invitation to join him for coffee and hurried back to her own cabin. She sat, trying to read, while the children fell asleep and the sounds of laughter and piano playing echoed out across the black waters, and she pushed all thoughts of Gabriel Foster from her mind. She resolved to stay well away from him for the rest of the voyage.

But next morning, as she came around the corner of the deck, Gabe stepped out in front of her.

"Your hunger got the better of you last night, or did you decide that that doddering old fool was less of a temptation than I?" he asked.

Fighting to control her temper, she took a deep breath. "I think that you and I have very little in common, Mr. Foster, and see no point in furthering our relationship."

His eyebrows shot up with obvious surprise. "Might I inquire if I have said or done something that has offended you, ma'am?"

"What you have done would offend any person of sensibility and morals, Mr. Foster," she said.

"Please explain yourself, madam," he said. "It was my understanding that I have treated you with the very soul of politeness and decorum."

"I have no complaints about the way you have treated me, Mr. Foster. It's your treatment of others I cannot condone."

"Meaning what?" he demanded.

"I think you might have told me that you are a gambler."

He looked amused and relieved. "I make my living at what I do best," he said. "By my quick hands and my quick wits and my knowledge of human greed."

"There are many professions where you could use those skills and remain honorable," she said.

"Are not all men gamblers to a certain extent, Mrs. Hugh Grenville?" he asked. "Your father, the fine Boston businessman, has he never taken a gamble in his business dealings? And your husband—are not the gold fields the greatest gamble man has ever undertaken?"

"That's different," Libby snapped.

"In what way?"

"In my world it is not considered acceptable to cheat at cards," she said bluntly.

"You call it cheating because I do it better than most."

"I saw you," she said, looking at him without blinking. "I saw you bring the queen from your sleeve."

"Really?" he asked. He still looked amused. "Then you have quicker eyes than most. Would you swear to the fact that I brought a card from my sleeve? You actually saw me extract it?"

Libby considered it. She had seen the slightest of movements, but. . . . "You had a queen and a five," she said. "Then you had two queens."

His smile broadened. "One thing you must learn, if you intend to travel into the West," he said, "is that it is not etiquette to look over a man's shoulder while he is playing cards. Men have been gunned down for less."

She looked at him in amazement. "You are not even repentant," she exclaimed. "You admit your guilt."

Gabe sighed. "You know little of human nature, Mrs. Hugh Grenville," he said. "The young fool was driven by greed, much farther than he should have gone. He'd won enough—I'd let him win enough, but he was convinced he could clean me out, that he was smarter than me. I had to show him I was the smarter. They never know when to quit, you see. That's how I make my money—I trade on greed. Is that so wrong?"

"It is to me," she said.

"Then we must beg to differ," Gabe said. "You will find, I think, that this is not Boston, Libby. In this world there is precious little honor, few men you can trust, and no guarantee that life will not finish tomorrow with a bullet in the back."

"Then if I were you, I would rather be the one spark of honor in a dark world," Libby said. "If I feared death at any moment, I would rather be prepared to meet my maker."

"I do not fear death," Gabe said, "and I am as ready to face my maker as any man that I know."

"I don't think there are any card parlors up in heaven," she said dryly.

"No? Then it will be a very dull place," Gabe said. "Besides, I think I like warmth. Perpetual fires sound rather more appealing."

"You are incorrigible."

"And you, Mrs. Hugh Grenville, are quite delightful," he said, laughing. "I hope I can persuade you to like me better."

"Fortunately you will not get the chance, Mr. Foster. After this voyage we will never see each other again," she replied and stalked past him to her cabin.

For the rest of her time on board, Libby stayed in her cabin or sought out the company of the other women passengers, suffering through long and boring accounts of their troubles with servants and dressmakers and their varied illnesses, rather than risk coming face to face with Mr. Gabriel Foster again. When they docked in St. Louis she hurried

the children ashore and made her way along the
levee to find the first ship going up the Missouri to
Independence.

In her diary she wrote: *May 30, 1949. I have learned
a valuable lesson. From now on I take nothing at face value.
When I meet the next Mr. Gabe Foster, I will be ready for
him!*

# CHAPTER
# 5

THE NEXT SHIP was very different from the *Mississippi Belle*. Up to this point the journey had presented relatively few of the hardships and dangers which had been rumored in the drawing rooms of New England. Libby's safe arrival in St. Louis almost convinced her that the end was in sight. Soon she would set off on the wagon train to California and find Hugh and live happily ever after. Her introduction to the steamer *Amelia* made her realize that maybe the real journey was just now beginning.

On the dockside a frightened mule had broken free from its owner and was braying loudly while it kicked out at the stacked piles of freight around it. From the lower deck of the ship came the bawl of oxen, the braying of mules, and the shouted curses of the deckhands. Wagons piled high with barrels and boxes were waiting to be loaded and men pushed past Libby and the children as if they too were pieces of freight. The men were loaded down with guns and knives and they shouldered their way past each other up the crowded gangplank. Libby clutched her two bags and her children more firmly.

"Stay close to me, darlings. It's now or never," she said and joined the human tide flowing up onto the ship.

"I don't want to go onto that ship. I don't like it," Bliss screamed, bursting into tears and wrapping herself around Libby's legs.

"We're going to find Papa. Don't you want to see Papa?" Libby coaxed, trying to release the little hands that clutched at her.

"I want to go home. I want to go back to Grandmama," Bliss screamed.

"Come on, Mama will carry you," Libby said, picking up the screaming child. Bliss fought and kicked. "Put me down. I want to go home," she yelled. "I don't like it here." Libby tried to hold the two bags in her other hand while she fought to control Bliss.

"That's enough, Bliss," she said severely. "You have to behave. Young ladies do not have temper tantrums in public."

"I don't care. I don't care," Bliss screamed, kicking more wildly.

Libby inched her way toward the crowded gangway. Men with bundles and trunks surged past her, hardly giving her a look, not one offering to help. She stumbled onto the deck, almost falling over the piles of boxes and sacks which were threatening to cover the entire surface. Eden hit her shin on a tin box and started to cry. Libby looked around for a steward and, finally seeing a man in uniform, she called to him.

"Can you take me to a cabin please. This disturbance is very upsetting for the children and they would tell me nothing when I bought my tickets."

The uniformed man looked at her with interest. "I don't think you'd want a cabin, lady," he said bluntly.

"Why on earth not? The journey takes a week doesn't it?"

"We're sleeping 'em eight to a cabin right now," he said, "and the other other seven would be men."

"Then what am I to do?" Libby asked.

"If I was you, lady, I'd find myself a little patch of deck out of the way and stay there," the man said. "And if I'd got any belongings, I'd sit on 'em. These guys aren't fussy about what they help themselves to."

"You aren't suggesting I sit outside on a deck for seven days?" Libby demanded angrily. "You want me to expose two little children to the night air?"

"If you want my advice, it would be to stay home, leastways until all this craziness is over," the man said. "Every ship for the past couple of months has been overloaded. I reckon half the states must be on their way to California by now."

"I can't stay home, since my home is in New England," Libby said shortly, "and I too am joining my husband in California."

"Then the sooner you toughen up those little ones by sleeping them in the open air, the better," the man said, "because that journey over the plains is awful hard on those who aren't in tiptop shape. They say there's a grave for every mile of the trip already."

"Thank you for your advice," Libby said coldly. "Come children, we'd better find ourselves a place to sit on deck before every inch is taken."

From below an ox started bellowing, the noise echoing alarmingly in the iron hold of the ship. Bliss wrapped her arms around her mother's neck, near-

ly strangling her. "I don't want to ride on this ship.
I want to go home," she screamed. "This is a nasty
ship, Mama."

"We must be brave. It won't be for long," Libby
soothed. "Look, we can make ourselves a little house
under that lifeboat."

She hurried them across the deck and spread out
her cloak for them in the narrow space under one of
the two lifeboats the ship carried. The girls immediately thought this was fun and happily played house
with the two little dolls she had brought along for
them.

All day long men and cargo kept on coming aboard
the ship until there was not a spare inch of space on
any deck. When the *Amelia* cast off, toward evening,
she left behind a crowd of would-be travellers who
yelled and cursed, waving their fists in anger as the
boat drew away from its dock with much grinding and
thrashing of its paddle wheels.

Libby and the girls sat without moving under the
lifeboat until darkness fell and the *Amelia* dropped
anchor for the night.

"I'm hungry, Mama, when's supper?" Bliss demanded, having quite forgotten her fears about the ship.

"We'll go and explore, if you like," Libby said, climbing out stiffly from their hiding place and extending
her hands to them. "I expect our bags will be safe
enough." When Libby took the girls below, she was
glad that she had taken the seaman's advice to stay
on deck. The smell of unwashed bodies, mingled
with strong liquor and smoke coming from the public rooms was almost unbearable after such a short
time on the river, and loud, drunken singing echoed
out across the peaceful water.

"I don't think we'll try and get dinner in there," Libby whispered to the girls. "I'll see if a steward can bring us up some sandwiches instead."

When she found a steward and gave him this request, he laughed at her.

"This ain't New York, lady," he said. "Meals is served in the dining room and you get what comes out of the pot!"

"But I can't take my daughters in there," she exclaimed, indicating the rowdy, smoke-filled interior.

The steward looked with more compassion. "I'll see what I can do," he said. "I expect there's some bread I can get my hands on, and maybe some cold meat."

Libby thanked him as he hurried off.

She kept her daughters close to her side as she crept along the passageways and back onto the deck again. After that, the first night passed not too unpleasantly.

In the morning they stopped at a small settlement along the river and had a chance to go ashore. The girls ran up and down the wooded bank while Libby managed to buy a loaf of fresh bread, six hard-boiled eggs, and some dried apples. She felt relieved that she no longer had to worry about taking the children into the public rooms on the boat to feed them and she enjoyed a good cup of coffee before the bell rang to get everyone back on board. The Missouri was a prettier river with more varied scenery than its bigger sister. In places, the banks rose to steep yellow cliffs and then fell to peaceful wooded coves. The sandbars were also covered with trees and once Eden spotted two deer having a drink. She called out to her mother and instantly every man on the deck grabbed a rifle and began shooting. The deer bounded away in fright and Eden started to cry.

"They are horrid men, Mama. They shot at the baby deer."

"Out here it's different, precious one," Libby said, hugging the sobbing child. "Here they must shoot for food. Where we are going there will be no butcher shops."

By the middle of the next night Libby discovered that the voyage was not going to be a peaceful one. She woke from fitful sleep, curled as tightly as humanly possible under the lifeboat, to feel boots run past, vibrating the deck close to her face. Farther down the deck loud groans were followed by the sound of more boots passing. There were murmurs of "doctor" and "dying." In the morning three of the passengers were now covered with their blankets.

"What happened?" Libby asked, assuming the men had gotten into a fight.

"It's cholera," a small, frightened-faced man hissed as he passed her. "The cholera's come aboard."

Libby hugged the children close to her. "We'll eat and drink nothing more on this ship," she said, "and we'll not come out from this lifeboat until we can go ashore."

At first light the wrapped corpses were carried ashore for a hasty burial in a sandy bank beside the river. Libby leaned on the railing, staring down at the incongruous scene. Willows and cottonwoods spread shade over a grassy clearing. Swallows skimmed low over the swiftly moving water and a pair of mallards paddled along the edge, under the trailing strands of willow leaves. It was the sort of scene for lovers and dreamers and summer picnics and yet there were now men with shovels piling up mounds of sand as they hastily dug a grave.

"At least they've got themselves a pretty burial place," a man behind her commented, "better than in the heathen lands out West."

Libby watched the men now shovelling sand back into the holes. It doesn't matter where you're buried, she thought. Dead is dead.

News of cholera on board had the effect of instantly quieting the noisy men. There was no singing and laughing that night, just the groans and screams of more dying men. In the morning there were four more bodies to be buried. Libby hurried ashore too and was almost tempted to take the girls off the boat to wait for a safer one. A farmer's wife was hanging out washing nearby and came over to see what was going on, on the riverbank.

"More poor devils not even getting a decent Christian burial," she commented to Libby, folding her arms across her broad chest.

"It seems to be happening all the time on this boat," Libby said. "I'm beginning to think I should wait for another boat to come along, for my children's sake."

"They're all the same these days," the farmer's wife said, shaking her head. "There's cholera raging up and down the whole river. Nobody's safe anymore. Too many dirty strangers, packed in like sardines," she added tersely. "I wish they'd go west and have done with it and leave us poor settlers in peace."

Then she went back to her washing, leaving Libby alone on the bank not really sure what to do for the best. She managed to buy some fresh bread and milk from a trader. She washed the children thoroughly before they boarded again and kept them as far away from the other passengers as she could.

When they were only one day out of Independence,

the steamer ran aground on a sandbar which jutted out from the shore. The captain had gangways lowered and ordered all the passengers to disembark to make the ship lighter. Ropes were dropped from the upper deck and men passengers joined the crew in trying to pull the ship free. As one sweating team did not succeed, other men stepped in to take their place and by late afternoon they had succeeded in refloating the *Amelia*. Not wanting to risk it happening again with the water level so low, the captain made them all walk a mile or so up the riverbank until the water was deeper and they could reboard. The mile walk along a leafy path relieved a little of Libby's anxiety. Only one more night and they could escape from the stinking pigpen the ship had become. She looked forward to the plains now as clean and breezy and free of disease. Before they got back on board, they passed another farm and the farmer's wife gave the children a drink of milk and a big peach each.

Libby had just dozed off to an uncomfortable sleep on the hard wood of the deck when she was woken by a gentle touch. "Mama?" Eden's frightened little face peered into hers. "Bliss doesn't feel well."

Libby shot upright, banging her head against the lifeboat above her. "What is it, darling?" she asked.

"My tummy hurts bad, real bad," Bliss said. Her little face was flushed and puckered up with pain. "Make it stop, Mama," she begged.

Libby felt cold sweat break out. "Stay with her, I'll go find a doctor," she whispered to Eden. Treading her way cautiously over sleeping men, she found a young doctor sitting by another cholera victim. The man was shaking with convulsions. "You'll let my wife know, won't you, Doc?" he asked, gasping between vomits. "Name's Anson, just outside Buffalo. They all know me. Tell her I tried my best. . . ." Then he convulsed once more and lay still. Libby stared in horror. It was the first time she had ever seen a person die. She wrapped her shawl around her shoulders, shivering in the night air, and touched the young doctor lightly on the shoulder.

"Can you come quickly? It's my little girl," she said.

A look of concern spread across his boyish face. "Little girl, you say?" He shook his head and followed Libby across the deck. Bliss was lying doubled over, holding her stomach. "It hurts, Mama, make it go away," she wailed.

The doctor bent down to examine her. "Any vomits? Diarrhea?" he asked. He prodded her stomach.

"Don't," Bliss complained.

He straightened up, looked at Libby, and smiled. "Has she eaten anything she is not used to?" he asked.

"A peach, this afternoon," Libby said.

The smile broadened. "Just a good, old-fashioned case of colic," he said. "Do you have any peppermint? A couple of drops should be all it takes."

"Thank God," Libby said, hugging the child close to her.

## CHAPTER
# 6

WHEN THEY DOCKED at the upper landing near Independence the next morning, the first sight that attracted the attention of the passengers crowded against the rails was not the town they expected to see, but a gentle countryside completely covered with tents. The tent city stretched as far as the eye could see in every direction. The smoke of hundreds of campfires hung in the humid air and a steady stream of men passed to and from the river, collecting water.

"Holy cow! Looks just like an army," a young man beside Libby commented. "Waitin' ready for battle."

"What are they all doing there?" Libby asked, still scanning the improbable scene.

"They're waiting to join companies, ma'am. Waiting for their chance to set off."

"Is that how this works?" Libby asked, delighted to have found somebody who seemed to know something, "One joins a company?"

"That's right, ma'am," the man said. "You signs yourself on with a company that's already formed, if you don't have enough men to form one of your own, and that way you gets across safe and sound."

"Is that what you're going to do?" she asked.

He grinned, the fresh, hopeful grin of a young man with adventure about to face him. "You bet ya," he said. "I aim to sign me on with the biggest and best company I can find. That way I'll eat well and not get myself scalped by Injuns."

"What does this cost?" Libby asked, thinking of her money, now down to just over two hundred dollars, tucked carefully in a pocket inside her blouse.

"They say the companies usually ask a hundred dollars," the young man said. "That's fair enough, I reckon, although it sure seems like a lot of money to a farm boy like me. We could get us a hired hand for a year for less."

"You're from a farm?" Libby asked, enjoying watching the excitement on the young, freckled face.

The young man nodded. "South Carolina. Loveliest country on God's earth," he said. "I got me a chance to buy the farm next to my pa's if I can raise the money. I aim to make a fortune quick as possible then go home and marry Bonnie Birdwell."

"Good luck to you," Libby said.

"From what I hear, we'll need it," the young man said, pushing his hat back on his head as his turn approached to walk down the gangplank. "I already lost my partner to cholera and him the fittest, toughest farmhand you ever did see. One morning he was talking and laughing and playing cards down in the saloon. Next morning we was carrying him ashore to bury him."

The line of people reached the top of the gangplank. "I'll be happy to give you a hand with your bags, ma'am," the young man said to Libby. "Seeing as how you've got the two littl'uns."

"Thank you very much," Libby said, gratefully handing them to him.

At the bottom of the gangplank the young man tipped his hat. "Well, goodbye to you, ma'am. Nice talking with you. Luke Hollister's my name."

"I'm Libby Grenville, Luke," Libby said. "I'll see you in California, maybe."

"You're heading for Californy? A little bitty woman like you?" Luke stammered. "My mam didn't even want me to go, telling me I was too young. Her eyes would pop clean from her head if she saw these young'uns going."

"How old are you, Luke?" Libby asked.

"I'm nineteen, almost," Luke said proudly. He touched his hat again. "Well, goodbye to you, Mrs. Grenville. Nice talking with you. God willing we will meet again out West."

The moment they reached the shore, Libby directed her children into town, away from that tent city. Her first priority was to have the children safely housed in a respectable hotel before she went out looking for a suitable company to join. It was a mile or so walk into the city of Independence, along a delightful sandy road, shaded by oak trees and looking very like any country road in New England. To begin with, she enjoyed the cool shade and soft sand under her feet, but as the heavy bags began to weigh her down and the straps cut into her hands, she found herself wishing these really were New England woods and that she was not alone here. All her confidence and bravado of a few moments earlier evaporated under a great rush of homesickness at finding herself in

such familiar countryside so very far from home. She
found herself remembering outings along such leafy
lanes, picnics under such spreading oaks—civilized
picnics with checkered cloths and wicker hampers of
cold meats and lobster and chilled champagne. . . .

The little girls spotted squirrels and bright birds
and danced along as if they were on an afternoon's
outing. From beyond the woods came the rough
shouts and laughter of men, the constant braying and
snorting of mules. Libby looked at the two little figures
dancing ahead of her and seriously considered not
going any farther. She could find employment easily
enough in Independence, she reasoned. The children
could live in a real house in a real town and she'd write
to Hugh to tell him to join her as soon as possible.
Then she reminded herself why she had come on this
journey. Hugh would not leave California until he had
made his fortune. For the first time she found herself
wondering whether he had reached California safely
by now. Who would know if he had been carried from
a river steamer, wrapped in his blanket to be buried
in a sandbar or had died unnoticed in that tent city?
Doubts crept into her mind that her journey might be
for nothing and she might never see Hugh again.

"There's nothing for it but to go on," she said,
emerging from the cool woodlands with a sigh and
gathering the children as she approached the bustling city.

Main Street looked as busy as Boston the week before
Christmas. Heavily laden wagons groaned through the
dusty streets. The air resounded with the crack of
whips and the harsh curses of wagon drivers. Horsemen galloped up, weaving skillfully past the wagons
and pedestrians. People were hurrying to and fro

with packages and sacks, going in and out of stores
and banks. But the shoppers were all men and they
each carried a gun at their sides. Libby was turned
away from the two respectable-looking hotels.

"I don't think you'll find a vacant bed in town,"
she was told. But at Ma Zettel's Boarding House,
in a small back street at the edge of town, they
had better luck. Ma Zettel was a big woman with
hair severely scraped back into a bun and skin like
tanned leather. She looked formidable as she stood
in her doorway with big arms folded across her chest,
but as she looked down at the two timid little figures
holding onto Libby's skirt, her stony face softened and
creased into a thousand smile lines. "Well, ain't you
the prettiest things I seen in a month of Sundays,"
she said, bending down toward Bliss. Bliss held out
her little hand. "How do you do, I'm Bliss Grenville,"
she said. "I comed a long way in a big boat."

The outstretched hand convinced Ma Zettel. She
straightened up and looked Libby in the eye. "I can't
let them sleep along of a lot of heathen men," she
said. "I'll squeeze you in somewhere." She led them
up to a tiny room in the attic which was normally a
storeroom. "I'll get a couple of camp cots put in here
before day's out," she said, shifting a pile of trunks to
one side with her tree-trunk arms as she spoke. "At
least you won't be bothered up here."

Libby now knew what she meant and nodded gratefully.

Ma Zettel looked at Libby with interest. "Your husband's out getting stocked up, is he?" she asked, then
went on, before Libby could reply, "Well, if he hasn't
got his mules yet, my brother-in-law has a fine pair
he'll sell for a hundred and twenty the pair, and that's

a bargain the way things are going around here, as anyone will tell you."

"I don't have a husband or a team with me," Libby said. "I'm going out to join my husband and I'm hoping to join a company to travel with."

"My dear Lord!" the woman said. "You've got spunk. I'll say that for you. Two little precious dears across all that waste and no man to protect you. Still, I've watched many a party set off over the past few years and there's been women among them you'd have thought would blow away with a breeze. But they've made it through to Oregon or California, and sometimes had a baby along the way, while their big strong husbands are the ones stricken with every sort of ague and fever."

Libby laughed. "I'm tougher than I look too," she said.

"I'm sure you are, my dear," Ma Zettel said. "Now, what do you say to a nice cup of coffee? I was just going to pour one for myself."

Libby took the girls down to the parlor and enjoyed the cool, leather chairs while the coffee revived her.

"Now I have another favor to ask," Libby said, when her cup was empty. "I have to find a company to join and I've no idea how to set about it. Would it be too much of an imposition to leave the children here? They are very good and amuse themselves easily."

"No trouble at all," Ma Zettel said. "I'll take them into the kitchen with me and they can help with the baking. You'd like that, wouldn't you, my precious ones?" she asked.

"Yes please," Eden said, looking at her mother as if someone had just offered her a present. "Cook never let us help with baking at home."

"Right then, off with you to the kitchen," Ma Zettel said. "And good luck to you, my dear, in your plans."

Libby hesitated, not sure what to do next. "I find a company that's about to leave and see if I can get a place with them, so I've heard?" she asked.

"That's what they all seem to do," the landlady said.

"And there's no public stage line for travellers on their own?" Libby asked.

"A stage line?" A smile twitched on the leathery face. "I did hear talk of getting one started but I don't think it ever amounted to anything. They'd lose too many coaches and drivers to make it profitable."

"Oh," Libby said.

"You're worrying that you won't be able to handle your own team?" the landlady asked.

"My own team?" Libby looked horrified.

"That's what they do. They get their own teams and then sign up along with a company. But maybe you could find yourself a man to drive your wagon."

"Buy my own wagon as well as the hundred dollars to join a company?" she stammered.

"Oh yes. The joining fee just pays for supplies and protection. They all have their own wagons."

"They must cost a lot of money," Libby said hopelessly.

"Prices are real inflated right now," the woman agreed. "Most of the men will pay anything to get started to the gold. You're looking at two hundred for the wagon and another hundred for the team at least."

"And if I can't afford that much?"

"Then you don't go, or you walk," the landlady said flatly. "Unless you could find someone with space to spare, to take you along with them."

"Oh," Libby said. She put out her hand against the doorpost to steady herself. Despair was fighting with anger that she had not troubled to find out the facts before she set out on such a crazy journey.

"Don't give up heart now, my dear," the landlady said, putting a big, heavy hand on Libby's shoulder. "I hear there's a fine, well-equipped party about to set out this week, run by a Mr. Sheldon Rival—a big-wig out of Chicago, so they say. He had a dozen wagons shipped here and a hold full of supplies with him which he aims to make a fortune with in California. He might have wagon space for the children at least. You could walk alongside. The wagons don't move fast if they're pulled by oxen which these are."

"Thank you," Libby said. "I'll go and try to convince this Mr. Rival to take me with him. Any idea where he's camped?"

"Camped?" Ma Zettel asked. "He's at the Independence House—best hotel in town. He's taken the whole second floor."

Libby felt hopeful and excited as she made her way to the big brick building on Main Street. At least Mr. Rival was a civilized man from Chicago—a business-man like her father. She could talk to him as one cultured person to another. The desk clerk pointed her in the direction of the restaurant when Libby asked for Mr. Rival's rooms.

"He's taking his lunch," he said. "You can't miss him. Big fellow, dressed real swanky."

Libby went into the restaurant. It was spacious and cool, decorated with large potted palms and marble pillars. She stood behind one of these as she looked around for Mr. Rival. He was, as the desk clerk had predicted, very easy to spot; a large red-faced man, probably in his forties, with at least three chins, into the last of which a napkin was now tucked as Mr. Rival bent over, slurping soup noisily from a bowl. Libby could see the glint of gold at his cuff links and watch chain. The top of his head was starting to bald although the rest of his hair was very black, making Libby guess that he dyed it. He was accompanied at the table by two wiry young men who looked like Libby's impression of a cowboy. They both listened politely as Mr. Rival spoke nonstop between slurps of soup.

"I don't intend losing one bag of that flour, you hear me? Not one bag. You'll get your pay when I roll into the streets of Hangtown and not before. Understood?"

"Yes sir, Mr. Rival," two voices chorused like children in a school.

Libby walked over and stood before him. Seeing her shadow, he raised his eyes, soup still dripping down his chins. "Watta you want?" he growled.

"How do you do?" Libby said politely. "I'm Elizabeth Grenville and I understand that you are shortly setting out for California. I'm travelling there alone and thought you might have space to take me on one of your wagons, for a fee, of course."

She was very conscious of the way Sheldon Rival looked her up and down, then licked the soup from his lips. "Thanks, little lady, but it's more profitable for me to transport flour than fancy girls," he said. "Flour will make more for me than you will."

"How dare you!" Libby said, almost having to restrain herself from slapping his face.

Sheldon Rival looked amused. "Why else does a lady on her own go out to California right now?" he asked.

"There's good money to be made in 'entertainment'."
He put such meaning into the last word that the two
men with him laughed.

Libby's face had flushed bright red. "I'd like you to
know that I'm a respectable married woman from a
good Bostonian family," she said, "and I'm travelling
to California to join my husband. I was not asking
for your charity or your patronage. I can't manage
my own wagon and I thought you might have room
in one of yours if I pay my way."

"Like I said," Sheldon Rival drawled, already looking down at his food again, "my wagons are full of
supplies. A sack of flour is worth more to me than
what you'd pay me. And sacks of flour don't talk
back." He laughed as if he'd made a good joke and
the other men dutifully laughed too.

"I can see I'm wasting my time here," Libby said in
her best Bostonian manner. "I thought I'd be dealing
with a civilized man, but I'm talking to an overgrown
monkey in civilized clothing. Good day to you, Mr.
Rival."

She heard laughter from a table behind her as she
turned to make a dignified exit from the dining room.
She gave a frosty stare in the direction of the laughter
and found herself looking at the smiling face of Gabe
Foster.

**CHAPTER**
**7**

"WHAT ARE YOU doing here?" Libby blurted out before she remembered that she had sworn never to speak to Gabriel Foster again.

Gabe's smile broadened. "I thought I'd take a trip out West and see for myself what the frontier looks like." He leaned back in his chair, looking up at her with obvious enjoyment. "Besides which, I heard that there were all these men sitting around with nothing to do all day. So I thought I'd volunteer my services and do them a good turn by amusing them with a few little card games."

"You are still despicable," Libby said.

"And you are still adorable," he said, "although I see it was misplaced concern on my part to worry about you surviving in the wilderness. I watched you dealing with old Rival there. It's a wonder he wasn't turned into an instant snowman with that icy stare you gave him."

"The man is an uncouth idiot," Libby said, "I feel myself fortunate that I was able to observe his true

72

character before I signed on with him."

"It was my impression he turned you down," Gabe said, grinning.

"Believe me, Mr. Foster, now that I have seen the man, I would not have signed on with him at any price, even if he were riding to California in a golden coach with half the U.S. cavalry at his side."

"So what are you aiming to do now?" Gabe asked.

"I'll find another company that can take me," she said. "There are enough men out there to find one with civilized manners and a kind heart."

"I wouldn't count on it," Gabe said. "Gold and kind hearts don't go well together."

"Pray don't concern yourself about me, Mr. Foster," she said. "I am a very determined woman."

"I don't doubt it for a moment," Gabe said, "and I've no doubt at all that you could walk all the way to California if you had to. But you've two little girls with you that need looking after. I hear you had a narrow brush with cholera on that damned ship. I'll ask around for you, if you like."

"I can do my own asking, thank you," Libby said. Then a worrying thought struck her. "You didn't follow us this far to keep an eye on us, did you?"

"Whatever gave you that idea?" Gabe said, laughing. "As a matter of fact, things got a little too hot for me in St. Louis. The young man on board I helped part from his cash turned out to be the son of a judge—a hanging judge. And since I rather like my head and neck just the way they are, I thought I'd take me a little trip westward. So you see, I've got enough headaches in my life without having a mean-tempered, high-moraled, ice-cold woman to worry about."

Libby flushed. "Then I bid you good day, Mr. Foster," she said, nodding her head slightly.

"I was just about to eat," Gabe said. "I don't suppose you'd care to join me, or would you still consider that to be one step away from supping with Old Nick himself?"

Libby looked longingly at the white cloth, the polished silver and thought of the last time she sat in a proper restaurant, eating good food and enjoying civilized company. She was aware that Gabe Foster represented the one familiar face in a sea of strangers, also that his presence still strangely disturbed her, however much she might despise him. She actually found herself thinking, what harm could there be in a cup of coffee? before she took control of herself. Aside from any other consideration, she was not going to give Sheldon Rival the satisfaction of seeing her dining with a known gambler, especially such a handsome one.

"I'm sorry," she said, "but I've left my daughters alone and must return to them right away. Please excuse me. I wish you good luck, Mr. Foster."

"And I you, Mrs. Hugh Grenville," he said.

She spent the rest of the day walking among the campsites, seeing if any party was willing to take on three extra female passengers, but nobody seemed at all willing to divide their precious supplies with three extra mouths, even for money, and even less willing to be saddled with the extra responsibilities of three helpless females. "We don't aim to stop for nobody, ma'am," one man said, looking away rather than face her pleading eyes. "If you or your kids gets sick, I couldn't hold up the wagons for you and I couldn't provide a doctor for you either. I'd sure hate to watch little kids die, or you for that matter."

She tried reasoning with him, assuring him that she was as tough as any man, but it was clear that he, like the other men she spoke to, had made up his mind. They were after gold, they had brought enough supplies to get them there, and they were not going to be tied down. Libby came back despondent as night was falling. All around her campfires glowed like red eyes in the dark.

The next morning her luck changed. She was taking Eden and Bliss out for an early morning walk when she heard someone yelling down from an upstairs window. At first she ignored the yelling, sure that it could not be directed at her, but when it went on, she hesitated and looked up.

"Yes, you—who else did you think I meant!" boomed the voice, and there, at the open window of the second-floor suite, was Sheldon Rival, still in his shirt and suspenders with rolled up sleeves and no collar or tie. "You wanted to join my party yesterday. You still want to?"

Libby longed to say that there was no way she would ever consider joining him again, but she remembered all the flat rejections of the day before. "Come up and talk about it, if you do," Sheldon Rival shouted. "Those brats yours?"

Libby nodded. "Then leave 'em downstairs in the foyer. Can't stand whining brats around the place."

Libby led the children inside. "Stay right here on this sofa, children," she said gently. "Mama will be down in a few seconds. Eden, take care of your sister."

"Yes, Mama," Eden said. She lugged Bliss, like a sack of potatoes, onto the velvet sofa. "Sit still, sissy,

and I'll tell you a story," she said. Libby smiled fondly at both of them, then went up the marble staircase
to Sheldon Rival's room. On hearing her knock, he
boomed, "Come in." She opened the door. Rival was
seated at a table near the window, a half-eaten peach
in front of him, a fat cigar dangling at his lip. He did
not get up, but beckoned Libby to come over to him.

"Now then," he said. "Things have changed since
I talked to you yesterday. My cook's come down with
cholera."

"I'm sorry to hear that," Libby said.

Rival shrugged. "Silly fool. I told him not to drink
the river water. So what I want to know is, do you
want his job?"

"You don't expect him to recover?" Libby asked,
shocked by his callousness.

"Probably not," Rival said. "Not many do, from my
experience. Anyway, even if he does, I don't want him
back as my cook. He could be carrying the disease and
infect my food. I presume you know how to cook?"

"Yes, of course," Libby said, secretly going over in
her mind the rare occasions she had been allowed in
the kitchen and the little cakes which were her repertoire.

"I like to eat well," Rival said. "I'm very particular
about my food. I've got me the best-stocked expedition ever to cross this Godforsaken wilderness and I
aim to eat well all the way across. I've got scouts and
sharpshooters and ox drivers and God knows what,
but none of them know how to cook anything more
than bacon and beans. So do you want the job or not?"

"On what terms?"

Rival's eyes narrowed. "You get to California, of
course. You get food and protection. You eat what

I eat. You provide your own bedding but you get to sleep in a wagon."

"I see," Libby said. "That sounds fair enough."

"You leave the brats behind, of course," he added.

"What?"

"Those kids. I don't have room for two extra bodies."

"You want me to leave my children behind? What sort of man are you?" Libby demanded.

Rival looked amused. "It's either them or my flour and my flour is worth more to me. You'll find someone in town to look after them until you come back for them. Or get someone to adopt them. You're young enough to breed yourself a whole army more."

Libby opened her mouth to tell this man how vile and disgusting she found him, but she closed it again. She was not going to let Sheldon Rival get the better of her. She'd take him on at his own game and she would beat him.

"You don't have much choice, do you?" he asked, picking up his cigar which still smoked away in his ashtray and puffing a cloud of smoke in her direction. "There's nobody else who'll take you to California. I hear you've been asking around all the companies. If you want to get there, you'll have to go along with my terms or not go at all."

"Very well, Mr. Rival," she said. "When do you propose leaving?"

"Tomorrow morning by ten o'clock," he said, picking up the peach in one hand, while he took another puff on the cigar. "I'm having everything loaded today so we get an early start. You'll know my wagons—they're bigger and better than anyone else's. Ask any of the men. They'll tell you. Ask my trail boss. His name's Jimmy. He'll tell you where to stow your stuff.

Now get going. I've got business to conduct. I'm nego-
tiating for extra oxen and a string of pack mules."

Libby hurried down to her children and took them
outside. Then, with the knowledge that she was getting a free passage, she went into outfitting stores
and bought blankets for each of them, some gingham
to make dresses, and a sturdy man's shirt for each
of them, since there were no jackets small enough.
She did manage to purchase three sunbonnets and
laughed at her children's faces when they all tried
them on. "Now we really look like three pioneers,"
she said. "How your father would laugh if he could
see us now." She did not mention what Mr. Rival had
ordered her to do with her children.

After she had deposited the children back with Ma
Zettel, she rolled up their belongings in the new cloth
and blankets and went to seek out Rival's trail boss
and wagons. As he had boasted, they were bigger and
finer than any others, long bodied with metal-rimmed
wheels. She found the trail boss supervising the loading of several kegs of water. "Make sure you lash these
down good," he yelled at a team of hard-looking men
who were clambering over the freight with ropes.
"You let the cargo shift on one of those passes and
the wagon's gone. Then Rival will have your hides."

"Are you Jimmy?" Libby called to him. He turned
around and eyed her with interest. He was very tall
and lean, much younger than she had expected but
tough and rugged looking as if he had spent all his
young years in the outdoors. His face was deeply
tanned and had a perpetual frown from being out
in bright sunlight and his expression showed what
he thought about having a woman along on the trip.
When she announced that she was Mr. Rival's new

cook, he gave a sardonic smile as if he did not believe her duties would be confined to cooking. "You can put your stuff in there," he said, indicating with a nod of his head a wagon piled high with sacks and boxes of food. "That's his personal food wagon."

"They're fine wagons," she commented, trying to establish a friendly relationship with the man. She had the feeling that it might be good to have an ally on the trip.

Jimmy sniffed. "Too fine if you want to know. I told him he'd need six oxen per wagon to get them over the divide, but now he's got them loaded down with so much stuff, I wouldn't be surprised if he didn't need eight. Lighter is better, I've always found. I see you travel light."

"That's because I had no choice," she said. "But I can see now that it is a big advantage."

He smiled for the first time, the smile making him look almost boyish. "What's your name?"

"Libby," she answered.

Jimmy stretched out a lean, brown hand. "Well, Libby, welcome aboard. I just hope you know what you're doing."

"I hope so too," she said, laughing at the absurdity of it.

He smiled encouragingly. "We'll get along fine if Rival listens to me."

"You've done this trip before?"

"Not this exact trip," he said, "but I was born out on the frontier and I've crossed the plains enough times. Of course, I didn't have all this clutter with me." His eyes strayed back to the line of loaded wagons.

"I'll take a look at the food wagon, if you don't mind. I want to get things arranged so I can find them and see if I've got everything I need on board," she said.

"Oh, I think you'll find everything you need." His tone indicated that there would be far more than she would need, far more than was necessary or sensible.

Libby climbed up onto the high bed of the wagon. She looked quickly over the sacks of meat and sugar, slabs of lard, barrels of apples and potatoes, at the big black cooking pots hanging on hooks, then she glanced up to see if anyone was watching her before rearranging the stuff to make a little clearing in the middle, boxed in safely on all sides. She covered it with a board and then put a tray of peaches on top of it.

"Fine," she called to Jimmy as she clambered down again. "He's certainly got enough supplies there."

"And he's taking a cow along, so he can have fresh cream and butter," Jimmy called back. "You know how to milk a cow?"

"Heavens no," Libby said.

Jimmy laughed. "It ain't hard. One of the guys will show ya. Most of them were born and bred on ranches and farms. Besides, old Rival won't get milk for long, when the cow has to walk twenty miles a day. Still, he'll learn soon enough, I reckon."

The excitement flowing through her gave Libby renewed energy. She hurried back to Ma Zettel, where the little girls, decorated liberally with flour, were rolling out dough at a big kitchen table.

"Handy little things, they are," she called, beaming as Libby walked in. "Made quite a passable cornbread."

"Which is more than their mother can do," Libby acknowledged. "I'm afraid I'm in for trouble when he finds out the extent of my cooking. You can't give me a quick course, can you?"

Ma Zettel laughed. "I can tell you some of my recipes," she said. "Of course, cooking on the trail is not like when you've got a big stove at your disposal. You make your bread in a dutch oven, for one thing. I think I've got a recipe for it in my big book over there. You're welcome to study it, if you've a mind to."

Libby gratefully took the book and began to scribble down recipes. She wished that she had paid more attention to domestic matters when she was growing up. Just how much was a pinch, or a gill or a peck? How did one scald milk or render fat? Her mother had tried to stress to her the importance of knowing how to run her own kitchen one day, how to order food and plan menus, but she had been glad to leave all that to her mother while she went out riding or for walks in the park. Now she tried desperately to recall which dishes she had enjoyed at home and which she could possibly make for a critical Sheldon Rival.

I'll tell him he'll have to eat what I prepare or starve, she thought bravely. Although when she considered it, she decided that Mr. Rival would probably not be squeamish about dumping her along the trail if her cooking didn't please him.

In the middle of the night she woke the children and dressed them in the darkness. "We're going for an exciting adventure," she whispered, "but you both have to be very brave and very quiet. Can you do that?"

Two sets of big eyes stared at her and they nodded silently. She felt a great rush of tenderness and concern well up in her throat as she tied their cloaks. Was she really doing the right thing, risking their lives in this way? Surely, Ma Zettel would look after them, as Sheldon Rival had suggested, for a fee, and she could come and pick them up on her way back with Hugh and all the gold.

"We're ready, Mama," Eden whispered and slipped her warm little hand into Libby's, making Libby realize that she had not left them behind in Boston, where they were in perfect safety, and she was not going to leave them behind now.

"Come on, then. Let the adventure start," Libby said, and led them silently down the stairs.

The camps were full of sleeping men and restless animals. Dying campfires gave enough light for Libby to pick her way around them. Dogs growled from time to time, but sniffed at the children and relaxed again. Sheldon Rival's wagons glowed white, like huge sails, in the light of a waning moon.

"This is where we have to be very, very brave," she whispered to the girls. "I'm going to hide you in a little secret room, because they don't allow children on this trip. If they find you, they'll leave us all behind and we'll never get to Papa. Do you think you can play quietly in a little secret room for a couple of days? Mama will be right there and will come to you whenever nobody is watching. Mama will sleep next to you at night."

"All right, Mama," Eden said. "I'll make sure sissy stays quiet."

"I can stay quiet on my own," Bliss said a little too loudly, then put her fingers to her lips, giggling as the others both tried to shush her.

Libby went around to the back of the food wagon and lifted the children in. She lifted the tray of peaches, moved aside the box of hard biscuits, and had the children crawl through to the little space she had lined with blankets. "See how cozy it is?" Libby whispered as she tucked them in. "You just go to sleep. Mama is going into town say goodbye to Mrs. Zettel and then I'll be back. As soon as it's light, we'll start moving. You can peep out through a little hole I've made in the canvas for you and I'll walk right alongside."

"What if we need to go pee-pee?" Bliss whispered in her mother's ear.

"There's a pot in the corner," she whispered back, smiling. Then she kissed both children and replaced the box across the opening.

I've done some crazy things in my life, but this has to be the craziest I have ever attempted, she thought as she glanced back at the silent wagon.

# CHAPTER 8

NEXT MORNING, ON the stroke of ten, the wagons moved off. Sheldon Rival had made his appearance around nine-thirty, walking down the line of wagons for a brief inspection before taking up his place beside the driver of the lead wagon. He was still dressed like a city businessman with highly polished boots, a gold stickpin in his silk cravat, and his big golden watch chain draped across a stripe-vested stomach. His eyes narrowed when he saw Libby perched on the running board of the cook wagon.

"Didn't think you'd show up," he said.

"I told you I would," she said coldly.

"Got rid of the brats then?"

"You don't see them, do you?"

"Smart woman. You know what's good for you," he said. "Maybe you'll do after all." Then he walked on, leaving Libby with her heart hammering.

For the first time she was able to see just what constituted Mr. Rival's expedition and she had to admit it was very impressive: twelve wagons in all, each covered with a bowed white canvas top, each pulled by six oxen, a couple of men to each wagon, twelve spare ox teams, a string of pack mules, well laden, several riding horses and the milk cow brought up the rear of the party. Several men rode alongside on mules or horses, their belongings packed in saddle-bags, their rifles slung across their saddles. Libby presumed they were the guards. They all looked weather-beaten and tough, as if they were used to frontier fighting.

The wagons moved away at a snail's pace, to the accompaniment of much cracking of whips and shouts of encouragement or curses from the wagon drivers. As they passed other campsites men came out of their tents to watch the departure, clearly impressed by the size and equipment of the expedition. They greeted the passing wagons with whistles, catcalls, and the occasional gunshot. Libby shrank back inside the wagon, knowing what sort of remarks they'd make if they spotted her. Also, at the back of her mind, was the thought that she did not want to be seen by Mr. Gabriel Foster. Having told him that nothing on earth would make her ride with Sheldon Rival, she did not want him to have the satisfaction of gloating, which he surely would do. So she sat unmoving in the shadow of the awning, as the wagons passed the last campsites and joined the sandy trail westward.

It was undulating country with bluffs and wooded valleys and the going was very pleasant. Libby walked beside her wagon, going to whisper something to the children when nobody was watching her. The pace was very slow and from time to time she climbed into the wagon and sat reading the cooking notes she had scribbled the night before, eyeing the big iron cook-pots anxiously. What if he found her cooking so terrible that he sent her back?

It would just have to be good enough, she told herself firmly.

As the hour for camping came closer, Libby began to feel something close to panic. She went over the food supplies she had seen in the wagon and tried to come up with at least one good meal to impress Mr. Rival. She was fairly sure that Rival would not make too much fuss about the children if her cooking was good enough. If it was bad they might find themselves all walking back in the direction of Independence, with no prospect of getting a free ride with another company. She had just decided that even she could not go wrong with a steak and was wondering whether potatoes or rice would be less lethal beside it when a horseman drew level with her.

"Don't tell me it's Mrs. Hugh Grenville!" said a familiar voice. Libby looked up to see Gabe Foster, seated on a very elegant white horse, looking more like a Boston gentleman out for an afternoon in the park than a man embarking on a trek across a wilderness. He still wore his dark jacket and striped trousers although he had traded the silk top hat for a wide-brimmed black felt. Libby was surprised and angry at the momentary surge of hope and joy that had shot through her and which she rationalized as the relief in finding a familiar face in a wagon train of strangers. The joy was very short-lived, however, because Gabe went on, in his calm, cultured voice, "Well no, of course, it can't be, since Mrs. Hugh Grenville swore that she would rather die than ever attach herself to Mr. Sheldon Rival and his company, and you don't look at all dead to me. In fact, you look very solid and in the flesh. So I can only assume that you are Mrs. Grenville's twin sister." He took off his hat and made a sweeping bow down to her. "Do I have the honor, madam, of addressing Mrs. Hugh Grenville's twin sister?"

Libby gave him a withering stare which made him try to stifle a grin. "Not you again!" she said.

"Alas," he said, "like the proverbial bad penny, I do seem to keep turning up."

"What are you doing here?"

"Like yourself, heading to the promised land."

"You're really going with us to California?" Again she found herself glad. Gabriel Foster might be infuriating, but at least she sensed that she could trust him.

"Everyone else in the world seems to be going to see the elephant, so I thought I might join them," he went on. "When I thought about how willing they all were to part with their meager money before they started, I decided that I could just as easily part them from their fortunes when they had made them."

Libby bit her tongue and did not answer.

"Do you like my horse?" Gabe asked.

"He's very beautiful," Libby answered civilly.

"I won him in a card game last night," Gabe said. "It seemed like Providence's way of saying that I was to set out for the promised land."

"I'm sure Providence had nothing to do with it," Libby said dryly. "Don't they say the devil always helps his own?"

"I'm sure Old Nick would have provided me with a black steed, don't you think?"

Libby had to laugh at this. "So you've really joined Sheldon Rival?"

"It's common sense," Gabe said. "If you want to cross empty lands in safety, join the party with the most food and the most guns. This one has plenty of both. I anticipate a pleasant crossing and I put my horse at your disposal, whenever you are tired of walking."

"Thank you, but I can always ride on the back of the food wagon, since I am Mr. Rival's cook," Libby said.

Gabe threw back his head and laughed loudly. "You, a cook? That's a good one. When did you ever learn to cook?"

"Every woman can cook," Libby said frostily. "It's in the blood."

"Fortunately I take my meals with the hired hands," Gabe said.

"What convinced Mr. Rival to take you along?" Libby asked. "I understood that everyone here is in his entourage."

"So I am," Gabe said. "Resident gambler." He looked at Libby, his eyes dancing with amusement. "Don't laugh, it's true. One of the things he wants to do when he gets to California and makes his fortune selling shovels and flour to the poor provisionless miners, is to open a saloon and gambling den. He wants me to instruct him how it's done, having made his money until now in trading pork bellies and other such unattractive ways."

He looked around. "I don't see those two adorable young ladies whose acquaintance I hoped to further on this long, tedious trip. Are they resting?"

Libby looked straight ahead, wanting to tell Gabe the truth, but not daring to. "It was Mr. Rival's wish that I leave them behind," she said formally. "Mr. Rival does not like children."

Gabe stared at her, forcing her to look away. "So you want me to believe that you abandoned them in Independence?"

"That is what I was instructed to do."

"I don't doubt it," he said. "That Rival is a monster in monster's clothing. However, I feel that even after our short acquaintanceship I know you well enough to be sure that you would not leave those two children, even if their guardian angels showed up in person to act as their attendants. Come on, where have you hidden them?"

Libby kept staring straight ahead. "What I choose to do with my own children is my own business, Mr. Foster."

"You don't have to worry about me, Libby," Gabe said, dropping his voice. "Whether you know it or not, I'm really an ally." He spurred his horse on and moved up the wagon train, leaving her staring at his back.

They camped for the night in an attractive leafy grove. Sheldon Rival stood to one side, giving instructions to the men on the correct way to pitch his tent—an enormous palace of canvas which required the combined strength of all the hands to erect.

"I wasn't hired to play nursemaid and put up tents," one of the hands muttered after Rival had sworn at him for letting a guy rope go loose.

"If you don't like it you can ride right back to Independence and find yourself another party," Rival said easily. "Although I doubt there are many back there who will pay my kind of money if all these goods get through safely."

The man shot him a look of pure hatred and went back to the guy ropes. Rival disappeared into his tent with a bottle of brandy and Libby set about making her first supper. She had just started collecting wood for a fire when Jimmy the trail boss appeared with his arms full of large sticks.

"Here," he said. "Seeing as how you're new at all this, I thought I'd get you started with wood tonight. Mr. Rival hates to be kept waiting."

"Thank you very much," Libby said gratefully.

"Make the most of it," Jimmy said. "In a couple of days we leave all trees behind us and you'll have to do without wood."

"I see we have a little spirit stove," Libby said. "I suppose I have to use that."

Jimmy laughed. "You're really an optimist if you think one barrel of alcohol is going to last us to California. The spirit's for when the weather's too bad to get a fire going. Once we're on the plains you have to learn to cook with buffalo chips."

"Buffalo chips?" Libby asked. "How do you get chips off a buffalo?" She thought he was making fun of her.

Jimmy stifled a smile. "It's a polite word for dung, ma'am," he said. "You collect dung patties and use them for the fire. They burn real well although they sure smell funny."

"I see," Libby said, still not sure whether he was teasing her or not.

The fire started easily and Libby decided on rice to go with the steak. She cut a generous slice from the hunk of beef in the sack and poured rice and water into the big, black saucepan. The steak sizzled and browned over the fire, making Libby feel proud of her cooking. When she looked at the rice, however, she found that it had already absorbed all the water and was starting to burn. Hastily she poured in more, then more and still the rice continued to grow. At last the steak was done and the rice was a huge sticky mess in the black pot. When she tried it, it tasted rather like schoolroom paste. In a flash of inspiration she shook salt, pepper, and then cayenne over it, in an attempt to give it some flavor, and hid it under the generous slice of meat.

Far from being pleased, Sheldon Rival scowled. "What's this?" he demanded.

"It's steak. All gentlemen like steak don't they?" she asked.

"If they are in their dining rooms at home," he said. "Out here it's a wasteful way to eat meat. How long do you think the beef is going to last if you serve it up at this rate?"

"I'm sorry," Libby said.

"From now on cook me dishes that use a little meat with the rice," he said. "Stews and fricassees."

"Yes sir," she said, hoping that humility would appease him.

He cut the steak and nodded. "Not bad flavor," he said. Then he took a forkful of rice, swallowed, then gasped. "What the devil is in this rice? It fair burned my mouth off!" he spluttered, taking a large swig of brandy.

"The rice?" Libby asked, fighting to stay calm. "Oh, I decided to cook it the spicy way. To ward off sickness on the trail. It's an old Bostonian seafaring dish."

"Is it, indeed. Well, you keep your Bostonian dishes to yourself and serve me good old regular food, you hear?"

"Yes, sir" she said.

But next morning all the men in the camp woke

feeling sick. They went about their duties clutching their stomachs, rushing to the bushes, and alternately blaming the camp cook and the water they had drunk. Even Gabe Foster could not managed a witticism for once. Sheldon Rival strode among them, giving orders, looking revoltingly healthy. He came over to Libby as she cooked bacon for his breakfast.

"It seems your Bostonian way of cooking did the trick," he said. "We're the only two able-bodied members of the camp."

Libby smiled to herself as she went on cooking. She managed scrambled eggs, since Rival was carrying a whole barrelful, stored in brine, and even flapjacks from Ma Zettel's recipe book.

Rival actually complimented her on the breakfast. "Not bad at all," he said, which she realized was high praise from him. She sneaked eggs and flapjacks in to Eden and Bliss while the men were striking camp and told herself that she had been worrying for nothing and that the whole journey would go smoothly. Any moment now she could bring them out in triumph to show Sheldon Rival that he could not get the better of her.

But next day, as they were in the middle of setting up camp, there was a sudden downpour. Libby had just started on what she hoped would be an impressive stew and suddenly found three extra inches of water added to it. Hurriedly, she dragged the heavy stew pot into the wagon and set up the little spirit stove. The storm raged on outside, sending wind and rain buffeting under the canvas of the wagon.

"Mama, I'm scared," Bliss called softly to her mother between the packing cases.

"Don't worry, we're quite safe in here," Libby whispered back.

"I'm here, Bliss," Eden whispered to her sister. "I'll take good care of you."

"But what if the wagon blows away?" Bliss whispered back.

"It won't," Libby said. "Remember how you both promised to be brave until you can come out? Well, it's very soon now."

She had barely finished talking when the wagon flap opened and Jimmy stood there. Libby spun around guiltily, wondering if he had heard her talking over the roar of the storm. He certainly looked angry enough. "Are you crazy?" he demanded, glaring at her.

"What?" She tried not to look too guilty.

"Cooking in the wagon, in this wind?" he went on. "Do you realize, lady, that you've got a barrel of alcohol right next to you? One big gust of wind and the whole thing goes up in flames."

"What am I to do then?" Libby demanded, relieved that it was only a fire in the wagon he was angry about. "Mr. Rival will want his dinner and I certainly can't cook outside."

"Then tell him you'll have to cook in his tent," Jimmy said, as if it didn't matter too much. "If he wants hot food tonight, his tent's the only thing that's big enough. I'm not risking a fire."

So Libby had to carry the stew-pot and the stove through to Sheldon Rival's tent. She was amazed how well it was furnished with almost all the comforts of home. There was a rug on the floor, a camp cot covered in a quilt, and a folding chair and table on which a bottle and glass were placed. Libby half expected to see pictures on the walls. She set up her stove under Rival's mocking gaze, feeling him watching her every move, painfully aware that her movements looked so unprofessional.

"I must say it's nice to have a woman about the place," Rival said as he drained his glass. "Gives it that final, homey touch, wouldn't you say?"

"Are you married, Mr. Rival?" Libby asked, not having taken him for the type of man who would become lyrical about the comforts of home.

"Me? Married? Why would I want to be married?" he asked, laughing. "I have a housekeeper and a flock of maids who do what I tell them and don't ask for money to buy new hats all the time. As for the other comforts of home—they can always be bought. Money buys everything, as I expect you've found out."

"Not entirely everything," Libby said. "The finer virtues can't be bought."

Rival laughed again. "There are no finer virtues when you come down to it," he said. "Put people in a position of survival and there are no finer virtues. Wait until you get to the gold fields, if you make it that far. You'll see."

"I like to believe differently," she said.

"Then you're either very naive, or a very good actress," Rival commented.

"What do you mean by that?" Libby asked.

"I mean that I haven't entirely got you figured out, Elizabeth Grenville," he said, looking at her with narrowed eyes. "Either you are a devoted little wife and mother, as you claim, or you are a very smooth-operating lady confidence trickster, gambler, bar girl . . . you tell me?"

"I am exactly who I say I am," Libby said, not bothering to look at him.

"Yet you leave your children at the drop of a hat," he said. "You know Gabe Foster."

"I only met Mr. Foster on the boat coming here," Libby said hastily. "I certainly do not know him."

"I see," Rival said with a low chuckle. "There's not much that passes my attention, Mrs. Grenville. I'm inclined to suspect that you and Foster are working as a team."

"What an absurd idea," Libby said shortly.

Rival went on chuckling. "So you really want me to believe there's a devoted little husband waiting for you, sweating in the California sunshine?"

"You can believe what you like," Libby said, stirring the stew savagely. "Where I come from, you can trust the word of a gentleman or a lady, but then I don't suppose you've had much experience with either."

"Watch that soup, it's bubbling over," Rival snapped. "Get on with your job."

"Gladly, *sir*," Libby said and went on stirring.

It rained hard all night. Libby cuddled close to her little girls while the wind blew in through the joints in the canvas and rain dripped from spots which had not been properly waterproofed. In the morning the rain eased to a fine drizzle but as they set out, they found that the track before them had turned to a sea of mud. The ox teams strained, the drivers cracked whips and cursed, but one by one, the wagons slithered and got stuck.

Jimmy rode up to Sheldon Rival. "Just like I told you, you've got them loaded too heavily," he shouted. "You'll have to lighten the load."

"I'm not lightening any load," Rival yelled back. "Why do you think I've got all this stuff along? For my own pleasure? The only reason for going is to sell it in California."

"You won't make it to the first ferry, let alone California, if you don't leave some of it behind," Jimmy said.

"Then take out all your own personal stuff and make the people walk."

"They are all walking, except for Jackson and he's down with a fever."

"Cholera? If you're keeping cholera from me, I'll have you horsewhipped."

"It's not cholera, keep your hair on," Jimmy said. "It's a marsh fever. He's got the shivers."

"Give him a mule and send him back to Independence," Rival barked. "I'm taking no liabilities and no sick passengers along with me. I'm taking no risks, understand me, boy?"

"But Mr. Rival . . ." Jimmy began.

"Remember who's paying you, boy," Rival snapped. "Get rid of him and tell the men to carry their own stuff until we're out of this mud."

"We won't be out of this mud," Jimmy said. "Every wagon that's gone ahead of us will have churned up the track until it's impassable. You've got to lighten now or we'll never make it. Do you want to come with me now and tell me what you want left behind or do you want me to do it for you?"

The two men glared at each other like fighting dogs, then Rival stepped down from his wagon. "We'll redistribute," he said. "I'm not leaving one shovel or one sack of flour."

They started down the train, past the straining and

sweating oxen. Libby held her breath as they came closer to her wagon.

"Maybe you could get rid of some of this food," she heard Jimmy say. "You've got an awful lot to feed just one person. Maybe you'll have to go without some of those luxuries."

"Very well, very well," Sheldon Rival said with a sigh. "I suppose I can sacrifice as well as the next man. This is one wagon I want to get through without mishap. What do you think I've got too much of?"

Jimmy leaped up onto the back of the wagon. "Well for a start," he began, then he pulled away a sack and stopped. "What have we here?" he asked.

Eden and Bliss crept out, wide-eyed with fear. Libby jumped and grabbed them. "They are my children," she said. "Mr. Rival wanted me to leave them behind. I couldn't do it."

Sheldon Rival's face was almost purple with anger. "You dared to try and trick me?" he asked. "When I said no brats, I meant no brats."

"They'll be no trouble," Libby said. "They can walk. They do not need to ride in your precious wagons. They can eat from my portion of food. We will ask nothing of you."

"Absolutely right that you'll ask nothing," Rival shouted, "and nothing's what you'll get. You can take them and . . ."

The sentence was cut off because Gabe Foster came riding up, pushing his horse between Rival and Libby. "Hey, there they are," he said, bending to scoop Eden and Bliss up onto his saddle. "My two favorite ladies. I knew they couldn't be far away. Come along, I've been telling all the guys about you and they want to meet the prettiest girls between here and California.

They're all looking forward to hearing you sing to them at the campfire tonight."

He turned his horse and started to head back down the wagons again. "Even you couldn't be that much of a rat, Rival," he muttered over his shoulder.

Sheldon scowled after him as he watched his guards crowd around the little girls and heard high childish laughter.

"You better keep them well away from me," he said, "and you try and trick me on anything else and I'll forget you're a lady, so help me."

"Don't worry," Libby said. "I have no further reason not to be straight with you."

# CHAPTER 9

LIBBY'S DIARY: *June 10, 1849. We do not seem to be progressing westward very quickly. Already we have become bogged down in terrible mud. The whole trail is churned up and littered. It is not pleasant walking through sticky mud, and the mosquitoes particularly seem to love our fair northern skin. The children and I are covered in bites which are soothed somewhat by plastering wet mud on them, making us look like strange, primitive tribes-people!*

It took a while to get going again after some of Rival's goods had been taken out to lighten the loads. The men had to bring up the spare ox teams to drag the wagons, one by one, through each patch of mud, and even when they spread out sacking over the track, it was hard going. It was clear that every party ahead of them had to similarly lighten loads to get through. All along the trail was a litter of abandoned articles—sacks of bacon, fancy clothing, even an iron stove.

"Pity I didn't bring an extra wagon just for the purpose," Sheldon Rival muttered. "Or even a fleet of extra wagons. I have a feeling I could have sold people back their own stuff when we reached California."

"You're all heart," Libby said, making him laugh.

When they camped for the night everyone was exhausted and even Sheldon Rival was too tired to complain about his food. They had only covered twelve miles in twenty-four hours.

Later the next day they came to the first ferry. Wagons were lined up for a mile or more along the bank. Men sat in the sunshine making repairs to wagon wheels, sewing up canvas into bags or shelters. Others stood waist deep in the river, washing clothes. Everyone seemed to be occupied with a huge spring cleaning.

They had to wait three days for their turn to cross. Rival offered to pay extra to the ferrymen to cut to the head of the line, but there were enough men waiting who stood fingering their rifles to convince him to get back to his place. Finally it was their turn to cross. The ferry was simply eight dugout canoes lashed together with planks on top. Onto this they loaded the wagons and swam the oxen and mules across. Libby thought the whole contraption looked very flimsy and would almost rather have swum across with the mules. She held on tightly to the children as the water lapped at the ferry boards, but all of Sheldon Rival's company made it across and struck out westward again.

Soon after, the soft, wooded countryside came to an end. Ahead was a sea of grass, waist high and sighing in the light wind. They could see wagons from companies ahead of them, their bowed canvas tops now truly looking like white sails on a green-golden ocean. Through the middle of this endless prairie a new line of brown was now drawn where countless wagons had already created deep parallel ruts in the rich soil. Sheldon Rival's wagons now started across this, the rocking of the wagons each adding to the illusion of sailing. Libby found all this evoked more painful memories of home; the creaking of sailing ships in Boston Harbor, the tangy ocean breeze, the beach at Cape Cod, picnics, beach parties—all so civilized and safe. All along this prairie trail were constant reminders of how very precarious life was at the present; not just castoff furniture, photos in heavy frames, sacks of food or tools, but graves, every mile or so, covered with new soil and primitive wooden crosses with crudely scrawled inscriptions on them— Josiah Weldon from Buffalo, New York. Died May 28, 1849. Aged 17 Years.

Libby looked carefully at each one, hoping not to see Hugh's name. As she stared down at the fresh red earth a new and more disturbing thought came into her mind. She found herself almost hoping that she would come across Hugh's name so that she need not subject her children to the terrible unknown ahead and could go home again with clear conscience.

"Poor devil," Gabe said, riding up beside her as she stared at a grave, lost in thought. "To think that his family back in New York is still imagining him filling his pockets with gold." He shook his head. "This whole thing is madness."

"But you chose to subject yourself to it?"

Gabe gave her that easy, laconic smile. "Don't you know the devil always protects his own?"

"Don't say things like that, even in jest," she said, shivering. She watched his back as he rode up and talked to Eden and Bliss, perched in the back of the wagon. She saw their faces light up and heard their laughter as he spoke with them. I don't know what to make of you, Mr. Gabriel Foster, she said to herself. I've never met anyone who confuses me as much as you do.

When they stopped to camp that evening, Jimmy had the wagons drawn into a circle. "We're moving into Pawnee country," he said.

"I'd like to see any damn Pawnee try to mess with me," Sheldon Rival said. "We've enough firepower here to blast the whole Pawnee nation to kingdom come."

"I'm not worried about an attack," Jimmy said. "I'm more concerned with a sneak raid in the night that carries off all our mules."

He came over to Libby. "From now on you start collecting buffalo chips," he said. "You won't see more than five trees between here and the Rockies."

"Come children," Libby called to the little girls. "You can help Mama get fuel for the fire."

"Watch them, though," Jimmy called after her. "You don't want them stepping on a rattlesnake. Keep them close to you."

"There are snakes here?" Libby asked, suddenly not anxious to leave the rutted camping area and set off into the waving grass.

Jimmy grinned, a very boyish grin in a weathered man's face. "Don't worry. They won't hurt you if you don't hurt them, but they do object to being stepped on."

Libby took down an empty sack. "Maybe you ought to stay and play here, girls," she said. "I don't want to be worrying about you when I have to work."

"We'll be very good and careful, Mama," Eden said.

"We'll stay right beside you as Mr. Jimmy said we should."

"Yes, Mama, we want to come," Bliss added, not wanting to be left out.

"All right, come on then," Libby said.

In half an hour they had filled the sack with buffalo chips. They were not as disgusting as Libby had feared they would be, but hard and herb-smelling. The girls, not knowing what they were touching, filled the sack while Libby searched.

Libby had gone a little way ahead, leaving the girls sitting beside the sack when she heard a sudden yell. "Mama! A snake! I've been bitten by a snake!"

Libby rushed back to see a terrified Eden jumping up and down, slapping at her legs. "Mama, it's biting me. Make it stop biting me!"

"Where? Where?" Libby struggled with Eden's pantaloons.

"On my legs. It's biting my legs."

"Both legs?" Libby succeeded in pulling down the long cotton panties.

"There's no snake here," she said.

"But it hurts, it's biting me," Eden protested, almost hysterical now. "Make it go away."

Little red wheals were appearing all over Eden's calves. Libby, calmer now that she could see no snake, spotted the problem. "It's only ants," she said. "Look, nasty little red ants. Hold still and I'll brush them all away."

"They hurt like snakes," Eden complained, scowling down at her legs.

"I'm sure they did," Libby said soothingly. "Let's go back to camp and we'll put some nice cold water on the bites."

She led the children back, glad that she had not obeyed her first impulse to yell for help. She could imagine how Jimmy would have grinned if she had panicked over a few ants.

For the next few days life settled into a pattern with nothing to break the monotony. They broke camp early in the morning and marched until the heat of the day became unbearable. Then they marched again at midafternoon before finding a safe camping spot for the night.

In her diary Libby wrote: *June 15, 1849. In the middle of nowhere, between Independence and Fort Kearny. I had thought dangers would be the worst part of the journey, but I can see that boredom is far worse an enemy. Nothing changes from day to day. The sun rises, the sun sets and we don't seem to have progressed at all. How I long for something to change the monotony. Anything to speed up the pace of this journey. How will I endure three months of this?*

The sun shone down on the back of necks and bare arms, turning them from white to red to brown. Libby kept her bonnet pulled forward over her face in the hope of at least keeping her complexion pale, but she noticed as she peered into her little hand mirror that there were already unsightly freckles over her nose. Apart from that minor tragedy, she was now getting used to the journey. Her feet no longer throbbed with blisters at the unaccustomed walking. She had managed to bake bread in the dutch oven. She was even developing muscles from scouring out the blackened, sticky cooking pots and was feeling rather proud of the way she was coping.

If Father could only see me now, she thought with a smile.

The little girls were also looking well, choosing to walk with Libby rather than ride in the wagon. Libby was fanatical about selecting what they ate and drank, always aware of those cholera graves beside the track.

From time to time they overtook other groups that had stopped to mend broken wagon shafts or change wheels. The strangers often invited them to share a cup of coffee, but Sheldon Rival always insisted on pushing on, showing no interest in either socializing or helping his fellow travellers. Once they overtook a party down with fever. Rival made his drivers push on the teams with all speed and he kept his handkerchief clamped over his own mouth until they were far away.

Then, on the eighth day of prairie, when they were not far from Fort Kearny, their first point of reference on an almost blank map, they came upon a group of about twenty ragged men, a couple of ox wagons, and a few tired mules heading back to Independence.

"If you've got sickness, keep well away," Sheldon Rival shouted as they jostled for space on the narrow track.

"Sickness will be the least of your worries," one of the men called back. "When your head and your shoulders are separated, you'll not have to worry about cholera or anything else."

"What are you talking about?" Jimmy demanded, riding up to meet them.

"Haven't you heard? The Pawnee are on the rise. They've slaughtered a great group of seventy emigrants and they say they're thirsting for more blood."

"Who says?" Jimmy asked, unmoved.

"Out past Fort Kearny. It's common knowledge out

there. We decided to come back rather than risk it. We're not going to be cut up by savages."

"A bunch of cowards," Rival sneered. "Let them go home. All the more gold for the rest of us."

"You'll decide who is a coward when you feel your scalp being peeled off," the man said.

"I'd like to see the savage that dares to attack me," Sheldon Rival said. "Do you know how much ammunition I carry? How many guards I've employed? Let the Pawnee prey on weaklings if they want to. We're pressing on."

The man shrugged his shoulders expressively, then cracked his whip for the oxen to move on. Libby looked longingly after them. They had represented a way back to sanity and she had not taken it. Now, it seemed, she had Indians to worry about, as well as all the other disasters waiting to happen. Jimmy was still talking to Rival and it appeared from their faces that neither was concerned.

"Do you think there's any truth in what they say?" Rival asked.

Jimmy pushed his hat back on his head. "These rumors go up and down the trail all the time," he said. "I don't think there's been a large-scale Indian attack since so many people took to the trail. They might have picked off a lone wagon, but there's safety in numbers, isn't there?"

Libby walked on, hoping their confidence wasn't misplaced. She wondered how many braves there were in the Pawnee nation and what would happen if they went on an organized warpath. Now as she walked, she kept her eyes open for dust clouds rising in the distance. She did notice, however, that Sheldon Rival posted guards that night for the first time.

Until that point the prairie had been singularly empty of wildlife. With so many travellers, any misguided grouse or pigeon that came near the trail wound up instantly in a cooking pot. Every day the men had been on the lookout for buffalo, full of exaggerated tales of moving carpets of animals where any shot would be guaranteed to bring down a beast. They were beginning to resent the monotony and ready for any form of excitement when there was a cry in the distance of "Buffalo! Hundreds of 'em!"

Without waiting they grabbed at rifles, mounted every horse and mule, and were off into the grass, leaving Libby and the children coughing in the cloud of dust they made. It was only as they disappeared that Libby realized that the men who had gone were the guards and the wagon train was now completely unprotected. She looked around nervously, then told herself that it was broad daylight and that there must be enough men left behind who could get to rifles.

Eden and Bliss were playing at tea parties with leaves and pebbles in the shade of the wagon, so she took the opportunity to collect her buffalo chips for the evening meal. She stayed close to the trail, her ears straining for any sounds of a buffalo hunt. She could hear very distant cries but they seemed to be receding. She bent to fill her sack and when she straightened up, she found herself looking into the faces of three Indians.

All of the stories she had ever heard, whispered around the drawing rooms of Boston or printed in the cheaper newspapers, came rushing back to her. Indians carried off white women and took them as wives. Would that be preferable to being killed instantly? Would it be preferable to being scalped and dying slowly? She tried to remain outwardly very calm and not run. The three braves, for their part, did not appear about to make any hostile move, but they had appeared from the grass so miraculously and silently that she could not predict what they were about to do next. She nodded to them and hoped that they would pass her by. But instead they came toward her, talking to each other in deep, guttural voices and, to her horror, one of them reached out to touch her head, saying something as he did so. Libby's heart was beating so furiously that she was sure it must be sounding out across the plains like a drum. She wondered what would happen if she screamed. Would any help come or would it make the Indians panic and kill her quickly, or, worse still, carry her off?

Then she was aware of someone at her side. Gabe Foster came up and Libby was glad to see that a brace of pistols was shining at his belt. Instead of grabbing her and running or gunning down the Indians, he walked over to them and began conversing with many gestures. One of the Indians again pointed to Libby's head. Gabe nodded. Libby felt as if she was about to explode with tension.

"Would you get me out of here?" she snapped to Gabe.

"In a minute, what's the rush?" Gabe answered. "I've never met real live Pawnee before."

"So you're going to wait around and watch me get scalped?" she demanded.

"What gave you that idea?" he asked.

"They keep pointing to my head."

"That's because they like the tortoise shell comb you're wearing. They've come to trade."

"Oh," Libby said, feeling rather foolish.

One of the Indians grunted again, pointing at Libby. Gabe listened, then laughed.

"What's so funny?" Libby demanded.

"He asked if you were my squaw and says that you make much noise."

"Most amusing," Libby said. "So how come you speak their language if you've never met a Pawnee before?" she asked, hating to be shown up to Gabe in a bad light once more.

"Oh it's simple, if you've got the gift," Gabe said, turning back to her with a superior expression on his face. "When they say 'we make trade,' I guess that they've come here to trade."

"I'm going back to camp, please excuse me to your friends," Libby said icily.

"Wait, don't you want to see what they've got to trade?" Gabe asked.

Libby pulled the comb from her hair, causing it to cascade over her shoulders. "Here," she said, tossing the comb to him. "You trade if you want to. I'm getting back to camp."

Shortly afterward, Gabe returned with two beautiful wolf pelts. "Here," he said, flinging them down onto the ground. "They'll help keep you warm when we pass through the mountains."

"You got those for one comb?"

"I got three," Gabe said with a grin. "I kept one for myself as commission." He started to leave. "You'll be pleased to hear that the chief of those braves now has your comb stuck in his oily locks," he said. "I thought it suited you better."

He laughed as Libby gave him a cold stare.

She headed for her own wagon. "Look what Mama's

got, girls," she called. Eden crawled out from under the wagon.

"Where's sissy?" Libby asked. "Did she get too hot?"

"She went to you, Mama," Eden said. "She wanted to help you."

"But I didn't see her." Libby had visions of Indians, slipping away with Bliss under one arm. "Bliss!" she yelled. "Baby! Where are you?"

She stared helplessly at the sea of grass, realizing for the first time that it was taller than a small child. Bliss could walk in and be lost, a few feet from the path. In panic she ran up and down, then sprinted after Gabe. "Gabe, you've got to help me," she begged, grabbing at his arm. "Bliss has gone. Do you think those Indians could have taken her?"

Gabe ran for his horse. "Don't worry, we'll find her," he said. "You search close to the track and keep on calling. Maybe she's just lost her sense of direction."

He spurred his horse into a lope, moving through the grass as if he were wading. Libby tried to make herself search in an orderly fashion, walking through the grass calling, "Bliss? Where are you?" every few steps. She could feel her dress sticking to her back as she ran on. Then she heard Gabe's shout. He came riding toward her with a little white bundle sitting in front of him.

"Look, Mama, I found pretty flowers," Bliss said, holding out a crushed sunflower in her little hand.

"You're a bad girl to go away from sissy," Libby said, taking her from the saddle and holding her close.

"Don't, you're squashing my flower," Bliss said, wriggling to get free.

"You must promise Mama you'll never leave the

wagon again without me," Libby said. "Mama was very, very worried."

"Sorry, Mama, I promise. Now can I go show sissy my flower?" Bliss asked.

Libby put her hand on Gabe's boot. "Thank you so much," she said. "It seems that I'm forever to be in your debt."

"Don't worry about it," Gabe answered. "You forgot yourself enough to call me by my first name. I can see we're progressing in the right direction."

"You are so infuriating!" Libby snapped, leaving Gabe laughing.

She had hardly calmed down after her double frights when she felt the earth beneath her feet vibrating. A cloud of dust was heading toward the wagons. Her first reaction was that the Indians had gone back to tell their people that the wagon train was unprotected and had come to attack. She yelled to Eden and Bliss to climb up into the wagon, then rushed to grab a rifle that was under the nearest seat and stood at the ready. But instead of Indians, the dust cloud revealed a brown, moving mass and a herd of buffalo thundered toward the wagons, heads down and packed close in flight. The size and power of the huge beasts was so overwhelming that Libby forgot to be terrified. They came closer and closer to the wagons, then, when it seemed they must crash through the line, they swerved at the last minute. A shot rang out, and Libby noticed that there were men riding alongside. Beside the large beasts they looked puny, like hounds around a stag. More shots rang and one huge bull swerved away from the herd, cutting through between the wagons with the men after him, whooping crazily like Indians. They

came up on either side, shooting as the bull swerved
and faltered. Finally, he dropped to the ground while
the men rode around in circles, screaming wildly and
firing in the air.

Libby was both excited and sickened by what she
had seen. She couldn't help feeling sorry for the
bull who had been so majestic and had been tak-
en so unfairly in a hail of bullets. At least when
Indians hunted with arrows it was a fairer contest,
she thought. The men, however, were delighted, slapping each other on the back, each claiming their bullet
had felled the buffalo and their bravery had stopped
the herd from breaking away and being lost. In the
midst of the chaos Sheldon Rival strolled up.

"You know how to cut up a buffalo?" he asked
Libby.

"I'll do it if you show me the way," she countered.

"Just make sure I get the best steak for my dinner,"
he said, moving past her to kick at the carcass with
one polished boot.

In her diary that night Libby wrote: *June 21. I longed
for excitement and change. Today my request was granted
a little too well. Now I will be content with many days of
boredom ahead.*

## CHAPTER
# 10

AT LAST THE prairie came to an end. Ahead was a dryer landscape, dotted with strange rock formations rising sheer from the ground like exaggerated sand castles made by children. Dust now replaced mud on the trail. It rose from the plodding hooves and hung as an ever-present cloud in the air, coating faces and clothing and making the men constantly clear their throats and spit.

Bliss thought this was great fun and practiced until Libby caught her. "Don't do that, it's not nice," she said.

"Everyone else does it," Bliss said, "and the dust keeps getting in my mouth and making it taste nasty."

"Then hold your kerchief across your mouth," Libby said. "Ladies don't spit."

"I'm not a lady. I'm going to be a cowboy," Bliss said.

"She's right, Mama," the normally timid Eden

**113**

chimed in. "There are no ladies here. It doesn't matter what we do."

"I am a lady," Libby said, frowning at her daughter. "I will always be a lady and so will you. We were born to be ladies and we will remain ladies, whatever unfortunate surroundings we find ourselves in. Please don't forget it."

"No, Mama," Eden said, giving Bliss a grin. "Come on, sissy, let's go see if Mr. Foster will give us a ride."

Libby shook her head as they ran off. Sitting alone on the backboard of the wagon, she took out her diary, reading it through as if it were someone else's life, someone who had lived very long ago and far away from here. Then she wrote, in jerky scrawl as the wheels lurched and bumped: *July 2, 1849. The hardest thing is being entirely alone. There is nobody here I can talk to, nobody whose advice I can trust. I think I'd even be grateful right now for one of father's lectures.*

A picture of the drawing room at home swam painfully into her mind; Father sitting there with his pipe, his gold watch chain stretched across his broad stomach. "Pay attention to this, young lady," he'd say, wagging the pipe in her direction so that her mother had to look up from her sewing to comment, "Watch the ash, Henry."

*Such a small life we led then*, she wrote in the diary. *Our definition of a crisis was if the ribbon on a bonnet broke when you wanted to wear it, or if there were no lobsters available when you had planned lobster for dinner. And they wanted to make me as small as that—to have me married and domesticated and content with so little.* A sense of excitement shot through her because she realized that she had come so far on her own, without any help or advice and was her own mistress in a giant world of infinite danger and infinite possibilities. She closed the diary and put it away.

The danger, unfortunately, was all too real and all too frequent. Every day they passed other parties that had stopped beside the road to mend broken axles, to replace dead animals, or to wait for someone in the group to recover or die. Once they passed the only party they had met so far that contained a woman. They were camped under a canvas awning and the woman looked tired and old, although Libby suspected she was not much older than herself. She was crouched by a makeshift bed on which a small child lay deathly still.

"He fell off the wagon and the wheel went over him," she told Libby. "We've done all we can but it's only a matter of time." She looked up with empty, hopeless eyes. "Such a delight he was too. So full of life and mischief. I put him in the wagon because he would keep wandering off into the grass and I was scared he'd get himself lost." She gave a deep, shuddering sigh. "We already gave up one child on this trip. My other boy came down with cholera back in Independence. Now there's just our Alice. . . ." She looked across at a solemn ten-year-old who sat in the corner, staring down at her hands, saying nothing, not moving.

Libby was shaken and horrified. She brought the remains of the stew she had made to the woman, also a couple of eggs and some brandy. "Maybe some nourishing food would help," she suggested.

The woman gave the ghost of a smile. "You're most kind," she said. "I think prayer is all that can help us now. I'm sure the Lord knows what he's doing." But her voice faltered and the girl in the corner sprang up to run over to her. "Don't upset yourself again, Mother," she whispered, putting her arms around the woman as if their roles were reversed.

Libby came out of the shelter to find Sheldon Rival had walked back to see what the holdup was. He was furious when he found she had given away some of his food. "If you start handing out charity to every beggar along the route, we'll all die of starvation," he said. "This is the West. This is every man for himself."

"How fortunate that I'm a woman then," Libby said, looking at him steadily. "There was a dying child in there. I'll just have bread for the next few days if you begrudge the food."

She walked proudly past him as if he didn't exist.

"We're not stopping again for anyone or anything, and that's an order," he called after her.

Now they began to experience the problems of being late-comers to the crossing. Earlier parties had used up all the grass for animal feed. The whole trailside was lined with human debris, everything too heavy, or broken, or spoiled was cast aside and even the dust began to smell of decay. The only source of water was the muddy Platte River which flowed beside them in a wide dusty valley. The water holes, dug beside campsites, were foul and muddy. Cholera was everywhere and the number of graves increased to almost one a mile. Besides the dead humans were the dead and dying animals, oxen and mules that had tried to pull too heavy a load too far with too little food and water.

"Can't we do something, Mama?" Eden cried desperately, as they watched an ox lying beside the trail, lifting his huge head in an entreating groan as the wagons passed.

Libby, suffering with her daughter, took a dipper of water from the barrel and tipped it into the ox's mouth. She knew it was a waste of water and would not prevent his death, but she felt better as she walked on. She realized how lucky they were to have Sheldon Rival's supplies with them. The water from his barrels was sweet and pure, while the men had to boil up muddy river water and complained that all their food tasted of mud. Libby encountered the problems with mud when she tried to wash some clothes during a halt. The little petticoats and pantaloons came out browner than they had started. She had just spread them to dry on the back of the wagon when Sheldon Rival came past.

"Come over to my tent. I've got some washing that needs doing," he said.

"You hired me as a cook, not a washerwoman," Libby said indignantly.

"I also hired you without children," he said, puffing cigar smoke at her as he spoke. "I can drop you all off right here, if you like."

"You wouldn't dare."

"I wouldn't put that to the test, if I were you. These men know who's paying them. In the end they'd do what I wanted, believe me. The clothes will be in my tent."

Seething with anger, yet not daring to challenge Rival too far, Libby went down to his tent to pick up the dirty clothes. She had never washed men's underwear before and it revolted her to have to handle Rival's smelly, sweaty undergarments and shirts. She relieved her tension by beating them mercilessly on a rock at the edge of the river, as she had watched the men do.

When they were finally dry she carried them back to his tent. In answer to his, "Come in" she entered with the pile of clothes.

"Just don't complain that they are not white anymore," she said. "The water here is brown and everything washed in it turns brown too—" She broke off as Rival got up from his chair. He was naked except for a small towel around his waist.

"Oh, excuse me, I thought . . ." Libby muttered.

"Bring the things over to me," Rival said. Then, as she hesitated, "What's the matter? You never seen a man undressed before?"

"No," she stammered.

"Your husband went to bed in his clothes?"

"My husband was a gentleman in every sense of the word," she said. "He always undressed in his own dressing room. When he came to bed he was already in his nightshirt."

Rival half stifled a guffaw. "Sounds like a proper sissy to me," he said. "Did his nightshirt have lace around it too? So tell me, who fathered the kids? The milkman? The candlestick maker?"

"Your clothing, sir," Libby said, thrusting it into his hands.

"Wait, aren't you curious to see what the rest of a man looks like?" he asked. "Now's your chance. The best bits are still hidden. . . ." He put down the clean clothes and lowered his hands to his towel.

"Good day, Mr. Rival. I have to get back to my chores," Libby said and fled, red cheeked, to the sound of his laughter. She reasoned that he was just having fun at her expense, but she decided that she would take care in the future to keep away from him when there were no other men around. This was not

always easy, as the nights were now getting cold and
Sheldon Rival spent a lot of time alone in his tent,
drinking, eating, and reading. The rest of the men
were sociable around the campfire in the evenings,
but Rival never joined them, or invited them to join
him for a drink, except for Gabe Foster. When she
carried in his dinner, he seldom missed an opportunity to taunt her, using deliberately crude language
and looking at her with hooded, reptilian eyes.

"So tell me about this husband of yours," Rival
asked one evening, pausing to refill his brandy glass
as she put a casserole down on the table in front
of him.

"My husband?" she asked, surprised.

"Yes, the one you claim you're going out to in
California. The one with the lacy nightshirt."

"Why do you want to know?"

"He intrigues me, with his lacy nightshirt. Does he
know what to do underneath that lacy nightshirt?
Does he enjoy a good poke?"

"I beg your pardon?" Libby asked.

Rival laughed coarsely. "You know what I'm talking
about so don't pretend that you're affronted. I'm talking about a good poke, and I don't mean the fire—
or at least not the fire in the hearth. The fire in a
man's loins, and a woman's. Does he enjoy it, your
husband?"

"What goes on in the privacy of my bedroom is my
own business," Libby said shortly, her face hot with
embarrassment, "and a gentleman would never think
of mentioning the subject."

Rival laughed. "But, as you've said before, I'm no
gentleman. There are no gentlemen between here
and your precious Boston. We're now in the land of

take-what-you-can-get and shoot when someone else takes it first. That's the only law out here. I bet that even your husband is pulling off his pants quickly enough with the first bargirl he meets. No more lacy nightshirts out West."

"I'm sure I can trust my husband perfectly," she said.

"Then he must be a pansy boy," Rival said. "No real man can go for months without a poke—no real woman either. Can you look at me and tell me that you don't miss it? That you wouldn't, if the time and place and person were right?"

"I'm sorry, but I'm not coming in this tent anymore if you insist on being so crude and disgusting. I'll have one of your men bring your food in the future."

Rival laughed again. "You see, I've caught you. You didn't deny that you missed it. What you need is a good poke from a real man. It might make you into a real warm woman."

"I'll let you know if ever I meet a real man," Libby said coldly and made her exit.

How dare he! she muttered as she stalked back down to the fire.

"Hey, what's the hurry?" Gabe Foster asked, grabbing at her arm as she swept past him.

"You men are all alike," Libby snapped. "Why can't you all just leave me alone and treat me like one of the men?"

"Very well, if that's what you want," Gabe said. "There's a poker game tonight after supper and Jake's breaking a new keg of rum. How about it?"

"Oh, go away," she said, pushing past him, her anger softened.

That night she thought about the conversation

again. The worst thing was that Rival had been right. She did miss having a man in her bed. But certainly not Sheldon Rival. Not if he were the last man on this earth. She found that her thoughts had wandered to Gabe Foster and the way he looked at her that was so unnerving . . . No! she told herself firmly. Think of Hugh. Think of poor Hugh with a pickaxe in his hand, his palms all blistered, digging gold. Think of how surprised he'd be. How happy. . . . But when she tried to conjure up his face she found that the image was already vague and indistinct, like someone seen through a fog.

# CHAPTER
# 11

AT LAST THE broad, dusty valley of the Platte began to narrow and the trail began to climb into a desolate country of steep hills clad in somber evergreens. The river itself swirled and thundered as it was channeled through its narrowed bed and each small stream that flowed into it presented a difficult crossing. Sometimes they had to raise the wagon beds to keep the contents dry, and it was a job to stop the oxen from being swept away in the fast-flowing water. At least they had enough to drink for a while and there were patches of grass which parties ahead of them had overlooked, so that they could progress faster than they had done for several days. The ride was now bone shaking as they jerked over crevices and boulders along the path.

Now she had seen what could happen to a child left in a wagon. Libby chose to walk almost all the time, her little girls close beside her. The girls, however, had become more adventurous and constantly wanted to run off and explore. Best of all they liked to ride ahead with Gabe, coming back with tales of deer or antelope they had spotted in the forest. Almost every day Gabe offered Libby the chance to ride his horse and every day Libby refused.

"I don't know why you don't like Mr. Foster," Eden said. "He's the nicest man I ever met."

"I like him better than Daddy," Bliss chimed in. "Why can't he be our daddy instead?"

"That's a foolish thing to say, Bliss," Libby chided. "Your daddy is working very hard for us and we're going to help him. Mr. Foster is being very nice to you children, I agree, but if we were back in Boston, he would not be the sort of man we could mix with socially."

"But we're not in Boston, Mama," Eden said. "You can mix with anyone you like out here."

"That's enough, Eden," Libby snapped. "I'm beginning to wish that we'd brought Miss Hammersham along to keep you two in order. You're already turning into little savages and we've only been away from home for two months. You'd never have answered back at home."

"You're turning into a savage too, Mama," Eden said, grinning at Bliss. "Look at your dress and you don't even wear a corset anymore."

"I have to dress to stay comfortable," Libby said primly, "but I remain a lady at heart. So should you. Now let me hear you recite your times tables again. Begin with seven."

"Aw, shucks," Eden said, causing Libby to look at her sharply.

"Eden Grenville, I do not wish to hear language like that," she said. "If you can't behave properly, I'll have you sit in the wagon and practice your sewing stitches all day."

She looked up to see Gabe's face. He tried to hide his amusement as she frowned at him.

"Can we ride with Mr. Foster, Mama?" Bliss asked.

"No, you cannot. I want you to sit inside the wagon and do your lessons," Libby said. "If you were home it would be lesson time right now. Your father will be very disappointed if you have forgotten all that you have learned. Go along—help Sissy into the wagon."

When the children had run on ahead, Gabe rode up to Libby. "You're going to have to give them some freedom, you know," he said. "They've got to survive in very tough circumstances. You're not helping by keeping them as prissy little Boston misses, holding your hand all day."

"Mr. Foster," she said, turning coldly toward him. "I am trying to bring up my children the way that I see fit. It is my belief that we shall only survive if we keep up our standards. By that I mean standards of cleanliness and manners and morality. I want my children ready to step back into the highest level of society when we return and I aim to keep them safe and sound until we do."

"You're going to have to unbend, Libby," Gabe said quietly. "You can't spend every moment watching and worrying over them."

"So you're suggesting that I let them get lost or step on snakes or fall off wagons like that poor little child in the shelter?" she demanded. "But then you seem to take a very light view of life and of people. People only exist for your amusement and profit, don't they? That must be why you have never made any attachments to hold you to one place. Since you have none of your own, I'll thank you to keep your views on child rearing to yourself, Mr. Foster."

Gabe raised his hat. "Good day to you, ma'am," he said and rode on.

Later that day they had to cross the Platte River itself. There was a long line of wagons waiting for the Mormon ferry. Sheldon Rival refused to be delayed again, and rode ahead to negotiate. He came riding back with a beet-colored face, brandishing his whip. "Those damn crooks!" he blustered. "Call themselves religious? They're nothing but cheap crooks. Not only would they not consider taking us out of turn, but they have the gall to demand five dollars per wagon to ferry us across. Five dollars! Can you imagine sixty dollars, just for the wagons?" He slid from his horse and handed it to the nearest man. "Get Jimmy and tell him we're going to ferry ourselves across right here. I'm not waiting to pay those crooks five dollars a wagon."

Jimmy wasn't too happy about the prospect of the company crossing the Platte by themselves, but Rival refused to change his mind. It was no easy task to have a horseman swim across the swift-flowing stream and secure a couple of strong ropes to trees on either side. When this was done, Jimmy had his men take the wheels off the wagons and seal the cracks in the wagon beds with tar. Then they were pushed into the water to float them across. Men stationed at the front and back of each wagon grasped the ropes to stop it from being swept downstream. Libby held her daughters close to her as she watched the first wagons try this insane crossing. Mules and oxen were thrashing and squealing in the icy, swirling water as their teamsters tried to drive them across. One heavily laden mule got

caught in the current and was swiftly carried downstream and out of sight, his eyes rolling in panic as
he disappeared.

"Do we have to cross like that, Mama?" Eden whispered, for once not needing to be told to hang onto
Libby's skirt.

"There doesn't seem to be any other way," Libby
said. "I expect it's safer than it looks."

Gabe rode up to the bank. "I'd offer to take the
girls across on my horse," he said. "He's a very strong
swimmer. But I know you'd call my offer interfer-
ence, so I won't upset you by making it."

Then he urged his horse down into the stream and
was soon striking out strongly for the opposite shore.
All Libby could do was to ride across in her wagon,
trying to conceal her terror as the stream threatened
to tear the rope out of the men's grasp and icy water
seeped around her feet, through cracks which had
not been properly sealed. When they made it safely
to the other side, Gabe was waiting to lift down the
children. He then reached out his hand to escort her
to shore.

"Thank you, I need no help, Mr. Foster," Libby
said. As she was about to step ashore the current
caught the wagon and swung it around so that there
was now a gap too wide for her to step across. She
had to go to her knees into the icy water, wading
ashore with her skirts lifted in a futile attempt to
keep them dry.

"Nice ankles," was Gabe's only comment as he
walked away.

Libby collected her sodden skirts and gave him a
stare to match the temperature of the water.

When the wagons were reassembled and the teams

gathered, they started off again, leaving the valley of
the Platte behind them. The country grew progress-
ively wilder and dryer. There were no more dark fir
trees on the mountains and the vegetation shrank to
occasional sagebrush which the animals could not eat.
The heat was intense. It reflected off rock surfaces
and made the white wagon-tops blinding to look
at. The men peeled off their shirts and rode or
walked in pants only, their torsos turning from red to
dark brown. Libby looked at them longingly. She had
already dared to walk without her corset and was now
down to one petticoat under her lightest dress, but the
thin fabric clung to her back and the tight sleeves were
like a torment. She watched the girls skipping happily
in their light ginghams and decided that she would
make herself a dress like theirs, however strange it
looked.

The end of a day without water came. The men
licked dry, cracked lips and looked resentfully at
Sheldon's water wagon as he dipped at his own barrel
of pure water. He even splashed some over his face,
deliberately, Libby thought, to show that he was boss
and owned luxuries they did not.

As the sun sank behind western peaks they saw a
pool of water gleaming ahead of them. The first
teams ignored the shouts and whips of their drivers,
lurching crazily toward the water. "Stop them! Get
them back! Hold their heads!" the drivers yelled to
each other, risking thundering hooves, trying to control the animals and grab at their heads. Libby wondered what all the panic was about until the stench
hit her, making her press her hand to her mouth, her
stomach heaving with revulsion. All around the pool
were the bloated carcasses of dead animals, their legs

straight in the air, their flesh crawling with maggots. Some of the spare oxen, unhampered by a wagon behind them, reached the pool and started drinking before they could be dragged away. By then it was too late. Within a few minutes they were writhing in agony, bleeding from their noses, and dying.

"What is it?" Libby asked in horror as one of the men fought to restrain the frantic mules.

"Alkali pools," the man shouted back. "There's no good water between here and the Sweetwater, and we won't reach that for a couple of days."

It took half an hour to force the desperate animals on past the lake and by then the poor oxen were so exhausted that two of them flopped to their knees and would not get up.

"Idiots!" Sheldon Rival yelled. "Now I'm down to three spare teams. How am I going to cross the desert?"

"You'll have to leave some of the stuff behind, like I've been telling you," Jimmy yelled back, his face and chest running with sweat that had carved channels through the coating of yellow dust. "We'll have to ditch some of that flour and some of those shovels and combine the load."

"You're crazy!"

"Then we ditch your food and you eat moldy flour and beans with the rest of us."

"Do what you must, then," Rival growled. "Take out some of the shovels and bury them. I'll pay someone to go back for them when I'm set up in California. Make it look like a grave, then nobody will steal them."

"Nobody will steal them," Jimmy said scathingly. "They're all trying to lighten their own loads right now. Nobody would be fool enough to take on extra."

Libby tried to cook dinner in the bitter stinging wind that whipped up dust and grit. The wind kept threatening to take the fire and sweep it into the surrounding tinder-dry brush, however Libby arranged screens around it. Consequently, she didn't dare do more than fry some bacon quickly, then fry eggs and bread in the grease.

"What's this supposed to be?" Rival demanded. "Am I wrong or is it supposed to be dinner and not breakfast at seven P.M.?"

"It's a choice of that or wagons flambé," Libby said shortly. "You try keeping a fire going safely in this wind."

Rival took a mouthful. "It tastes gritty," he said, but Libby was already walking away, past caring. She lay in the wagon that night, listening to the wind peppering the canvas with a constant barrage of grit, feeling her tongue and lips swollen and coated while she fantasized about water; water in hot baths, water in babbling brooks, gentle waves breaking over her at Cape Cod, iced pitchers of lemonade in summer. She still would not waiver from her promise to share her food and drink ration with her children and so most of her water had gone to them.

In the morning the wind had still not died down and everyone rubbed red and swollen eyes as they tried to break camp. The animals had to be whipped to make them get up and move off.

"If we can do fifteen miles today we'll make the Sweetwater by nightfall," Jimmy encouraged.

Libby kept the children in the wagon and wrapped a scarf around her face to keep out the worst of the dust. At times it swirled around them thick as fog, so that the wagon in front looked like a ghost ship, plowing through a phantom ocean. Libby looked longingly at the wagon, safe and secure with its flaps tight, but she could see that the animals were laboring with the load they already had, their nostrils and flanks flecked with foam.

By midafternoon the dust storm intensified, blotting out the sun and forcing all of the men to tie handkerchiefs over their faces. They staggered by their animals, coughing and retching and cursing. Just when the air was thicker than any midwinter Boston fog, Libby noticed something lying beside the path.

"Wait," she called, but the wind snatched away her little voice so that nobody heard or waited. She went over cautiously and saw that a body was lying there, half covered with sand, unburied. She ran up to Sheldon Rival. "There's a dead man beside the path."

"So? What can I do about it?" Rival asked.

"We should bury him, not leave him there for the wolves."

"He's dead. He won't know the difference."

"It's only common decency."

"I'm not stopping now," Rival shouted as the wind picked up. "If we don't make the Sweetwater by nightfall, we'll all be dead."

The wagons plodded on. Libby hesitated, then grabbed a spare piece of canvas from the wagon. At least she could cover him. That was the least one could do.

"What is it?" Gabe asked, passing her as he led his horse.

"A body," she said. "I thought we should at least cover it."

"I'll come with you," Gabe said.

Libby went forward hesitantly as Gabe knelt beside

the body. She shut her eyes, remembering the maggots on the cattle carcasses. Then she opened them again as Gabe gave an exclamation.

"He's still alive," he called. "Hey, Rival!" he shouted at the disappearing wagons, "this man's still alive. Hold on a minute, we must get him aboard."

"I'm not stopping," Rival called back, "and I'm not taking him with us. He could have cholera for all we know. Keep those wagons moving," he yelled to the men.

Libby looked at Gabe. "I'll get him some water," she said. She ran and scooped up a mugful. Gabe raised the man's head while Libby tried to pour a little through the swollen lips, then washed off the encrusted face with her kerchief. The man coughed, then licked his lips as if he could not believe his senses. His eyes opened suddenly and focussed on Libby and Gabe. They were young, blue eyes and they looked bewildered.

"Here, don't try to talk. Drink this," Gabe said. The man took a couple of quick gulps. "God bless you, sir," he muttered.

Libby finished sponging his face and looked at him more closely. She had a sudden remembrance of a cheeky grin and a southern voice drawling, "I'm nineteen, ma'am. Almost . . ."

"Luke!" she said in horror. "You're Luke, aren't you?"

"You know him?" Gabe asked.

"I met him on the river steamer. He's from South Carolina and his name's Luke something."

Hearing his name, the young man turned wearily to look at Libby. "Bonnie?" he asked, puzzled. "I thought you was back in South Carolina. I was going to get gold for you, Bonnie. You shouldn't be here. It's no place for a woman . . ."

"Bonnie?" Gabe asked, giving Libby a quizzical look.

"I think that was the girl he was going to marry," she whispered. "He thinks I'm her."

"What happened, Luke?" Gabe asked gently.

"Danged gun went off," Luke mumbled. "The wind blew it over and it went off. Got me in the side. They went on without me."

Libby glanced down and saw that his left side was dark with blood under the encrusting sand. "Your friends just left you here?" Libby demanded.

"They didn't have much choice. There was no water left. Anyways, I'm better now," he muttered. "It don't hurt no more. Now I got that water in me, I'll catch up with them soon enough. I'm going to be fine, ain't I?"

"Just fine," Gabe said, patting his hand.

"That's good," Luke said, licking his lips. "I'll be in California in no time at all."

Libby looked at Gabe's face. He drew her aside. "You go on," he said. "You don't want to lose sight of the wagons. I'll stay with him."

"I'll stay too," she said resolutely. "You can't move him alone."

Gabe shook his head. "He's not going anywhere," he said in a low voice. "He won't last much longer. He's lost too much blood."

"We can't just leave him here," Libby said. "Maybe there would be a chance if we caught up with a company who had a doctor with them . . . maybe just some good food and drink?"

Gabe shook his head solemnly. "I've seen enough dying men, Libby. We can't move him. You go ahead.

I'll stay with him until the end."

"I'll stay too then," Libby said.

"Libby, the shape he's in right now, my horse can only carry one person," Gabe insisted. "I'd rather you kept with the wagons. We don't want to risk three corpses instead of one." He touched her hand. "There's really nothing you can do," he said. "I'll rig up a shelter around him and give him water and that's about all anyone can do, I'm afraid."

"But what if he doesn't die for days?" Libby asked.

"He won't last the night," Gabe whispered. "Believe me, Libby. You go on. I'd rather you were safe. Go on, or you'll miss the wagons in this dust."

Libby looked at the dim shapes fading into obscurity, then back at the young man. He was lying peacefully with eyes closed now. She bent over him. "I have to go now, Luke," she said softly, "but I'll be back real soon." Then she gave his forehead a gentle kiss. He didn't speak but a little smile spread across his lips. Gabe's eyes met hers. She got to her feet, brushing off the sand and began to walk after the wagons.

They camped for the night by a mineral spring a couple of miles farther on. The water was too bitter for humans to drink but it had been trampled around the edges and was not surrounded by bloated corpses so Jimmy decided they could risk letting the animals drink a little. The men, however, tried boiling it but spat it out again, choosing to finish the last drops in their canteens.

All the time she was getting a fire going Libby kept looking back for Gabe. As it got dark she began to worry about him. What if the dust storm was worse over the lip of the hill and had blotted out their trail? She could see how easy it would be to lose one's

way in this featureless landscape. Then there were
rattlesnakes, there were reports of wolves, although
they had seen none, but they came upon graves that
had been dug up and the bones scattered. That was
blamed on wolves. And of course, there were desperate men out here, men who might have gotten
themselves separated from their own companies and
who would risk anything for a horse, or a gold watch
chain, or even a water flask.

Sheldon Rival complained that she had slopped his
coffee into his bread when she carried the tray to him,
but she hardly heard him, her ears straining for the
thud of horse's hooves over dry ground. She collected
Rival's tray and ate her own meal. She washed up in
water from the spring that stung her dry, sunburned
hands and she tucked the girls in for the night and
still he hadn't come. The men settled down around
their campfire on the other side of the circle. Someone got out a banjo and they started singing, laughing at what were apparently crude lyrics. She could
see the lamp glowing inside Rival's tent as he sat and
drank alone. At last the campfire died down to a red
glow and Sheldon Rival turned out his lamp. Libby
hesitated, agonizing between wanting them to send
out a search party right away and not wanting them
to see her concern.

She climbed into the wagon beside the girls and
pulled her blanket over her, shivering in the bitter
night air, but she lay wide awake, watching a new
moon rise over black hills, listening to the moan of
wind in sagebrush and the sound of an immense
silence. It must have been past midnight when she
thought she heard rocks tumbling on the path above.
She leaped out of bed and watched a dark shape

coming down the gentle incline toward them. The
dark shape defined itself into a man leading a horse.
"Thank God," Libby muttered and let the canvas fall
quickly back into place. She heard the chink of a harness, the soft snort of a horse's breath, and the scrape
of Gabe's boots on rock as he came past her wagon.
The footsteps paused for a moment, then kept on
going.

# CHAPTER 12

THEY STRUCK THE Sweetwater next day. Men and beasts alike went crazy splashing and drinking in the good, icy water. The men fished and gave Libby two beautiful trout for dinner. She grilled them over the fire and they looked truly appetizing, with moist pink flesh showing through crisp, wood-smoked skin. Finally I should get a compliment from the Old Bull on this, she thought as she put the fish on a bed of rice and handed it to one of the men to take in to Sheldon. But the meal came back half eaten.

"Mr. Rival's not feeling good," the man said, putting the plate down beside Libby. "He's got the fever bad and he'd like some of that spruce-needle tea."

"Very well," Libby said. She put water on to boil and then carried the tea into Rival's tent. Rival was lying on his cot, already in his nightshirt. His face was flushed and he scowled as he looked up.

"There you are at last," he said. "I could have died before you got here."

"Water takes a long time to boil up here," Libby

136

said. "I made it as fast as I could."

"I need some company," Rival said. "It's damned lonely for a man, all alone when he's feeling ill. Feel my forehead—do I have a fever?"

Libby knelt to put down the tea then reached across. "A slight one," she said.

"My head aches like the devil."

"They say that's from the altitude," Libby said. "We're supposed to be very high here."

"Altitude, my foot," Rival said. "It's a sickness you've brought to this camp from stopping with that dying fellow."

"The man was shot in the side. He had no sickness."

"Poppycock. I'm the fittest man on earth, usually," Rival said. "Either you brought in the fever or you're poisoning me with your cooking."

"Mr. Rival, I eat what you eat and I am perfectly healthy," Libby said. "If there's anything wrong with you, it probably comes from drinking too much."

"Nonsense. I've not been drinking enough," Rival said. He propped himself up on one elbow. "In fact that's what I need right now. Not any pansy-boy tea, but another glass of brandy. Bring the bottle over here."

"Have you already been drinking?" she asked as he picked up an empty glass.

"Of course I've been drinking."

"It's really not good for a fever or a headache."

"Woman, don't tell me what I need," Rival said. "Hand me that bottle." He indicated the half-empty bottle on a packing case.

"I really don't think that's wise, Mr. Rival," Libby

said, but Rival leaned over. "The bottle, dammit," he said.

"Careful, you're going to fall out of bed," she said, bending to grab him as the cot teetered. He put out a hand to steady himself, holding onto her shoulder. Suddenly, it was as if he had become aware that a woman was kneeling beside him and he had his hand on soft white flesh. The bloodshot eyes moved slowly down her body. "On second thought," he said, slurring his words slightly, "maybe I don't need another drink."

"Very sensible," Libby said, reaching to pick up the tea. The pressure on her shoulder increased.

"And I don't need any tea either," he said. "I know just the way to work off a fever." Libby had taken to leaving the top buttons of her dress undone because of the heat. As she bent over, Rival suddenly grabbed at her, trying to force his hand down inside her dress. Libby was so shocked that she opened her mouth to scream but no sound came out. She grabbed at the hand, trying to drag it away, but he laughed as he fought to undo her buttons with his other hand. "So soft," he murmured. "Do you know how long I've gone without . . ." He lost patience with the buttons and jerked the fabric so savagely that the buttons came flying off, pinging like missiles against the tent side. The light fabric of her dress front ripped. His hand slid inside her camisole and closed around her breast.

"Stop it, let go of me," Libby gasped, trying to lift away his hand and push his face away from her at the same time.

"Come on, don't play coy with me. Don't pretend you don't want it," Rival murmured, his mouth open

hungrily, like a fish gasping for air. He tried to pull
her exposed breast toward him, the cot tipped, and
he fell heavily on top of her. His weight knocked the
breath from her as she tried to scream and immediately he crushed his lips on hers, one hand still trapped
around her breast, the other scrabbling wildly to lift
her skirt. Libby tried to turn her head this way and
that to get herself free. Rival was moaning with impatience, already moving on top of her.

Get the tea, Libby was telling herself. Find the hot
tea. Throw it over him. It must be right here. She
reached out her hand over the floor, trying to locate
the mug without knocking it over, trying not to give
in to panic. Rival was already tugging at the fasten-
ings on her undergarments.

Then the voice spoke, loud and clear from the
doorway.

"Mr. Rival, sir?"

"Go away, dammit," Rival growled.

"I distinctly remember you asked me to come and
play cards with you at nine," Gabe's voice came clearly
across the tent, "and it is nine. So I came. But I can
see that you're otherwise engaged at the moment."
Libby looked across at him imploringly. "Good evening, ma'am," Gabe said easily. "So I'll come back later,
will I?"

"Get lost, Foster," Rival muttered, half moving off
Libby to glare up at him. Libby finally managed to
get a hand free and struggled to sit up.

"Get away from me, you animal," she said, her voice
breaking into a sob.

"It's just that you did say nine, and I know how you
value punctuality," Gabe said. "So I gather you don't
want to play cards this evening?"

"Don't be a fool, Foster. Can't you see we're busy?" Rival demanded.

"It's just that I get the impression that the lady isn't as interested in being busy as you are," Gabe said. "Am I right, ma'am?"

"If she knows what's good for her," Rival mumbled. "She's my property right now, Foster. Mind your own damn business."

"I didn't think the duties of a cook included so much," Gabe said. "Remind me to hire myself one."

"I said get out, Foster. Remember who you're working for."

Gabe's hand played with the silver pistol at his belt. The crisp click as he cocked it made Rival look up in alarm. "Get your hands off her, Rival," Gabe said evenly, "or one little bullet will mean you'll never do it again. Do I make myself clear?"

Reluctantly, Rival rolled over and sat up. "Go to the devil, Foster."

Libby scrambled to her feet, trying to smooth down her skirts and hold her ripped bodice up over her breasts.

"I'll walk you back to your wagon," Gabe said.

"I can manage," Libby mumbled, ashamed as if she had been the cause of the scene.

Gabe ignored her and fell into step beside her. "Are you all right?" he asked gently.

"Thank you, yes," Libby answered, looking away. "Really, I don't need you to walk with me. . . ."

"That's all right then. I'll just accept your undying gratitude, then I'll go."

"I got the impression you were enjoying yourself at my expense," Libby said.

"I was rather," Gabe answered, "but I fully intended to rescue you."

"Did it occur to you that I didn't need your help?" Libby demanded. "You love to interfere, don't you?"

"So you were enjoying it? I didn't get that impression."

"I meant that I was perfectly able to save myself. I was about to throw a mug of hot tea over him when you walked in."

"And if he had liked being bathed in hot tea?" Gabe stopped and put his hand on her arm. "Libby, you're not in Boston now. There are no more gentlemen and there are too few women. It's no good thinking you can appeal to decency because we've left it behind, and any man can take what he wants from you in a struggle—even a flabby specimen like Sheldon Rival. You have to face the fact that you're not invulnerable. You need protection. You're a woman."

His grip on her arm tightened so that he was almost shaking her. "Libby, you can't act as if you're made of stone all the time. It won't work. You've got to bend. . . ."

Tears that she had suppressed for so long sprang stinging into her eyes. "I can't bend," she managed to say in a choked voice. "If I bend, I'll break."

Then she ran to her wagon and climbed in before he could see her cry.

They followed the Sweetwater upward for a week and, at the end of July they crossed the Great Divide.

"South Pass," Jimmy said excitedly, riding up the column on a slim little piebald he had got in trade from an Indian.

Libby looked around at the desolate jumble of bare

rocks and weather-worn hills. It wasn't even clear that the trail beyond went down again. It was not what she had expected of a mountain pass, especially not of the crossing from East to West. "How can you tell?" she asked.

Jimmy screwed up his eyes against the harsh light. "We experienced scouts learn to recognize every inch of the trail," he said. Then his face creased into a grin. "Besides," he said, "someone before us has scribbled South Pass on that rock over there."

Libby laughed with the relief of knowing that they had reached the top of the trail. She peered ahead almost expecting to see the Pacific Ocean between the peeks. "That's good news," she said.

"Isn't it just?" Jimmy said happily. "It's nice to know we've made it halfway."

"Halfway?" Libby blurted out.

Jimmy looked amused. "Didn't you know that the Rockies are halfway? At least we get to go downhill for a while now, although we've got the worst part ahead of us."

"Oh," Libby said, turning away in disappointment. She already felt as if she had been in this world of unreality for half her lifetime. She had been strong and brave for as long as she could and she really longed for a return to the civilized world of afternoon tea and carriage rides and new bonnets. Then she remembered how she had chafed at that world, impatient with its pettiness and smallness. "Where do I belong?" she muttered to herself. "What do I want?"

She sent Sheldon Rival another trout in for his dinner, refusing to go anywhere near his tent. After her terrible experience she had acted as if he did not exist and it appeared that he too was somewhat embarrassed by it, since he seemed to take pains to avoid her as well. After the dinner was cleared away and the men had settled into a card game around their fire, Libby told the girls a bedtime story, then wandered around, strangely restless. A fat, yellow moon was rising over black peaks and the night was completely still. Coarse laughter came from the card game. Horses whickered, oxen snorted, and hooves clattered on the hard ground. Libby had a sudden desire to be away from it all. She began to walk up the slope of the nearest hill until she stood on its bare summit and looked back at the pinpoint of red glow that was the fire. Above her stretched an immense canopy of black velvet sky, hung with stars so thick and bright that she almost felt she could reach up and pluck one.

How insignificant we are, she thought, looking back at the firelight in the sea of blackness. Nobody in the world knows we're here. Then the thought went one step further. Is there anyone in the world, back where the lights are on the other side of the blackness, who is thinking of us right now? Are my parents worrying about me? Does Hugh think I'm safe in my Boston bed?

But even Hugh and her parents seemed more unreal than the granite under her feet and the stars above her head. She sat down on a boulder, leaning back to study the stars. Up here the Milky Way made a clean line across the heavens. She remembered her first governess, Miss Danford, saying that the stars were the cracks in the floorboards of heaven. She had always found that a comforting thought when she was a small child. Later, when Miss Danford still persisted in saying it, she had thought it stupid and babyish.

Now she was no longer sure that Miss Danford hadn't been right. After all, Libby thought, it was she who predicted I'd come to a bad end if I didn't curb my impulsiveness, and look where I am now. A million miles from anybody who loves me or even knows me.

She could not have imagined it possible to feel so completely alone. She had not let herself give in to fear until now, but up here, away from the noise of the camp, the fear and the hopelessness threatened to swallow her up. She wrapped her shawl tighter around her and started to go down back to the noise and the fire, when she saw a dark shape, coming up the hill toward her. She realized at once that nobody would hear her if she called out and she had not gotten into the habit of taking a gun with her, as all the men did. She picked up a rock, holding it firmly in her right hand. If it was an animal, a thrown rock should scare it off.

"Who's there?" she asked, her voice sounding unnaturally loud.

"Libby, is that you?" Gabe asked.

"What are you doing, following me around?"

"I didn't know you were here," Gabe said, coming the last few steps up the slope in large strides. "I came to look at the stars and to get away from the camp. What are you doing up here? It's not very wise, you know."

"I came to get away too," Libby said, "but I was just on my way down."

"Don't go because of me," Gabe said. "I can find myself another hill if you want to be alone. One thing we have enough of around here is empty hilltops."

"I really was on my way down," Libby said. "It was just too lonely up here. It overwhelmed me."

Gabe sat on the rock Libby had been sitting on. "Yes, it is daunting, looking out over so much empty land, knowing there is not a soul who cares whether we live or die." He leaned back. "But the stars are beautiful up here, aren't they? They look near enough to touch."

"I'd better leave you to your stargazing."

"You always run away from me," Gabe said. "Am I such a monster?"

"No, you're not a monster," Libby said.

"Are you still angry with me for interfering the other night?"

"Of course not. I'm grateful to you. It's just . . ."

"Just what?"

Libby sighed. "Why do you have to be a gambler, Gabe? You have so many good qualities. You're kind and you're obviously smart. Why couldn't you have been something respectable?"

Gabe laughed, his laugh bouncing off the polished surfaces of the rock. "You sound just like my mother. She wanted me to be a bank clerk," he said.

"But you didn't want to?"

"My father died when I was young and we lived in what were politely called 'reduced circumstances'." Do you know what that is? It means pretending you are not poor when you are. Not very enjoyable. When we had someone to tea we had to pretend we weren't hungry because there was only one cake, and that was for the guest. Anyway, my father had been in a bank and she arranged for me to start as junior clerk in the same bank after school. I stuck it out for three months." He laughed again. "Imagine me—starched collars, columns of figures, Yes, Mr. Blakely. No, Mr. Blakely. You're two minutes late, Foster. Lateness will not be tolerated. I felt as if I was suffocating. I had to get away."

"So what did you do?"

"You name it, I did it," Gabe said. "I tried my hand at most things. When I was a deckhand on a river steamer, I started playing poker and I realized how very stupid and very greedy most people are. They would always give themselves away when they thought they held a winning hand and they would never know when to quit. I decided that there couldn't be an easier way of making money."

"But it's not always easy, is it?" Libby asked. "You had to flee from a hanging judge. From the way you handled that gun, you've obviously had to use it."

"Those things don't worry me," Gabe said. "I've never shied away from danger. In fact I welcome it. Danger gives spice to life. It's boredom that I fear, Libby—routine and pettiness and being tied down. But I have to admit that the loneliness isn't always easy to handle. Nobody wants to get too close to a gambler because he'll always be moving on."

He fell silent and they both stared out into the blackness while the wind sighed through the rocks.

"So tell me about your Hugh," Gabe said at last. "He must be quite a man to make you come so far after him."

"Hugh is . . . Hugh is different," Libby said. "Have you ever seen a drawing of Puck? You know, in *A Midsummer Night's Dream*? Hugh is like that. He's somehow not affected by the real world. He goes through money like a sieve, and he will have forgotten to pick me up from the milliners because he was writing a sonnet. He can be quite exasperating at times. He's quite impractical. That's why I have to go to him. He won't have a clue how to survive in a mining camp. He probably won't have a clue how to dig up gold—he wasn't born to be a laborer."

"And you were?"

"I was born strong," Libby said. "I was headstrong, even as a little girl. My governess said I'd come to a bad end."

Gabe laughed. "Seeing you here, she'd probably say that she'd been proved right."

"I was just thinking the same thing."

"So you're off to rescue an impractical, exasperating man who spends money and writes sonnets," Gabe said. "He must have some good qualities too, or you'd have said good riddance and begun searching for a replacement."

"He has many good qualities," Libby said. "The most wonderful curly hair, for one thing."

"Has anyone ever crossed a continent for curly hair before, I wonder?"

"And he has the nicest nature," Libby said firmly, conscious that Gabe was teasing her. "He looks at me as if I am the most wonderful thing on the earth, and he adores the children. He acts as if they can do no wrong, and as if he is the only man who has ever fathered a child." She smiled at the memory of him, suddenly sharp and clear, with Bliss astride his shoulders, playing at horsey. "I'm a very lucky woman," she added. "Not many women can say they've a husband who still adores them after seven years."

"I'd say he was a very lucky man," Gabe said quietly. "Not many men have a wife who would tramp halfway across the world in search of him."

"As I told you before," Libby said, "I was brought up on duty and loyalty, although had I known what terrible things lay ahead, I doubt I would have been so eager to set off."

"Yes you would. Once you'd made up your mind to go, wild horses wouldn't have stopped you. You are the most stubbornly determined woman I've ever met, Libby Grenville."

"Am I to take that as insult or compliment, Mr. Foster?"

"We've known each other for a thousand miles and the nearest person is a half-mile away. Can't I now be Gabe?"

"Very well—Gabe," she said softly.

"Much better."

"I still have to thank you for what you did for Luke," Libby said. "You showed that you could be very caring and very kind. I really appreciated it."

"Thank you," Gabe said. "So does that mean we're not enemies anymore? You don't hate me?"

"I don't think I've ever hated you."

"Is there then a possibility that we can be friends for the rest of this journey at least?"

"I think I would be unwise to turn down any offer of friendship right now," Libby said.

"Shall we shake on it?" Gabe asked and extended his hand to her.

As she took his outstretched hand and it closed around hers, it was as if a jolt of electricity ran up her arm and spread throughout her whole body.

"I, er, really should go back now. My daughters might wake and wonder where I've got to," she said shakily, pulling her hand away.

"I'll walk down with you," he said.

They came down the hill in companionable silence.

# CHAPTER 13

*AUGUST 5, 1849. At last we are moving along at a good pace, now that the weather is cooler and there is enough water. I was despondent at first when I learned that we had half our journey ahead of us, but the air up here is very bracing and everyone is in good spirits. I think we all reason that downhill is preferable to uphill! Beautiful, majestic scenery—mountain peaks tipped with snow and strange rock formations that look like the columns of an ancient city. The men are shooting plenty of game at the springs we pass. I have a horrible feeling that I'll have to learn to pluck wildfowl and skin rabbits before long. So far the men have been kind enough to do this for me.*

The days in the high country were the most pleasant portion of the journey so far. There was no more mention of cholera and everyone seemed to have overcome the mountain sickness so that they went about chores whistling and addressed each other with good-natured insults. There was feed for the animals and everyone seemed to think that California was almost within reach, if they kept up a good pace.

It was hard to say when all this changed. One by one the good springs died out. There were several frightening descents into steep valleys. The drivers would lock the rear wheels and let the wagons slither down behind their terrified, complaining teams while everyone else stood well out of the way. But then came the terrible descent to Goose Creek. From above it looked insane to even consider taking wagons down.

"There must be a better way," Rival shouted.

Jimmy shrugged. "If there is, nobody's found it yet. We have to follow the valley and this is the valley."

"Take good care of my provisions, you hear," Rival shouted after him. "You better not spill one sack . . ."

They took down the first wagon with teams of men using ropes to keep it from sliding into the animals, who could barely keep their feet. It took agonizing minutes to get it down and then the same thing had to be repeated with the second wagon, and then the third. When it came to the water wagon, either the ropes had been tried to their limits or the cargo was just too heavy. Suddenly, there was the groan of snapping rope, the cries of the men, and the wagon going faster and faster. The men on the other rope tried to hold on, but they were dragged down the rocks as the wagon slithered sideways, hit a rock and tipped, rolling over and over, dragging two of the screaming oxen with it and spilling water barrels which bounced and broke in a cascade all the way to the bottom.

Sheldon Rival was beside himself with impotent rage. "Fools! Incompetent fools! Look what you've done! My water! My precious water," he yelled, running to try and salvage the last drops from shattered barrels. He paid no attention to the dying oxen, thrashing to free themselves from the shafts, nor to the men who clambered down with scraped arms and legs.

"You were paid to get my stuff through safely," he shouted to Jimmy. "Now I'm damned if I'll pay you at all."

"You'll not live to finish the journey if you don't pay the men what you owe them," Jimmy shouted back. "They did their best. The wagon was too heavy. I kept telling you that. Now you'll just have to drink spring water like the rest of us. You'll survive."

The camp was in a somber mood when they stopped that night. It had been very reassuring to have a wagon full of water barrels. Now there was no guarantee of fresh water, no way of carrying it if they found it, and the true desert lay ahead. The six oxen from the wrecked wagon all had to be shot and the men stewed the tough, stringy meat, putting out strips of meat for jerky to dry on the hot rocks.

When they set out again, they travelled as fast as they dared, eager to reach the Humboldt River. That river was supposed to take them almost into California, through many miles of near desert. But the meeting up with the Humboldt, as August was drawing to a close, added to the depression that settled over the company. They had been looking forward to following a major river down to the lowlands, confident that a constant source of water flowed beside them. The Humboldt turned out to be a muddy, salty stream, not much more than a trickle in places, too bitter for humans to drink. On a rock beside it was scrawled Humbug River, so obviously previous parties had been equally disillusioned.

Each day Libby could sense that morale was getting worse. The men slunk about their chores muttering to each other. Nobody whistled. A scout was sent out ahead to look for a camping site with good water. When he didn't come back, a search party was sent for him. They found him among rocks with an arrow in his back. There was no sign of his horse. "Digger Indians" was whispered around camp and that night the guard was doubled. Rumors about the Diggers spread and inflated in the darkness. It was said that they crept into camps and murdered everyone in their sleep, or that they stole all the animals and left expeditions to die. They could move so silently and invisibly through the rocks that they could get past any lookout.

"I say we go after 'em and hunt 'em down like the animals they are," one of the men yelled. "We should avenge poor old Joe."

"Don't be stupid," Jimmy's big voice answered. "They know this country like the back of their hands. They'd melt into the rocks and you could spend a month looking. We'll just press on as quickly as possible."

Gabe brought his bedding roll and saddle over to Libby's wagon. "I think I'll sleep better away from all that noise," he said. Libby recognized that he was guarding her and the children and she was grateful.

For the next days they moved with armed guards riding up and down the column but they saw no more signs of Indians. There were dead animals in plenty beside the trail, but these had obviously died from exhaustion rather than arrows. The trail began to be littered again as parties ahead had to consolidate provisions into fewer wagons with fewer animals to pull them. The smell of spoiled food and other human debris, as well as the dead animals rotting quickly in the scorching sun made the going very unpleasant.

"Mama, it smells bad," Bliss complained. "There's bad drains here."

"Stay inside the wagon and hold up your handkerchief like I do," Libby said, laughing at the thought of drains in the middle of a desert.

The two girls let down the wagon flaps and Libby held her scarf to her mouth, trying to stare at the majestic skyline of bare mountains ahead rather than look at the pathetic sights beside the trail.

At last the Humboldt River petered out into a scummy salt marsh in a desert. The animals tried to drink, then backed away again. There was no choice but to press on.

"No more good water between here and California," someone muttered.

Just before nightfall they saw a magnificent lake stretching out ahead of them, covering the whole valley with blue water. Distant peaks were reflected in it and it shimmered in the pink evening light. The men jumped from wagons and mules and rushed forward yelling like schoolboys on the last day of school.

"Come back!" Jimmy yelled, spurring his horse after them. "It's only a mirage. It's not real."

The sun set and the lake vanished. The men came back dragging their feet, hot, dusty, tired, and embarrassed to have been taken in so easily. There was no singing around the campfire that night.

Libby knew something was very wrong the moment she emerged from her bed in the wagon. Although it was light, no campfire was blazing with coffee cooking for breakfast. The oxen were still foraging nearby. Angry voices were coming from Sheldon Rival's tent. Men hurrying past Libby looked scared.

"What is it?" Libby asked.

The man glanced back over his shoulder at her. "It's Johnson and his mob. They've beat it."

Still not much wiser, Libby hurried over to Rival's tent.

"And you just let them go?" Rival was screaming.

"I knew nothing about it until I woke this morning," Jimmy answered, his own voice shrill with anger. "I can't stay awake all night, you know."

"I thought I told you to post guards. What about them? They just let half my men walk out of here?"

"The guards were with them," Jimmy said. "It was Bob Barclay. He's a great buddy of Johnson."

"Fools!" Rival shouted. "What do they think they can accomplish alone?"

"Apparently they think we're travelling too slowly with wagons. They want to make a quick dash across the desert. They thought you wouldn't pay them when they got to California, so they've taken mules and supplies instead."

"What did they take?"

"Whatever they could carry," Jimmy's tired voice answered. "All the mules, spare rifles, a couple of sacks of flour and the dried meat. They'll probably make it."

"I hope they rot." Rival spat. "I hope we come across their bloated corpses. I wish them damned to hell."

"Wish all you want," Jimmy said. "It doesn't alter the fact that we're down to ten men and we'll have to leave wagons behind."

Rival strode out of his tent before Libby could move away. He caught sight of her and pointed. "You! You think you could drive a team?" he asked. "I'll make it worth your while."

"I suppose I could try," Libby said. She had been watching the drivers for so long that she was sure she could imitate any command. Besides, the tired oxen were reduced to such a slow plod that she reasoned all the driving required was an occasional flick of the whip.

"Good," Rival said. "That's one more wagon we can take. What about Foster? Did he go with them?"

"Foster's still here," Jimmy said, following him out of the tent.

"He can drive too, and so can you. Tie your horses on behind."

"So can you, for that matter," Jimmy said.

"I will, if I have to, dammit," Rival said.

"Let's get going, then," Rival added, "before the day gets too unbearably hot."

"If you take my advice, which you haven't so far," Jimmy said in a tired voice, "you'll rest up during the day and make the desert crossing by night."

"And what if we lose our way?" Rival asked. "What if we pass the Carson River in the dark?"

"If we make for the mountains, then head south, we can't miss it," Jimmy said. "Anyway, that's less of a risk than losing all your animals to heatstroke."

"Very well, do what you want," Rival said.

They spent a miserable day, lying in the shade of the wagons to get away from the sweltering heat. As the sun sank they set off. Eden and Bliss were delighted that their mother finally had been promoted to wagon driver and wanted to sit beside her on the driver's seat. Libby remembered all too clearly the child who fell under the wagon wheels and made them stay inside.

"But it's so hot in here," Eden complained.

"I'm thirsty, Mama," Bliss said pitifully. "My mouth's all dry and crackly."

"You have to be patient, darling one," Libby soothed. "We'll find water soon and then you can take a lovely long drink."

Gabe came over to her as the first wagons set off. "Are you sure you can handle this?" he asked. "You don't have to if you don't want to. You could ride in my wagon and let Rival's supplies go to hell."

Libby managed a weak smile. "I don't see why not," she said. "I used to handle a pony and trap pretty well in the park at home."

Gabe shook his head. "I don't think the two have much in common. If you lost your way in the park you went on until you hit the railings."

"I'll manage," she said.

"I knew you'd be stubborn," Gabe muttered. "Very well. I'll go right ahead of you. Stay close behind me. We'll stick together, no matter what."

Libby nodded. She cracked her whip and the oxen lumbered off, grunting unwillingly. The last light faded and it was hard to make out the shape of the wagon in front. The animals' hooves crunched through the crisp salty surface into sand beneath.

Libby's own mouth was painfully dry and her tongue felt as if it were swollen to double its real size. Her eyes stung with blowing sand and when she rubbed them, no tears came. At first the thought of driving a wagon had seemed like a challenge, almost like a game, but as the night deepened around her, she realized how very easy it would be to stray from the track and become lost in wasteland. With nightfall the temperature dropped rapidly and her hands became so cold it was hard to hold the reins. She sat shivering as she strained her eyes for the ghostly white shape ahead. Then she heard the sound of singing: "Oh Susannah, don't you cry for me. I'm off to Californee with my shovel on my knee!"

It was the song she had heard many times from many camps along the trail, but the voice was now unmistakably Gabe's. She smiled to herself and urged the oxen to catch up with him. All through the night the snatches of song floated ahead, rousing her every time her eyes began to nod shut. The desert trail seemed to go on and on, unchanging, plodding hooves, ghostly rocks, sand and grit. In the darkness Libby's eyes played tricks on her and she saw Indians moving between rocks, rattlesnakes slinking across the path, even lights dancing in the distance.

As the night wore on, she was even glad of the cold, because she was too uncomfortable to fall asleep. Every time Gabe's singing died down she tried some of her own or she recited every childhood poem that Miss Danford had made her learn. In this way she managed to keep going until the sun came up, rising as a harsh red ball behind the eastern mountains. They continued on as the whole valley was lit with flame and only called a halt when they finally struck water. Her mouth parched and her head singing with tiredness, Libby climbed down stiffly from her hard perch and staggered down to join the men. The water turned out to be a hot spring, boiling as it came from the ground. It was a strange place of rising steam and twisted mineral columns. The smell of sulfur hung heavy in the air.

"Do we have to camp here?" Rival demanded. "There must be a better spot than this."

Jimmy shook his head. "No more water until the Carson," he said.

"Then let's press on and try to make the Carson by nightfall."

"The animals would die."

"But they can't drink this."

"They'll have to. We'll scoop up water with every pan we've got and leave it until it's cool enough to drink."

Eden and Bliss came to join their mother.

"It smells bad here, Mama," Eden said, wrinkling her nose. "Can't we stop somewhere else?"

"We have to stop where there's water," Libby said.

"I want a drink, Mama," Bliss begged.

"We have to wait a while," Libby said. "Hold Mama's hand. The water's very hot."

The men cursed as they carried bowls of scalding water and it slopped over them. Rival noticed Libby, standing with her children in the shade. "You made it then," he said. "Might as well make the most of all this hot water and get my washing done."

"If you want me to drive all night, I intend to sleep all day," Libby said. "Do your own washing."

She caught Gabe's eye and he winked at her.

"I enjoyed your repertoire of singing, Mr. Foster," she said, "although I'd have preferred a little opera and not so many barroom songs."

"My apologies, madame," he said, bowing, "but my Mozart is a little rusty and I had not realized I had an audience. I was singing purely to keep myself awake. I hope I didn't disturb you?"

"On the contrary, I found it very reassuring," she said, returning his smile.

"I thought from time to time that I heard a cricket chirping behind me," Gabe added, his eyes teasing. "Did you hear it?"

"I can't say that I did," she replied, walking past him to take a pail of water to the shade of the wagon.

The water was foul tasting, and never really cooled enough to be refreshing, but it was better than nothing. They spent a miserable day lying in the shade, splashing themselves with warm water to try and get cool. As the sun set, they started off again in a repeat of the past night's march.

The second night was almost unbearable. Libby had hardly slept during the heat of the day and now her head throbbed and she swayed with tiredness. Every few minutes she found herself dropping off to sleep, the reins slipping from her hands. Once, one of the oxen stumbled and the wagon lurched, almost sending her sprawling forward off the seat. She only just managed to grab at the footboard to stop herself from falling under the hooves. That frightened her awake for a while, but as dawn approached, sleep overtook her again. She woke with a start when a voice yelled. It was still dark, but the eastern sky was etched with a thin line of approaching dawn. She had no idea how long she'd slept, but the wagon ahead of her had stopped and there were shouts and screams echoing off the rocks.

Cautiously, she reached for the rifle under her seat. A figure came running toward her. "Hey, put that down. My singing didn't offend you that much, did it?" Gabe shouted.

"What's going on?" Libby asked. "What are all those shouts?"

"We've found the Carson," Gabe shouted back. "The men are going crazy. Come on, come and get wet." He put up his arms to her and lifted her down. She was very conscious of his hands on her waist and that they lingered there, long after her feet had touched the ground. "You can let go of me now, Mr. Foster," she said, laughing uneasily. "I'm quite able to stand on my own."

"I've noticed," he said and slid his hands from her.

# CHAPTER
## 14

EVERYONE ENJOYED THE fresh water, the oxen standing knee deep or wallowing in satisfaction and the men, stripped to the waist, splashing each other like little boys. Libby would have loved to join in the fun, but she felt uneasy among so many exuberant men, especially since these men were now little better than naked and had been without women for two months. So she had to content herself with bringing pails of water back to the wagon, where she and the girls washed themselves in privacy.

"We have to start looking respectable again soon children," she said, "because we're almost in California. We just have to follow this river up into the mountains and then California is on the other side. In a few days we'll be safely there and we'll find Papa again."

"Does that mean we'll have to wear pantaloons and underskirts again?" Eden asked, wrinkling her nose with disgust.

"We can't go on dressing like savages forever," Libby said.

"I like being a savage," Eden said.

"Me too," Bliss added.

Libby looked at them. They had survived remarkably well, she thought. They were very different from the pale, chubby daughters who had set out, dressed in their laces and velvets. They were both skinny and suntanned like little native children, but they were fit enough and Eden seemed to have grown.

I hope their father won't have a fit when he sees them in this condition, Libby thought. I must try to clean up their proper dresses so that they look respectable when he sees them. And me, she added. I must look like a savage too. She ran her hand through her hair which she now wore in a braid, like a schoolgirl, and which was sun-bleached strawberry blond at the front. When she thought of dressing up again, of wearing her corset and her hooped skirts and layers of undergarments, she shuddered.

She wondered if Hugh had become a savage too, then shook her head. Hugh would probably still be insisting on starched white tablecloths and polished silver as he worked in his gold mine. He'd probably be shovelling up gold with lace cuffs on his shirt. It would take more than a wilderness half a world away from civilization to make Hugh forget he was an English gentleman. Then she found herself smiling at the thought of him. He had been less and less in her thoughts as she faced the hardships of the journey, but now that the journey was almost over, she realized how much she wanted to see him again, to get back to being normal and safe with a man to protect her.

They waited several days for the animals to get back their strength before they moved on down the Carson River with the bare faces of the mountains coming closer and closer on their right. At last they came to the place where the river entered the dry valley. It was the first week of September when they set off, up the steepest, most rugged mountains they had yet encountered. The pass over the Rockies had been so gentle that they had hardly been aware of it. The pass over the Sierra Nevada Mountains went straight up. Beside them the river cascaded down to the dry plain in a series of trickles and falls. There was no trail to follow. The only route went over and around boulders, some as big as a man, some as big as a wagon. At times it was hard enough for a person to find footing. The oxen slithered and bellowed and had to be dragged and pushed and whipped while the wagons bumped and lurched behind, more often on two wheels than on four.

After a day of sweat and bruises the plains seemed to have barely dropped away. The top was nowhere in sight. But the men who stayed with Rival were in better spirits now and everyone felt that California was literally just around the corner. They had been on the road for more than three months and they were anxious for journey's end. Also there were fears of snow. Until this moment, all they had worried about was the heat. Now the men muttered about rumors of parties snowed in at the summit, freezing to death or dying from starvation only miles from the promised land.

"As long as we make it over safely before fall starts, we won't have to worry," Jimmy told them.

At last, battered and exhausted, they reached the summit. They stood on top of the world and stared out in all directions—the dry, parched desert world behind in muted tones of yellow and gray contrasting with the world ahead, a world of granite peaks, splashes of snow, towering pines, and small blue lakes. It was enchantingly beautiful but not what any of them wanted to see. They wanted to see a clear road leading down to towns where chimneys were smoking. Instead, the rugged country went on, peak after peak into the blue west.

They set up camp in a high alpine meadow, wrapping themselves up as the temperature dropped with the sunset. The fire of dry pine branches flared up into a big blaze and Libby secretly hoped that the blaze would attract settlers from hidden towns nearby, who would arrive with fresh food and warm clothing and invitations to shelter. That night Libby lay in a dream. She was at a concert, back in Boston, and the orchestra was playing. It was a rousing piece with much clashing of cymbals and banging of drums. When it finished the crowd broke into applause. Libby opened her eyes and the clapping went on, accompanied by a final drum roll. There was a bright flash, lighting up the whole wagon and Libby sat up.

"What is it, Mama?" Bliss asked, waking too.

"It's only a thunderstorm," Libby said, realizing that the dream clapping had been the sounds of rain on the canvas top of the wagon.

Bliss moved closer to her mother as the storm raged on. A wind sprang up and tore at the wagon flaps. The rain fell harder and harder and from outside came the sound of branches breaking and falling. Eventually, they drifted back to sleep and woke to complete and overwhelming silence.

"The storm's over," Bliss announced, sitting up.

Eden opened her eyes. "What storm?" she asked.

"You slept through a thunderstorm last night," Libby said, smiling.

"That's funny. I thought people were clapping in my dream. It must have been thunder," Eden said.

"I had the same dream," Libby said. "Thank heavens it's stopped now."

"It's awful cold, Mama," Bliss said. "Is the sun shining, do you think?" She pulled back the flaps and let out a yell. "Look, Mama, it's snowing!"

The other two joined her. The world outside was eerily white and still. Snow was falling so thickly that the other wagons were just hazy shapes. The big pine trees were already bowed with white branches.

"Can we play in it? Can we build a snowman?" the girls begged excitedly.

Jimmy came up, not looking excited. "We must get going," he said. "There's more snow in those clouds and we don't want to find ourselves trapped up here."

"But how will we find our way with all this snow?" Libby asked.

"We'll have to risk it. One good storm and we might be cut off for weeks."

"But it's only September. How can this happen?"

Jimmy shrugged as if he wasn't responsible for the weather. "We're pretty high up here," he said, "although it's not usual to have snow this early. Let's just hope it's a freak and it soon melts."

Libby was glad to get out her old underskirts and camisole and her Boston dress. Even with the woolen shirt and her shawl over her, her fingers were soon numb as she tried to help with harnessing the oxen. Two of them were so exhausted by the climb and the long journey that they refused to get up. They lay there, pathetically covered with a coating of snow and would not move, however much the men tried to cajole, force, or whip them.

"Leave them," Libby cried at last, when the whips had drawn blood on their backs. "Can't you see they can't go on?"

In the end they had no alternative but to leave the oxen. That also meant leaving one wagon. With the expectation that the journey would end very shortly, Rival agreed to leave his own cook wagon behind, having Libby drive the wagon loaded with flour sacks. Rival had his brandied fruit and bottles of brandy brought across and there was scarcely room for Libby's belongings, much less the children. Libby perched them on top of flour sacks and wrapped them in rugs. "Stay warm," she commanded.

They began to cross the Sierras with only two teams to each wagon. The going was nightmarish. The animals slithered and stumbled, scared to put down their feet on a trail they could not see. Snow blew into everyone's faces and found openings in wagon flaps so that it piled and melted inside, making everything wet. Shoes which had held up for more than three months of crossing the wasteland now leaked and fell apart. The men pulled on several pairs of socks over their boots to help them keep their footing as they pulled the bullocks between boulders. Snow blew straight into their faces and in minutes they were soaked through.

"Get back in the wagon, you can't handle this," Gabe shouted to Libby as she attempted to coax her team forward.

"There's no one else to do it," she shouted back.

"Then leave the damn wagon. You'll freeze to death. You'll catch pneumonia."

"I'll manage," Libby said, although she was shivering so violently that she could not keep her hands still.

By midday they came to a man-high drift. While the men got out shovels to dig, Libby made them all hot coffee on the spirit stove. She noticed that there was almost no spirit left. If they had to spend another night up here, how would they keep warm? Eden and Bliss were huddled in blankets, covered in the wolfskins Gabe had bartered for. If she'd known how useful they'd be, she'd have traded the rest of her hair combs and even her mirror, Libby thought ruefully. She cradled a coffee cup in her hands, trying to restore feeling to them. Her legs and feet still felt numb. She had to keep moving, keep active. She poured more coffee and ferried it down to the men working at the drift.

"It's a bugger, ma'am. Pardon my language," one of them said, wiping the sweat from his brow. Libby stared at the forbidding wall of snow. Then, as she watched, the two men working at the front dug through and they were looking at the long valley below. With renewed energy the men cleared a path wide enough for the wagons and soon they were heading downward. On the other side there was just a dusting of snow, as if Mother Nature had put this last obstacle in the way and then given up.

They camped in another mountain meadow and dried clothes in front of a big fire. Next morning they woke to blue skies and no more trace of snow ahead. "Downhill all the way," someone shouted and the men encouraged their teams to move faster. There was even more hint of a road here. In several places wooden bridges spanned ravines and at one point the road was built out from the rock face with wooden spikes. It was not easy going. The road was never wider than a wagon and pebbles slithered and bounced down thousand-foot drops as they passed over.

Only one more day of this, Libby kept chanting to herself. She was convinced that she only had to survive this steep-sided valley and everything else would be easy. She sat gripping the reins, willing the oxen not to stumble, not daring to look at that dreadful drop.

She made it safely over the wooden bridge and gave a prayer of thanks. Ahead was a clear road cut into the mountainside. The team ahead of Libby began to move ahead faster. She heard the driver's shouts and the crack of a whip. Her own team responded, lumbering after the disappearing wagon ahead. "Whoa," Libby yelled, dragging on the reins. She could feel the wagon picking up speed and jammed on the wheel lock. Sparks flew from the rear wheel, but she was not strong enough to stop it from turning. The wagon started gaining on the weary animals, one of them stumbled and the wagon slithered sideways, one of its wheels hanging out over the drop.

Libby leaped from her seat. She could feel the weight of the wagon pulling at the animals. "Help!" she screamed. "Eden! Bliss! Jump to Mama!"

Slowly, the wagon began to slide backward, hanging out over the drop. Men came running from other teams. Arms reached out to help Libby to the ground. "The children!" She reached out desperately toward them.

"Mama, my dolly!" Bliss yelled. She tried to go back into the wagon. Desperately Libby grabbed at her skirt.

"Forget the doll. Jump! Jump to Mama!" Libby shouted, dragging Bliss down from the seat.

One of the men caught Eden as she jumped. Hands grabbed at the bullocks' heads. A shower of pebbles cascaded downward, bumping off hidden rocks below. Libby dragged the children back to the rock face, an arm around each of them. The tired animals were no match for a laden wagon.

"It's no use, it's going!" men shouted.

"Cut them loose," someone shouted. Knives hacked at the harness straps. The wagon inched backwards, teetered for a moment, then, with a groan, it disappeared over the edge, taking the animals with it. There was a horrible crash, then all was still. Libby put her hand to her mouth, feeling that she might vomit any second. The vision of that disappearing wagon kept haunting her, knowing that Eden and Bliss had escaped death by seconds. Bliss was crying. "I want my dollie!"

"Don't worry, sissy, we'll get you a new dollie," Eden's wise little voice comforted. Libby could not stop trembling. She was trembling so violently that she wrapped her arms around her to steady herself.

"Are you all right?" Gabe asked, running up to her.

"Oh, Gabe," she whispered and buried her head in his shoulder.

His strong arms closed around her. "It's over. You're safe," he muttered, stroking her hair.

Sheldon Rival arrived, panting, up the hill.

"My wagon!" he gasped. "What did you do to my wagon?"

"There was only one team. They couldn't hold it," men explained. "We're lucky it didn't go over with the little girls in it."

"It was *her* wagon?" Rival demanded. "I might have known. You stupid woman. What about my flour? What about my potatoes?"

Libby broke free from Gabe. "Your flour?" she screamed. "My children nearly lost their lives and you're worried about flour? What sort of man are you? You're not a human at all, you're a monster! My only regret is that you didn't go over that cliff with your precious flour!"

She took her children by the hand. "Come on, children," she said. "We'll not stay with this man another minute. We can find our own way from here. Goodbye Mr. Rival. May you rot in hell!"

"Mama—where are we going? What about Mr. Foster? How will we find the way?" Eden demanded.

"My dollie!" Bliss wailed.

Libby kept both hands firmly in hers and kept walking, past the wagons and into the pine trees. Moments later she heard the clip-clop of hooves behind her and there was Gabe on his horse.

"Wait up, you walk too fast," he called after her.

"What are you doing?" she asked with a tired smile.

"Keeping an eye on you."

"I don't need keeping an eye on."

"Where do you intend to sleep tonight? What do you intend to eat?" Gabe asked.

"We're in California. We'll find a settlement by nightfall."

"Hardly. We're about three days away from the nearest settlements."

"Are you sure?"

"That's what Jimmy says."

"Oh," Libby said, realizing that they had no possessions and no food. "Then we'll gather berries, I suppose."

Gabe laughed. "Gather berries! And what if you meet a grizzly bear while you're gathering your berries? What if you meet bandits? You can't take these children through country like this with no man to protect you. Besides, I've lost interest in Mr. Rival."

"But you were driving one of his wagons!" Libby exclaimed. "What's going to happen to it?"

A big smile spread across Gabe's face. "For all I care it can sit on a mountain pass until kingdom come," he said, "or Rival can yoke himself up and pull it down."

He looked at Libby and they both burst out laughing.

With the girls riding Gabe's horse, they made good mileage. They camped for the night under towering pines on soft beds of needles. Gabe shot a rabbit which they grilled over a fire. Libby did not find any berries. Next day they pressed on and by day's end the landscape had begun to change. Golden hillsides and oak groves were replacing pines and granite. Best of all, as they stopped for the night under a large oak tree, they could see a spiral of smoke on the western horizon.

"Civilization tomorrow," Libby said, staring out at it.

"People yes, I'm not so sure about the civilization," Gabe said.

"People, houses, food, beds," Libby said. "I can't wait for this journey to end."

"No, I don't suppose you can," Gabe said slowly. His tone made her turn to look back at him. "In a few days now you'll be reunited with good old Hugh, living in a snug little cottage, making mountains of gold and you'll forget that I ever existed."

"I won't ever forget you, Gabe," Libby said, gazing at him. "I wouldn't have made it without you."

Gabe laughed, a light, brittle laugh. "But when we come upon each other again, I emerging from my gambling parlor, and you with your shopping bag and children at your heels, you will pretend that you don't see me and you'll pass me by."

"That doesn't mean I'll forget you," she said, smiling at him.

"You already think me beyond hope, so I'm going to ask you one thing," Gabe said, turning to her.

"Which is?"

"Something I've been longing to do since that first evening in New Orleans. . . . May I kiss you, just once, before we part?"

"I don't think that's wise, Mr. Foster," Libby said, stepping back from him.

"What happened to Gabe?"

"We're coming back to civilization," Libby said, looking away from him as she tried to pinpoint that wisp of smoke. "We have to remember that I'm a married woman and you're not a friend of the family." She glanced across at Gabe. "Is that so amusing?" she asked.

His smiled broadened. "It's just that I didn't take you for the kind of woman who cared what people thought. You wouldn't have started on this journey if you listened to gossip."

"I don't care for me," she said. "It's Hugh I'm thinking about. I kept looking for his grave all the way. I didn't see it, so I have to hope he's already here, working hard for me and the children. Think how hurt he'd be if he heard rumors of his wife amusing herself with a gambler during the lonely hours of the trail."

Gabe's smile turned to a chuckle.

"You find me funny?"

"I still find you adorable," he said. "I cannot think that you are hardhearted enough to send me on my way without one token of affection between us. Just one delicate brushing of the lips—is that too much to ask?"

"Maybe it is," she said seriously.

"You find me so repugnant?" He took her arm, fiercely.

"You know I don't," she said. "It's the opposite. I'm scared of waking feelings that are best left asleep."

"I think you're fooling yourself if you think those feelings are not already awake," he said softly. He put a finger under her chin and drew her face gently toward him, then he leaned forward just enough to brush her lips with his. "I suppose I dare not ask or expect more than that," he whispered, his eyes warm and teasing, his face still inches away from hers. "That one little kiss will have to last me through my lonely, declining years."

Libby gave a half sob, half laugh and wrapped her arms around his neck, bringing her lips up hungrily to meet his. They stood there together, not moving, arms wrapped tightly around each other, lips locked together, for what seemed like an eternity. Then, reluctantly, they broke away.

"That kiss will certainly last me a lifetime, Mrs. Hugh Grenville," Gabe said shakily.

That night Libby lay awake, looking up at the stars through the filigree of leaves and branches. She was

very conscious of Gabe lying beside her. Her whole
body ached with longing. After so long, to be kissed
and held in strong arms, to be desired so strongly,
was almost more than she could bear.

I didn't want to like you, Gabe Foster, she thought.
Now I don't think I can ever be content without you.

# CHAPTER
# 15

THE NEXT DAY the trail dropped steadily downward, the hot air rising to meet them, smelling of sage and bay. Libby went ahead and Gabe led his horse with the two little girls perched among his baggage. It was pleasant going, cool and shady under the trees with the flash of blue jays and large hawks circling overhead. Small songbirds twittered in the trees and the blue jays' harsh cries echoed from the valley sides, unnaturally loud after so many weeks of hearing no sound except the wind. Gradually, they were aware of other noises—the distant ring of pick and shovel on rock, shouts echoing up steep canyons. They came upon an empty cabin, the path became clearly defined and by midday they could glimpse clusters of tents and crude shacks along the creek sides. The next day they walked into the main street of Hangtown.

"Welcome to civilization," Gabe said quizzically as Libby looked around her in dismay. She had expected a town, maybe not as old and established and neat as New England, but something that bore some resemblance to the towns she knew. This was more like the tent city at Independence. It was a jumble of structures, perched in random order on any flat piece of ground. The term *structures* was more apt than buildings, because apart from a few log cabins, most of the buildings consisted of wooden frames between and over which canvas was tacked. This even applied to the grandly named Empire Hotel which was two stories of canvas with red calico draped in place of window glass.

Several dirty, unshaven men were sitting out on the unfinished wooden porch, filling glasses from a bottle they passed between them. One of the men leaned over the edge of the porch and spat onto the dust below, which was littered with every imaginable piece of garbage from old sardine cans to empty champagne bottles. None of the men seemed to notice Libby, Gabe, and the children. There was no real main street but in the dusty track which passed for a main street, men were busy digging deep holes, as if this were a mine and not a town. As Libby and Gabe stared, one of the men popped his head up with a shout. "Told ya I'd strike something here, didn't I!" he yelled, holding up something in his hand that was too small to see. Instantly, several other men leaped up from the porch of the Empire Hotel and ran across to join him in digging.

Gabe touched Libby's arm. "What now?" he asked.

"What can I do?" Libby said, looking around as if for inspiration. "I'll have to take the children to that so-called hotel and make enquiries about Hugh. Everyone says this is the crossroads and that any news comes through here. I should have thought men who looked and talked like Hugh were rare enough to be noticed." She looked up at Gabe. "And you, what will you do?"

"Me? Oh, I'll give myself some time to look around," Gabe said. "Maybe I'll stay a few days in the Empire too. Get the feeling of the place—see if they're interested in playing cards here."

Just as he spoke a horseman galloped up and flung himself from his horse, yelling, "They got her. Looks like they're bringing her here."

"Honest Injun?" one of the diggers asked, leaning on his shovel. "Did she confess?"

"She did it right enough," the horseman said excitedly. "They found two bags of dust under her mattress and Fat Joe swears one of the bags looks like the one Pete brought in with him."

"She claims she won it fair and square in a card game, so I heard," another of the men said. As if by magic, a crowd began to form in the middle of the street. Many of the men were carrying bottles from which they took frequent swigs and the noise level rose as if it were a big party. Gabe stopped a young fellow as he hurried to join them. "What's going on here?" he asked.

"They caught Rosa Montez," he said excitedly. "You know—the gambling-house girl who murdered poor old Pittsburgh Pete. I reckon she thought she could get away with it, seeing as how she's a woman, but I don't think she will. The boys are all riled up, on account of old Pete being so generous with his liquor."

A distant roar could be heard on the other side of town, like an approaching parade on the Fourth of July. Libby glanced at Gabe and he pulled his horse, with the children still perched in the saddle, off to the shelter of one of the half-finished buildings. Soon they could see that it really was a parade approaching. A whole seething mass of men in colorful blue and red shirts, with bandannas tied around their throats, came up the street, yelling and firing guns into the air. They were unkempt with long matted beards and wore misshapen hats pulled down over their faces. Libby's first reaction was that they were some sort of brigand army.

Some of the men at the front ran to the Empire and came out with a table decked in red calico and several chairs which they put down in the middle of the street. After a certain amount of arguing and jostling, five men were pushed over to the table and sat down. Then from the middle of the crowd two men dragged a beautiful young woman. She was dark skinned, dark eyed, and had long heavy black hair flowing down over her shoulders. She was dressed in a skimpy red satin dress with a black-fringed shawl over her shoulders and she looked as out of place, among this slovenly band, as a swan among the chickens. Her eyes darted around nervously as she was pushed forward to the table.

"We found her trying to run off down to Diamond Springs," one of the men said. He was a tall, skinny fellow with a long, drooping moustache and was dressed head to toe in black.

"Did she have the money on her?"

"No, but we found these here bags under her mattress," another man said, holding up two leather pouches. "One of them looks just like the bag Pete had on him."

"I no keel him!" the Mexican girl exclaimed. "Why I want keel him? He good man. Pay good money."

One of the men at the table stretched out long, booted legs. "I reckon you thought you didn't get enough out of him at cards last night, so you'd help yourself later," he said. "I've got men who will swear they saw Pete going up to your bedroom."

"So? Was wrong? He pay me," the girl shrieked. "If I go keel him, why I not keel him in my bed? Why I keel him after, eh?"

"If you didn't kill him, why were you trying to run off when we came for ya?" the first man demanded.

"I know you no believe what I say," she said. "I Mexicano. I foreigner. You think all Mexicanos bad."

"Who else would want to kill old Pete? That's what I say," the man in black insisted. "I say she's a no-good whore and she should get what's coming to her."

One of the men at the table, gray haired and more distinguished looking than any of his fellows, glanced around. "Do you think we should call some witnesses?" he asked. "Maybe there was someone who saw Pete leave the hotel. Maybe someone was seen to follow him."

"Heck no, Doc. We heard all we need to hear," the man in black insisted. "Me and the boys want justice for old Pete."

"That's right. String her up. Get it over with," several other voices shouted.

The gray-haired man looked at his companions. One of them shrugged. "If that's what they want, you'd better go along with it, because they'll do it anyway," he said.

"We should at least try to get her a priest," the gray-haired man insisted.

Libby had stood in the shadow of a small wooden cabin, not fully understanding what was happening until one of the men stepped forward with a rope. She stared at it in horror and disbelief, then she strode out into the sunlight. "You can't be thinking of hanging this woman on such vague evidence," she said.

The effect was instantaneous. There was an intake of breath, like a giant sigh, from the whole crowd and the noise level dropped to whispers. Libby was conscious of many pairs of eyes, all staring at her as if she had just popped out of a bottle, like a genie.

"It's a woman. Look, a woman," was whispered at the front of the crowd and those at the back pushed and shoved to get a better view.

The older, gray-haired man stood up and removed his hat. "You'll have to excuse them, ma'am," he said. "Many of them haven't set eyes on a woman in months. Not a real lady like yourself, that is."

"Then it seems as if I've arrived just in time," Libby said, looking around at the faces and trying to determine if they were friendly under all that hair and dirt. "Have you been away from civilization so long that you can think of hanging a lady without a proper trial?"

One of the men took off his hat and stepped forward, clutching it to his middle as if he were going courting. "Begging your pardon, ma'am," he said, "but this ain't no lady. This is one of the card dealers from the Fandango House. They're all a bad lot. Any one of them would stab you in the back for a couple of ounces."

The Mexican girl looked at Libby with imploring eyes. "Tell them I no do nothing," she said. "I no keel."

"If I am not mistaken, California is now part of the United States, so she's entitled to a fair trial, whoever she is," Libby said with her best Boston haughtiness. "Where is the judge in this town?"

Several of the men grinned. "Ain't no law in this town 'ceptin' us," someone drawled. "We make our own law and those who don't like it, just ride on out of town again."

"Please step aside, ma'am," the man clutching his hat said. "I wouldn't want you to get hurt. The boys are itching for a hanging and a hanging it's going to be."

"Come on boys, take her over to the tree," the first man shouted. "Let's get this over with and then I say free drinks all round with poor old Pete's gold." A great roar went up from the crowd. Libby tried to step forward to reach the girl but the men surged around her like an inflowing tide. Libby heard a scream as they dragged the girl away. She started shouting in Spanish, alternately pleading and cursing as she was dragged down the street.

"No! Wait, come back," Libby shouted as she tried to fight her way through the crowd. She felt a restraining arm on her and Gabe held her fast. "Let it be, Libby, there's nothing you can do."

"But they're going to kill that girl."

Gabe's eyes were solemn. "I know, but there's nothing we can do to stop them. You can see how they've all been drinking. Look at their faces—this is fun to them. They want it."

"But that's horrible," Libby said, shuddering.

The last of the men hurried after the procession. They were bright and excited, joking with each other as they ran. "I'll wager ten to one she don't die in five minutes," Libby heard someone shout. One of the last men turned back to Libby and Gabe. "Don't fret about it. She deserves all she's going to get whether she killed old Pete or no," he said, grinning pleasantly. "These fancy card dealers who come in here and cheat a miner out of his hard-earned gold . . ." He paused and spat on the dirt. "Hanging's too good for them, that's what I say."

The crowd noise faded as the men ran down the street and around the corner. Libby and Gabe were left alone outside the hotel with the calico-draped table and the five empty chairs.

"Now we know why they call it Hangtown," Gabe said. "I get the feeling I'd get a warmer welcome someplace else."

Libby hadn't considered before that he might be in danger. "Gabe," she said, touching his arm gently, "do you have to go back to being a gambler?"

A broad smile spread across his face. "What would you have me do? Break my back digging all day in an icy stream when I can earn the same amount or more by a quick flick of the wrist and the luck of the cards?"

"But you saw what they think of gamblers here," Libby said.

He looked down at her tenderly. "Don't worry about me. I know how to take care of myself, and don't forget, Old Nick takes care of his own. I'll do just fine, I'm sure."

"Then I hope for your sake that all the settlements aren't like this," she said.

"If they are, I'll head down to San Francisco," Gabe said. "I hear it's a city known for its sinful ways. I should be right at home there."

Libby managed a weak smile. Don't go, she wanted to say to him. I need you here with me. I don't want to be left in this place on my own. I don't want to be without you. But she managed to keep silent. "I suppose I should go and check in to the hotel," she said. "And you should be on your way."

"I suppose so," Gabe said. They stood there facing each other, neither moving. "Look Libby," Gabe said at last. "I'll stay if you want me to, until you meet up with your husband."

"Oh, no, I'll be just fine," Libby said lightly. "Besides, it would only start rumors if you were seen around here with me. I think it would be best if you got right away."

"If that's what you really want," Gabe said.

"It's what I really want."

Gabe took a deep breath. "Right. Then that's that. I'll get on my way and try to find a friendly spot for the night," he said. "You're sure you'll be all right?"

"I'll be fine. We'll all be fine. I'm sure we'll find Hugh really quickly and everything will be fine," Libby babbled, horrified that she might cry if he stayed any longer.

"What about money?" Gabe asked. "You lost all your things. Do you need money?" He started to reach into his inside pocket.

"I have money," Libby said quickly. "I always kept my money on my person, thank heavens. I've enough to pay for a hotel until we find Hugh. I expect he's already got some sort of shelter for us. We'll survive very well."

Gabe ran over to his saddlebag. "At least take these," he said. "This is the wolf pelt we traded for your comb, and these are a couple of other skins I got later. I wouldn't like to think of you cold in winter."

He held them out to her. She hesitated. "Take them, please," he said. "Besides, I'm going to be offered so many warm, soft beds that I won't need them."

Libby laughed and took them.

"Were you about to tell me I was incorrigible or insufferable?"

Libby shook her head. "No," she said.

"Then I'd better be on my way," Gabe said. He held out his hand. "Goodbye, Mrs. Hugh Grenville. It was really nice knowing you."

Libby took his hand, although her own was trembling. "Goodbye, Mr. Foster. I wish you every happiness."

"And I you, Mrs. Grenville," Gabe said. He walked over to his horse and lifted down the children, kissing each in turn as he set them down. "Bye, princesses. Be good to your mommie. Take care of her, won't you?"

Eden tugged at his coat. "Do you have to go?" she asked, her lip quivering.

"I'm afraid so. You'll soon have your daddy here to take care of you. You don't need me."

He swung into the saddle, dug in his spurs, and set off at a brisk trot down the street. Libby watched until the cloud of dust behind him had settled. Then she took the children and went into the hotel.

"I'd like a room for a few days," she said as a huge man in a leather apron appeared.

"Passing through, are ya?" he asked

"I've just arrived from Boston. I'm coming out to join my husband," Libby said.

"That wasn't your husband I saw arrive with ya?" he asked, a spark of interest flickering in his eyes.

"He was just a kindly fellow traveller who rescued me and my daughters after an accident along the trail."

"You crossed the plains all alone?" The man looked impressed.

"We came on ahead of the main party," Libby said. "They were travelling slower with oxen. They'll be coming down the pass."

"I expect you could do with a good meal then," the hotel keeper said. "Pretty poor food out on the trail, right?"

"We'd love a meal," Libby said, "and a hot bath."

"I'll have hot water sent up to your room," the man said. "What would you like for your meal?"

"There's a choice?" Libby asked, amazed.

"Lady, you can get anything here you want," the man said. "Oysters, ham and eggs, steaks, peaches. You name it, we've got it."

"I don't believe it," Libby exclaimed in wonder. "You've really got oysters?"

"Real favorite of the miners, they are," the man said. "They like them fried up with ham and eggs."

"That sounds really good," Libby exclaimed. "I'll try it. And maybe a boiled egg each for the little girls?"

Soon they were sitting on a real bed in a room that had a wooden floor but canvas walls and roof. Red calico draped across the window frame gave the room a pleasant pink glow and made it feel like an exotic tent. A Chinese servant appeared with a hip bath and hot water, adding to the exotic atmosphere. Libby looked at him with interest. She didn't ever remember seeing a real Chinese person before and was fascinated by his loose pants and jacket and the long black pigtail down his back. He, on the other hand, displayed no interest at all in pouring water for a strange woman. When he was done he gave the slightest of bows and left. Libby looked at all that hot water.

"Come on, you lucky ladies, time for a bath," she said, starting to undo Bliss's dress.

"I don't want a bath. I like being dirty," Bliss protested.

"If you don't have a bath your papa will not recognize you," Libby said sternly and pulled the dress over her head.

With her daughters clean and wrapped in towels, Libby allowed herself the luxury of sitting without her clothes in warm, clean water. Then, of course, she wished she had clean clothes to change into.

"We'll have to go shopping tomorrow, children," she said.

"I need a new dolly. You promised," Bliss complained.

"And we need new dresses, Mama," Eden added. "Mine's too small and it's all dirty."

"We'll see what we can do," Libby said. "I hope there's a store in town that sells clothing. We'll have to be careful with our money. We don't know how long until we find Papa."

"Mr. Foster offered to give you some money, but you wouldn't take it," Eden said accusingly.

"We couldn't take Mr. Foster's money. We don't accept money from strangers," Libby said.

"Mr. Foster wasn't a stranger. He was nice," Eden said firmly.

"He was very nice, but it still wouldn't have been right to take his money. He'll need it himself and we'll be fine," Libby said.

She shook as much dust and dirt as she could out of their clothing and went down to the dining room. The hotelier, who told her his name was Big George, waited on her personally, making her feel that she had stepped back into Boston for a second. Libby could not remember when anything had tasted quite so delicious; the moist oysters with their salty taste of ocean and the juicy ham and fresh eggs, together with real bread to mop it up with. Although it was a man-sized plate, Libby cleared every morsel. So did the two girls. As she finished eating and washed it down with a big mug of coffee, men began to return up the street, talking loudly, reminding her that she had been bathing and eating while a hanging had been taking place.

Have I already become so callous, so insensitive? she wondered. Survival had been such a primary concern for so many months, she decided it had truly been a case of everyone for himself with no time or energy to think too much about others. If I had wept for every grave along the way, I should have no more tears left, she thought. This is a harsh world and I have to live in it for a while.

She finished the last of her coffee, then looked around the room. The interior walls were also calico draped and there was a potted fern in the corner to try and convey some elegance to the primitive wooden trestle table and the mismatched chairs. On the doorframe a slate was tacked. It read: Oisters 1 doller apeese. Eggs 75 sents. shampayne ten dollers a bottel.

"I don't believe it," Libby said, getting up hurriedly from the table. "It must be some sort of joke."

She walked through to the reception area where

Big George was now talking to three other men, listening to their vivid descriptions of how the hanging had gone. They all fell silent and looked at Libby as she approached.

"Good meal, missus?" the hotelier asked.

"Very good," Libby said. "Would you like me to pay for it right now or with my room bill?"

"Suit yourself," the hotelier said. "You'd have trouble skipping town without paying. Women are as rare as hen's teeth out here. Everyone would know exactly where you were."

"I'd rather pay as I go," Libby said. "What do I owe you?"

The man sucked at his teeth. "By my reckoning it comes to ten dollars and fifty cents."

"For one meal?" Libby asked, unable to keep her composure any longer.

"That's the prices around these parts," George said, still smiling pleasantly. "Most folks is surprised at first, but the miners are willing to pay anything to get luxuries from home. Supplies are real short, see. If I can bring peaches up from Chile and oysters in tins around the Horn, then I can charge what I like for them, for you'll not find them anywhere else."

"I see," Libby said. She managed a gracious nod. "You may add the meal to my bill."

The sound of scuffling outside the open door made her look around to see the doorway crowded with staring faces. "See," she heard a loud whisper. "I told ya there was a real live woman in town."

"Who does she belong to?" another whisper asked.

"Ask her if she's a widder."

"No you, I don't know how to talk to women anymore."

Libby realized that this was a good chance. She smiled at them. "Good day to you," she said. "My name is Mrs. Hugh Grenville. I've just arrived from the States and I've come to join my husband. I wonder if any of you know where I might find him. His name's Hugh Grenville. . . ."

She saw a big grin spread over all the ugly faces.

"What's so amusing?" she asked.

"Pardon me, ma'am, but none of us goes by his proper name here. We're all Frenchy Joe and Pious Pete and Little Jim. We don't know a thing about each other and we don't want to know."

"They sing a song here, ma'am," another man said. "Go on, sing it, Willie!"

A young boy blushed but sang in a good voice:

"Oh, what was your name in the States,
Was it Thompson or Johnson or Bates,
Did you flee for your life or murder your wife?
Say what was your name in the States?"


"But my husband should be easy to find, even if he has no name," Libby said. "He's an Englishman. An English gentleman, very proper. He talks very correctly and likes to dress well. . . ."

"You know anyone like that, Frenchie?" one of the men asked.

Several of them guffawed so that Libby couldn't hear the muttered answer.

"We'll keep our eyes open, ma'am. If we find him, we'll tell him you're staying here, will we?"

"Thank you, I'd appreciate that," Libby said.

The men ambled away. Libby turned to the hotelier. "Once they spread the word, it shouldn't take too long, should it?"

Big George shook his head kindly. "I wouldn't hope for too much," he said. "Chances are, even if they know where he is, they wouldn't tell you."

"Why on earth not?"

Big George shrugged. "Plenty of men come to the mines to get away from their wives. They'll probably think you're a no-good, interfering woman out to spoil a man's fun, if you'll pardon my saying so."

"Then I'll have to start searching myself," Libby said. "I've come this far. I'm not going to give up now."

**CHAPTER
16**

IT WAS ONLY after a week of exhaustive searching
that Libby finally realized how hopeless a quest she
had taken on. On the way to California she had imagined the mines as one little area, like a coal mine,
but not as deep, with all the men crowded together
digging. Now as she enquired, she found there were
hundreds of little settlements stretched up and down
a hundred miles of rugged country and new settlements being formed with every new gold strike. Some
of them were not even named yet. And as for Hugh
standing out because of his English accent—every
stretch of river had as many Germans and Swedes
and Frenchmen and Englishmen and Mexicans and
Chinese digging on it as it did Americans. There were
hundreds of men who seemed to be called English Joe
or London Louie or Frenchie or Sauerkraut. Libby
tried to fight off the feeling of despair that threatened
to overcome her by poring over the map in the hotel
lobby and trying to put herself into Hugh's head. If
he'd started from Independence, it was likely he had

191

come into Hangtown. If so, he would have gone to
the first big strike he heard about. She tried asking
George when the various discoveries were made, but
he was vague and unhelpful, claiming that men were
finding new places to dig every day.

It was with a feeling of grim determination that she
marched the children down to the livery stable and
rented a horse for herself. She chose a big, steady
bay and set the children up in front of her, not wanting to leave them alone in the hotel room. Although
Hangtown was almost deserted by day, excitement or
violence could flare up at any moment and the evenings were always rowdy. A man would run through
town yelling that he'd struck it rich and suddenly it
would be rifles fired into the air and free drinks all
round. Or a quarrel would flare up over a claim or
even over a small insult and men would go for their
guns. Libby could not believe the matter-of-fact way
that dead men were dragged out of the road, as if
they were pieces of litter. In the evening she would
hear the talk floating up from the barroom downstairs
that "poor old so-and-so had copped it today." Then
someone would comment that he shouldn't have claim
jumped and the matter would be forgotten. It seemed
that life was as impermanent as the tent cities that
were springing up.

Each day of her first week in Hangtown Libby
headed the horse out in a different direction, trying to talk to as many people as possible. It was hard
going up and down mountainsides on trails only just
wide enough for a single horse. Luckily, she had cho-
sen a good horse and he was very sure-footed as they
slithered down sandy slopes and had to ford rushing streams. She soon found that all settlements were

deserted during daylight. Every able-bodied man was out working on his claim. Only the sick lay in their tents or cabins and Libby was not too anxious to get close enough to question them.

The miners who were working did not welcome her either. Gold was the number-one priority and they wanted to get as much as they could before the winter rains came in earnest. They stopped work just long enough to look at her curiously, but when she asked about her husband they all shrugged or shook their heads and excused themselves to get back to their work, so that she began to believe what George had said was true. They had a code not to ask questions about anyone and certainly not to betray him to his wife.

After six days of journeying around under a hot September sun, Libby sat on the hotel bed and stared at the wall, trying to decide what she should do next. The little girls lay asleep, relaxed as only children can be whatever their surroundings. She took the last of her money from her pouch and spread it out on the bed. By the time she had paid the hotel and food bills there would be precious little left; enough for a couple of weeks of board at the hotel.

"I can't go back," Libby muttered to herself. "I've no money to pay the fare and I couldn't subject the children to that trip again. I can't afford a boat either, so I have to assume I'm stuck here." She looked down at the sleeping faces. "And somehow we've got to survive, even if we have to take up gold digging ourselves."

In the morning she sought out George.

"Any news about your husband yet?" he asked before she could say anything.

"Not yet," she said. "This is taking longer than I planned. Can you suggest somewhere cheaper to live, where I could maybe do my own cooking?"

George looked down at her and shrugged his big shoulders expressively. "There are a couple of boarding houses, but they board ten men to a room or to a tent, as the case may be, in bunks," he said. "The men don't care where they sleep right now—a barrel, a tent, a few branches over them. That will all change when they see what the rains are like." He grinned, then looked at her with pity. "There's no place for a woman here yet, or for little children. My advice to you would be to take the stage down to Sacramento and then get a ship down to San Francisco. I hear they're getting quite citified there. You'd feel more at home."

Libby wanted to say that she'd do that if she had the money, but she tossed back her hair and looked proudly at George. "I'm not leaving until I find my husband," she said, "and I know I could do it if some of you men would only help me."

"I'll keep my ears open," George said, "but why don't you wait for him down in San Francisco, or at least in Sacramento? There are plenty of women down there."

"We're staying here," Libby said, "if it's at all possible. Even if I have to start digging gold to pay for my board."

George looked horrified. "You could never do that!" he exclaimed.

"Why not? I'm strong. I'm not afraid of work," Libby said, eyeing him haughtily. "I'm not even afraid to show my ankles, like some women."

George shook his head. "I don't think you realize

what's involved," he said. "It's no longer a case of swishing around some gravel in a pan. The surface gold's all been picked up by now, at least in the settled places you can get to. Right now the men are digging up tons of earth, spade by spade, day after day. They're loading it into the rockers, they're sifting it and they're throwing it away again. It's backbreaking. It would kill you."

"Then what do you suggest?" Libby said angrily, because she had seen something of what the miners were doing and knew in her heart that it was beyond her. "What I need is a job. Could you use more help here in the hotel?"

A smile spread across George's face. He shook his massive head. "Lady, you'd cause me more headaches than you'd be worth. I'd have to stand over you with a shotgun day and night to keep the drunken miners away from you. And you can't blame them, poor devils. They've been without women long enough. If you worked here, they'd think you were one of the fancy girls and there for the taking and I'm sure you wouldn't want that." A slow grin spread across his face. "Of course, if you're interested in that direction, you could make yourself all the money you want. There's not enough of them to go around."

"Certainly not!" Libby said, and stalked from the room.

She walked through the town hoping for inspiration. At the far end a new tent had been set up with the sign, Trading Post. M. Hopkins Proprietor, tacked up. Barrels and sacks were piled up around it and inside it was stacked almost to the roof with pans and shovels, tobacco, whiskey, boots, and tough denim work pants.

Libby peered inside and a scholarly looking face with a high serious brow and a neat little beard looked up at her in surprise.

"My word, you gave me a fright," the man said, grinning pleasantly. "I thought I'd been away from the real world so long that I'd started hallucinating. I certainly didn't expect to see a woman here."

He got to his feet and Libby saw that he was very tall and thin, older than most of the men she had seen around and far too distinguished looking to be a storekeeper.

"I've been in town a week," Libby said. "I came to find my husband, but I hadn't realized how hard it would be. Nobody wants to tell me anything and it's so hard to get around and it costs so much . . ." Her eyes went to a crude price list tacked to his wall: Shovels $15 each. Pants $12.

"It's insane," Libby said. "How in good conscience can you charge men so much?"

"I know it's insane," he agreed, "but that's the way it is up here. Gold is king. As long as the gold keeps on coming they don't care what anything costs. I aim to make a tidy fortune in keeping them supplied with what they need." He reached out a hand to Libby. "Mark Hopkins at your service, ma'am."

"How do you do, Mr Hopkins, I'm Libby Grenville. I came from Boston to join my husband. You must see lots of men in your store. You haven't seen him, have you? His name's Hugh and he's an Englishman—tall, slim, and lots of dark curly hair?"

Mark Hopkins shook his head. "By the time I see them, they all look the same, all hidden under straggly beards and black hats," he said. "I could have served a gorilla here and not known it."

"If you ever do hear of him, you'll let me know, won't you?" Libby asked.

"I'll try. Where are you staying?"

"I'm at the hotel, but I've got to move out. I can't afford their prices any longer."

Mr. Hopkins smiled. "I'm sure you'd have more than enough offers of bed and board, but I don't think they'd be what you had in mind."

Libby found him immediately likable and pleasant and realized what a strain it had been to be constantly on guard with every person she had encountered for four whole months. She suddenly felt the burden of the overwhelming responsibility she had shouldered since setting off from Boston five months ago. Before that she had not known what responsibility was. Her parents ran their household. Choosing a governess for the girls had been her only major decision, except for deciding that she wanted to marry Hugh. She hadn't liked the governess after she hired her and Hugh had probably been a mistake too.

"You don't need an assistant here, do you?" she asked hopefully.

He looked at her with understanding. "Not yet I don't. I came up here with one cartload of supplies. When I sell them I aim to go back to San Francisco and stock up with two cartloads, then four, until I make my fortune. I'll need assistants later, but now I have to save every penny for the next step." He gave Libby an embarrassed smile. "I'd really like to help," he said, "but up here, if you don't take your chances when you've got them, you lose out forever."

"I understand that," Libby said. She started to walk away, then hesitated, not really sure where she was going. What would she do when the money finally ran out? She had never felt more completely alone and empty.

"I tell you what," Mark Hopkins's voice called after her. "I could let you have some canvas at cost, enough to make yourself a tent. That would keep you dry, at least. Do you have household stuff with you?"

"It all went over a cliff with a wagon up in the Sierra," Libby said. "We were lucky not to go with it."

"I've got a nice big dutch oven I'll let you have," he said, "and a couple of blankets. You can pay me what I paid for them."

"But I can't accept favors from you."

"I'm a good businessman, not a monster," he said, already picking up a bolt of canvas and then adding blankets and the cook pot to it. "Don't worry about me. I'll just add a little onto the price the miners pay to cover it."

"There're lots of other things I need," Libby said, "but I'd feel better if I paid the real price for them. I'll need a knife and an ax and plates and cutlery and food. . . ."

"I can't help with the food," Mark said. "I'm strictly a nonperishable man. You'll have to go to Herr Otto at the trading post for that, and pay what he asks, I'm afraid. He's got the monopoly on food around here because he knows a Chilean sea captain and he gets whatever is shipped from Chile."

Mark took down a large, lethal-looking knife and handed it to her.

"It's a little large, maybe," Libby said hesitantly. "I only want it for cutting food."

Mark looked at her steadily. "You might need to defend yourself," he said.

Libby had not considered that aspect. Would she

really be able to defend herself against wild animals or bandits or whatever else roamed these hills? If only Gabe would come back, she found herself thinking. He'd know what I should do. But it was unlikely Gabe would bother to come back to a town where they hanged people so readily, especially after rumors of cheating at cards.

With a heavy heart Libby carried her goods back to the hotel. On the walk, her mind racing like a fly, trapped against a closed windowpane, she came to the decision not to put up her tent in the town, where there were always drunken men. She had to find somewhere that was safe for herself and the girls. The trouble was that she wasn't sure where was safe.

At the hotel she handed over most of her money to pay the bill. It came to one hundred and twenty-five dollars. Then she divided all the items she had bought from Mark Hopkins into three bundles, a large one for herself and smaller ones for the girls.

"You'll have to be big girls and help Mama," she said.

"We're big girls, aren't we, Eden?" Bliss said, taking her bundle and trying to throw it over her shoulder as she had seen men do.

Libby laughed and ruffled her hair. "Come on, let's get going," she said.

They set out away from town, up a small wooded valley, far above the nearest miners' camp.

"Where are we going, Mama?" Bliss asked. "Are we going to Papa now? When are we going to find him?"

"Soon," Libby answered with a tired sigh. "But as for now, we're going to make ourselves a nice little home."

# CHAPTER
# 17

WHEN THEY CAME to a clearing, surrounded by live oaks and tall pine trees, Libby dropped her heavy bundle to the ground.

"I suppose this is as good as anywhere," she said. "At least it's private here and sheltered. Now let's see if we can make a tent."

"Are we going to be Indians, Mama?" Bliss asked excitedly.

Libby smiled at her. How wonderful to be four years old, she thought. How wonderful not to worry all the time. She managed to cut a couple of straight branches and make a crude tent. Then she took the girls back into town and spent the last of her money on supplies at a trading post behind the hotel. She didn't even bother to ask this man for work; he was a fat German with an unfriendly face and a cigar hanging from his mouth, reminding her of Sheldon Rival. She wondered for a moment about the latter. She had expected Rival to arrive in town any day and was glad that she would not be there to face him. Looking at the

200

prices posted on the wall, she cautiously bought only what was absolutely necessary: some rice, flour and sugar, beans and bacon. As the man unwillingly dug flour from a barrel for her, she noticed something moving in it.

"What's that?" she asked, stepping back in horror.

"Weevils," Herr Otto said, as if it was too unimportant to mention.

"I don't want moldy flour!" Libby exclaimed.

"It's all moldy by the time it gets here," he said. "The miners like the weevils. They say it saves them the trouble of going out and shooting meat."

"It's disgusting," Libby said.

Herr Otto stood with the scoop poised in his hand. "Do you want it or not?" he asked.

"I suppose I've no choice," Libby said with a sigh.

"That's right," he agreed with an unpleasant grin.

When she asked for potatoes, Herr Otto bent under the counter and handed her one, as if he were bringing up a large gold nugget. "That will be a dollar," he said.

"A dollar? For one potato?" Libby shrieked. "That's absurd. Look at it—it's so old it's sprouting."

Herr Otto shrugged his massive shoulders. "These are the only potatoes between here and San Francisco," he said, "and they get like that by the time they've come around the Horn on a ship. Do you want it or not?"

"What other vegetables do you have?" Libby asked.

"I got some onions," the storekeeper said, "but they're also a dollar each. I can't keep vegetables in the store. The moment I get them, everyone buys them."

"Forget it," Libby said. "I'll make do without." As she walked back to the tent, she almost wanted to laugh at the absurdity of the situation.

The children thought living in a tent was a big adventure. They loved playing in the outdoors and were excited by every bird and squirrel they saw. Libby was frightened to let them roam at first, aware of rattlesnakes and bears and wolves, but as the peaceful surroundings soothed her and the sun shone from a perfect blue arc of sky, she gave in and let them run and climb to their heart's content. They had their first narrow escape that evening when Bliss came running up to her mother excitedly. "Come see, Mama. I've found a dear little kitty." Mystified, Libby followed her daughter and found a large skunk waddling through the trees. She tried to imagine what would have happened if Bliss had decided to pick it up.

The nights were cold and Libby was glad she had accepted the pelts to sleep on. She would lie awake, staring up at the stars in the clearest of clear skies and worry about what was going to happen to them.

"I'll have to give up," she said each night. "I'll have to admit that I'll never find Hugh and that he has either learned to survive or given up and gone home or died by now." She realized how ironic it would be if he arrived back in Boston only to find she had gone to California. "How stupid I was," she muttered over and over. "How little I knew in those days." But it was no good blaming herself or thinking what might have been. She was stuck in the gold country and she had to decide what to do before winter came and she could no longer live in a tent. The big question, of course, was whether she could ever go home. Would her father take her back, if she managed to get that far? That was another thing to worry about, if she ever raised the money for the fare, which at the moment seemed impossible.

If she had not been so terrified about the future, the clearing would have been a delightful spot. It would have been an ideal picnic site, sheltered by giant trees, with the sweet smell of pine, manzanita, and bay and a thick carpet of pine needles, if only one could have packed up the picnic and gone home to a real house and a real bed at the end of the day. Libby could not afford a lantern, so the day ended at sunset and the nights were unbearably long. She kept a candle for emergencies only and prayed there would be none of those.

The next morning she served the girls flapjacks and tea for breakfast. She knew she had better do something soon. They would soon get sick on such a poor diet. She fought with her repugnance and now reconsidered an idea she had pushed firmly to the back of her mind until now. She wasn't selling her body for anyone or anything, so all she could do to get money was wash the miners' clothes. That was something they certainly needed.

She thought of the sweat-stained, mud-stained garments and shuddered at the thought of touching them, but it was something they might be glad to pay for, so it had to be done. She set out for the nearest mining settlement and went up to the men as they worked.

"Morning, ma'am," they called politely. "Any news of your husband yet?"

"Not yet," Libby said. "I wanted to tell you that I've set up house nearby while I wait for him and I'm taking in washing. Do you have anything you need washed?"

"Yeah, and I'm wearing it," one old-timer said.

The men laughed loudly. "He ain't changed his long johns since he got here, I reckon," another commented and they laughed again.

"If you decide to purchase a change of clothing and would like this one washed, you can find me off the trail to Coloma," Libby said frostily.

She met with the same reaction at the next diggings she came to. One man muttered that he'd never have a dime to send home if he had to pay for something he didn't really need.

Libby continued down the river but got no takers. She was about to go home, discouraged, when Eden and Bliss, who had been playing farther down the bank, came running up in excitement. "Mama! Come see. We've found gold. Lots of it. We'll be rich, Mama. You won't have to do any horrid washing."

Trying to hold back her excitement, Libby ran after them. It will be someone else's claim, she told herself. We won't be able to keep it.

One or two of the men threw down their shovels and ran after them to see the discovery.

"Look there, see," Eden called, pointing down to the sandy bottom of the stream, where golden flecks gleamed in the sunlight.

"Oh," Libby said, speechless. There did not seem to be anyone working this little cove and no tools signified an active claim. She bent down and reached into the water, scooping up a handful of sand. The golden flakes rose and swirled as she disturbed the water.

"That's not gold you've got there," one of the men muttered, peering over her shoulder. "That's fool's gold."

"Fool's gold?"

"It's pyrite, another mineral altogether. We call it fool's gold. It's worthless."

"You can always tell if it floats like that," the other man said, more kindly. "Gold's heavy, see. It sinks."

"I see," Libby said, stepping back from the bank. She gathered up her skirts. "Thank you for your trouble, gentlemen Come children, we must be heading home."

She noticed they were looking after her as she walked.

On Sunday morning she was awakened by polite coughs outside the tent. "Mama, there's strange men out there," Eden whispered.

Libby looked around for the knife.

"What is it?" she called.

"Washing, ma'am," came a gruff voice. "We all change our clothes on Sunday. We'll pick it up tonight."

Libby looked out of the tent at a large pile of dirty clothes.

The men nodded politely to her.

"We even got Old Buck out of his long johns," one of them said, grinning. "He's sitting under a tree naked as a jay bird until you get them washed. Let's hope they don't fall to pieces."

"I'll have them ready for you," Libby said.

As soon as they had gone, she carried the clothes down to the creek below, lit a fire, and set a pan of water on to boil. The clothes were filthy beyond recognition and had to be boiled and scrubbed until they showed any trace of their original color. She worked without stopping until at the end of the day she had raw, red hands, an aching back, and a pile of clean clothing drying in the sun. That night she was twenty dollars richer. She went into town and bought eggs and canned butter, plus some cloth to make the girls some clothes.

The same thing was repeated the next Sunday. She did not dare canvass for more work because she knew she could not get it done in a day. Each time the men passed her, they would enquire politely whether she had found her husband yet. She heard that rumors were flying up and down the creek about her: that her husband was really a British prince run away from ascending the throne; that she had murdered her husband and was hiding out in California; or that she was a widow and was waiting for a man to strike it really rich before she got her claws into him. Libby realized how dangerous for her these rumors could be. If they didn't think she was respectably married and searching for her husband, she would become easy picking with no protection.

So she went to extra lengths to talk about Hugh and describe him to everyone she met. She realized that Hugh was her talisman and shield. As a married woman whose husband was at the diggings, she was safe from all unwanted attentions. Men respected another man's wife as they did his claim. The moment they thought she had no husband, she was no longer safe. In all her dealings with them she made sure she maintained a frosty distance. She behaved to the miners as her father did to his coachmen at home, polite but distant and unapproachably above them. If they ever happened to make a crude joke in her presence, or use a swear word, her look made them mumble an apology. She knew that there were some men at the diggings who could have become her friends; not all were humble farmers and laborers, but she didn't dare let down her guard. The miners started calling her Lady Muck, behind her back at least, and she did little to discourage this.

One day a man for whom she had done washing came up to the tent, panting hard from the climb up from the creek. "I heard of an Englishman over at Kelsey," he gasped. "Sounded just like your old man—dark, curly hair, English as they come."

"That's him!" she exclaimed. "How far is it to Kelsey?"

"Couple of miles over the hill that way," the man said.

"Thank you very much," Libby said excitedly. "I'm very grateful to you for your trouble."

She called to the children and told them that they were finally going to Papa. It was a rugged path over the hill and as she dropped down to the diggings at Kelsey, her heart was beating so loudly she was sure all the men would hear her coming and look up. Old doubts surfaced as she came down the final slope. What if he wasn't pleased to see her, if he'd planned to run away?

"I hear you have an Englishman working on this stretch of river," she called to the first men. "I'm his wife. I've been looking for him."

"Honest Injun?" one man said, nudging his neighbor. He yelled down the line of men. "Hey Charlie. Get up here. Got someone to see you."

Then he winked at his neighbor again. "I reckon Charlie's in for the shock of his life."

"Wot did yer want to see me about?" A sharp voice demanded and a little dark man swaggered up the line of men towards Libby.

"Your missus is here," one of his companions shouted.

Libby and the man looked at each other in dismay and then Libby said, "This is the wrong man" at the same time as the cockney said, "This ain't my old lady."

Libby kept her composure all the way home, but back in the tent she flung herself down on the ground and cried, no longer able to keep her disappointment and despair from her children.

# CHAPTER
# 18

IN MID-OCTOBER the first real winter storm rolled in from the Pacific. All night long the wind howled through the branches and tore at the canvas, sending driving rain into the tent. In the morning they were cold, wet, and miserable, and Libby was not able to get a fire going. Bliss started coughing. The storm continued all day, turning paths down the hillsides into rivers which threatened to sweep away the tent. When Libby tried to go into town next day, she found that the track was now impassable mud.

The creeks continued to rise, even after the rain had stopped, as water came down from the High Sierra, and miners found their digging sites either under water or swept away. As they waited impatiently for the water to go down, they had nothing to do but household chores, and Libby found that they no longer needed her to do their washing.

That night Bliss developed a fever and lay tossing and moaning. Libby sat huddled in a wet blanket, staring out at the drops dripping from the branches, sunk into despair so deep that she felt as if she were drowning.

"It's hopeless," she said softly. "They're going to die and it's all my fault. Oh, God, forgive me for my pride and recklessness," she whispered. "Punish me, but spare my children. Don't leave us to die."

In the morning it really did seem as if her prayer had been answered. The storm had passed over, leaving clear blue skies and new grass sprouting and the men anxious to get back to work. When they got down to their sites they found many of them unrecognizable. The water had swept away tools and stream banks and piled up debris where there had been none. This added to the frustration of enforced idleness and fights broke out. Libby was carrying her pan to get water just above the nearest diggings when two men emerged from the undergrowth right in front of her.

"I'm warning you, you just stay away," one yelled.

"It's my claim, I'm telling you," the other snarled.

"Prove it! Where's your tools?"

"Can I help it if the danged storm swept them away? I know my claim when I see it and you're jumping it."

"You're out of your head. Your claim never came that far down the creek."

"It did so. Right to that big pine."

"It never did."

"You calling me a liar now?"

The first man drew his gun. "I'm saying that I'm working that stretch of river now and if you don't like it, that's too bad."

"Think you can scare me?" the other man demanded. He drew his own gun.

"You'd never dare use that thing," the first man taunted. He was a skinny, shifty-looking type with long, drooping moustaches. "You're as lily-livered as they come."

"You take that back," the other man said. He was small and fair skinned, freckled from the sun.

"Lily-livered, that's what I said," the first man repeated.

Suddenly shots rang out. It was impossible for Libby to see who fired first, but both men dropped to the ground. Libby rushed over to them shouting, "Stop this madness!" But it was too late. The skinny one was lying dead with blood trickling down his moustaches. The other appeared to be dead too, but as Libby bent over him, he opened his eyes and tried to focus on her, as if he didn't really believe her presence.

"He got me," he murmured.

"You got him too," Libby said. "He's dead."

A faint smile passed the man's lips. "No kidding?" he asked. "They always said I couldn't shoot straight." He groaned in pain, holding his side and coughing.

"We've got to get some help for you," Libby said. "Where are your friends working?"

"Get me back to my cabin," the man whispered. "It's right here, just through the trees."

He tried to get to his feet. Libby helped him, draping his arm over her shoulder. He was not a big man and she managed to half drag him up the hill to a small log cabin among the trees. It already had a roof and two wooden walls, a stove and a crude bed, but only canvas draped over the front and one side. Libby laid him on the bed.

"Do you have a partner I can get?" she asked.

The man shook his head. "Only me," he said. "I'm here by myself. My partner died of cholera back on the trail. I've been alone since I got here."

"You lie there, I'm going for help," she said. "I'll try and get a doctor to you."

The man shook his head sadly. "Won't do no good," he said softly. "I'm done for, I can tell. Just stay here with me, will ya?"

"Of course," Libby said, squatting down beside him. He grabbed her arm urgently. "I want you to do something for me," he whispered. "You look like the sort I can trust. I've got three bags of gold sewn into this mattress. I want you to send them to my wife."

"Where does she live?" Libby asked. "Do you have the address written down somewhere?"

His grip on her forearm tightened. "It's Hettie Jacobsen," he said, his eyes pleading. "Snowdrop Farm, just outside Harrisburg, Pennsylvania. See it gets to her." He broke off, coughing again.

"Don't worry, I'll see it gets to her," Libby said.

"You promise?" the man insisted.

Libby put her hand over his. "You can count on me."

He nodded. "That's good," he said. His eyes opened, alert and clear blue. "Shame to go now, just when the claim was starting to pay," he said with a sigh. "Why don't you take it? Lots of gold waiting to come out of that creek . . . just waiting . . . gold."

He closed his eyes and sank back again. "Where is it?" Libby asked. "How would I know it?"

"It's down next to that big old. . . ." His voice faded away. He was dead.

Respectfully, Libby covered him and went down to the nearest creek to find men to dig him a grave.

When they came up to the cabin it seemed that
nobody really knew him. He was a loner who didn't
like to drink, they told her. If any of them had an idea
where he had been working the river, they were not
telling Libby, in spite of her subtle questions. They
buried him along with the other dead man on a bank
behind the cabin and then hurried back to their claims
again, leaving Libby alone.

"I'd better get that gold and send it back to his
wife," she murmured to herself. She ripped open
the side of the mattress and took out the three heavy
bags. I wonder how many ounces there are here, she
asked herself. The bags sat round and heavy in her
hands and slowly an idea began to creep into her
mind: she did not have to send the gold. Nobody
except her knew it existed. She and the girls could
get a passage down to Sacramento for the winter,
down to a warm, snug house and good food and
new clothes. Then if they decided to sail back to
Boston, she could send the woman some money from
there. . . .

Even before she had finished reasoning it out,
she dismissed it. She remembered the man's face,
his pleading eyes and she remembered saying, "You
can count on me." Whatever happens to me, I was
not brought up to cheat and steal, Libby thought.
I can't do it, even if my children's lives depend on
it.

Slowly, another realization came to her, spreading
through her with warmth and excitement. She might
not take his gold, but he had left behind a cabin—a
cabin which nobody else could claim. He didn't have a
partner. He was a loner, the others said. She looked in
wonder at the stove, at the barrel of flour, at the bed

and table and it looked like a palace. As fast as she
could, she ran back to get the children. She got the
stove going, made some hot tea, and put on the rabbit
she found hanging up to start a stew. She tucked Bliss
in the bed, wrapped in warm quilts.

Within a few days her cough and fever had completely gone. As soon as Bliss was well enough to be
left Libby wrote a letter to the man's widow and took it
into town. She also took the gold with her to the Wells
Fargo office to have the gold sent back to the widow.
It came to almost a thousand dollars. As it was being
weighed, Libby watched wistfully, thinking what she
could have done with so much wealth. But on the way
back she decided a cabin was even better than a fortune. She now had a place of her own that would keep
out storms, that nobody could take away from her.

After the tent, the cabin seemed like a palace. The
bed was only strips of rawhide nailed to a frame and
way too small for the three of them, but it had a mattress stuffed with pine needles and it was off the wet
ground. They managed with the two girls snuggled
at one end and Libby at the other. The table kept
the food away from ants and rats and there was even
one high shelf behind the stove where the miner
had stored his most prized possessions like tobacco,
ammunition, coffee, tea, and sugar. His rifle hung
on a hook on the wall. Best of all, there was some
dry wood and the stove gave out steady heat. Libby
joined the canvas from their former tent to rainproof
the last two walls and stood looking around her in
delight.

"Our own home at last," she said.

"Are we going to live here forever?" Eden asked
suspiciously. "What about Papa?"

"We'll find him," Libby said, "but we can't travel during the bad weather. We'll be snug here."

"I want to go home to Grandma and Grandpa," Bliss said suddenly, sitting up in the bed. Her face was still red and blotchy but the deep cough on her chest had improved with hot broth. "I miss my toys. We don't have any toys here. And I want ice cream again. I want to go home." Her little lip quivered.

Libby felt like crying too. She wanted to say that she agreed completely with Bliss—she missed her own things and the good food and, above all, the company of people she felt at home with. She knew how to make small talk at dinner parties. She knew that wherever she went in Boston she would be treated with respect. Here, she was never sure from day to day. The miners were polite enough to her at the moment because they still thought she was Hugh's wife, but just how long would they go on being polite if no Hugh showed up? As she sat warming her hands in front of the stove she considered seriously for the first time that she might never see him again and was embarrassed that she did not feel an overwhelming sense of loss and desolation. She would miss him, of course, but her main emotion was the empty fear of having nothing and nobody.

She stood up and went over to Bliss, giving her a beaming smile. "We'll find Papa and be home and safe before you know it," she said. "Remember that big house in England I told you about—the one waiting for Papa? We'll be going there and choosing ponies for you girls and a nursery full of toys."

"Can there be a dollhouse?" Bliss asked, her eyes lighting up.

"Definitely a dollhouse," Libby said.

When she had cleared away the evening meal that night, Libby sat down to sew. She was in the middle of making the girls dresses, but she put that aside and got out the scraps of calico and gingham to make into two crude dolls. She realized that at the moment some things were more important than looking neat and clean.

The dolls were a big success, although nobody could say that they looked beautiful. Bliss named hers Annabel, after her favorite doll at home, and took it everywhere with her, dangling by one hand. Consequently, hers soon got very dirty, while Eden's, tucked into the bed during the day, remained pristine. Bliss didn't seem to mind. She was happy and she was well again and it warmed Libby's heart to watch her scampering through the woodland. She worried more about Eden. Eden never said much and never gave away what she was feeling, but Libby could tell the child worried about their future by the occasional questions she asked and the way she bit her lip at the answers Libby gave.

"What will you do if there's no more washing?" she asked Libby. "How will we eat?"

"We'll manage," Libby said. "There's a barrel of flour in the cabin and plenty of beans."

Eden made a face. "I hate beans," she said.

"I'm not very fond of them myself," Libby agreed, "but they are better than starving. We'll have to try and get some meat. Maybe I could shoot a rabbit."

"Shoot a little rabbit?" Eden asked in horror. "You couldn't shoot a nice furry little rabbit, could you?"

"If we have to, we have to," Libby said. "We need meat, Eden."

"I'll eat beans then," Eden said stubbornly.

Libby considered the possibility of hunting for their food as they walked down to the creek for water together. They often saw wildlife in the woods—ground squirrels and doves and quail and rabbits, also the occasional deer, although the deer had become very wary of humans and their guns. Would she have the nerve to shoot them? she wondered. Then she knew she would if her children were starving. It would be just another thing she would have to do to be added to the list of things she never dreamed she was capable of doing.

October became November. In between rainstorms the weather was mild and beautiful. It seemed that the moment a storm passed by, the sun came out like the middle of summer and even in November it was warm and pleasant. It even became too hot inside the cabin with the stove going, so Libby rolled back the canvas front of the cabin to let in the fresh air and prepared her food in the open.

One afternoon Eden had been out alone and came running back to Libby excitedly. "Mama, I found berries. Are they good to eat? They look good."

"You didn't taste any, did you?" Libby asked, hurrying over to see what Eden held in her hand.

"Not until you told me they were all right," Eden said.

She held up her hand and Libby relaxed. "Why, they're blackberries," she said. "You must have found a late bush. Are there more?"

"Lots more," Eden said.

Libby went to get a pail. "Come on, show me where you found them," she said. "We can make a lovely pie. Much better than beans." She slipped her hand around her daughter's shoulder and Eden grinned up at her.

An hour or so later the pie stood cooling on the table, sending out a wonderful aroma. The smell must have wafted down the trail on the light breeze because it wasn't long before a miner came stomping up the path, pausing and scratching his head in wonder when he saw the pie.

"You just bake that, missus?" he asked.

Libby nodded.

"What's in it?"

"Blackberries," Libby said.

"I'll give ya this nugget for it," he said, holding out a sizeable lump of gold in his hand. "It's about an ounce."

"You want to give me that for a pie?" Libby asked in amazement.

"It's worth it to me," the miner said. "My wife used to bake the best pies and I'm mighty homesick for a good one."

"Then it's yours," Libby said. Still rather dazed, Libby handed him the pie with instructions to bring back the plate. She put the nugget in her pocket.

"Mama, you sold our pie," Bliss complained.

"She made a lot of money, Bliss," Eden said. "The man gave her a lump of gold. Now we're rich, right Mama?"

"Not rich," Libby said, "but we've a little money now, and you know what? We're going hunting for all the blackberries we can find and were going to bake as many pies as we can."

They only managed to find enough blackberries for four more pies, but Libby sold them all with ease and went into town to get the gold weighed. It came to

almost five ounces and Libby came out of Wells Fargo
with seventy-five dollars in her pocket. She looked for
the familiar tent at the end of town and was told that
Mr. Hopkins had sold all his supplies and gone down
to San Francisco to get more.

So he's already on stage two of his plan, Libby
thought, happy for him, but missing the one friendly
face she could count on. A big new wooden building
was going up along what had become a main street,
not draped with calico and canvas but with thick log
walls and a sturdy porch. Libby paused to look at it
as she passed.

"I see someone struck it rich," she commented to
a man who was working on it.

"Going to be the biggest hotel in the whole gold
country," the man said. "This guy's supposed to be
rolling in money."

"Lucky for him," Libby said. She went into the German's grocery store, trying to decide what supplies
would give her best value for her money.

"Still no vegetables?" she asked.

Herr Otto shook his head. "Only potatoes right
now. The mules can't get up from Sacramento anymore. The roads are too bad."

"And the potatoes are still the same old ones at a
dollar each, I suppose?" Libby asked.

"The same."

Gradually, an idea was forming in Libby's mind: a
picture of sprouting potatoes.

"Give me fifty," she said.

"You want fifty potatoes?" the man asked. "You got
the money?"

Libby put down fifty dollars on the counter and carried her potatoes home in triumph.

"Yippee! Potatoes," Bliss said when she saw them. "Can we have them baked with butter on them?"

"Not these potatoes," Libby said. "I've got something else in mind for them." She started cutting them into pieces, around each sprout. The children watched, mystified. Then she took the spade and worked solidly all afternoon, turning over the soft sandy soil in front of the cabin.

When the children saw what she was going to do, they were horrified.

"Don't plant our potatoes, Mama. We want to eat them."

"What will we have to eat if you put them in the ground?"

"Maybe we can spare just one to eat now," Libby said, softening. "If this works out well, we'll never have to worry about food again."

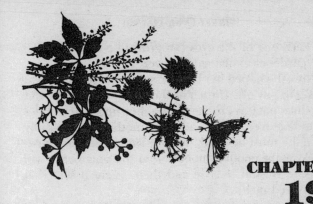

# CHAPTER
# 19

THE THOUGHT OF potatoes growing outside her door lifted Libby's depression and gave her something to aim for again. She knew nothing about planting things, but she dimly remembered, back in her very early childhood, hanging around the gardener at her grandmother's big estate.

"You want to see magic?" the gardener asked her.

Staring at him wide-eyed and a little afraid, she had nodded silently. He had taken a big old potato from his pocket. "Here," he had instructed. "Drop that in the ground and when you come back next time, you'll see magic."

When Libby had returned several months later, she had hurried out to find the gardener. Grinning at her from a mouth with most of its teeth missing he had beckoned her to follow him. Then he put a fork into the soil and where the potato had been, lots of perfect new potatoes were growing instead.

"How did it do that?" she had asked, as if she had just witnessed a miracle.

"Each one of the eyes can grow into a new plant," the gardener explained. "Clever, ain't it?"

Now she hoped her brief lesson in horticulture was going to pay off. If each of those segments really did produce potatoes in the spring, her financial worries would be over. If she had heard nothing of Hugh by then, he must be dead, or gone home, she reasoned. She'd make enough money from the potatoes to sail back to Boston in style and then . . . she'd see what happened next.

Another worry was relieved with the new cabin. After days of relentless rain, it was comforting to hear it beating on a shake roof with only a few drips coming through and only the occasional blast finding a gap in the canvas walls. Even if a blast came in, it didn't matter, because the stove was giving out comforting heat. Libby felt like a child in her first playhouse and realized with a jolt that this was her first real home that she had not had to share with her parents. Knowing it was hers gave her the incentive to improve it. She tried her hand at making a bench for the girls to sit on and, impressed with her success, decided she would make a second bed if she could get someone to give her some rawhide.

Winter had now set in. It was cold all the time. There was only a brief hiatus between storms and the creeks did not go down. Some miners gave up and moved down to Sacramento for the winter. Others, who could not afford to go, hung around in their cabins, playing cards, whittling, and doing chores to while away long days. There was no more washing to be done because nobody was getting fresh gold to pay for it. Hunger began to be a problem. It was also a major concern for Libby. She had plenty of flour and beans, but she knew that children needed a nourishing diet. She had to get meat from somewhere. When she saw a pair of miners go past, dragging the carcass of a deer, she suggested that she'd make them a venison pie if they gave her some of the meat.

"We'd like to help, but there's five of us at the cabin," one of the men said. "It's hard to find deer these days. They've all been driven right up into the mountains."

Libby took the girls out hopefully scouting for edible plants, not really knowing what she was looking for, but the high winds had stripped and flattened anything that might have been edible. She found some acorns under a grove of big oaks and tried roasting them. They tasted quite pleasant but they all had stomach pains that night so she didn't dare try it again. She watched the mourning doves up in the trees and wondered if she could ever manage to shoot one of them with the rifle. Secretly, she began to practice behind the cabin, aiming at a target on a tree trunk until at least she could fire the rifle without it slamming into her shoulder.

One morning she heard a twittering just outside the canvas and peeked out to see a flock of quail, feeding happily in the grass. They were enchanting plump little birds with adorable black crests, like question marks, bobbing on their heads as they communicated with each other. Swiftly, she grabbed a length of cloth she was about to cut out, opened the canvas suddenly, and threw it over the birds. Some managed to escape, running peeping into the forest, but the fabric still twitched with the remaining birds. Cautiously, she reached under it and her hands fastened around a bird. It struggled as she lifted it up, then lay limp in her hands. She could feel its tiny heart hammering against her fingers and noticed how beautifully it was marked with a delicate little crest on its head.

How can I possibly kill it? she asked herself, her heart racing almost as fast as the bird's. She slipped her thumb and forefinger around the little neck, but before she could apply any pressure the crested head fell back and the bird lay there, dead in her hand. It was frightened to death, she thought, feeling guilty and elated at the same time. She had never believed it could be so easy. She lifted the cloth and found that two more birds had died. The others scurried around in panic but she let them go. It took her ages and much revulsion to pluck the three little birds, but they made a good stew to which she added dumplings.

Although the cabin was removed from the nearest settlement, Libby had not felt alone or threatened until one night. Shortly after dark she heard snuffling sounds right outside the cabin. She lifted the canvas a fraction to peer out and found herself looking at a huge grizzly bear. His head was massive and she could see four-inch-long claws glinting on his front toes. He had obviously smelled the food inside the cabin and was trying to see how to get at it. In terror Libby realized that one slash with his claws would open up the cabin like a sardine can. Her eyes went to the rifle on the wall. It was such a puny little thing compared to the size and strength of the bear. What if she shot and wounded him and he charged, enraged? Trying to control her panic she shoved a pile of dry kindling into the stove and held her breath while she waited for it to burst into flame. Then very steadily she lifted the canvas on the front and went around to the bear. He turned his giant head toward her with a surprised grunt, then reared up on his hind feet, at least eight feet tall.

"Shoo! Go away!" Libby screamed, waving the burning brand at him. Bravely, she took a step forward. For a second, time seemed to stand still, the bear poised above her, the flames flickering. Then he grunted again, dropped to all fours, and ambled off into the forest. Back in the cabin Libby collapsed onto the floor, shivering with shock.

"I can't go on forever alone," she whimpered. "I can't keep on like this. I need someone to protect me and take care of me!" Her thoughts wandered to Gabe, riding up with Bliss on his saddle, not to Hugh. Where was he now? she wondered. She imagined him sitting in a barroom, surrounded by handsome Mexican bar girls, gold piled up all around him, never thinking of her at all.

Christmas came and would have passed unnoticed if Libby had not heard drunkenly sung carols coming up from the settlement down by the creek. It seemed that even in this time of hardship, the miners always seemed to have money for drink.

There was not even one present or treat for the children. She found her thoughts going back to Christmases at home. Her parents had always held a huge celebration with goose and plum pudding, guests and parlor games, and always lovely presents. Libby wiped away a tear and found that she was crying for herself as much as for her children.

Around the first of the new year they woke to find the land blanketed in snow and more flakes falling thick and fast. There was almost a foot of snow on the roof of the cabin and the boughs of the pine trees were weighed down with their white mantle.

Rocks and bushes were now unrecognizable bumps in a smooth landscape. It kept on snowing all day and all night, at times accompanied by winds that swirled the flakes and plastered the sides of trees. By next morning the snow was piled halfway up one wall of the cabin and when Libby went outside, she soon sank in past her knees.

"We'll just have to wait patiently until it goes away," she said to the girls, and scooped snow into a pan to melt for water.

"I don't want it to go away," Bliss said, looking expectantly at her sister. "I want to play in it."

"You have no warm clothes," Libby said, "and no snow boots."

"Just a little play, Mama, and then we'll come in to the fire again," Eden begged. So Libby let them make a snowman outside the cabin. After a few minutes they were glad enough to come in again, shivering.

"I wish we had something good to eat," Eden said. "I hate bean soup."

"At least it's hot," Libby said. "I'm afraid we're stuck with bean soup until we can catch something or get into town."

She looked at the girls worriedly. They had no energy and they both looked pale and drawn, like little old women. "As soon as I can, I'll try and see if I can get down to the mining camps and do some mending or baking in return for meat," she said. "Maybe they're all tired of doing their own chores by now."

Darkness came so very early and the nights seemed to go on forever. Libby would often lie awake, staring at the red glow coming from the stove. Somehow they had to keep on going until spring. What if the snow lasted for weeks as it sometimes did in Boston?

How long could they live on beans and rice? What
would happen when there was no more dry wood
to be found? Shadows flickered at the corners of the
firelight and the shadows were heavy with demons.

On the third snowy night Libby had settled the girls
down to bed and was sitting, trying to sew by the light
of one sputtering candle. She hated to go to bed too
early, for that meant so many hours of lying, thinking. As long as she was up and active, thoughts could
be kept at bay. Suddenly she looked up, her needle
poised above her sewing as she heard a noise outside.
Something was crunching through the snow. A bear?
Didn't bears hibernate when the weather got too bad?
It sounded like something too large for a coyote or a
fox or any other of the animals that sometimes hung
around at night. Her gaze went to the rifle on the
wall. Slowly, she put down her sewing and reached for
it. Since the grizzly incident she always kept it loaded. The crunching and slithering seemed to be coming closer. She held her breath. The sound seemed to
have stopped. She waited a moment, then very cautiously pulled back the canvas front of the cabin.

She peered into the darkness, gasped and slid her
finger onto the trigger of the rifle. A man was prowling around the cabin, trying to be silent and cautious.
She cocked the rifle. The man heard the click and
spun around.

"What are you doing here?" she demanded.

"Looking for the front door," came the muffled
reply.

"There isn't one."

"Then how am I supposed to knock?"

"Who are you? What do you want?" she snapped,
her nerves stretched taut.

The figure came toward her. He was snow encrusted and ice hung from his moustaches. "It's Santa Claus. I'm a little late," said a muffled voice.

"Don't come any closer. This thing is loaded," Libby said threateningly.

"I see your temper hasn't improved over the last couple of months," the voice said. Libby opened the canvas flap wider. It threw a triangle of light onto the white snow. "Or have you forgotten me already?" the man asked.

"Gabe? Is that you?" Libby's voice trembled. She lowered the gun.

"See, you've already forgotten what I look like," Gabe said and stepped into the light. "Is it safe to come closer now, or will you blast my head off with that dangerous-looking weapon?"

# CHAPTER
## 20

"WHAT ARE YOU doing here?" Libby asked, unable to conceal her delight.

"I tramp for hours through snowdrifts to see if you're surviving and you ask me what I'm doing here?" he asked. "Woman, my hands are about to succumb to frostbite, I might never have the use of my toes again. Are you going to keep interrogating me on the doorstep forever?"

Libby laughed. "Come on in," she said, "only talk quietly. The children are already sleeping."

Gabe put his hand to his lips and dropped his voice to a whisper. "How are my favorite princesses?"

"They're both well, thank God. I worry about them a lot, but they seem to be surviving everything."

"They must be tougher than they look, like their mother," Gabe said, smiling at her. She held open the canvas and Gabe stepped inside. "Very cozy," he commented. "Don't tell me you built this whole thing single-handed. I knew you were a remarkable woman, but not this remarkable."

"I inherited it," Libby said. "Here, let me take those snowy clothes before they cause a flood on my floor. Sit down by the fire. Would you like coffee or tea?"

"You inherited it?" Gabe asked, holding his hands over the stove. "From whom? Hugh built it?"

"I didn't find Hugh," she said. "At least, not yet. I'm still looking but it's so hard to get information. The rains put a stop to travelling." She went ahead of him to the stove and put on water to boil.

"Except for hardy people like me," Gabe said.

"As you say, except for hardy people like you," Libby agreed, looking at him fondly. "What are you doing travelling around in weather like this?"

"I was down in Sacramento," Gabe said, "and the water started rising. When it reached my second-floor window I decided that I had better get out. So I thought I'd head back up here and see if there were a lot of idle miners who had nothing better to do than play cards. I passed through Hangtown and I just happened to ask whether anybody knew about you. The young man at the trading post said you lived a mile or so out of town, on your own, so I thought I'd pay you a visit. Just to make sure you were all right, you understand."

"You came all this way on foot?"

"Believe it or not, there isn't any snow down in the town. If I'd known what I was going to encounter, I'd never have set out."

"I'm glad you did," Libby said.

"I thought I was going for an afternoon stroll," Gabe said. "That's a good old-fashioned mile to your place. More like twenty."

Libby watched him, remembering with pleasure

how the laugh lines around his eyes always crinkled when he smiled.

"It was very nice of you, Gabe."

"I'm actually a very nice sort of fellow," he said, coming across to the stove and putting down his pack on the table, "apart from my unfortunate habit of liking to gamble. So tell me all. How have you fared since we parted?"

"Oh, I've managed very well," Libby said airily. "We lived in a tent to start with and I took in washing."

"You—a washerwoman? I'd love to tell them that in Boston." He threw back his head and laughed.

"You'd be surprised at what I can do," Libby said. "I baked pies. I do mending and cooking sometimes. We're just fine since we got the cabin."

"Ah yes, the cabin you inherited," Gabe said. "Tell me about that."

"It was luck, or fate if you'd rather," Libby said. "Two miners got in a fight and they shot each other. I helped one of them back here and he died. He lived here all alone, so I just took it over."

"How convenient," Gabe said. "You're sure you didn't shoot him when you were waving that formidable rifle around."

"I'd like you to know that I shoot very well," she said. "I've been practicing. I even shot a rabbit."

"My congratulations," Gabe said. "I see that you are now doubly dangerous and able to take care of yourself." He reached into the bag beside him. "I did, however, bring some stuff up from Hangtown, just in case the snow had prevented you from hunting your dinner." He grinned up at her and produced several packages from the bag. "Dried meat," he said.

"Dried apples and . . . a can of oysters! What do you say about that?"

Libby's eyes lit up. "I don't know what to say. You really are Santa Claus," she said. "Can we open the oysters now? We can share them."

Gabe laughed. "I eat these things all the time," he said. "One gets rather bored with them after a while. I'll watch you eat them." He rummaged in the sack again. "I will, however, join you in a glass of champagne, if you can produce two glasses."

"French champagne!" Libby exclaimed in amazement.

"It's quite the rage up and down the mining camps," Gabe said. "Whenever a miner strikes it really rich, only French champagne is good enough for him. It doesn't matter that he's never drunk anything other than beer or whiskey in his life before and that he doesn't even like the taste of good champagne. Success means champagne, so he drinks it."

Libby went over to the shelf and took down two tin mugs. "No glasses, I'm afraid. We'll have to pretend these are crystal."

"No problem," Gabe said. He wrapped his handkerchief over the cork, twisted, and it came off with only a faint pop. "There," he said with satisfaction and began to pour.

Libby watched him, not able to take her eyes off him for a second. She noticed the greatcoat he had been wearing was of good cloth and had a big fur collar. His cuff links glinted gold and he had on a clean, crisp shirt.

"You must be doing well to be able to afford champagne," she said.

He looked up at her. "Not bad, as they say. If I

make money at the same rate all winter, I plan to go down to San Francisco next summer and start buying land down there. If there has ever been a boom town, it's San Francisco. It's just going to double and redouble in size and prosperity and I think I'd like to be in on it." As he talked he produced a knife from his pocket, opened the can of oysters, and tipped them onto a plate. Then he pushed the plate toward Libby.

"Sounds like a good idea," Libby said.

"And you?" Gabe asked slowly. "What will you do after the winter?"

"I'll start looking again," Libby said. "I have a little venture going that should make me some money. If I make enough, I'll be able to travel up and down the entire length of the diggings or even hire other people to go looking for me."

"Searching for Hugh, you mean?"

"What else?" Libby asked.

"So you're not going to give up on him yet? You don't think he died along the way?"

Libby's gaze met his. "Until I have proof he is dead, I have to assume he's still alive and I'm still his wife," she said.

"Very commendable," Gabe said. He lifted his tin mug to his lips. "Your health," he said.

"And yours," Libby replied, lifting her own mug.

It was almost like a dream, she thought, to be sitting opposite Gabe eating oysters and sipping champagne. Surely, she'd wake and find herself curled in the narrow bed with the stove almost out and cold beans for breakfast.

"So where are you going now?" she asked him, her voice slightly unsteady.

"If I make it back to Hangtown successfully and do not get buried under any new drifts, I'm heading down south to the southern mines," he said. "I hear the weather is milder down there and it doesn't rain as much. Also the rivers aren't running as high and the men are still digging, which means they have gold in their pockets." He scowled at her reproachfully. "Don't sigh like that. You know that the leopard can't change his spots. You are not going to turn me into a preacher, especially when I have landed myself in gambler's heaven."

"So the other places aren't as hostile as Hangtown?" Libby asked.

A broad smile spread over Gabe's face. "Oh, I've made a few hasty exits and I have a bullet hole in my hat to prove one of them, but on the whole, I find the men lining up for the privilege of having their gold taken away. I made five hundred dollars one Sunday, if you can believe."

"Gabe! And on the Sabbath too," Libby said, shocked.

Gabe laughed again. "Sorry, my dear, but in the mines Sunday is gambling day, not church. Anyway, doesn't the Bible say he who hesitates is lost?"

"I think that was Benjamin Franklin, not the Bible," Libby said, laughing too. "You really are a rogue, Gabe Foster."

"And you are really glad to see me. I can see it in your eyes."

"I'd be glad of any friendly face at the moment," Libby said guardedly. "When you've been alone as long as I have, stranded up here with just two little girls for company and knowing that you dare not make friends with any of the miners in case they get the wrong idea."

Amusement flickered in Gabe's eyes. "By the way, do you know what they call you in town?" he asked. "Lady Muck."

"I know," Libby said, "and I'm glad that they do."

"How come?"

"As long as they think of me as an unapproachable, stuck-up snob, I'm fairly safe from unwanted attentions. Lady Muck is my shield—that and Hugh."

Gabe took a long, slow drink of champagne. "And if you don't find him this summer? You'll go back home?"

"I suppose so," Libby said slowly. "This is no place for a woman, or for little children."

"I thought your father had forbidden you to darken his door again."

"Maybe my absence will soften him," she said, "and Mother would want me back. Maybe I'll go and claim Hugh's house in England and start a new life there with the children." She stared at the red glow from the open stove door. "And you? Will you go back to New Orleans when you've made your pile?"

"I don't think so," Gabe said. "I've nothing to go back for. I think this is the future. I'll make my fortune and turn respectable businessman, if a bullet doesn't get me first."

"Don't," she said, shivering.

"Let's not talk about the future," he said. "Look, you're not eating your oysters. Here," he stabbed an oyster with the fork and held it up to her mouth. "Come on, open wide," he said. The gesture was somehow so intimate that she felt a shiver go all the way down her spine.

"Shouldn't you be getting back?" she asked. "It takes a good hour to walk down, even in fine weather."

"You're not thinking of sending me back tonight?" Gabe asked in horror.

"You were not thinking of staying here? There's only this one room."

"And?"

"What will people say?"

"There are not too many people around to see, are there? The nearest camp must be down on the creek."

"But they knew in town that you were coming up here. If you don't show up until morning, there will be talk."

"So? Let them talk."

"But you don't understand, Gabe. If they think I've entertained one male visitor for the night, then I'm vulnerable. Any of them could try their luck."

Gabe laughed. "Let's hope they're luckier than I've been," he said.

"It's no joking matter," Libby said, getting up and walking across the room to his coat. "I'm all alone here, completely alone, and I don't know how long I can keep going like this. So please go. You'll be able to follow your footprints. You'll get back quickly. . . ."

Gabe came over to her and took his hat from her hands. "Very well, if that's what you want, I'll go. I'll probably be able to find my way down to town again, although I think it's beginning to snow harder. If I fall into a drift, or lose the trail and they find my frozen body in the morning, don't worry about it. Just think of it as the ultimate sacrifice I made for you. Good-bye, Mrs. Grenville." He took his coat from her and started for the door. "Thank you for a most pleasant visit."

"No, wait," Libby called, grabbing his arm.

"You don't want me to go after all?"

"Yes. No. I don't know," Libby said with a sigh. "I don't want anything to happen to you, but I'm scared if you stay."

Gabe's eyes narrowed. "After all those nights on the trail when I could have crept into your wagon any time, you're still scared of me? Don't you trust me, Libby?"

"It's not that," Libby said, turning her face away, hoping he wouldn't see the blush rising in her cheeks. "I don't trust me."

"Ah," Gabe said slowly. "So Lady Muck really is human. That's comforting to know."

"Of course I'm human," Libby said.

"Then wouldn't it be an act of humanity to allow a poor frozen traveller to sleep on your floor for the night?" Gabe asked, taking his coat from her. "See, I'll spread out my coat over here and curl up in my little corner." Very slowly and deliberately he spread out the coat on the floor. "There," he said. He came over and sat beside the stove again. "Let's talk some more, you and I. I'm sure you are starved for good conversation as you are for—other things."

"Yes," she said hesitantly perching herself on the bench. "Sometimes one does get weary of talking only to children."

Gabe laughed. "You should see yourself, sitting up poker-faced and poker-backed as a schoolmistress. Relax, Libby. Let's enjoy each other's company while we can. We might never have this chance again."

"I know," she said softly, "Do you think I don't realize that? This is so hard for me, Gabe. Having you sitting here beside me and forcing myself to keep thinking of Hugh."

"Hugh's not here right now, I am," Gabe said. "You've been in my thoughts often, Libby Grenville. I can't seem to forget that kiss, on the hillside, before we said goodbye. I expect you've forgotten all about it?"

Libby looked down at the red glow of the stove and shook her head. "I've tried to make myself forget," she said in a low voice. "I've tried not to think about you, Gabe."

"Libby," Gabe said softly. He reached over and took her hand. "Do you know how lovely you look in the firelight? Your hair is glowing like spun gold. Do you know what you're doing to me right now?"

Libby pulled her hand away. "Don't, Gabe," she said. "Please don't." She got to her feet and turned away from him, her hands to her face.

"Very well." He rose to his feet too. "You don't have to worry about me, Libby," he said, gently touching her arm. "I don't want to upset you. I'll go over to my place in the corner, if that's what you want." She was conscious of his closeness, her hand still on his arm.

"What I want and what is right are not always the same thing," she said. "I'm still married until somebody tells me I'm not."

"Libby," he said, gently stroking her cheek, "you're trembling. Do you want me to go to my corner now?"

"You know I don't," she whispered, closing her hand over his hand that still rested on her cheek. Slowly he bent his head down to her, bringing his lips toward hers. Libby gave a shudder as his arms came around her. His lips were warm and demanding and she could feel his hands fumbling with the buttons at the back of her dress, but she had no power to resist him. She had never felt such overwhelming desire in her life. She was conscious of Gabe lowering her down onto his coat on the floor, his lips kissing a trail down her neck as he eased her dress over her shoulder.

"I've wanted you from the moment I first saw you," he murmured. He moved to unbutton his pants while his lips still played over her shoulder, nuzzling down to her breast.

Libby was lost in a red haze of desire. She was not conscious of the hardness of the earth floor beneath them or of the cold air blowing in under the canvas wall. All she knew was that she felt as she had never felt before and that this man was awakening her body like a skilled musician fine-tuning an instrument. Then she was aware of something else. She heard a whimper come from the bed on the other side of the room and a little voice called, "Mama? Are you there?"

Hastily, they scrambled apart and Libby righted her dress. "What is it, darling?" she called back.

"Mama, I had a bad dream," came Bliss's voice. "Are you coming to bed now? I can't sleep unless you're here."

Libby looked at Gabe and gave a rueful smile. "It's no use," she said. "I don't think fate wants us to be together."

"They'll go back to sleep," Gabe whispered.

Libby shook her head. "I can't, Gabe," she said. "Not with them in the room. I don't know what came over me."

"I do. You finally admitted that you're a woman for a few seconds," he said.

She touched his arm. "Don't be angry. Try to understand."

He got to his feet. "I think I will try and make it back into town tonight after all," he said.

"But Gabe—all that snow."

"I need to cool off," he said shortly, "and all that snow is the next best thing to a cold shower."

He put on his coat and pulled his hat down over his ears, then walked out into the night.

# CHAPTER
# 21

THE JANUARY SNOWSTORM proved to be the the last gasp of winter. After a few days all trace of snow melted and the wind that blew in from the west was already mild, scented with blossom. New grass began to appear on the hillsides and sun-bleached gold of last year's grasses was replaced with soft green. Rainstorms came, but not so frequently and cleared to blue sky and cloudless sunshine. The midday sun was warm enough to make Libby and the children take off layers of clothing and the first green sprouts showed in the potato patch. Libby weeded and watched as if she were guarding her children.

Although the weather down in the diggings was mild and springlike, the creeks and rivers still ran high with melting snow from the higher mountains and many of the miners were still idle. It was a hard time for them; no gold was coming in and game was getting scarcer all the time. The boredom and enforced idleness made some of them drink more than they should or spend their days playing cards. Others resorted to playing outlaw, riding around the countryside and taking what they needed from the more prosperous. It was a rare day when Libby did not hear shots echoing through the hills and never knew whether they came from deer hunting or a violent quarrel or marauding bandits. She always kept the rifle loaded, just in case.

Food was becoming a problem. They soon finished the dried meat Gabe brought and an occasional dove or quail was not enough for the three of them. In spite of practice, Libby was still not good enough to shoot a rabbit. She noticed that the girls were becoming listless.

"Why don't you go out and play?" she would ask.

"I don't feel like it today," came the tired answer and Libby would watch them in concern.

The concern changed to alarm when Eden complained, "My teeth hurt me," and Libby found her gums were bleeding.

"And I got boo-boos on my legs," Bliss complained, annoyed that Eden was getting the attention. She held up her skirts and Libby noticed that there were far too many bruises for the number of times she fell or hurt herself. There was a nagging ulcer on her own shin and for the first time she tied it in with her children's problems.

To the children she tried not to show any alarm, but later she went for a walk alone, striding through the woodland, trying to get her thoughts in order. It was imperative that they get a better diet, but there was no money and no real hope of getting money until the miners went back to work. All the diggings on the creeks nearby were still idle and the men had all the time in the world to do their own washing and mending and cooking.

"I have to get some work," Libby thought desperately. "I can't wait for the potatoes to grow. Somebody must hire me."

She left the children in the cabin, feeling that they would be safe enough if they stayed inside, and set off down to Hangtown. The path was still muddy in places and she had to wade across several streams that had not been there in the fall. She made it with no mishap, meeting nobody on the route. The town had grown since she saw it last. Most of the tents had been replaced with sturdy log structures. There were now three saloons instead of one and the fine new hotel was complete. When she sought out her friend Mark Hopkins, she found that he had moved from tent to wooden store.

"I see your plan's progressing on schedule," she said, looking around the well-stocked shelves.

Hopkins spread his hands wide in a gesture of hopelessness. "Now if only the water would go down and the miners would get money to buy this stuff. I spent every penny of my profits to get all this up here. You've no idea what they are charging for freight these days."

"Almost as much as you are charging for these pants, I expect," Libby said, picking up a new pair of blue overalls with a ten-dollar price tag.

"Ah, well these are special pants," Mark said. "They are made extra strong for the miners—and notice the little rivets at the seams and pockets. They'll hold up through anything, at least that is what Mr. Levi Strauss down in San Francisco promises me."

Libby looked out to the empty street. "So I take it

you haven't reached the stage of needing an assistant yet?"

"Not until some buyers appear," he said. "How are you managing up there in the cabin?"

"We're keeping going, but only just," Libby said. "We're all beginning to suffer from lack of fresh food."

"You're not the only ones," Mark said. "What with the floods down in the valley and the bad trails, we haven't had any shipments of fruit or vegetables since Christmas. You go to Herr Otto's store and all he'll offer you is rotten pork or green bacon. He's even sold out of canned peaches at two dollars a can!"

"Oh dear," Libby said. "I was hoping to find some work down here and at least be able to buy food."

"The roads should be open soon," Hopkins said, "and there are several new businesses in town, although I'm not sure you'd want to work in them—they are all saloons or gambling places and I really don't see you as a bar girl."

"What about that big new hotel I saw?" Libby asked. "They must need maids and cooks there."

Hopkins shrugged. "I hear the owner went down to San Francisco and hired straight from there," he said. "He's got Chinese help and he probably only pays them room and board."

"Who is the owner?" Libby asked.

"Not a very pleasant man. Name of Rival," Mark said.

"Sheldon Rival?" Libby asked. "I came across the plains with him. I wondered when he'd show up."

"He's already made a fortune selling supplies on the new diggings up beyond Grass Valley, so I hear," Hopkins said, "and now he's building hotels and saloons in all the major towns. The man looks as if he aims to take over the whole gold country."

"I hope not," Libby said. "He's one of the most obnoxious, heartless individuals I've ever met. I'm glad I spoke to you before I went looking for a job at his hotel."

"I wouldn't worry," Mark said. "I hear he doesn't run these places himself once he's got them started up. He puts in managers and just checks on them from time to time. He's having himself a mansion built, down towards Sacramento, well away from the primitive conditions at the diggings."

"As long as it's well away from me," Libby said. "I've seen quite enough of Mr. Rival to last me a lifetime."

She left Mark Hopkins's store and came out into the main street. Although more buildings had sprung up, there had been no attempt made to relieve the squalor of the town. Castoff clothing, broken tools, and empty sardine cans littered the streets and there were still yawning potholes where men had hopefully mined for gold. It seemed that small-scale dry digging was still going on around town, for new pits had appeared and piles of gravel were mounting up behind and between buildings. But these pits were idle at the moment, probably because it was much harder to separate the gold without running water. This problem was obviously being addressed, as a series of flumes was being built. Men were working on high trellises as they constructed a wooden channel to carry water where they wanted it. Libby stared up at the ambitious wooden waterways and decided that they must have cost a fortune to build. Obviously, gold mining was no longer a one-man operation. It was already turning into big business.

At one end of the town the sickly smell of incense came from the new Chinese quarter. Libby looked curiously at the expressionless Oriental faces as they walked past her, not seeming to notice her presence at all. Some of them were patiently working through the gravel which had been cast up by previous diggings. They squatted there, meticulously digging and sifting, then throwing away and digging some more. As Libby paused to watch, one of the men called out excitedly and held up something in his hand. She could see it looked like a good sized nugget. Immediately, the other Chinese came running over and started digging next to the lucky man. But Libby was not the only one who had witnessed the discovery. From the hotel porch several men materialized, strolling up to the Chinese digging, as if they had all the time in the world. When they reached the spot, however, they fanned out, encircling the diggers.

"What you got there, Chinky?" one of them drawled.

The Chinese looked up suspiciously.

"Show me what you got, boy," the man commanded, taking his pistol from its holster.

Unwillingly, the Chinese opened his hand to reveal the nugget.

"Well, lookee here," the first man said, whistling. "I think Chinky just struck pay dirt. This claim's too good for dirty foreigners, don't you think, boys?"

His companions nodded, walking forward menacingly, fingering their own guns. Most of the Chinese backed away, but the finder of the nugget stuck his ground. "This not your claim," he said. "This all used up. You don't want."

"Obviously it ain't all used up if it produces stuff

like this," the man said. "OK. Hand it over."

"Is mine. I find," the Chinese said bravely. "Law says no claim jump."

The men laughed. "What law?"

"United States law!" The Chinese said defiantly.

The laughter continued. "United States law is for Americans," the man said. "It don't apply to no dirty Chinese."

"Excuse please. Chinese people not dirty. Chinese people wash more than white peoples. Very clean."

The laughter faded at this direct insult. Another man stepped forward to join the first. "You're scum. Killing Chinese is the same as shooting deer. Nobody cares."

"Now, are you going to hand it over like a good boy, or am I going to have to blow your hand off first?" the first man asked.

Unwillingly, the Chinese opened his hand and the first man snatched the nugget. "Now, get out of here and don't come back," the man said. "If I catch you digging here again, I'm going to shoot first and ask questions afterward."

"Is free country. Part of America," the Chinese man said. The miner raised his arm and brought the butt of his gun crashing down on the Chinese man's head. As he fell he kicked him viciously.

"This one's a troublemaker, boys. Better make sure he don't make no trouble again," he growled.

The other men closed in. Libby had watched unseen from the side of the street. Now she could stand by no longer.

"Leave him alone," she shouted, running up to the men who had closed in. The Chinese man had rolled himself into a ball, trying to protect himself from the

vicious kicks. She didn't stop to think of her own possible danger as she grabbed the leader's arm. "Stop it
at once!" she shouted. "It's cowardly and disgusting.
You're a disgrace to your country."

The men broke into laughter, but they stopped
their attack to look at her.

"Well, ain't that nice. It's Lady Muck herself. Sorry
you had to witness this, ma'am, but the little varmint
was helping himself to gold he had no right to."

"It was an old digging and you know it," Libby said.
"Besides, he gave you the nugget. Let him go."

Bravely she pushed between them and held out her
hand to the Chinese man. "Come on, get up and go
while you still can," she said. "They won't kill you
while I'm here. Hurry. Get out of here."

The little man scrambled to his feet and scurried
away like a frightened animal. The watchers roared
with laughter and gave a final swing with the boot as
he went past.

"He won't be around here again in a hurry," one
of them said.

"And we got us enough gold here for a couple of
bottles at least."

Slowly, they began to drift back toward the hotel.
Libby, her face still bright red and her heart still
pounding, headed back to her cabin. She hurried
as fast as she could, unable to shake off the uneasy
feeling that she was being followed. Several times she
was conscious of little sounds—the snap of a twig,
the bouncing of pebbles down a slope. But when
she stopped and looked back, she saw and heard
nothing. She began to worry that one of the men
she had stopped was coming to get his revenge and
the moment she reached the cabin, she took down

the rifle from the wall, putting it beside her on the table as she fixed the evening meal.

Eden and Bliss ate a few spoonfuls of pureed beans and coarse bread, then went willingly to bed. The docility worried Libby even more. It seemed as if they were just slipping away from life and that one day it would just be extinguished. She cleared away the half-eaten food and was washing off the remains outside the cabin when she was sure she heard a noise in the oak grove beyond. She dropped her pan and ran in to get the gun. As she came out again a shadow darted between trees.

"I know you're there. You'd better come out and show yourself before I shoot," Libby shouted.

"No shoot," pleaded a little voice and out of the shadows stepped the Chinese man she had rescued that afternoon.

"Oh," Libby said, completely taken by surprise. "It's you. What do you want?"

The Chinese made her a solemn bow. "You save life," he said. "Ah Fong thank missee. I stay here now."

"Stay where?" Libby asked.

"I stay here with you."

"But you can't stay here," Libby said. "I've only got this little cabin. No place for you here."

"No worry," Ah Fong said, with the slightest of smiles. "I build own place sleep and eat, but I belong you now."

"What do you mean?" Libby asked anxiously. "You don't belong to me."

"Yes," Ah Fong insisted. "You save life, now it belong you. I come be your servant. I make good servant. Take good care of missee."

"But Ah Fong—is that your name? I really don't need a servant and I can't pay you."

"No need pay. Ah Fong not need pay. Ah Fong need food. That all."

"But I really don't have food for you, Ah Fong," Libby said, exasperated by his patient insistence. "We don't have any good food left. Myself and my two daughters are only eating beans. We're getting sick."

"So?" Ah Fong said. He put down his bundle beside the cabin. "Not worry," he said. "Ah Fong fix."

Since he obviously wasn't going to leave, Libby went back into the cabin again. It was getting dark and she could hardly send him back down to town at night. She scooped up a plate of beans and rice and took it out to him. He was already busy pulling down pine branches and making himself a little shelter. He accepted the food cordially.

Next morning he was nowhere to be seen, although the shelter now stood with woven sides and a thick pine roof and his bundle of possessions inside. Around midday he showed up again and came straight into the cabin without knocking or waiting to be asked. He opened his shirt and tipped out various plants onto the table.

"Here," he said, picking up some small round leaves. "You eat."

"What is it?" Libby asked.

"Good food," he said. As if to demonstrate, he picked up a leaf and munched it, nodding all the time. "Make well again," he said.

Then he held up some evergreen needless. "Make good tea," he said. "Good for childrens."

He brushed Libby aside and poured out water into a pan, adding the needles to it. The children didn't like the taste, but the next day they did seem brighter and Eden's gums weren't bleeding as much. Ah Fong showed up with more leaves and roots he said were good to eat and spent hours putting out snares all around the cabin. By the end of the week the snares had caught a rabbit and a squirrel, both of which he skinned and cooked for them. He refused Libby's offer to join them as she served the rabbit, but took his own plate outside, eating it squatting in his shelter. Libby felt guilty about his living in such a flimsy house, but he made it very clear to her that there was a distance between them. He was the servant and lived in the servant's house and that was how it should be.

As she watched him, delicately eating rice with his chopsticks, she wondered if he was really some sort of genie in disguise. Incongruously, she found herself thinking back to her childhood. When she was a small girl her governess had read her the story of Aladin and his lamp. When she went to bed that night, she noticed her bedside lamp and, in horror, imagined what it would be like if a great, huge genie billowed out of it. The horror mounted until the evening breeze blew through her net curtains, sending them billowing out, just like a genie. Libby had screamed hysterically and brought the whole household running.

"It's just a story," her governess had said scornfully. "There is no such thing as magic lamps or genies. Now go to sleep."

Maybe she didn't know everything, Libby thought, looking with wonder at Ah Fong. Maybe I finally said the right magic words and now I have my own personal genie who's going to make everything right.

# CHAPTER
# 22

LIBBY SOON FOUND out that Ah Fong was not going to be like a genie—devoted and willing to grant her every wish. As she should have suspected from the way he stood up to the bullies in town, he was not at all shy about speaking his opinion and telling her when she was wrong.

"Why you spoil good rabbit by stewing to death?" he asked her.

"It makes a good broth that way," Libby said.

"Sure, good broth, but meat—like eating leather. Here, I show you." Then he sliced up the meat and sauteed it lightly with some wild garlic, serving it with watercress that he had found in a stream. It tasted delicious beyond Libby's wildest imaginings.

"Next time you go town, you stop by Chinese house," he said. "I give you message and they give you spices. Make food taste better."

Libby didn't think the food could taste much better and she gladly let Ah Fong take over more of the cooking. The girls were responding to his additions

to their diet and were already more feisty again. They
were a little scared of Ah Fong at first, but after a
week or so it became obvious that he had adopted
them and would let them do all sorts of things their
mother would not.

"Let's play horsey, Ah Fong," Bliss would yell and
would climb on his back while he patiently galloped
round and round.

"That's enough, Bliss, you're tiring Ah Fong," Libby
would call, but Ah Fong would look up, his face glis-
tening with sweat. "Ah Fong no tired, missus. Ah Fong
like play with little missee."

Another thing Ah Fong took over as his own was
the potato patch. He was horrified at the condition
of the soil Libby had planted her potatoes in. "How
they going to grow in lumpy bed?" he asked. "What
they got to eat?"

"Plants need to eat?" Libby asked.

"Sure," Ah Fong said. "We need dung. Make soil
rich!"

So he had Libby and the girls walking up and down
the trails, picking up the horse and mule droppings
to be dug into the potato patch. The young plants
seemed to like the attention because they sprouted
healthy leaves and began to show white flowers. Libby
found that she was looking forward to the future with
anticipation for the first time in months. She really
believed that the arrival of Ah Fong had been a turning point and that from now on, everything was going
to get better and better.

One day she took her washing down to the stream
below the cabin. It was still running fast and deep, far
above the summer bed the miners had worked. Libby
found a pool out of the main swirl of current and sat

with her bare feet dangling in the cold water as she washed the girls' clothes. It was an idyllic spot, overhung with willows decorated with the most delicate new green leaves. A kingfisher sat on a low bough, staring down at the water and a flock of tiny birds, no bigger than thimbles, hopped twittering through the branches. With the hot sun beating on the back of her neck, the water looked so inviting that Libby decided to wash the dress she was wearing also. It would soon dry in the sun on the bank. She took it off and slid into the water in just her camisole and underskirt. The water was icy cold but refreshing and she laughed as she bobbed up and down in it, splashing it over her face.

When her feet and legs were beginning to tingle with cold, she decided reluctantly that she had better get out. She hauled herself up the steep bank and found herself facing four grinning faces. She recognized at least one of them from the incident in town. Then, they had at least been polite to her. Now there was an animal quality to their grins.

"Well, lookee, boys," one of them said. His eyes went over Libby's body, to which her wet undergarments now clung revealingly. He was a heavyset man, dressed from head to toe in black and he wore a gun belt decorated with Mexican silver. Two silver pistols hung at his hips. "What have we got here?"

"Looks like we just caught ourselves a mermaid," another man added.

"You all alone, little lady?"

Libby tried to act as if their presence was not alarming her. She nodded politely to them and then bent to gather up her things. She noticed one of them was carrying a bottle.

"She's all alone. Ain't that sad?" one of them said and the others laughed.

"What she needs is a little male company," the first man suggested. He was slurring his words. The silly grins on the other faces indicated that they had all been drinking. Libby just prayed that drink had dulled their wits and made them slow.

She was now clutching her bundle of wet clothing to her chest and she tried to walk past them. "Thank you, but I'll have male company very soon, when my husband returns," she said, stressing the word *husband*.

The men were straddling the path, barring her way.

"What husband?" the man in black demanded. "You ain't really got no husband, have ya? You're all alone out here—just like us. We're all alone and we've been without a woman too long."

"There are bar girls in town now, so I understand," Libby said frostily. "I'm sure they'd be delighted to entertain you."

"Yeah, but they cost money," one of the men complained. "Do you know how much they're charging these days? No one's got any money until the creeks go down."

The man in black grabbed at her underskirt as she tried to push past them. "Besides, why pay for what you can take for free?" he asked. Libby caught the sickly smell of alcohol on his breath and wrenched herself away from him. He went to grab at her, but misjudged and stumbled. That fraction of a second was all that Libby needed. She sprinted ahead of them up the path to her cabin. Her breath was coming in gulps and the pain in her side stabbed as she ran, but she did not slow, all the way up the hill. She had the feeling that if only she could reach the cabin, she'd be safe.

When she got there, she found it all closed up and no sign of Ah Fong or the children. They liked to go with him and find food. With trembling fingers she untied the canvas flap and let herself in, running across to take down the rifle. With its cool metal barrel in her hands she felt more secure and she stood there, feet apart, gun at the ready, waiting as she heard the blundering feet, the ribald comments, and the curses come up the hill toward her.

"Don't be shy, little lady," one of the voices called out to her.

"You're going to like it as much as we are, darlin'," another added.

Libby cocked the rifle.

"Don't come any closer," she commanded through the canvas. "I'm warning you! Stay away. I've got a gun and I swear I'll shoot the first man who comes through this door!"

"Oh, she's got a gun. Ain't she sweet?" a slurred voice said and there were drunken giggles. "Oh, we're so afraid."

"I like a spunky woman. It's so much better after a struggle." A big hand reached in to pull back the canvas and the man in black stepped into the cabin. "Come on now, baby. You ain't going to shoot old Bart now, are ya?" he crooned.

"Get out!" Libby shouted. "I mean it. Get out or I'll shoot!"

"She don't mean it. She couldn't hit a. . . ." He was going to say *fly*. He lurched toward her, his mouth hanging open in anticipation as Libby pulled the trig-

ger. There was an incredibly loud blast and the anticipation on his face turned to surprise as he clutched
at his middle and crumpled to the floor. The other
men peered in with stunned faces. Libby stood facing
them, still squarely on both feet, rifle still aimed.

"I've plenty of ammunition and I'll do the same to
you if you don't go away," she said. "Now get your
friend out of my cabin and go."

She motioned to them with the rifle. Still stunned
by what had happened, they dragged out the lifeless
man and Libby heard them slithering back down the
hill. When she was sure they had gone, she sat down,
shaking. She had actually shot, maybe even killed a
man, and it had not been hard.

She was amazed how calm she was. She played
through the scene again in her mind and it was as if
she were a spectator at a play, not personally involved
at all. She felt nothing, neither guilt nor fear. She put
the rifle back on the wall and scraped away the blood-
stained earth from the dirt floor just as if she were a
machine and not a person at all. She had just sat down
with a cup of tea when she heard voices and the children came bursting in with Ah Fong in hot pursuit.

"Look, Mama, look what we found for you," Bliss
yelled. "Ah Fong says that these leaves taste good."

"And Mama, I picked you flowers. Aren't they
pretty?" Eden added, holding out a sagging bouquet
of wild flowers to Libby. Libby took them and smiled
graciously. She smiled and nodded at everything they
told her, determined to say nothing about what had
just happened.

When Ah Fong asked her later, "Something wrong,
missee?" she turned on the smile again. "Wrong?
What could be wrong? Nothing's wrong, everything's

fine," she said, so forcefully that he went about his chores without saying anything more.

It was late in the afternoon when Ah Fong looked up from the stove, where he was frying rice. "Horses coming," he said.

Libby listened and then she heard them too, a faint drumming of hooves along the trail, getting louder and closer. Her eyes went to the rifle again. She had held off four men, but could she hold off more?

"Get under the bed, girls," she commanded, "and don't come out until I tell you to."

"What is it, Mama?" Eden asked fearfully. "Is it bad men coming for us?"

"It may be," Libby said. "Just do what I tell you."

Ah Fong shot her a querying look. "You stay out of the way too," she said.

The horses galloped into the clearing.

"We know you're in there," shouted a man's voice. "Come on out with your hands up."

"Go away!" Libby yelled. "I don't know who you are, but I'm not being tricked into coming out. I've still got my rifle and I've still got bullets."

"Don't be a fool," the voice shouted. "We've got the place surrounded. Come out and surrender before it's too late."

Libby glanced back at the children cowering in the corner and Ah Fong by the stove. She couldn't risk any shooting with only canvas to protect them. Cautiously, she opened the canvas. "What do you want?" she asked, looking up at strange faces.

"Is this the woman?" the leader asked.

"That's her," a voice replied and Libby saw one of the men who had chased her up from the creek.

"Come with us please," the leader said.

"What for?"

"You're under arrest for the murder of Bart Jackson."

"But he attacked me. It was self-defense," Libby said in outrage.

"You'll be able to tell your side at the trial," the man said. "Now get out here before we have to drag you behind the horses."

Libby looked back at Ah Fong. "Take care of the girls for me," she said. "Don't let anything happen to them until I get back."

"Don't worry, missee. Ah Fong take good care," he said. "You don't let them devils push you around. You got law of United States for you."

"I hope so, Fong," she said, letting the canvas flap fall.

The leading man reached down and dragged her up roughly onto his saddle, then they set off at a gallop back down the trail. It was an uncomfortable ride for Libby, held like a sack of potatoes in front of the man, and she was shaken and bruised by the time they rode into the main street of Hangtown.

"Here she is. We got her," members of the posse shouted as they rode into town. They shot off guns into the air and men came running from the bars into the main street. Someone brought out a table and chairs. The man let Libby slide from his horse and someone pushed her to the front of the crowd. The whole scene was assuming a nightmare quality. It was such a close reenactment of the trial she had witnessed on her arrival in Hangtown. She remembered the way they had pushed the Mexican girl to the front of the crowd, the way she had stood there defiantly, fear gradually overtaking defiance as she realized what was going to happen to her. Libby looked around the faces of the crowd; they had the same excited, eager look that she had noticed before, as if they were about to witness a sports event. She realized then that they wanted another hanging.

Five men took their places in the chairs, one of them the doctor who had shown the only spark of justice and compassion at the last trial. Libby looked around the crowd, hoping to see other familiar faces, but there were none.

"State your name please," the man in the center chair asked.

"Elizabeth Grenville."

"Elizabeth Grenville, you are charged with the murder of Bart Jackson earlier today. We have in the crowd three men who saw you kill him. Is Slim here?"

One of the men stepped forward. "I was there, along with Billy Bob and Dutch," he said. "We saw her gun him down in cold blood."

"That's not true," Libby began.

"Shut up and let the man speak. You'll get your turn," came from the table. "How did it happen, Slim?"

The man looked at Libby. There was now no sign of the drunken grin. His eyes were hard and sharp as they watched her. "We was walking down by the creek," he said, "and we was passing this little lady's cabin and we knowed she was all alone there, so Bart said why don't we pay a call on her and see how she's getting along? So we called out to her and she yells out something we can't quite hear, so Bart pulls open her door and steps inside and before he can speak— bang—he's lying dead on the floor and her standing there holding a rifle in her hand. And she looks up, cool as a cucumber and says to the rest of us, "Get him out of here or you'll end up the same as him. I swear to God."

Libby ran over to the table. "Don't listen to him," she begged. "It wasn't like that at all. They tried to grab me down at the creek. They were all drunk. I ran all the way back to the cabin and got my rifle. I told them not to come in but the man in black came in anyway. He was laughing and he said I couldn't shoot a fly. It was when he reached out to grab the gun that I shot him. I didn't mean to kill him but it was self-defense. They were going to. . . ." Libby's voice trailed off, unable to go on.

"Is this right, Slim? Billy Bob? Dutch?" the doctor asked, looking up from the table.

The three men looked at each other and grinned. "We were just having a little fun, that's all. We didn't mean no harm. There was no call to go shooting any-one. It was coldblooded murder. I say hang the bitch."

"That's right. String her up. Let her get what's com-ing to her." Voices from the crowd took up the chant.

"But if it was self-defense," the doctor tried to shout over the noise of the crowd. "A woman has a right to protect her honor."

"Nobody touched her," Slim yelled. "It was all in her head. I tell you, she's got a crazy idea about men looking at her—comes from being too long without a man. If you let her go, she'll like as not gun down any miner who happens to look her way—I swear it."

"That's right. It ain't safe to let her go. Get rid of her," voices from the crowd picked up again.

Libby looked from one face to the next. They wanted to hang her, she could see that. They were itching for the excitement of a hanging. It didn't

matter whether they thought she was innocent or
not. She thought of her children, with only Ah Fong
to take care of them. She thought of Hugh and wondered if he would ever know what she did for him,
however misguided and stupid it had been. Then she
thought of Gabe. If only things had been different,
she thought sadly, and wished she had not sent him
away that night.

"Take her down to the hanging tree," someone yelled. Pistols were fired off into the air.
Horses neighed and stamped around uneasily. Hands
grabbed her and the crowd surged forward, sweeping
her along with its momentum so that her feet hardly
touched the ground. Buildings flashed past her and
a large oak tree loomed ahead. Men were already
attempting to throw a rope over a branch that jutted
out over the street.

"Wait! Listen to me!" Libby screamed, but the roar
of the crowd drowned out her voice. She wondered if
it would hurt much and if it took long to die. The rope
was secured. "Bring her over here," called the man
with the noose. A hefty push in the back sent Libby
staggering forward. She stumbled and the crowd
roared and jeered. She remembered the Mexican
girl's proud defiance and brushed herself off, turning to stare at them with equal disdain. "You're all
animals," she shouted. "There is not one person here
who is worthy to be called a man."

"Shut her up. She talks too much," a drunken voice
yelled.

Hands jerked the noose over her neck.

"Hold it right there!" a voice commanded and a
bullet spat into the dust right at the feet of the poten-
tial hangman. Gabe Foster stepped between Libby and

the crowd, both pistols cocked. "Nobody moves until I've had my say," he shouted.

"Get him out of here. We've heard enough," men shouted from the crowd.

Gabe faced them calmly. "I think enough people have seen me shoot," he said. "Just be quiet and listen to what I have to say."

The crowd muttered and fell silent. Gabe did not look at Libby, but stepped in front of her, facing the crowd. "Which of you have come across this woman before?" he asked.

Several hands were raised sheepishly.

"And what was your impression of her until now?"

"Stuck up," someone muttered. "Kept to herself. Didn't like to joke with the miners. . . ."

"In other words," Gabe said, "she was what you would call a real lady. Am I correct?"

Several murmurs from the crowd.

"She still gunned down Bart," growled a voice at the back.

"Can you blame her?" Gabe shouted. "Would you expect a proper lady to act any differently if she was attacked and grabbed by a band of drunken miners and had to fight for her honor?" He scanned the group, his gaze moving from left to right. "I think you've all been away from civilization too long," he roared. "What would you feel if this was your sister, or your sweetheart, or your mother, or your wife? Would you want one of them to have to go through what this lady's been through? Would you condemn her because she tried to defend herself from the ultimate degradation? She has lived here alone, bravely taking care of two little children with nobody to protect her or look after her."

His gaze swept the audience again. Several miners hung their heads, not wanting to look at him. "This lady is not a criminal and you know it," Gabe went on. "I beg you not to make this terrible mistake. If you allow this to happen now, then one day, as God is my witness, I swear to you that your wife, or your sister, or your little daughter will suffer as this lady is suffering, and you will realize that it is God's justice and judgment coming back to punish you. Revenge is mine, says the Lord. Do you dare to trifle with Him?"

The doctor pushed his way through the crowd to join Gabe. "You've heard him," he said. "He speaks with the voice of reason. All those who think she acted in self-defense say aye."

There was a murmured aye from the crowd.

"All those against?"

There was silence. The doctor went over to Libby and took the noose from her neck. "My dear. You are free to go," he said.

# Chapter
## 23

THE CROWD STARTED to drift away. Libby just stood there under the tree, too overwhelmed and dazed to know what to do next. The doctor patted her shoulder. "I'm very glad for you, my dear. I hate to see these miscarriages of justice, but when they've been drinking, it's not easy to stop them." He turned to Gabe still standing with both pistols in his hands. "You have this gentleman to thank for your life, I think."

She looked at him with wonder as his eyes lit up with a smile.

"You really are my guardian angel, aren't you?" she asked. "How on earth did you manage to materialize just when I needed you most?"

Gabe tucked the pistols back in their holsters. "Oh, you know us angels," he said. "We just hover around, playing our harps until needed."

"In which case, what took you so long?" she asked, not knowing whether to laugh or cry with pent-up emotion. "A few more minutes and I'd have been swinging from that tree."

"Well, it takes a while to change out of my wings and white nightgown," Gabe said. He slipped his arm around her shoulder. "Actually I was asleep in my room at the hotel. I keep pretty late hours and I usually take a nap in the afternoon. I heard all the noise and asked what was happening."

"You're staying at the hotel? Here?" she asked.

"The new hotel," he said.

"Sheldon Rival's place?" she asked in disgust.

"That's right. He asked me to get his gambling parlor going for him, so I've been here about a month."

"And I didn't know," she said. "But I thought you despised the man as much as I do."

"Sure I do," he agreed. He started to lead her across the street toward the impressive wooden front of the new hotel. "But he made me a very good offer and I saw no reason not to help part him from his money. I have a fine suite and my meals and a generous cut from the takings. I'm going to take you there now and get you a glass of brandy for the shock you've just had."

Libby allowed herself to be led in through the front door of the hotel and across the elegant lobby, decorated with palm trees and brass spittoons and leather chairs. Along one wall ran a mahogany bar, well stocked with bottles.

"A bottle of your best cognac and two glasses sent up to my room, Carlo," Gabe called to the man at the bar. "This lady's had a bad shock and needs to recover."

"Very good, Mr. Foster," the man called after them.

Gabe led Libby up one flight of stairs and pushed open a door leading to a sitting room, well furnished by frontier standards. Curtains at the far end were half open around a large brass bed. Libby sank gently into a red plush sofa as Gabe brought over a little table.

"Now what would you like as the first meal of your new life?" he asked. "Anything you want you can have. Oysters? Steak? Trout?"

Libby put her hands up to her face, laughing hysterically. "This doesn't make sense," she said. "None of this makes sense. Two minutes ago I had a rope around my neck and now you're calmly offering me oysters."

"All the more reason to enjoy life while you can," Gabe said. "You've just understood firsthand how precarious it is. All we can do with it is make the most of every moment. So what do I tell Carlo? Oysters followed by steak followed by brandied peaches?"

Libby's hands were still on her cheeks. "I can't stay here, Gabe. I have to get home to my children. They'll be worried about me."

"They're all alone?"

"No, Ah Fong is with them, but . . ."

"Ah Fong?"

"I've got a Chinese servant," Libby said. "He just attached himself to me after he said I saved his life."

Gabe looked amused. "Then everything's fine," he said. "When Carlo comes in with the cognac, I'll have him send somebody out to the cabin with the news that you are fine and you'll be back later. Does that meet with your approval?"

She nodded.

A tap at the door announced the arrival of the cognac. Gabe gave the orders to Carlo, then poured the amber liquid into two glasses, holding Libby's glass up to her lips as if she were a small child who had to be fed. "You'll feel much better when you've finished this," he said.

Libby coughed as she swallowed, but she felt warmth spreading throughout her body and she obediently finished the glass. The light was fading in the room as the sun sank behind the hills and Gabe got up to light the candle, placing it on the table and pulling up a chair to either side. It seemed no time at all before dinner was brought in, hidden under silver tureens on a white-napkined tray. A bottle of champagne accompanied it and Gabe let Carlo uncork it, pouring a glass for each of them. Then he escorted Libby over to the table and served her oysters.

"They go down very easily, especially with champagne," he said. "Known remedy to steady the nerves."

"My nerves are surprisingly steady," Libby said, "considering what they have been through today."

"If I'd known what tough fiber you were made of, I'd never have tackled you in the first place," Gabe said, smiling. "I'd have walked right past you in New Orleans and not stopped."

"I'm glad you did," she said. "Although I've brought you nothing but trouble."

"But the most enjoyable kind of trouble," Gabe said. He picked up his glass. "To you, madame. May all your troubles now be over."

Libby lifted her glass to touch his, not taking her eyes from his for a second. They worked their way through the courses, neither of them saying much, but when Libby looked up, she saw Gabe watching her, his eyes warm in the candlelight. The juicy steak, the shoestring potatoes, the baby carrots all slipped down with no effort, and brandied peaches replenished the glow of the cognac. The candlelight flickered, making the shadows dance in the corners, contributing to her feeling of unreality. Since she had gone down to the creek to wash clothes that morning, nothing had seemed real anymore. She had gone through such extremes of fear that she felt like a person rescued from drowning, each new breath a miracle.

When she finally put down her glass with a sigh of content, he looked at her appraisingly. "I suppose that now you've eaten you are going to give me your usual speech about morals and duty and run out on me," he said.

Libby got up and walked across to the window. The hills outside were only black outlines against the pearl-gray sky, but they were dotted with the lights of miners' camps, like fireflies. "I have lived by my morals and my sense of duty all the time I've been here but they haven't protected me," she said flatly. "I'd have died a horrible death by now, if you hadn't saved me. You risked your life for me, Gabe." She turned to look back at him. "Ah Fong said that his life belonged to me, because I'd saved him. Maybe the same is true for you—you saved me, so my life belongs to you."

Gabe leaned back in his chair, eyeing her speculatively. "If you are only staying in this room because you feel grateful, then please go now," he said. "You don't owe me anything, Libby."

She walked slowly over to his chair. "You know I feel more for you than gratitude," she said. "I think what you said was right, about making the most of each moment. You might be dead tomorrow. I might be dead tomorrow, but we are both here right now and this moment might never come again. If I walked out, I'd regret it for the rest of my life."

Deliberately, she began to undo the buttons at the front of her dress. He took her hands away. "Let me do that," he said. Then, in impatience, "Why do women have to have so many buttons?"

"You have buttons on your shirt too," she said, laughing.

"Ah, but the difference is that I can remove my shirt over my head without undoing any buttons, like this," he said and demonstrated, slipping it off easily with one fluid movement. She admired his bare torso, noting with pleasure the muscles that stood out at his shoulders and the black curly hair on his chest. She smiled and stepped out of her dress.

"And why do women have to wear so many clothes," he said. "It's not as if it's cold here." His fingers deftly worked at the buttons on the front of her underbodice until he could slip it off her shoulders, down to her waist.

"I've never let a man see me naked before," she said, turning away in embarrassment.

"Never? And you've been married how many years?"

"Hugh always respected my delicacy in such matters," she said primly. "He always changed in his dressing room and I in mine."

"How very boring," Gabe said with a chuckle. "But the human body is nothing to be ashamed of, especially when it looks like yours, my dear." He put his hands on her shoulders and turned her to face him. "Why hide something that gives so much pleasure?" and he ran the tip of his finger around her nipple. Libby was unprepared for the jolt of desire at the pit of her stomach. Gabe was already unbuckling his belt.

"And now you'll have to excuse me if I'm a trifle impatient, because I don't think I can wait much longer," he said. "Later tonight we'll have all the time in the world for play." He swept her up in his arms as if she weighed nothing and carried her over to the bed, swiftly removing the last of their garments before he lowered himself onto her.

Libby had not known that such passion existed before. Her whole body was on fire, she was moving urgently with him, arching her back to feel her naked breasts against the coarse hair of his chest, her mouth seeking out his chin, his neck, his ear as he nibbled at her neck and shoulder. She heard herself cry out, though she was not sure whether it was from pain or pleasure. Then she was lost in a red whirl of desire, her head ready to explode. She was laughing deep in her throat as she felt the world break apart into glittering shards. Gabe gave a shuddering sigh and collapsed onto her.

For a while they lay there, holding each other tightly, breathing as one. Then Gabe propped himself up on one elbow, looking down into her eyes with tenderness. "Do you always laugh when you make love?" he asked.

"It's never been like this before," she said.

"Never? Not even with . . ."

"Never," she cut him off. "I didn't know it was possible to feel like that."

"Ah, well, it takes a master," he said, grinning wickedly, "although you weren't bad, for a beginner. Next time we'll be much better."

"I don't see how it could be."

"You'd be surprised at all the things you don't know and I will be delighted to teach you," he said, stroking back a damp curl that had fallen across her forehead. "What I have to teach you could last a lifetime." He rolled away from her, onto his back, lying with hands behind his head, staring at the ceiling. "What a sweet life we could have together, Libby. I'm going to be very rich, you know. I can give up gambling soon and build a fine house on a hill in San Francisco. We'll own property. We can travel. Doesn't that sound fine to you?"

"Very fine," she said, "but I can't commit to you until I've done that final search for Hugh."

"But you love me," Gabe said, leaning over her again. "You never loved Hugh the way you love me. Admit it. Hugh never made you feel the way you do with me."

"I admit it," she said. "I feel as if I've been asleep all my life and I've just woken up. You told me once that I would know real love if I'd ever experienced it, and you were right."

He bent to kiss her forehead. "I've told many women that I loved them, but it's never been true until now. I love you, Libby Grenville. I don't ever want to be parted from you. In the morning I'm going up to the cabin for your things and I'm going to bring you down here, where I can watch over you. Then we can decide whether we move to . . ."

Libby put her fingers on his lips. "Let's not talk about the future anymore," she said. "Let's make the most of now. Who knows what tomorrow will bring?"

"But you'll let me bring you down to town where I can keep you safe?" he asked.

"But what about my potatoes?" Libby demanded.

"Potatoes?"

"I'm planning to make my fortune growing pota-toes. That old rogue at the store sells them for a dol-lar each."

Gabe laughed. "A fortune growing potatoes. I love it. Who but my sweet, crazy Libby would dream up a scheme like that. I tell you what—we'll ask your devot-ed Chinese to live up there and guard your potatoes, if that makes you happy."

"Being with you makes me happy," she said. She snuggled up to his chest and he wrapped an arm around her.

"Then I'll never leave you again," he said.

# CHAPTER
# 24

LIBBY OPENED HER eyes to slatted sunlight shining on a white-painted wall. The clean sterility of her surroundings was in such contrast to the peeling logs and flapping canvas she was used to that for a moment she had no idea where she was. Then, as it gradually came back to her, she reached out to her left and touched only cold sheets. She was alone in the big brass bed.

"Gabe?" she called softly. The events of last night were still cloaked in unreality. Had she really lain in his arms and heard him say that he would never leave her? Already her body ached for him again. If I hadn't stayed last night, I'd never have known, she thought in wonder. I'd have lived my whole life without knowing what it means to be truly, wonderfully happy and fulfilled. He really is the most remarkable man.

She let her gaze move around the empty rooms. Someone had cleared away the remains of last night's dinner and her clothes were now neatly hanging over the back of a chair. Gabe's clothes were gone. She sat up, remembering how Hugh had run off without a word of goodbye. Had all those things Gabe said last night been just words? Was he the sort of man who lost interest once he got her into bed? She smiled at her own thoughts and shook her head firmly. Gabe might be a scoundrel and he might have no conscience in some things, but he was not a coward. He was not the sort of person who would ever slink away without saying goodbye. That was one of the things she liked so much about him. She knew where she stood with him. He made it perfectly obvious what he liked and disliked, what he wanted and did not want—and she knew that he wanted her. It made her feel warm inside. If any nagging thoughts of the future came into her mind, she pushed them away to a safe compartment at the back where they could not intrude on her happiness.

She had just finished her inspection of the room and lain back again on the soft feather pillows when the door opened and Gabe came in, carrying a tray.

"You're awake," he said. "I had planned to wake you gently with a kiss. Now you've deprived me of one pleasure."

"I'll go back to sleep again if you wish," she said, smiling at him. She lay back on the pillow and closed her eyes. "There. I'm sound asleep."

He put down the tray and tiptoed over to her, bending to give her the most delicate of kisses on the forehead. She opened her eyes to look into his warm, brown ones and his lips moved to fasten onto her own.

"Whoa, steady there," he said, breaking away as she wrapped her arms around his neck. "I've got breakfast waiting on a tray. Don't get me excited now or the eggs and bacon will be cold before we get to them.

Besides," he went on, playfully pulling her upright, "it's never done before breakfast in the best of households. Surely you remember that from Boston?"

He took her hand to lift her up from the pillow.

"Gabe, I'm naked. I can't get up," Libby protested. Gabe laughed and fetched his own silk gown for her, easing her into it like a little child. Still holding her hand he took her through to the table in the sitting room and seated her as if he were a head waiter at a good restaurant. "I hope this is to your liking, madame," he said.

Libby shook her head as if he had produced a miracle. "Do you know how long it's been since I had either eggs or bacon?" she asked. "After beans everything looks wonderful."

"No more beans," Gabe said firmly. "As soon as you're dressed, we're going to rent you a horse and go up to bring down the children and your things to the hotel." She opened her mouth to speak but he put a finger on her lips. "No ifs or buts, that's an order. I leave you alone for a few minutes and you start shooting people and getting yourself hanged, so it's clear to me that you ought not to be left alone. You are dangerous to yourself and to the population at large. Therefore I'm going to keep you under my wing until we can make more permanent plans." She went to say something again but again he cut her off. "And don't say what will people think. People can think what they like. You're a damned sight safer in my care than you are being prim and proper out at that cabin."

Libby stuck a generous strip of bacon on her fork. "I hope you're not always going to be this bossy."

Gabe laughed. "Just where your safety is concerned," he said. "You've been let loose too long. I aim to take good care of you."

She laughed and pretended to be busy with her breakfast, but inside she still could not shake off the sense of wonder. He really loves me, she thought. He wants to take care of me. And she felt like crying.

After breakfast she washed and dressed, enjoying the luxury of hot water and real soap and soft towels. She wished she had something prettier to put on, very conscious of her homemade dress and its lack of style. I'll have to get some better clothes if we're coming to live in town, she thought and was amazed at the calm way she was accepting this radical step in her life. It was as if her near brush with death had eradicated all of her past and she was now a newborn person, planning a future completely free from past restraints. She brushed her hair and tied it back with a ribbon, noting in the mirror how girlish she still looked with her freckled nose and her long red curls. Her eyes were still the wide, hopeful eyes that had looked back from her mirror before she married Hugh.

Gabe had gone to see about the horses and told her to join him at the stable when she was ready. With a last look around the room she went down to meet him. As she crossed the lobby of the hotel, two miners came out of the dining room, their saddlebags slung over their shoulders. They nodded respectfully to her as she swept past, then one of them ran to catch up with her.

"Pardon me, ma'am," he said, touching her arm lightly, "but wasn't you the lady riding around the camps last fall, looking for an Englishman?"

"Yes, I was," she said, blushing and wondering if this man had seen her go up to Gabe's room.

"And you never found him?"

She shook her head.

A big smile crossed his unshaven face. "Then I think I might have news for you," he said. "I was coming up from Sonora and the southern mines. I spent the night in a place called Angel's Camp and I heard about this young English guy who bust his leg up pretty bad. Seems he's been laid up all winter after a bad fall. They said he was a real gentleman and he spoke real refined. Looked as if the wind would blow him away, one of the guys said. They call him Gentleman Jim. That sound like him?"

Libby's heart was beating so fast that she could hardly breathe, let alone speak. All she could do was nod. "Yes," she said at last, "that sounds like him."

"Then I think you'll find him at the hotel down in Angel's Camp," the miner said.

"Thank you," she mumbled.

The miner tipped his hat. "I'm very glad to have been of service, ma'am. I bet he'll be mighty glad to see you."

"Yes," she said, "I'm sure he will."

She managed to walk out, past the other miners, keeping her face composed. Once outside, however, she ran down the street to the stable. Gabe was just coming out leading two good-looking bays. He saw from her face immediately that something was wrong.

"What is it?" he asked, catching her as she almost stumbled.

"I've just met a man who's seen Hugh," she gasped.

"You're sure it was him?"

"It sounds very like him," she said. "The man said he had broken his leg and been laid up all winter."

"Where is he?"

"At a place called Angel's Camp, down south of here."

"Angel's Camp? Yes, I know it," Gabe said. "Good gambling place."

There was a pause as they stood looking at each other. Then Gabe said, "So what are you going to do?" at the same time as Libby said, "Gabe, I've got to go to him."

Gabe nodded. "Yes, I guess you'd have to."

She turned her head away, afraid to look at him anymore. "It was like a dream, wasn't it?" she asked. "Too good to be true."

"Maybe it's not him," Gabe said.

"Yes, maybe. But I've got to go anyway."

"I understand," he said. "I've just rented you a horse. Wasn't that lucky."

"Very lucky," she said mechanically.

"So you'll go right away?"

"I have to know," she said. "Can we send word out to the children? I know Ah Fong can take care of them for a couple of days."

"I'll go out there myself, if you'd like," Gabe said.

Libby drew a circle with her toe in the dust. "I was wondering if you'd come with me."

"You want me to come with you?" Gabe asked, his eyes narrowing.

"I'd like you to. It's a long way to go on my own."

"You're asking a lot of me, Libby," he said flatly. "It's not in my nature to be that generous and deliver a woman I love back to her husband."

"I know I'm asking a lot," she said, blinking back the tears. "It's just that I want to be with you for as long as possible, but if it's too hard for you, I understand."

He looked at her with longing. "You know I'd do anything for you," he said. "We've got the horses. We'd better get going. It will take us a couple of days. I'll just let them know at the hotel and have someone go out to your cabin. . . ."

He handed her the bridle and strode up the street. Libby watched him go, noting every little detail about him, the way his coat hung well from his broad shoulders, the way he walked with fluid grace, the way the hair curled over his collar. She didn't know how she could ever live without him.

It was a perfect spring day as they set out, the colors clear and bright, the soft green curve of the hills etched against a clear blue sky. It seemed as if all nature was conspiring to mock their despair; bright carpets of orange poppies and purple lupines decked the sunny slopes, giant gold and black butterflies flittered around them, bird song resounded through the tall pines and old oaks. The horses hooves made a muffled thud on the soft yellow earth of the trail as they rode side by side and the warm sun threw black shadows beside them, shadows of a man and a woman that merged as the horses walked together. Neither of them spoke. When Libby glanced across to Gabe, he was staring straight ahead, his eyes focussed on the path. She knew she shouldn't have asked him to come, but she couldn't bear to let him go.

This was a gentler country than Libby had seen so far with none of the steep ravines they had encountered on their first journey or the rocky hills around Hangtown. At times it seemed that all it lacked to make it like the familiar New England countryside was some cows or sheep in the rich grass and little white churches nestled in the hollows.

The trail wound up and down hillsides, crossed over foaming streams on frail-looking wooden bridges and forded gentler streams where bare-chested miners were back at work and where dragonflies darted in flashes of green and red. From time to time they passed through settlements, some no better than tent cities, some already turning into real towns: Diamond Springs, Eldorado, and then Plymouth and Amador City. Some were deserted, while in others men still lounged idly on the hotel porches or even dug hopefully in the town streets. Nobody showed much curiosity as they passed. They were a couple out for a visit and, as such, nothing out of the ordinary.

Libby noted that there were already women in some of the towns. Tired-looking, sun-browned faces peered from the occasional tent and once several ragged children ran out. A sign tacked to a large tent read: Ma White's Boarding House. All The Comforts Of Home. Reasonable Rates. Inside, bunks were stacked to cram in as many miners as possible and an awning covered a kitchen table and stove where a scrawny middle-aged woman was kneading dough. She looked up at them and gave Libby a weary smile as she wiped a streak of flour across her forehead.

By late afternoon they had reached the town of Sutter Creek. Gabe looked critically at the line of hotels and saloons.

"Which do you fancy?" he asked. "I'm no expert on this region, so take your pick."

Libby took in the shaded sidewalks and the aura of civilization most places still lacked, then she turned to Gabe. "Would you mind very much if we just had something to eat and then we went on?"

Gabe's face clouded. "You are so anxious to complete the journey?" he asked. "We won't do it tonight, however hard we press the horses."

Libby smiled at him. "No, it's not that," she said. "It's just that I don't feel that I could face hotels and strangers and noisy saloons. The weather's really mild—couldn't we just camp for the night away from everyone and everything? I'd like to remember those nights on the trail together."

"As you wish," Gabe said stiffly, then he grinned as if aware of the black humor in their situation. "If you hadn't been so stubbornly self-righteous in those days, think of the wonderful time we could have had together."

"Hardly, with all those men looking on."

"I don't know," Gabe said speculatively. "We could have crept away often enough. Still, it doesn't do any good dwelling on what might have been, does it?"

"I'm afraid it doesn't," Libby said.

They stopped just long enough to get a meal, then mounted again, riding on until the sun began to sink across the plains, which could now be glimpsed stretching out as far as the eye could see, glowing pink in the setting sun. They brought the horses to a halt as Libby stared out to the west.

"I suppose Sacramento must be down there," she said.

"A little farther north," Gabe answered, putting up his hand to shield his eyes from the sun. "And Stockton's farther south. There's nothing in between."

Libby shielded her eyes too. "All that empty country," she said. "It seems a waste to leave it uncultivated."

"I don't think much would grow there," Gabe said. "It floods every winter, and it gets no rain all summer.

All the Californios do is run cattle. They don't attempt to grow things on those big ranches of theirs."

"The Californios?"

"That's what they call the Mexicans who originally settled this place. They have huge land grants up and down the valley, although I gather most of them have left their cattle for gold, which is more productive."

Libby sighed. "I'd like to have a house in a place like this and feel that I was looking out over the edge of the world."

"Too far from civilization for me," Gabe said, laughing. "How would I make a living out here? I need life around me." He jammed his hat more firmly onto his head against the evening breeze which swept in from the west. "You see, we have nothing in common," he said. "It's probably a good thing that we are forced to part. We'd soon get tired of each other."

"I'm sure you're right," Libby said. Then she made the mistake of looking at him. She bit her lip and turned away again.

"Do you want to stop here then?" Gabe asked. "No sense in pressing on until it's dark."

"Here looks fine to me," Libby said. "We could spread out the saddle blankets under that big oak tree and sit and watch the sun set."

"Your wish is my command," Gabe said formally. He slipped from his horse and helped her down, leading the two horses up onto a mound crowned by an oak. Then he unsaddled them and tethered them to graze, placing the saddles side by side against the gnarled trunk of the oak.

"Comfortable?" Gabe asked when they were both sitting with the saddles as backrests.

Libby nodded. "As comfortable as I can be at this

moment," she said. "I'm sorry, Gabe. I shouldn't have begged you to come with me. It was selfish and I had no right. . . ."

He reached across and took her hand, squeezing it but saying nothing. It was their first contact all day. As they watched, the sun became a ball of red fire and sank into the haze. The sky turned from pink to light blue to pearl. The trees faded to silhouettes. A brisk wind rose from the valley.

"I hope you haven't made a mistake," Gabe said.

"I hope so too," Libby said, "but I have to go, don't I?"

"I meant about sleeping out," Gabe said. "It's still only spring. I hope you won't find it too cold."

"I've got you to keep me warm," Libby said. She shivered. "I want you to hold me, Gabe."

He slipped his arm around her shoulder and pulled her close to him. She nestled her head against his shoulder, noting the way the soft cloth felt, the way he smelled, every detail about him, as if she were compiling a mental scrapbook to preserve the moment forever. For a long while neither of them spoke, then Libby said, slowly and deliberately, "I want to tell you something, Gabe. I want you to know that I have never loved another man the way I love you and that I will never love another man the way I love you. Whatever happens in the future, I want you to know that."

"Then why go back to your husband?" Gabe asked softly. "This is not Boston, Libby. This is the Wild West. Nobody knows or cares here if a woman is divorced. Tell him the truth and ask him for a divorce. If he's a decent man, he'll let you go. God knows we've given him enough grounds. . . ."

Libby gave a shuddering sigh that went through her whole body. "I don't know, Gabe," she said. "I can't decide anything until I see him again."

"If we're put on earth to be happy, Libby, why deny both of us our happiness?"

"I do love you, Gabe," she said, "but sometimes duty has to come before happiness. I did make a vow, you know. I suspect many soldiers would be happier running away from a battle, but they stay because it's their duty to stay."

"Dammit, Libby, don't start all this sanctimonious stuff with me," Gabe said forcefully. "The man ran out on you. You don't owe him anything. If you'd still been home, waiting for him all this time and hearing nothing, wouldn't you have looked around and considered which of your male friends might make a suitable replacement? We don't even know it's him. We don't even know if he's holed up with a nice little Mexican bar girl."

"Don't," Libby said, sitting up and pulling away from him. "Don't be angry with me, Gabe. I'm really confused. I don't know what I should do."

"It's very simple," Gabe said. "We find the fellow and if it is Hugh, then you tell him that you've fallen in love with another man and you're going to live with him in San Francisco. Simple as that."

"I wish it were simple," Libby said. "What if he takes the children back to Boston, as he has every right to do? If I go with you I have no legal rights to them at all."

"I don't know," Gabe said, thumping his fist against the saddle in frustration. "It's just that somehow it's got to work out. I love you and you love me, Libby." He took her face in his hands, looked at her long and hard, then brought his lips crushing down on hers. She cried out in pain, but she didn't push him away. They fell back together onto the grass. This time there was none of the playful lovemaking of the night before. They came together with a desperate urgency that left them both gasping and clinging to each other, their hearts hammering.

"I can't let you go," Gabe murmured into her ear. "Promise me you'll tell him, Libby."

"I can't promise until I've seen him," she said, "but I promise I'll do everything I can, because I don't see how I can live without you either."

He pulled the rug around them and they fell asleep in each other's arms.

# CHAPTER
# 25

BY THE MIDDLE of the next day they were descending the steep hill that led into Angel's Camp. It proved to be a bustling community with several hotels and stores lining a main street with wooden sidewalks. Horses were tied at the rails and men came in and out with bags of gold and bundles of supplies.

"I was right about the southern mines producing better," Gabe said. "They don't get the snow down here so the rivers go down sooner." He looked across at a large saloon at which the gambling tables were in operation, each with a beautiful Mexican girl as dealer. "Doesn't look like a bad place to be, in fact."

Libby said nothing. She was finding it hard enough to breathe.

Gabe slid from his horse. "You can wait here, if you like. I'll go find out where he is."

Libby nodded silently as Gabe strolled into the nearest bar. Soon he came out again and motioned across the street. "The Angel's Hotel is across the street." he said. He led the horses over to a new, balconied

287

wooden building. "Not bad," he said, looking at the lace curtains which decorated the windows and the carpet on the floor. "I can see he's got taste."

He reached up his arms to help Libby down from her horse. Slowly, he lowered her to the ground, then released her unwillingly. "I'll stay here with the horses," he said. "You can't always trust people in places like this."

She looked at him, wide-eyed, and nodded in understanding. Then she took a deep breath and walked toward the hotel. A pleasant older woman came out of a back room in response to Libby's ringing the desk bell. "Can I help you?" she asked, wiping her hands on her apron as if she had been caught in the middle of washing up.

"I understand you have an Englishman staying here," she said.

"That's right," the woman said, her expression already becoming guarded.

"I think he might be my husband," Libby said. "I came out to join him and I've not been able to find him. Do you know his name?"

The woman smiled. "They don't go by names out here much," she said. "Around here he's known as Gentleman Jim, or at the hotel we just call him Jimmy. But if he's your husband, you'd best come see for yourself." She smoothed down her apron. "He's out back on the porch," she said. "Through here, please."

Libby followed her down a narrow hallway.

"I understand he's hurt his leg?" she asked.

"Hurt his leg?" the woman said scornfully. "When they brought him in here, he was hanging between life and death. Been crushed in a cave-in, so they say. They didn't discover him for a couple of days and he was in a bad way. No one expected him to live. Out of his head for a while he was there, not knowing where he was and a raging fever. Anyway, I took care of him and he hung on until the leg got gangrene in it. They thought they'd have to have it off, but the doctor we've got is wonderful skilled and they managed to save it. He's walking again now with a cane. You'll see for yourself."

She opened a screened door onto a shaded porch that looked out over the stream and the valley. Wicker chairs were placed along it and one of them was occupied by a young man, his eyes closed as if asleep. His leg was still wrapped in bandages and propped on a stool. A newspaper was across his lap. His dark curls fell across his forehead. His face was deathly pale.

"There he is," the landlady whispered. "Is that him?"

Libby stood in the doorway like a statue. "Yes," she whispered back. "That's him."

She tiptoed across the wooden porch and knelt beside the sleeping man.

"Hugh?" she said softly, touching his hand which now seemed so slender and frail that it almost looked transparent.

The sleeping figure stirred and the dark eyes opened, focussed on Libby, blinked and tried to focus again. "Yes?" he asked. "What do you want?"

"Hugh, it's me. It's Libby," she said.

"Libby?" he sounded confused. "Libby who?"

Libby looked up at the landlady who still stood in the doorway.

"The doctor said he lost his memory when he had brain fever," she said.

Turmoil was raging inside Libby. One voice was

whispering, "Get out while you can. He doesn't even remember you. You're free. You can go back to Gabe and say it wasn't him and ride away forever!" While an answering voice insisted, equally forcefully, "You can't leave him like this. You're his wife. He needs you more than ever now." And in Libby Grenville, nee Parsons, of an old Boston family, the voice of duty won out. She touched his hand again.

"Hugh, it's Libby. Your wife. I've come to find you."

Hugh's brow creased as if he were thinking hard. Then he said, "Libby? My wife?" Then he shook his head. "My wife's in Boston."

Libby grabbed his shoulders impatiently. "Hugh, look at me. I'm Libby. I'm your wife. Don't you know me?"

Slowly, his dark hollow eyes scanned her face. He frowned again and blinked several times. "Libby?" he asked, cautiously putting out a hand to touch her face. "Is it really you?"

"Yes, it's me," Libby said, laughing with pent-up emotion. "Don't you know me, Hugh?"

"Yes," he said. "Yes, I know you. Libby! What are you doing here?" He shook his head as if he were trying to make sense of the unfathomable. "I dreamed about you so many times, when I was lying here and I thought I was going to die. I dreamed you were coming to rescue me."

"And I was, Hugh," she said. "I came all the way across the plains because I sensed that you'd need me. I've spent the whole winter searching."

"And now you've found me again," he said, laughing too. "It's like a miracle, Libby. You mustn't mind if I cry. I'm just so overwhelmed. I thought I'd never leave this place. I had nowhere to go. . . ."

"I've a cabin up north of here," Libby said. "I've come to take you home."

Tears began to run down Hugh's cheeks. He wiped them away in embarrassment. "I don't know what to say," he said. "It's a miracle. I thought I'd never see you again. I thought I'd die as a stupid, blundering failure and you'd be better off without me."

"Don't say that," she said gently. "We'll get you out of here and then we'll concentrate on getting you well and strong."

"That's right," he said. "I've got to get well and strong because now I've got reason to be well and strong. I've got to get back to Boston, to my little darlings. How are they, Libby?"

"They're not in Boston. They're here," Libby said. "They're back at the cabin waiting to see their papa."

"They're here? Eden and Bliss are here?" Hugh said. He covered his face with his hands. "It's all too much for me . . . after so long."

"Can you ride a horse, do you think?" Libby asked. "You can go get your things and then we can start for home."

"I can do anything if you're with me," Hugh said. He lifted his leg off the stool, then struggled to stand upright. With effort, he started to walk down the porch, shrugging off her attempt to help him. But when he got to the doorway he looked back at Libby. "You won't go away, will you?" he asked. "I can't believe you're real."

Libby bit her lip. "I won't go away," she said evenly. "I'll go tell the landlady."

She watched Hugh making his way upstairs, one stair at a time, then she hurried out to the front of the hotel. Gabe was sitting on a bench in the shade,

close to the two horses. He got to his feet as she came
out, trying to read the news from her expression. He
sensed the truth before she said anything by the way
she walked with heavy, measured steps.

"It's him?" he asked.

"It's him."

"And?"

"He's very sick, Gabe," she said quietly. "He nearly
died. He still looks terrible. I can't leave him like this.
I have to take him home and take care of him."

"I see."

"No you don't see," she said angrily, grabbing his
sleeve. "I feel like I'm being torn in two. I don't want
to lose you, but I can't leave him here. Please understand. Please . . ."

"I'm trying to," Gabe said flatly.

Her grip on his arm tightened. "If you really love
me," she said softly, "then please don't make it harder
on me than it already is. Would you please go now?"

"Very well," he said. "Only this time it really is
goodbye. I'm not going to appear again when you
need me. I'll go get my things from Hangtown and
then I'm gone."

"Where will you go?" she asked.

"Who knows? There are plenty of places for a gambler to make a fortune out here, hundreds of mining camps I haven't been to yet. And then there's San
Francisco. They say that's a city of sin."

"I see."

They stood looking at each other.

"I wish you every joy, Gabe Foster," she said. "I
hope things go well for you, wherever you are. I'll
never stop thinking about you, as long as I live."

"Nor I you, Libby Grenville," Gabe said. "I'm not

going to kiss you goodbye. We already said our good-
byes last night."

He untied his horse with a swift jerk at the reins
and swung into the saddle. Then he spurred the horse
into a gallop and disappeared down the main street in
a cloud of yellow dust.

Libby waited until the dust had settled before she
went back into the hotel. The landlady was at the
front desk. "I'll be taking him home right away,"
Libby said.

The landlady nodded. "If you'd like to settle up
what he owes me," she said, pulling out the visitor book. "It's four hundred and forty dollars, if I
remember correctly."

"Four hundred and forty!" Libby exclaimed in horror.

"He's been here four months," the woman said.
"That's a long time."

"And he paid nothing at all?" Libby asked. "He
came with no money?"

"Oh, he had gold on him when they found him,"
the landlady said briskly. "But that all went in the doctor bills and the first weeks when he was delirious."

Libby looked at the wall, hoping for inspiration.
"Look," she said at last. "I don't have that sort of
money. Can we work something out? Maybe I can
pay you a little at a time?"

The landlady gave an embarrassed half smile, half
shrug. "I'd like to help you out, but I don't own this
place anymore. I used to run this as a boarding house,
but this fancy eastern gentleman made me a good
offer and kept me here to run the place. He's the
one who's done it up so fancy you wouldn't recognize how it was. And I have my orders from him—

nobody's allowed to leave without paying their bill."

"You mean Hugh can't leave until he pays?"

"That's what Mr. Rival said."

"Sheldon Rival? He owns this hotel?"

"You know him?" the landlady asked. "They say he's going to be the wealthiest man in the mines. He's buying up hotels and gambling saloons in every town. But he's a hard man."

"I'm not leaving my husband here," Libby said. "Do you know where I can find Mr. Rival right now? I'll arrange to pay him somehow. Maybe he'll give me some time if I explain things to him."

"Maybe," the woman said doubtfully. "I only know I have to follow his orders. If he tells you differently, then good luck to you. He was here a couple of days ago and then he was heading south, so I'd guess he was overseeing that new mine of his at Columbia."

"How far away is that?" Libby asked.

The woman shrugged. "No more than fifteen, twenty miles, I'd say. Not easy miles, mind you, but I'd say you could be there and back by nightfall."

"Then I'll go," Libby said. "Which is my husband's room? I'll tell him that I'll be back for him by nightfall."

Columbia was already a big, sprawling camp, set in a narrow valley among tall hills. The noise of machinery echoed from the steep rock walls above it as Libby rode into town, her dress plastered to her back with sweat. Sheldon Rival was standing on a rock, his cigar hanging, as usual, from one corner of his mouth, his hands stuck in his pockets. He watched a sweating group of men maneuver a length of metal rail into position. As Libby walked toward him, she felt the

revulsion again for this man rise in her throat. She
wished that he was seeing her on more equal terms
for once. She was very aware that she looked tired,
sweaty, and disheveled, while he looked immaculate
and very prosperous. She was not used to riding and
this second long ride made her legs feel as if they had
turned to jelly.

His face creased into something like a sneer as he
recognized her.

"Well, well," he said. "I wondered when and where
you'd turn up. I'm amazed, frankly, that you've kept
going so long. Found your husband then?"

"Yes, thank you," Libby said with icy politeness.

"And you were looking for me—or is this just a
happy coincidence?"

"I have to speak to you," she said. "About my husband."

"What about him?"

"He's been staying at a hotel you've just bought,"
she said. "The landlady says she's not allowed to let
him leave until the bill is paid."

"And?"

"The bill is over four hundred dollars."

"So? He ought not to have eaten and drunk beyond
his means," Rival said crudely. "That's his problem,
not mine."

"You don't understand," Libby said, fighting against
her anger. "He's been very sick. They brought him to
the hotel when he was half dead and he's spent all this
time recovering."

"So what you're saying is that he can't pay? Is that
what I'm hearing?" Rival asked bluntly.

"He hasn't been able to work all winter," Libby said.
"All I ask is a little time, Mr. Rival. It makes no sense

not to let him leave until he pays. He'll just be running up a bigger bill and be no nearer to paying at the end of it."

Rival sneered again. "Then he'll have to do what other men have done—come and work for me until it's paid off."

"Doing what?"

Rival jerked his head. "See all this?" he asked. "Miners scratching in the beds of streams—that's all over. Mining is going to be big business from now on; we've learned to get gold out of solid rock. I'm digging into the hill over there and I'm getting the machinery set up to crush the rock and melt out the gold. He can work in my mine until he's paid up."

"Don't be stupid," Libby blurted out, unable to stay calm any longer. "I just told you that he nearly died. He can still barely walk. He couldn't work in a mine." Then she swallowed hard, realizing that anger would get her nowhere with this man. He enjoyed seeing her angry and seeing her squirm. "Look, Mr. Rival," she said. "Let me take him home and I'll give you my written word that we'll pay you."

"How?" He eyed her appraisingly.

"Just give me a little time," she said. "and I have prospects of making a lot of money."

"You've got a claim that's paying well?"

"Almost as good as that. I've a crop that should be ready for harvest soon. You know what vegetables are selling for up here."

Rival actually chuckled. "You must think I'm very softhearted all of a sudden," he said. "Vegetables, you say? One hailstorm can flatten vegetables. One invasion of gophers or rabbits and you've lost them. Sorry, lady, but vegetables are not good collateral."

"Maybe I'll find someone else to lend me the money—someone who does think that vegetables are worth something," she said. "A little time—that's all I ask, because if you make my husband work now, it will surely kill him and then you'll never get what's owning to you."

Rival eyed her critically. "Tell you what," he said. "I could always use you instead."

"In a mine?" Libby asked.

Rival laughed loudly. "A mine?" he demanded. "What use would you be in a mine? I'm talking about in one of my saloons. I can't get enough bar girls for the demand, and when the water goes down and the miners are digging up gold again, they'll all be coming into town and wanting a little of what they've been hankering for. So what do you say?"

Libby eyed him coldly, amazed that it was possible to loathe another human being so violently. If she had been holding a gun at this moment, she would have found it very easy to pull the trigger. "You're suggesting that I come to work for you as a prostitute?" she asked.

"Sure, why not?" he asked. "You're not bad looking, if you were tarted up a bit, got some decent clothes, and had someone do something with that hair. Besides, you'd make a change from the Mexicans. The men like a bit of lily-white flesh now and then."

"You are an obscene and disgusting man," she said. "I think you delight in the corruption and destruction of others."

"I confess it gives me a certain pleasure to watch a snooty high society queen put in her place," he said. "You shouldn't have refused me, back on the trail.

Now we've a score to settle and it would give me great pleasure to watch you getting laid by any miner who had the money. So what's it to be—him or you?"

"The answer is neither," Libby said. "I'm going home right now and I'll come back with the money, some way or other. I would rather die than be in your debt and I would certainly kill myself right away rather than work in one of your disgusting bars."

"Your friend Gabe Foster didn't feel like that," Rival said, his grin spreading as he watched her reaction. "He was a sensible man when it came to making a buck. He knew a good deal when he saw one. He's working for me right now."

Libby was not going to give him the satisfaction of driving in this additional wound. "I think you'll find that he's just quit," Libby said, enjoying the surprise that registered on his bloated face.

"Who said so?"

Libby smiled. "You think you know everything, Mr. Rival, but you don't. I'll be back with your money."

She swept away from him, to her waiting horse.

# CHAPTER
# 26

BACK IN HANGTOWN, Libby made a desperate round of the banks, but got the same reaction from each of them. They would lend money against a good claim, but not against a vegetable patch. She looked longingly at Rival's new hotel as she passed it, wondering if Gabe was up there in his room or if he'd already left. She fought off the temptation to go and find out. At last, in desperation, she went into Mark Hopkins' store. He looked surprised to see her.

"I'm glad to see your head is still attached to your neck," he said, smiling at her. "I was down arranging for shipping in Sacramento and when I got back the town was full of talk. They said you'd nearly gotten yourself hanged. I couldn't believe it."

"It was true," Libby said, thinking how long ago it already felt. "But now I'm in almost as much trouble again." She blurted the whole story out to him. He looked at her with compassion.

"Sheldon Rival, eh?" he asked. "I know the man. He wanted to buy this store, but I told him to get walking." He shifted from one foot to the other. "I'd really like to help out, Mrs. Grenville but I've already ordered my next load of supplies to be delivered at the end of the month. I have to go down to Sacramento and pick them up from the ship and I have to pay cash for them—every penny of my profits."

"But you'd lend me money until the end of the month?" Libby asked hesitantly. "I swear I'd pay you back by then."

"But your potatoes won't be ready by then, will they?"

"I'll get the money somehow," Libby said. "Just let me pay off Rival and bring my husband home and I swear I'll find a way to pay you back by the end of the month."

Mark Hopkins stared past her, out the open door for a moment, then looked back and smiled. "That's what life is all about, taking risks, isn't it?" he asked. "I'll take the risk that you'll be able to pay me back in time and I don't have to send all those boxes of shovels back to San Francisco."

"I won't let you down, Mr. Hopkins," she said. "I can't tell you what this means to me."

A few days later, Hugh was safely installed in the cabin, being waited on by his delighted children.

"You amaze me, Libby," he said, looking around at the snug little room. "You've managed all this on your own. Who would have thought it, back in Boston."

"Back in Boston I always had my father to tell me what to do and my mother to fuss around making sure I did it," Libby said with a wry smile. "Out here it was a case of survive or die."

Hugh reached over and took her hand. "I can't tell you how I've dreamed about this moment," he said, holding Libby's hand as if he were drowning. "When I lay there half alive and half dead and I heard them talking about cutting off my leg, I said to myself, why bother? Just give up the fight and die before all that pain. But then I thought of you and the girls and I told myself I had to keep going, just to see you again."

Libby squeezed his hand but could find nothing to say. She tucked him in the bed with rugs around him, trying not to let her concern about the money show in her face. Hugh must have no idea of how she had to ransom him. In typical Hugh fashion, he assumed all was taken care of.

"They were wonderfully kind to me, back there in Angel's Camp," he said. "That landlady treated me as if I was her own son. I'd like to do something to repay her someday. Wouldn't it be fun to send her some silk or the latest shawl from England when we get there? But as for now, do you have writing paper for me to pen her a note or maybe I could even manage a poem now that I'm feeling better."

"Writing paper?" Libby asked, barely able to keep her temper under control.

Hugh didn't seem to notice the color rising in her face. He leaned back contentedly and went on. "Funny how I didn't feel like writing poetry at all, when I had all that time on my hands and nothing else to do. In fact the only poem I composed in four months was an epigram:

> The poet, Hugh Grenville
> Became instant landfill
> When a sandbank on himfell.

\*    \*    \*

Not too great, but to the point, as I gather they had to dig me out. Not that I remember anything of it . . . just a typical Hugh Grenville way of doing things, I suppose, not knowing what sort of banks collapse on people. Maybe I can put it all into a book now and sell it back on the East Coast. My dangerous days as a Forty-Niner, by poet Hugh Grenville. Yes. I'll get started right away. Paper, Libby!"

"Hugh, things like writing paper are luxuries out here. We've been at survival level with just enough to eat." Before he could answer she went outside with Ah Fong to inspect her potatoes.

"There's no chance they'll be ready in the next couple of weeks, is there?" she asked.

Ah Fong shook his head. "Right now only tiny potatoes, like bullets," he said. "Not make enough money from tiny potatoes. Wait one more month."

"Then I'll have to find some other way of making money fast," Libby said. "Do you think you can catch me some birds and rabbits?"

"I try," Ah Fong said. "Lot of hungry miners also trying catch things to eat."

Libby threw herself into a frenzied program of work. She baked bread and took it around to the miners every morning. She made pies with the game that Ah Fong managed to catch and sold the pies to the hotels. She went around the camps doing washing and brought mending home to do at night.

"You're killing yourself, Libby," Hugh said gently as she dozed off with a torn shirt in her hands. "Slow down a little. Don't work so hard."

"What choice do I have?" she snapped back, caught off guard.

"What do you mean?" Hugh looked at her with large, innocent eyes.

"I mean that someone has to pay off a huge hotel bill for you, and I'm the only person who can do it," she said and instantly regretted that she had. His face clouded over. "You mean my gold wasn't enough? I did find gold, you know. The claim was really going well until I tried digging into a gravel bank which collapsed on top of me. I had a bag of gold when they brought me in."

"It wasn't enough, Hugh," she said gently. "But don't worry about it. It wasn't your fault. There was nothing you could do about it."

The next morning she found that he had gone out to pan for gold and she was overcome with guilt, knowing that he was not fit enough to do anything. When he came back home his face was almost gray with exhaustion and the bandage on his leg showed it had been bleeding.

"For heavens sake don't do anything foolish like that again," Libby said, sitting him down and putting a mug of tea in front of him. "You know you can't start digging in rivers yet."

"You're right," he said with a sigh. "It wasn't any use, anyway. Every inch of these creeks is full of men right now. There's not a spot within miles that hasn't been prospected and claimed."

"You just concentrate on getting well," Libby said. "That's what you can do for us at this moment."

"But I want to help," Hugh said. "Let me take some of the chores off your shoulders. I hate seeing you scrubbing like a common kitchen woman."

"That's what I am right now," Libby said with a grin. "We're all equal out here. All laborers."

"I wish you hadn't come," Hugh said. "I wish I could have known you were safely home in Boston, living your normal life."

"And what would you be doing, if I hadn't come?" she asked. "You'd be working in Sheldon Rival's mine or you'd be dead."

"Either would have been a small sacrifice not to put you through all this," Hugh said. "Tell me honestly, Libby. Don't you wish you had stayed home? Don't you hate me for it?"

A picture of Gabe swam unbidden into Libby's mind. She pushed it away firmly. "I wouldn't have missed this for the world, Hugh," she said. "Until I started on this journey, I was only playing at living. Now I truly know what it feels like to be alive."

He gazed at her admiringly. "I must say you are looking wonderful," he said. "So blooming, so full of health." He looked down at the sleeping children, curled together on the wolf rugs on the floor. Libby had given Hugh sole occupancy of the bed, and had made the three of them beds in the corner behind the stove. "They're looking wonderful too. Thank heavens they take after you." His gaze shifted back to Libby. "Don't sleep down there with them tonight," he said, running his hand up her arm. "I want to remember what it feels like to hold you again."

"But Hugh, your leg," she protested. "It's such a narrow bed."

"Hold me, Libby," he whispered. He slipped his arms around her and pulled her toward him, nestling his head between her breasts like a child. "So good," he murmured. "This feels so good."

That night Libby lay awake with Hugh's arm tightly around her, his leg across hers, trying to make herself feel something for him. She knew it was only a matter of time before he would make love to her and she was terrified that he would notice her lack of response to him. "You are my husband," she murmured to herself. "I promised at the altar that I would love and cherish you. I was only eighteen. I was just a child. I didn't know what I was promising. Am I to be punished for the rest of my life for demanding my own way when I was a spoiled child?"

After that Hugh tried hard to be of assistance to Libby. He insisted on helping with the baking and the washing, often making the job twice as complicated for her, but it was hard to dissuade him. "I want to feel I'm good for something," he'd say. "Just give me another chance at kneading that dough. I know I can get better."

In spite of working seven days a week, Libby was still short of cash when the end of the month loomed ahead. Sheldon Rival's proposal and Big George's proposal before it crossed her mind more than once. Would it be so terrible to sell her body to a few men, just until she made enough to pay the debt? After all, did anything matter anymore, now that Gabe had gone? She felt as if her body had died with him. Did it matter if men paid to make love to a corpse? She wrestled with the idea as she rolled and pounded dough, scrubbed and wrung out washing. She had worked as hard as any human being could work, doing everything she could think of, and it was not enough. After this, a few nights in bed with strange men would seem easy money.

She made up her mind to go speak to Big George about it the next day. He was a decent enough man, by California standards. He'd select her respectable clients and she'd heard that a good saloon girl could make a hundred dollars a night in the gold towns. Then we'll get out of here and go to England, she told herself. Nobody need ever know except me.

In the morning she dressed with care and put up her hair, instead of tying it back as she had done for months.

"You're going out?" Hugh asked.

"I have some business to attend to in town," she said.

"What sort of business?"

"I'm trying to renegotiate our debt," she said shortly. She was just deciding whether to add her bonnet to the outfit when Ah Fong yelled from outside, "Missee. Come quick. Come quick!"

She dropped the bonnet and ran outside. "What is it?" she shouted, expecting to see men with guns, grizzly bears, or something equally dangerous. Ah Fong was dancing around like a crazy person.

"Come see potato," he shouted. He pointed down at the soil. "I think maybe this plant bigger than rest so I dig up carefully to see. Take look. You think this very fine potato?"

Libby looked down at the ground. The roots of the plant lying there were full of big brown perfect globes, bigger than goose eggs.

"Potatoes," Libby screamed. "They're wonderful, Ah Fong! Is this the only plant that's ready so far?"

"Maybe these two, three more," he said. "See they get best sun and water here. We go dig up and see, yes?"

"Yes," Libby said. "Dig them up and see."

So instead of setting off for town, Libby set off with a basket full of potatoes. By the time she had gone through two mining camps she had sold them all and she was thirty-five dollars richer. Plants continued to ripen all week and on the last day of April Libby was able to take Mark Hopkins his entire amount of money.

All through May the plants continued to yield well. Ah Fong would not let her dig them all up at once.

"Make people wait for them," he said. "Too many at once not valuable. Then price go down."

Rumor of the potatoes spread through the camps and Libby no longer had to go out peddling them. She sold them as fast as they came out of the ground and she set Ah Fong as guard at night, just in case any miner decided to help himself rather than pay her dollar apiece. As it was, nobody seemed to object to the high price. They were so much fresher and more appealing than the tired, moldy objects down at the store that the miners were delighted with them.

"You got any more vegetables, missus?" they asked. "We've been without decent vegetables all winter."

"I'll have some soon," she said. "I'm going to be planting summer crops."

She hurried over to Ah Fong. "What would grow fast and easily in this soil and this climate?" she asked.

"Melon," he said. "They grow like weed, and squash, and onion. Onion grow real good and easy."

"I'll see what I can find," Libby said. "I'll get Mark Hopkins to look around for me and find out where I can get seeds."

"Maybe Chinese get you seeds," Ah Fong said. "Chinese grow own gardens, have seeds too."

Ah Fong's enquiries came up with some watermelon seeds and some mung beans, which he said she could

sprout on a piece of flannel and eat after a few days.
Encouraged by this, she tried sprouting some of her
own dried beans and soon had a row of beans growing in her vegetable patch. Mark Hopkins came back
to report that most of the vegetables down in San
Francisco still came from Chile but that a broker in
Sacramento might be of some use to her.

"I'm going to find new things to plant, Ah Fong,"
she announced as she returned to the cabin. "Mr.
Hopkins thinks I might be able to buy seeds or little
plants in Sacramento."

"You get more plants you need more land," Ah
Fong said. "No sense buying just a few plants. Get
many, get rich quick."

"Where do I get more land?" she asked. "We've
almost reached the edge of the clearing."

"Dig up around cabin," he said as if it were a stupid
question. "What you need grass out in front for? I get
ready for you while you gone."

Then she took all her profits from the potatoes and
went down to Sacramento.

Sacramento was like a gold town, only larger. It
had grown into a large city, set out in ambitious
square city blocks but still half tent, half wood, busy
and bustling, incredibly smelly and dirty. Evidence
of the winter floods was still marked by the black
line halfway up the canvas walls and by the evil-
smelling mud in the streets. The wharf was full of
ships, from big river steamers to little sailing craft,
all unloading and adding to the enormous piles of
every kind of provision already stacked in the open
air. Obviously, some of the perishable foods had not
been sold soon enough and flies were settling on slabs
of green bacon and mounds of rotting peaches and

spoiled fish. Mosquitoes were everywhere. Libby felt her stomach turn as she picked her way over thick debris to find the food broker.

She found that he was one of the few who had managed to build a warehouse for his goods, in the hope of keeping them from spoiling. He did not seem to be succeeding in this because the temperature inside the big wooden hall was just as hot as it was outside. The air was fetid with the smell of rotting fruit.

"Seeds you want?" he asked Libby. "I don't have any seeds to sell, but I can let you have some corn. That would grow well here and I've some squash that are too big and old to sell now. You can take the seeds from them if you like . . . and these strawberries are just rotting on me. See if you can get new plants from them."

Libby bought those and a variety of dried beans and peas, to see which of them could be coaxed back to life, plus all the onions he had. Then, because she still had money to spare, she bought two sacks of flour and a box each of apples and peaches, remembering how easily she had sold the pies last fall. She was just paying him when the heat and the smell seemed to overpower her. Perspiration started to run down her forehead and she felt clammy all over. Saliva welled up in her mouth. The walls started to sway around and the next thing she knew, she was lying on the floor with several worried faces bending over her.

"You all right, missus?" a young man asked.

"I think so," Libby said. "It's just so hot in here."

"You'd best go lie down in a cool room," the older man said. "There's a lot of fever going around. They say there's cholera and typhoid and smallpox too, after the floods."

Libby sat up cautiously. "I think I'd rather get the stuff packed up and get out of here, back to the hills," she said. "I feel fine now."

She bought a mule and had the sacks loaded onto it, then she set off, leading the mule behind her rented horse, not stopping until she was on rising ground again and could spend the night at a hotel above the plains.

All the time she journeyed, she worried about getting sick. Even though she was clear of the city, she still could not shake off the clammy, nauseated feeling she had had before she fainted.

I can't have come so far to go down with a fever now, she told herself severely. Not now that we've almost made it. If these vegetables work out, I'll grow more and more. Like Mark Hopkins, I can make a fortune. But I can't afford to be sick.

Her stern pep talk seemed to be working, because she felt better as the air got cooler and by the time she rode up to the cabin the next day, she was feeling almost well again. Ah Fong greeted the vegetables with delight, showing her where they were going to plant the corn, where the squash was going to go, and how they had finished a new bed for the onions. They worked together, all five of them, all day to get everything planted. When they finished, by sunset, the little girls danced around with Ah Fong singing a nonsense song, "Planting all the melons, planting all the beans, planting all the good things, yum yum yum."

Libby watched them with a weary smile.

"You're tired," Hugh said. "You've had a strenuous time. Now maybe you can take it easy until these crops grow."

"I've got to keep on with the washing and baking in case they don't," Libby said with a sigh. She felt so tired that she could lie down and sleep for a week, and she still could not shake off the clamminess.

I've got to see the doctor in the morning, she decided. I can't risk getting sick now. I can't risk giving something to my family.

So in the morning she rode the new mule down to Hangtown, which was strange in itself, because usually she enjoyed the walk. The doctor greeted her civilly. "It's good to meet in happier surroundings than before," he said. "What seems to be the problem?"

Libby described how she had fainted in Sacramento and how she could not shake off the feeling. "I don't want to find that I've got some terrible fever, Doctor. I have to know, because I don't want to give it to anyone in my family."

"Let's take a look at you," the doctor said. "If you had cholera, or typhoid, I think you'd know it by now. That's not to say you haven't caught a lesser fever. Every germ in the world breeds down in the swampy country by the river."

He examined her briskly and efficiently. When she had dressed again, he motioned her to sit at his desk.

"You don't seem to be running a fever right now," he said. "Let me ask you one thing, when was your last menstrual period?"

"My what?" Libby asked, then blushed. "I'm not very regular, I'm afraid. I never have been."

"But not within the last month?"

"I don't think so," Libby said.

The doctor nodded. "Then I think I have happier news for you than a fever," he said with a smile, as if he were very pleased with himself.

Libby looked at him in disbelief. "Are you trying to tell me that I'm going to have a baby?"

"My dear young woman," he said. "Does it come as such a surprise? You are reunited with your husband after a long time apart. What could be more natural?"

"Nothing. Nothing at all," Libby stammered.

The doctor held out his hand. "My congratulations," he said. "I expect you'll both be hoping for a boy this time, eh?"

"Yes," Libby managed to say with a false smile on her face. "That would be very nice."

She got to her feet. "Thank you very much, Doctor," she said.

"I expect I'll be seeing you about eight months from now, eh?" the doctor asked jovially.

No, Libby said to herself, hurriedly counting from March. About seven months from now.

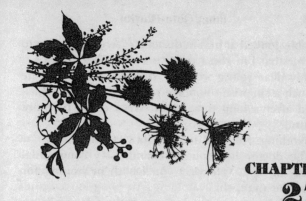

# CHAPTER
# 27

THE KNOWLEDGE THAT she was going to have Gabe's child should have shocked Libby. Instead it elated her. She often put her hand to her belly, as if touching it was in some way touching part of Gabe. "Now I'll always have something to remember you by," she whispered.

When Libby told Hugh, a month later, he was equally delighted, if very amazed. Libby was glad that they had made love, albeit very tentatively, so that he did not question that the child was his.

"It will be a boy this time, I know it will," he said happily. "Finally it looks as though everything is going to be fine, Libby. We've had a rough time but now our troubles are over."

Libby smiled at the irony of his words. Everything in the world has mended except for my heart, she thought. The garden is flourishing, the children are flourishing, Hugh is recovering, and the baby is growing. I'm the only one who can't flourish.

As the summer days grew longer and warmer,

Libby spent a lot of time in the vegetable garden with Ah Fong. Hugh had forbidden her to take in any more washing as soon as he learned about the baby, and it really did look as if the garden was going to produce magnificently. In a month the corn had already grown into strong green shoots, the squash and melons were sturdy little plants, and the onions had begun to flower. They had already begun to sell Ah Fong's bean sprouts, at first to very suspicious miners, then to repeat customers. Ah Fong looked after the garden as if it was his own child. He would not allow the tiniest weed to appear. He collected horse dung relentlessly and worked it into the soil. He dug irrigation ditches from a stream higher up the hill so that there was enough water flowing past the plants on hot dry days.

Libby's pies were also very successful. Both hotels in town would buy as many as she could bake and often she sold her entire stock before she ever reached town.

"If only we had a bigger oven," she complained to Hugh. "Maybe I'll get a brick oven built outside when the profits come in from the summer crop."

He put an arm around her protectively. "But Libby, darling, these vegetables and fruit are supposed to free you from slaving away. You don't want to spend your life baking pies, do you?"

"I want to make sure we are never desperate again," Libby said. "Vegetables are so precarious. One hailstorm would flatten them. One plague of rabbits would wipe us out. And my pies are selling so well. In this sort of place you grab what you can when you can."

"But you have to remember your condition," Hugh said. "You should be resting."

She walked away from him. He perched on the edge of the bed, looking at her with concern.

"Libby, please take care of yourself," he said. "You seem so different. So remote. Back in Boston you were always so gay, so carefree . . ."

"Things were slightly different back in Boston," Libby said. "I didn't have to worry every day that my family might starve."

He came up behind her, putting his hands on her shoulders and kissing the back of her neck. "It will all be over soon," he said. "If this crop works out as we think it will, then we'll have enough to go to England. We'll take that house my brother is offering and we'll bring up the children as little aristocrats. You'd like that, wouldn't you?"

"That would be very nice," Libby said politely.

"Isn't it what you want, Libby?" he demanded.

She stared out through the open door at the dappled green of the hillside, sloping away to the leafy valley. "I don't know what I want anymore," she said. "I'm sure it will be fine in England."

"But you don't seem very happy," he said. "Aren't you happy about the baby?"

"Oh, yes," she said with conviction. "I'm very happy about the baby."

"That's good," he said. "I'm sure it will be a son this time. Look how big you are already and how high you carry him." He put his arms around her, caressing her belly. Libby shivered. "Don't," she said and moved away. She caught a glimpse of his face and the hurt look in his eyes and she immediately felt guilty. She came across and took both his hands.

"I'm sorry, Hugh," she said. "I know I'm moody these days. I suppose my nerves have been stretched too far for too long and I don't know how to relax anymore."

"But the end really is in sight, Libby. Soon this whole business will seem like a nightmare when we look back on it. We've just got to keep us all well and strong until we can book a passage to England." He looked up as Ah Fong passed the front of the cabin, a hoe over his shoulder, singing a harsh Chinese song. "And we can take Ah Fong with us, if you'd like."

"Where Ah Fong goes is up to him," Libby said, "but I've been thinking about him. I think we should build him a better house. I'll see about the timber when I'm in town. And we should finish off this place too. These canvas walls are delightful in summer, but I assure you that they are not so delightful when the wind whips through them."

"You think we'll be here another winter?" Hugh asked. "I was hoping this summer's yield would be enough . . ."

"We have to plan for the worst," Libby said. "It might not be wise to travel when the baby is due."

"But we could be home by January if we left in September," Hugh said.

"All the same, I don't feel right about travelling in the last months," Libby said warily. "What if I fell in a storm? I'd hate to give birth on board ship."

"Whatever you want," Hugh said warmly. "Whatever makes you happy."

If only you knew, she thought and went back to her baking.

As the summer progressed the crops began to fulfill their promise. Under Ah Fong's instruction, Libby became expert at looking for signs of bugs, picking strawberries at just the right moment, and recognizing weeds the moment they sprouted. Hugh's leg was much stronger and he started making the deliveries, leading the mule with baskets full of beautiful produce strapped on either side. The miners could not buy enough of it and the hotels would take anything that was not snapped up on the way to town. By the middle of August Libby had two new log walls on the cabin and a real front door that could be bolted, Ah Fong had a little one-room house beside the vegetable patch and there was almost three thousand dollars in the bank. Hugh started making enquiries about ships sailing from San Francisco. Libby greeted the news of ships with a heavy heart. Part of her did not want to be trapped in this cabin for the rest of her life, but part of her could not bear to sail so far away from Gabe. She knew it was irrational to expect that she would ever see him again, but she could not face the finality of sailing to another continent. When she heard Hugh describing to the children the new life they would have and how they would go riding and learn to dance and be presented at court one day, Libby had to go outside and join Ah Fong pulling weeds among the vegetables.

The weather in August was so hot and dry that the wind felt like a blast from an oven. The little creek on the hillside dried up and they had to go down to the river with buckets to keep the gardens going. It became a morning ritual as all five of them stood in a bucket chain and passed the water up the slope to the plants. The first crops were now gathered and Libby looked speculatively at the bare earth where they had been, longing to put something in their place. But there was no point, if they were not going to be here for the harvest. She was feeling the heat very badly, the weight of the baby pressing against her too-tight dresses.

"I should get some gingham in the store and make myself something looser," she said to Hugh.

"Don't bother. We'll have you something made properly at a dressmaker in San Francisco before we sail," he said. "There are no proper fabrics up here. You can't wear gingham when we get back to civilization."

"I suppose not," she said, "and I suppose I'll have to go back to corsets again after the child is born."

"And put your hair up," Hugh said with a laugh. "You look about fifteen years old with it tied back like that."

"It will be hard to adjust to the real world again," Libby said. "There's so much we've forgotten about."

"Indeed there is," Hugh said. "The girls' table manners are quite appalling and their language! At least we'll be able to work with them on the ship so that they are presentable by the time they meet my family."

He started a campaign of instruction and criticism that both girls resented and fought against.

"You've let them run wild, Libby," Hugh complained. Libby agreed this was probably true.

"It seemed more important to keep them well and happy," she said. "There were so many times when we could have lost them . . . I wanted their childhood to be happy."

"They don't have to be unhappy just because I want them to eat with their mouths closed and not to tear at their food like animals," Hugh said. "Sit up straight, Bliss. When you're an English lady you'll not be allowed to slouch."

"I don't like you," Bliss said, scowling at him. "I liked Mr. Foster better. I wish he was our daddy."

"Bliss!" Libby blurted out.

"Who is Mr. Foster?" Hugh asked in a clipped voice.

"He was a man who helped us along the trail," Libby said quickly.

"He was very nice," Eden added. "Mama liked to talk to him."

"He still lives around here?"

"I've no idea where he is," Libby said. She tried to sound uninterested, but Hugh must have caught something in her voice. He looked enquiringly. "A gentleman?"

"Not in your sense of the word," Libby said. "A gambler."

"Oh, I see," Hugh said, looking amused. "No wonder he hasn't paid any social calls since I've been here."

"Meaning what?"

"A lady of your upbringing could hardly be seen to associate with a gambler, could she?" Hugh asked easily.

The incident was over and Hugh did not mention Gabe again. He continued to work on the girls' manners and deportment, but not with too much success.

"Don't worry about it," Libby said. "They'll pick it up very quickly when we're in England. Children ape what they see. They've only been exposed to miners with no manners for so long that they think it's the correct way to behave. When they see English gentlefolk, they'll want to be like them."

"I hope so," Hugh said with a sigh.

Eden came running up the path toward them, her pigtails flying and her gingham dress billowing out.

She had grown tall in the past months and no longer looked like the pale, skinny child of Boston.

"Look at her," Hugh said, shaking his head critically, "she's like a little Indian child, brown and skinny and running barefoot. Her aunts in England will die of heart failure when they see her."

"Mama, Papa, there are horsemen coming up the trail," Eden was yelling as she ran. "A whole bunch of 'em."

"Eden, you can't have a bunch of horses. That's not correct," Hugh said, but Libby interrupted.

"What do they look like?" Libby asked nervously. She had never told Hugh about the lynch mob and the way she had escaped death.

"Like an army," Eden said. "They've got uniforms and guns and things."

"Maybe they're a new company arrived at the gold fields," Hugh said, not showing much interest. "They often dress in military style. I'm surprised new companies are still coming out here. Don't they hear how overcrowded California already is?" He stuck his hands in his pockets. "Well, I can't wait around all day. This load of produce has to get down to the hotel before it spoils in this hot sun." He went around the house to begin loading the mule for its daily trip to town.

They could all now hear the chink of bridles and the muffled thud of horses hooves, moving fast. A horse snorted, the sound echoing loudly from the hills opposite. Then a well-armed band of men appeared, wheeling to a halt in front of the cabin.

"Keep those horses off my vegetables," Libby called out, moving around to protect her precious patch.

As they wheeled to a halt she could see that the men

at the front were smartly turned out in uniform but those behind them were a ragtag company riding an assortment of skinny horses and mules.

"We haven't come for your vegetables, lady," the leader said, a lean, weathered man in a blue uniform with a thick gun belt and rifles on either side of his saddle. "We've come for your husband."

"My husband? What has he done?" Libby asked in amazement.

"He ain't done nothing, lady," the man went on, grinning. "We just need to borrow him a while."

"Borrow him, what for?"

"Injun uprising, north of here near Lassen's place," another of the men said. "They murdered a bunch of settlers and set fire to a couple of towns. We're recruiting a force to go teach them varmints a lesson."

"I don't think Hugh would be interested," Libby said. "He's been very sick. He's only just walking again."

"Is he the guy who takes around the vegetables?" the first man demanded. There was no longer a pleasant tone to his voice.

Libby nodded.

"Then he can walk. Where is he? Tell him to go get his things."

"He's not going to fight any Indian uprising," Libby said, annoyed now. "Go and find somebody else."

The second man who had spoken urged his horse forward and showed her a badge. "United States Cavalry, ma'am," he said. "I have an authorization here from the President to recruit any men I need in case of emergency. Your husband doesn't have a choice. Tell him to get his things."

Hugh appeared at this moment, leading the mule. "What's all this, Libby?" he asked.

"Hugh, they want you to go fight Indians with them."

"No thank you," Hugh said. The men all laughed.

"I'm not asking you, I'm telling you," the leader said. "You've just been recruited, mister. Now get your things and saddle up that mule. We need to get going."

"I don't have to do anything of the sort," Hugh said angrily. "I'm an English citizen. I'm not bound by your American laws."

The cavalry man with the badge started to get something out of his shirt. "My orders say any able-bodied man. They don't specify what kind of citizen. Now get your things, or I'll shoot you on the spot."

"But you don't understand," Libby said, running over to the leader and tugging at his bridle. "He's been sick. He's not well enough to go and fight."

The man looked down at her, noting her condition. "Ma'am, it will all be over in a couple of days. I'm not asking him to come to the north pole with me. If we can round up a big enough force, we can blast those devils to hell and come back home again. But if we let this one tribe get away with murder, then the others will all try it and you and your children won't be safe up in these hills."

Hugh went over to Libby and led her away from the man. "It's all right, darling," he said. "If I must go, I must. I'll just pack some things together."

"Take the rifle," Libby said. "We don't have much ammunition."

"He don't need no rifle," the leader said. "We supply the arms and the ammunition," the first man said. "All we need is men to shoot them."

Hugh went into the house. When he came out again, he looked very pale and fragile, but he seemed calm as Libby helped him saddle the mule. "Don't worry," he said to her. "I'm sure it will all be over very quickly. Take good care of the girls for me, won't you? And take care of yourself . . . and my son."

"I will," Libby said.

He kissed her gently on the lips, then mounted the mule. The troop began to move off. At the edge of the clearing Hugh looked back and blew her a kiss.

It was a week later before Libby got news that he had been knocked from his saddle by an Indian arrow and trampled to death under the hooves of his companions' horses.

# CHAPTER
# 28

LIBBY RECEIVED THE news of Hugh's death with surprising calmness. Her overwhelming feeling was one of guilt, that she was not grieving more deeply for the man who had been her husband for nine years. She would miss him, she was sad for him, but her heart wasn't broken as it had been when Gabe left. If she felt anything else, it was anger at the waste and stupidity of his death. She accompanied the cavalry officer up north to see his grave, on a wild, rocky hillside, overlooking a narrow canyon. It was such a remote place that she almost accepted the major's offer to rebury the remains where she wanted them.

Poor Hugh, she thought, looking down at the crude wooden cross and the fresh yellow earth. It's not fair that your last place on earth should be so far from what you wanted. She seriously considered having his remains shipped over to England to be buried with his family, then she dismissed the idea. Hugh wanted to return home in triumph or not at all. If she took the children to England later, she would take him with her. Not that it mattered very much. She felt very strongly that Hugh was not there. He was already very far away, probably laughing at the irony of his stupid, unnecessary end.

When she came home again she was strangely lethargic, unable to show any interest in the profits which came in from the garden or for Ah Fong's great ideas for expansion.

"You going to leave this ground doing nothing, after I put all that good dung in it?" he asked her.

"We might not be here next year," Libby said. "It doesn't make any sense to plant stuff now."

"Doesn't make sense to leave good ground for the weeds," Ah Fong said. "How about we put in winter cabbage? Then if you go in winter, still get some money."

"If you like, Ah Fong," Libby said. "Do what you like."

The one positive outcome of Hugh's death was that it brought her community sympathy for the first time. Men made a point of stopping off at the cabin on their way to and from town, expressing their condolences, cursing "them varmints," and often leaving a present or even a gold nugget "for the girls and the little one that's coming." She had offers of firewood for the winter and a replacement for the mule which had been lost in the heat of battle. Libby never did hear whether the skirmish had been a success. She didn't want to know. If she had any emotion at all it was anger at the stupidity of wanting to punish a whole tribe for what must have been the anti-social actions of just one or two members, and was most likely a justifiable retaliation for brutal treatment by settlers in the first place. She knew that many of the miners talked of shooting Indians for sport, just as they would talk of shooting deer, and in her heart, she was on the Indians' side.

Among the procession of men who stopped by at the cabin was Mark Hopkins, looking very prosperous in a city suit with a gold watch chain and riding on a fine-looking horse.

"I just heard the news when I got back to town," he said, mopping his brow with a white handkerchief as he dismounted. "I came to say how very sorry I am. I really thought things were going well for you at last."

Libby nodded. "Thank you for coming," she said.

"What will you do now?" he asked.

Libby stared out past him, over the golden hills. "I don't know," she said. "I really don't know. I suppose I should take the children to England, because that's what Hugh wanted. . . ."

"But you don't want to go?"

"I'd be a foreigner there," she said. "I wouldn't know anybody. I'd have to wear a corset again."

Mark laughed.

"You know what I mean," she said, smiling too. "I've become so used to living out here with no restraints and no formalities. I'm beginning to wonder whether I wouldn't suffocate with all the restrictions of English upper-class life. I wouldn't even know which fork to use after eating from tin plates with spoons for all this while."

"If you don't go, will you stay on here?"

"I don't know about that, either," she said. "I can see that this is not an ideal place to bring up children. It's very isolated, there's no school, but at least I'm providing well for my family here."

"For the time being," Mark said.

"What do you mean?"

"I mean that we've already had the gold boom," Mark said. "From now on it's all downhill. Too many men and not enough gold. It will peter out and then they'll all drift away again."

"So what do you suggest?"

"San Francisco," Mark said, his face lighting up. "I'm on my way there now. I've come to say goodbye. I've sold my store here and I'm moving down to the valley. I'm having a store built in Sacramento to supply the mines, but I'm also looking for a home in San Francisco. Sacramento is no place to spend the winter, unless one is a duck. I'm also considering putting money into property down there, where the boom's just starting. You might consider doing the same."

"Me, buy property in San Francisco?" Libby asked.

"Why not?" Mark Hopkins asked. "Right now you can buy lots for a song. I'm thinking of buying a large stretch of sand dunes."

"What on earth for?"

He grinned, the same boyish grin. "Because the city has got to spread and when it does, my sand dunes will be worth millions."

She looked at him admiringly. "You really do like to live dangerously, don't you?"

"It's the only way," he said. "Risks are good. They make you feel as if you're truly alive. Calculated risks, of course. You do need a smart head on your shoulders to start with. But I think you have that too."

Libby smiled to acknowledge the compliment. "But from what I hear, San Francisco is hardly the place to think of bringing up children right now. All that corruption and violence and bawdy living . . ."

"It will outgrow all that soon enough," Hopkins said. "In the meantime, why don't you speculate a little. I'm sure you've made a tidy profit this summer. Let me put some of your money into lots for you. It doesn't have to be a great deal and I think you'll be surprised how quickly you can double and triple your investment."

"I don't know," Libby said. "I seem to have been saying that ever since Hugh died. I just can't make up my mind anymore. I was so decisive and head-strong when I came here and I seem to have turned into one of my own vegetables."

"You're still shocked and grieving," Hopkins said gently. "It's understandable. Healing takes a while."

"I think I'm more angry than grieving," Libby confessed. "And guilty too. I keep thinking I could have done more to stop them from taking him. He wasn't fit to ride all that way and I knew it. I tried to stop them, but I should have done more—got a doctor to forbid it or even lain down in front of the horses. He looked so frail when he set off. . . ." Her voice trailed away.

Hopkins put a comforting hand on her shoulder. "This country wasn't meant for people like Hugh," he said. "It eats people like him for breakfast and spits out the bones. You have to be tough like us to survive."

Libby looked down at the ground. A line of big black ants was attempting to move a grass stalk across the sandy trail. It seemed like a hopeless task but they kept going back patiently every time the stalk got stuck behind a pebble. "I used to think I was tough," she said in a small voice, "but I don't think I am anymore. I don't know what I want or where I want to be. Nothing seems to matter to me."

"Give it time," Mark said. "Take care of yourself. Have the baby and then decide. I'll give you an address in San Francisco where I can be reached. Look me up if you decide to come down there. Maybe you'd do better to spend the winter there if the baby's due soon—better doctors and less chance of getting stranded in the mud or snow."

"Maybe you're right," she said. "I'll think about it."

"Don't leave it too late."

"I know. I'll make up my mind soon." Libby said.

"Take care," he said and shook her hand warmly.

After he had gone the lethargy returned, enhanced by the Indian summer which came with a vengeance in late September. The sun beat down mercilessly, bleaching the dry grasses ghost white and shrivelling any plant that dared to show its head. The winds that came up from the Sacramento Valley were fierce, hot winds that seemed to snatch away breath.

"Now are you glad we didn't start a whole new garden?" Libby asked Ah Fong. "We'd have had to sit by and watch it shrivel."

"This not good place for garden," Ah Fong said. "We need place near big stream or good well. Then dig lots of little ditches and plants grow all time. We go find place like that, yes?"

"I can't decide anything until after the baby is born," Libby said. "It's too hot even to think."

She spent her days sitting under the biggest oak, splashing herself with water and fanning herself. She was sitting there when she saw a spiral of smoke rise from the valley below. It looked too substantial for the usual campfire smoke and was soon rising up and spreading out across the sky.

"Ah Fong, look. There's a fire," she called.

Ah Fong came running. "That down in town," he said. "Too bad. Wind's coming too."

As they watched, the spiral turned from white to gray to black, billowing out into angry clouds. Red tongues of flame could be seen dancing among the smoke billows and the smell of burning wood was carried to them on the hot wind.

"I no like," Ah Fong said, sniffing the wind like an animal. "Wind getting stronger and fire comes this way."

"Surely they'd put it out before it gets all the way up here?" Libby said, not feeling too much alarm. They continued to watch as the black smoke spread. They could hear the first sounds of fire; the clang of a bell, the neighing of frightened horses, and then the crackle and roar. The wind had live sparks in it.

Libby was just wondering whether they should do something when a horseman galloped up the trail. "All Hangtown's burning and it's racing this way almost as fast as I could ride," he shouted. "Get out while you still can."

"Where should we go?" Libby yelled back. The whole countryside was tinder dry and the wind was gusting as it always did at late afternoon.

"Get down to the creek," the man shouted. "Where it's all dug up and there's no vegetation. At least you can get in the water if you have to there."

He galloped on to warn the next settlers. Libby looked at Ah Fong. "Are the children still down at the creek?" she asked. The two little girls had found a favorite wading pool where they spent the hottest days.

"Yes, missee," Ah Fong said, staring at the approaching conflagration as if he were hypnotized.

"Then get down there and join them," Libby said. "Take them out to that bar in the middle—the one that's all gravel."

"What you do, missee?"

"I'm just going to check the cabin first," Libby said.

"Don't wait too long. Fire run faster than horses," Ah Fong said.

"I'll be right down," Libby shouted after him and picked up her skirts to run to the cabin. She stood inside, enjoying the semidarkness, looking at all the familiar objects. Two years ago she would have despised any of these things, thinking them too coarse. Now she looked with affection at the black stove which had kept them warm all winter, the rickety bed in the corner, the pans she had made her pies in.

"This is nonsense," she said to herself. "I can't risk getting burned alive just for a few objects. Objects can be replaced. People can't." She snatched the rifle off the wall and the ammunition pouch beside it, then impetuously took Gabe's wolfskins and ran down the hill, clutching them to her. Ah Fong looked at her curiously as she waded the shallow water to join him, but he said nothing about the strange selection process of the western woman's brain.

"The fire won't get to our cabin, will it, Mama?" Eden asked.

"I hope not," Libby said, "but we can't take any chances." She looked around in alarm. "Where's Bliss?"

"She was right here," Ah Fong said. "She was sitting there playing with the pebbles a second ago."

Libby scanned the empty stretch of beach. "Bliss!" she shouted. The only sound was the distant roar of the fire.

"Where can she be?" Libby screamed in panic.

"Perhaps she went back to get her dolly," Eden said.

"She did what?" Libby almost shook her.

Eden's frightened little face stared up at her in alarm. "She asked me if all our stuff would get burned up and then she said she didn't want her dolly to get burned."

"And you let her go?"

"I didn't see her go," Eden said, starting to cry. "I didn't know she'd go."

"Just stay here with Ah Fong," Libby shouted.

"Missee, you no go. I go for you!" Ah Fong yelled but Libby was already wading back, not attempting to pick up her skirts this time, which clung in a sodden mass around her legs. Gasping and panting, she scrambled up the hillside, steadying herself on the manzanita bushes which jutted across the path. The fire was all too real a danger now. She could hear the crackle of burning grass, the roar as it consumed a new tree and she could taste the smoke. Ashes floated and fell, some igniting new fires as they landed in the dry grass. When she glanced down the hill, it seemed as if the whole valley was burning and all the anger of hell was sweeping up to swallow her.

"Bliss!" she yelled hoarsely. "Bliss, come to Mama right now!"

The cabin door was open. Libby sprinted across the clearing. Bliss was crouched down on the cabin floor, her doll on the floor beside her.

"I can't find dolly's shoe," she complained. "I think it fell down the side of the bed."

"Come with me right now," Libby said, grabbing her daughter's hand. "Quickly."

"But dolly can't go without her shoe," Bliss said, starting to wail. "I want dolly's shoes." She struggled to get away from Libby's grasp.

"Damn dolly's shoe," Libby said, slapping her hard across the bare leg. "Do you want to get burned up?" She swept the crying child under one arm and staggered out of the house with her. Tongues of flame were licking up the hillside and sweeping along the creek ahead of them, barring the way they had come. Libby looked around in panic, then put down the frightened child.

"Don't leave me, Mama. I'll be good," Bliss screamed in terror.

Libby had already run back into the house and came back with a bucket of water, which she poured over the little girl, then over herself. Then she ran with the trembling child to an old oak tree, hollowed on one side by a lightning strike. She thrust Bliss inside first then crouched next to her, holding her wet apron over both their faces. She felt the heat as the grass around them burst into flame. Flames licked hungrily at the tree trunk and sizzled against the wet cloth. The roaring was louder than a storm wind and the smoke choked them, making them cough and retch. She heard the crackle as a branch above caught on fire. Sparks rained down. Libby's head was singing as she fought unconsciousness.

Then she noticed that the roaring had died down. Cautiously, she lowered her apron. The ground around them was blackened, but there was no more grass to burn. "It's all right, Bliss. It's passed by," she said, standing up and giving her hand to the child. Bliss came out, looking with fear and wonder at the black and smoldering world. "Dolly didn't get burned at all," she said happily. Libby's gaze went back to the cabin. A black stove jutted out above a pile of charred timber.

"It's all gone," Bliss said and started to cry. Libby started crying too. I didn't cry when my husband was killed, she thought, but I'm crying because I've lost my house. It doesn't make any sense at all.

After a while they made their way cautiously back down to the river, Libby carrying her daughter because the ground was still hot in places and Bliss wore no shoes. Eden met them with hysterical joy.

"I told her she no have to worry, you one very smart lady," Ah Fong said, but Libby noticed that he wiped away a tear when he thought she wasn't looking.

They spent the night on the bar in mid-river, not knowing where else was safe to go. Nobody came past, all the miners being presumably busy with their own tragedies. The children and Ah Fong managed to sleep, the little girls snuggled like puppies on Gabe's wolfskins, but Libby lay awake, her body racked with pains.

I won't lose this baby, I won't! she commanded herself as a tight band of pain shot across her stomach and back again. She lay awake all night, as if her will alone could prevent her from miscarrying the child. By early morning the pains had subsided although her back and side still ached. She watched the dawn come with a sense of wonder, as if she had fought a long battle and won. The child was still there, moving restlessly inside her as it had done for the past couple of months. She realized that her pains had not been premature labor at all, but more likely strained muscles as she carried a sturdy, squirming five-year-old across a rugged hillside. She was sleeping peacefully when the others woke.

The scene that greeted their eyes was one of utter devastation. As far as the eye could see in any direction was blackened earth and charred tree trunks. Only the biggest oaks had managed to survive with some of their leaves still green and unburned. There was not a blade of vegetation and the air still smelled of burning. Libby went with the children and Ah Fong back up to the remains of the cabin.

"Oh, Mama," Eden said, tears running down her soot-blackened cheeks, "it's all gone. Everything you worked for is gone. Now we've got nothing again."

"It's not all gone," Libby said, "Don't cry, Eden. We have plenty of money in the bank to start again," she said, "only this time it will be much better."

"Missee going to build new house?" Ah Fong asked suspiciously. "Here?"

A glorious vision swam into Libby's head: herself and Gabe standing on a hillside, looking out over the valley that went on forever. She heard herself saying, "I'd like to build a house someday." Now there was nothing to stop her from doing it.

"No, not right here," Libby said. "I've nothing to keep me near Hangtown anymore. We'll find a better place for a house, farther south where the miners haven't had a chance to sample my excellent produce yet. There are a lot of little towns all in a row there and it's easier to get around, a more gentle countryside than this. We'll go look for a site to build down there."

"So we won't be going to England now?" Eden asked.

"Would that upset you very much?"

Eden chewed on her lip thoughtfully. "I'd like to see Papa's house," she said. "And I'd really like my own pony, but sure don't want to learn all those manners."

Libby burst out laughing and hugged her daughter to her. "Exactly my feelings," she said. Then she attempted to look stern. "Of course, if we stay here long, we'll have to get a governess for you two. You can't grow up too wild."

"That's all right," Eden said, "as long as I don't have to wear shoes too often . . . and maybe I can still have a pony one day, if you grow enough vegetables?"

Libby smiled again. "We'll grow enough vegetables to feed the whole of California," she said. "We're going to be the richest women in the state."

# CHAPTER
## 29

THERE WAS NOTHING left of Hangtown as they made their way through it. Only the big safe in the Wells Fargo office and a couple of brick chimneys stuck out from blackened earth and rubble. Hastily pitched tents were the first signs of rebirth. Libby found herself feeling glad that it had all gone. The place held too many memories, both bitter and sweet, and she was anxious to put them all behind her. She noticed, however, that Ah Fong did look back, and realized that with all her own concerns, she had given little thought to him or his future.

"You don't have to come with me if you don't want to, Ah Fong," she said. "If you'd rather stay in Hangtown with your friends."

"You don't want Ah Fong around no more?" Ah Fong asked, surprised.

Libby laughed uneasily. "Of course I want you. I could never have survived this long without you. But I want you to know that you don't owe me anything any longer. You're free to leave whenever you want to."

"Where you think I go?" he asked.

"I don't know," Libby said with some embarrassment. "I just thought that maybe you'd rather go back
to your Chinese friends and try your hand at gold
mining again."

Ah Fong pursed his lips in distaste. "What I want to
do damn fool thing like that for?" he asked. "No place
for Chinese gold miners here. Chinese only allowed
to dig when everyone else has finished. I like better
making things grow. How you going to start new farm
without Ah Fong?"

"Not very well," she said, smiling. "But if you stay
you're not my house servant. You're now my farm
manager, understood? I want to pay you the proper
wage."

She held out her hand to him. Very cautiously and
solemnly he took it.

A few days later they were bumping along in a
newly purchased buckboard down the very route
that Libby had gone with Gabe. She had not realized how hard it would be to retrace those steps, but
every inch of the way cried out with memories. Here
they had seen a kingfisher, here they had stopped to
water the horses and Gabe had lifted her down from
the saddle as if she were made of finest porcelain.
"If only . . ." she found herself saying and wondered
what she meant by it. If only he was still around here?
She remembered his commenting that the southern
mines would be good for a gambler. Is that why I
want to come down here? she wondered.

I mustn't hope for too much, she told herself severely. It was just that if he ever came back to their hillside
again, she wanted him to find her there.

She found the place without difficulty and brought

the horse to a halt, looking out over the hazy flat lands below. Libby sighed as she climbed down from the trap.

"You want a house here?" Ah Fong asked.

"Yes. Isn't it beautiful?"

Ah Fong looked at her suspiciously. "No good for growing things," he said, kicking at the dry earth. "Too dry."

"But there's a creek we've just passed," Libby said. "It still had water in it and it's the driest time of year."

"You need flat land so water won't run away. We go farther down hill."

"But I want my house on a hill."

Ah Fong sighed expansively. "So we go down until we meet flat land. Then you build house up a bit and plant vegetable on flat."

Libby had to smile. "Very well. We'll go down a bit and see if we can find a place that you like as well as I."

Cautiously, she drove the trap down the slope, following the creek until it slowed its descent and meandered between willows.

"How about this, Ah Fong?" she asked excitedly. "This must suit you too. It's flat enough for crops down below and I could build my house right beside the creek here. Then I'd have a view of willows on one side and down to the plains on the other."

"Not wise build here," Ah Fong said. "Too near river."

"But I like it near river."

"River flood, sweep house away," Ah Fong said. "See. River get this big in spring!" He pointed across to the other bank which was cut away steeply high above the water level.

"Anyone would think it was your house, not mine," Libby snapped, feeling hot and tired now.

"Fine. So build house here. Enjoy trip when you float down to Sacramento," Ah Fong said, turning his back on her.

"All right. Have it your way," Libby said, "Only I want my view."

They paced up and down along the river until they found a spot that satisfied both of them. It was high enough to be clear of floods, Ah Fong thought, but the soil was good enough for crops down below the house. Libby had Ah Fong drive some stakes into the ground where the house was going to be, so that they had some sort of claim on the land.

"We must find out how we register land like this," she said. "We don't want someone coming in and digging up our backyard for gold. Although I don't think they've been finding gold this far down the valley."

As they were walking back to the trap, Ah Fong stiffened. "Horsemen," he whispered, "coming this way fast."

Libby followed his gaze, shielding her eyes against the fierce sunlight. She remembered rumors of bandits and wished she had not left the rifle under the seat in the buckboard. There were two horsemen, riding magnificent steeds. Their tails streamed out behind them as they galloped and the riders sat so well, they seemed to be part of the horses. Silver glinted from rider and horse in the sunlight so that they made Libby think of gods of some pagan religion, riding to bring vengeance. She watched entranced as they came nearer and it was only as they reined in the horses and drew their guns that she felt any fear.

"What you want here?" one of the men shouted in strongly accented English. Now that they were no longer moving, Libby could see they were Mexican Californios, wearing big black hats, dressed in fringed leather decorated with silver. Silver adorned their spurs and bridles and even their saddles; Libby couldn't ever remember seeing anything as exotic or as handsome. The faces, however, were not friendly.

"We are just travellers and we have no gold on us," she called to them.

She saw the younger say something to the elder and the guns were lowered. They urged their horses closer. "My pardon, *señora*," the older one said. His face was tanned and lined like old leather, his hair was gray, but his large drooping moustache was still black. The younger must have been his son, because his face was a younger copy of his father's. "We took you for cattle bandits."

Libby laughed. "Do we look like cattle bandits?"

The man smiled too, even more lines creasing his face. "Now that we see you, no. But everytime we see strangers on our land we cannot be sure. These gringos, these strangers who come here for gold—they think they can help themselves to our cattle too. Half our herd has been stolen since they came here. My best herdsman was shot in cold blood."

Libby was just taking in what he had said. "So this is your land?" she asked.

The man nodded. "I was granted this land twenty-five years ago by the government in Mexico. From the Cozumnes River south is all mine."

"I'm very sorry," Libby said. "I had no idea I was trespassing. I was looking for somewhere to build my new house. This seemed so ideal."

"Why you want to build house here?" the son asked. "Your man is digging at the gold?"

"My husband is dead," Libby said, "and I have been making money by growing vegetables. My cabin was just destroyed by fire. I was looking for a place with better soil and more room to start again."

"How much land you need to grow these vegetables?" the man asked slowly.

"Not too much to start with," Libby said. "There is just myself and my assistant here to work the land at the moment."

The older man said something quickly to his son. The son nodded, then spurred his horse into a gallop, disappearing quickly through the tall grass.

"Please," the older man said. "I am Don Miguel Flores. My son Manuel has gone to tell my wife. You come to my house and we talk."

She followed the Mexican across the golden hillside and down into the valley. Ground squirrels popped up from their burrows and vanished in terror as the buckboard's wheels passed by. The Mexican's horse danced impatiently at the slow pace. Then, in a dip in the grasslands, they could see a glimpse of red roof, surrounded by trees. Ten minutes later Libby drove the buckboard in through a white gate in a hedge of ferocious-looking cactus and up to a low white house with a red-tiled roof. Hens ran squawking in all directions from the horses hooves, dogs jumped up, barking from the shade of a big feathery tree. Don Miguel sprang from his horse with agility and helped down Libby and the girls. Ah Fong looked suspiciously at the house.

"I wait with horse, missee," he said.

Libby nodded. "Thank you, Ah Fong. I'll have them bring you something to drink."

"Please, come inside," Don Miguel said. "My wife will be so happy to see another woman and little children again."

He pushed open a heavy studded door and Libby stepped into a stone-floored room. It was a large room with deeply recessed windows. The furniture was all dark wood and leather and the floor was dotted with animal skins. A magnificent pair of horns and a fine spotted skin decorated the white wall. The surprising coolness made her gasp.

"Something is wrong?" Don Miguel asked in alarm.

"No. It's wonderful," Libby said. "It's just so cool in here."

He smiled with satisfaction. "Yes. It is always cool. That is the adobe walls. They keep out the heat." He looked around. "Conchita? *Donde es*?"

A little round woman came scurrying out of a back room, wiping her hands on a cloth, smiling nervously at Libby.

"My wife, Dona Conchita," Don Miguel said, holding out his hand to present her to Libby. "Conchita, *Señora* Libby Grenville."

She saw the children and her eyes opened wide with pleasure. She went over to them, releasing a torrent of Spanish.

"You must forgive my wife. She speak no English," Don Miguel said. "But she very happy to see children again. My daughters have married far away and my son have no wife yet." He turned to glare at the young man who had come in behind his mother.

The young man muttered something in Spanish, then turned to Libby. "I tell him, how I find a wife when I spend all day only with cows?" he asked.

Don Miguel bowed to Libby and extended his hand. "I expect you like cool drink," he said. "Come, we go out to my patio. Very nice in summer."

"Maybe I could take a drink out to my servant first," Libby suggested.

"He is welcome to come inside," Don Miguel said. "Manuel, go invite this lady's servant into kitchen and give him drink. And you *señora*, please come with me."

Libby allowed herself to be escorted out through a door at the back and again was overcome with wonder. "But this is beautiful," she said. "This is paradise."

The walled garden was covered with an enormous grapevine, hung with purple grapes and throwing the tiled area beneath into deep cool shade. A table and chairs, slung with leather, stood together under a large feathery tree and on the wall on the other side another large tree was festooned with yellow fruit.

"Why, it's lemons," Libby said in surprise.

"*Si, limone*," Conchita said, nodding excitedly. She held up the jug she had carried out from the kitchen. "*Limone, fresce.*"

"How wonderful to grow your own lemons," Libby said as Conchita poured out the lemonade and handed them first to the children. "I must plant a lemon tree first of all when I find a place for my new house. And grapes, just like these. I think everything grows to giant size here."

Miguel translated this for his wife, who laughed and said something in return. Miguel laughed too. "My wife says she think you grow fine strong baby here," he said. "Please excuse."

"Nothing to excuse," Libby said smiling. "I think it will be a fine strong baby. It certainly kicks hard enough."

Miguel pulled out one of the chairs for Libby, who seated herself gratefully.

"My wife says she is very sorry that you lose your husband at such a time," Don Miguel went on. Libby nodded to Conchita who looked at her with understanding and sympathy. "She thinks you look very simpatico. She say she like if you build house close by. Then she have children to play with."

Libby's face lit up. "You mean it?"

Don Miguel nodded. "I let you have that land you want," he said. "I'm happy if you live there. Now it's empty. I keep no cattle up there because always they get stolen. All my cattle now down in valley where no gold miners come. So that land no good to me. Take what you need. Build house. You make my wife happy."

"That is very nice of you, Don Miguel," Libby said, feeling that she might be about to cry at any moment. It was so long since she had met gentility and kindness that she found it overwhelming. "I think I will be very happy too to know that there is another woman nearby."

Eden and Bliss, with the unerring instinct of the very young, had followed Conchita back into the kitchen and now came running out again excitedly. "Look, Mama, the kind lady gave us cakes," Bliss cried,

"And guess what?" Eden asked, her face flushed with excitement, "they have kittens. Can we have one? Please?"

Libby laughed. "First we need a house and some furniture. Then we can think about kittens."

"But the kittens will be all grown by the time we have a house," Eden begged. "Can't I keep just a little one, Mama?"

Don Miguel smiled indulgently. "Ask your mama if you can choose one kitten and then it can live here until your house is ready."

"Can I, please?" Eden asked, beaming at him. "Oh, thank you. That would be wonderful. I've always wanted a pet of my own."

"You have never had a pet?"

Eden looked sorrowful. "No, never. In Boston we lived with Grandmama and Grandpapa and they didn't like animals, and since we came out here, Mama's been too busy to think of pets."

They lunched on the patio, Bliss and Eden each with a sleeping kitten in her lap. The air was scented with lemon blossom. Conchita brought out plates of cold beef, tomatoes, and flat bread, also a spicy relish Don Miguel called salsa. He poured red wine for Libby. "We make our own," he said. "Just for ourselves, but it is good, no?"

Libby sighed with contentment. "I could sit like this forever," she said.

"Why you not stay here until you finish house?" Don Miguel asked. "You are most welcome. My wife would be happy."

Libby got the impression that he would be happy too, but was too polite to say so.

"I couldn't impose on you," she said hesitantly. "I don't know how long it will take to build a house and there are hotels up in the gold towns . . ."

Miguel and his wife exchanged remarks in Spanish.

He frowned. "My wife thinks the gold towns are not good place for little girls. She think they better here. Good food. No shooting. No bad men."

"I'm sure you're right," Libby said, "and I would love to stay here, but it might take a long while until I can move into my own house."

Manuel had come to sit beside them. "I think you find, *señora*, that there are many men who want work," he said. "Too many men find no gold and need money. If you ask for carpenters, I think you do not have to pay them much and the house go up very quick."

"What sort of house you want?" Don Miguel asked.

Libby looked up at the red-tiled roof. "A house just like this," she said.

The men laughed. "Then you will indeed be our guest for a long while," Don Miguel said. "This house is built of adobe. Do you know what that is? It is the name for the clay soil we find by the creeks here. We make bricks of clay and straw, and let them dry. Then they make very good walls. Very thick—keep out heat in summer and cold in winter. But it takes a long time to make all these bricks. We start with little wood house and every day we make more bricks, build this house nearby."

"Then that's what I'll do," Libby said. "I'll start with a little wooden house and you can show me how to make adobe bricks."

"But ladies cannot make bricks. This is man's work," Manuel said in horror. "Especially not lady expecting like you."

Libby laughed. "There is not much that this lady has not tried," she said. "I've surprised myself during the past year. But the bricks will have to wait a while. It's most important that I get my planting done first if I'm to get next season's potatoes in. And I'd like to grow grapes like you, and fruit trees. I want to make sure that the miners never have to send down to Chile for their fruit again. From now on they buy from me."

# CHAPTER
# 30

As Don Miguel had predicted, there was no short-
age of men roaming the gold fields, disappointed,
hungry, and ready to work for a small wage. Libby
found a skilled carpenter to be her foreman and had
him select ten willing and strong men. Putting aside
her visions of a house like the Flores', Libby decided
to start simply, with a small wooden frame house, containing two bedrooms and living area. It was to be
connected by a covered walkway to another building
containing the kitchen and Ah Fong's quarters. He
nearly wept when he saw what she was planning for
him. "House of my own. This is too good," he said.

"Nonsense, Ah Fong," Libby said, smiling in embarrassment. "Of course my farm manager has to have a
house."

Ah Fong beamed at her. "Wait till I write letter
home to my village in China. They going to think
Ah Fong done pretty well here. I tell my father he
better start looking for bride for me."

"That would be wonderful, Ah Fong," Libby said,

enjoying his happiness. "You'll start your own family and your children can play with my baby."

"Better get house built first," Ah Fong said practically.

The timbers from the house were sent down from Sutter's Mill. Libby had the stove moved down from the old cabin and put in the new kitchen, but she also had a big brick oven built outside, knowing how hot the kitchen would get in the summer. In her own living room was a large brick fireplace and before she paid off her team, she had them cut and stack firewood for the winter.

It was all finished before the rains and she stood outside with her Mexican neighbors, looking at it with pride.

"Now all I need is furniture, dishes, cookware, bedding and it will be a home," she said, laughing excitedly.

"I expect these men could make you some furniture, if you tell them what you want," Manuel said.

"Oh, no." Libby shook her head. "I've slept on a leather-strip bed long enough," she said. "I want real furniture—a feather bed and proper carpets on the floor."

"Then you'll have to go down to San Francisco and see what you can find," Manuel said.

Libby nodded. "I have to go to San Francisco anyway," she said. "I want to arrange to have fruit trees sent up from Chile."

"You will undertake such a journey now?" Don Miguel said, looking with concern at the bulge in her dress. "Is that wise?"

"I still have almost three more months," Libby said. "I don't intend to stay away that long."

"But the journey by coach to the ship. So much shaking."

"I'll drive my own buckboard down," Libby said. "Then I can go as fast or as slowly as I want."

"But *Señora* Libby . . ."

"I'm a pretty tough woman, Don Miguel," Libby said. "I'll be fine. In fact I'm looking forward to going to the city. It will be a treat to buy clothes and eat well and maybe go to a theater."

She had wanted her fields plowed while she was away, but could not find a plow in the whole area. So she kept on some of the unskilled men to dig up the earth with shovels. They were glad of the extra work.

"Maybe you'd like to keep us on to work the fields after you've planted," one of them suggested.

"In the spring, maybe I could use you," Libby said, "but nothing happens all winter. I couldn't afford to feed you all while you did nothing."

After he had walked away, Ah Fong drew her aside. "Missee, I like to come San Francisco with you," he said urgently.

"You would?"

Ah Fong nodded seriously. "I want find good Chinese men, come and work these fields with me in spring," he said. "Those white men no good."

"They seem hard workers," Libby said.

Ah Fong shook his head even more violently so that his pigtail danced. "No, missee. They not take orders from Ah Fong. They not think Chinese man know nothing. They think Chinese man like dirt."

Libby considered the wisdom of this and decided he was right. No white man was going to take orders from a Chinese. "Very well, Ah Fong," she said. "You shall come down to San Francisco with me and select some workers for the spring."

Ah Fong grinned happily. "And I find Chinese food in San Francisco," he said.

They set off two days later, all four of them in the buckboard, dressed as presentably as was possible in their homemade ginghams. Sacramento was as smelly and chaotic as ever, dusty and plagued with mosquitoes and flies and garbage, but had already turned from tent city to permanent settlement. A levee had been built to keep out flood water and brick buildings were going up on all the streets. The new store that Mark Hopkins was building with a partner called Hutchinson was nearing completion, but the workmen told Libby that Mr. Hopkins himself was down in San Francisco.

The steamer ride down to San Francisco was pleasant and restful, with Libby sitting on deck and watching marshlands slip past. The girls were excited to watch herons and egrets flap lazily from the reeds and as the river opened into the wider waters of the delta and then the bay, they were amazed by the thousands of duck and geese that had already come south to these placid waters for the winter. As the river opened into Suisun Bay, hills rose up again and the steamer sailed between steep banks. Everyone crowded to the rails to get the first glimpse of the city. At last it came into view, with little wooden houses climbing up hills so steep that they seemed to hang there, one above the other. As they approached the dock, they had to sail past a forest of masts, where hulls of rotting ships lay, abandoned by sailors gone to try their luck in the gold fields.

Everywhere in San Francisco there was building

going on. One of the deckhands told Libby there had been a terrible fire just a month before and now everyone was building with brick and iron, in case it happened again. After the quiet and loneliness of life up in the gold country, San Francisco was almost overwhelming. Almost every building they passed on the way from the wharf to the hotel was a saloon and piano music spilled from every doorway to create a cacophony of sound in the street. It seemed everybody was either coming or going. Men with packs on their backs staggered ashore excitedly as other men, slouched and disillusioned, waited to board ships sailing round the Horn back home. Supplies of every description were piled on the waterfront, some rotting or spilled in the thick bay mud, making the area smell even worse than Sacramento.

As they moved away from the foul-smelling mud of the port, they started seeing the wealth of the city. The streets were boarded over to cover the sand, and in winter the mud, which had made travelling in San Francisco so treacherous. Tall new buildings were going up on Montgomery and Kearny Streets. Fashionably dressed men and women rode past in fine carriages. Restaurants might still be in large tents, but they had gleaming white tablecloths. There were seedy, hastily built sheds which advertised themselves as boarding houses, but there were already one or two fine hotels with mirrored foyers decorated with palm trees. Libby checked into the St. Francis on the corner of Clay Street, just off the central plaza, while Ah Fong disappeared up Dupont Street where a large Chinese settlement was rapidly springing up.

In such opulent surroundings, Libby was painfully aware of their shabbiness and countrified appearance.

She hurried the girls to a dressmaker and had them all
measured for complete new wardrobes, waiting until
one good outfit was ready before she conducted any
business. She obtained the name of the Chilean merchant who brought in most of the fruits and vegetables
and arranged a meeting with him for the following
day. She spent the rest of that first day shopping
for furniture. She found that precious little could be
obtained ready-made. What furniture there was had
come by ship around the Horn and was ridiculously
expensive. But she did get referrals to a German cabi-
net maker who seemed very obliging and told her he
could make her anything she wanted. She later found
out that he had a team of men stripping the idle ships
of their teak and mahogany cabin panelling for the
wood.

By the end of the day she was able to collect the first
of her new outfits from the dressmaker and although
she thought privately that she looked rather like a
ship in full sail, at least she no longer looked shabby.
Now that she had city clothes, she was emboldened
to send a card to Mark Hopkins. A cordial message
was returned, inviting her to dinner at Brown's Hotel,
just across the square. He arrived looking very distinguished in a suit and starched white shirt. Apart from
this he showed no signs of wealth, but the way the
headwaiter treated him convinced Libby that he was
already a person of stature in the town. Although she
was now well enough dressed and her hair was tamed
with mother-of-pearl combs, Libby still felt uneasy as
she was escorted to a table in a velvet-draped alcove.
Everyone else was chatting easily, sipping champagne
and scooping oysters from the shell as if these were
normal activities. Beside them she felt like a country

bumpkin, come to the big city for the first time. She found herself glancing across at the next table to see which fork to use.

"What's wrong?" Mark Hopkins asked her.

Libby blushed. "This sounds stupid, but I'm scared of making a fool of myself," she said. "It's so long since I ate in elegant surroundings. I'm not sure I know what to do anymore."

Mark laughed. "Why worry about it?" he asked. "None of these people do. Look at that old man over there." He motioned with his head to where a paunchy, florid man was sitting between two beautiful young women in velvet gowns, their high coiffures decorated with sweeping ostrich feathers. "See what he's using to eat his oysters."

Libby looked across discreetly and saw that he was clutching his knife like a dagger and stabbing each oyster before bringing it to his mouth.

"Anything goes here," Mark whispered. "Those girls are from the Pink Palace down the street. They get a hundred dollars a night."

Libby's eyes widened as she noted the emeralds on one girl's neck.

"And see the young woman who has just come in?" Mark whispered. Libby followed the progress of a gorgeous blond who seemed to have been poured into a red satin dress with a tiny waist and enormous hooped skirt. Around her shoulders was a velvet cape which swept to the floor behind her and she demurely fanned herself as she walked with a black lace fan. Mark put his hand up to his beard and muttered into it as she went past. "She is having herself a mansion built over in North Beach with the proceeds of faro dealing. They say she's the best gambler in the city."

The word *gambler* sent Libby's thoughts racing to Gabe. She stared out across the smoke-filled room, wondering where he was and whether she would ever see him again. Then she blinked and her heart lurched as she saw him. At first she thought her eyes were playing tricks, but as he stood for a moment surveying the scene, she realized that it was truly Gabe. He stood in the doorway leading to a back room, looking even more handsome than she remembered him. He was wearing evening dress with a white ruffled shirt. A diamond stickpin sparkled at his throat. A red satin-lined cape flowed behind him. Libby felt as if she couldn't breathe as he started to walk across the restaurant toward her. He was coming closer to her table. She wanted to cry out to him. She prayed he'd look her way. Then the miracle happened. He glanced in her direction. She saw him register surprise, a half smile, then with a polite nod he swept on.

Libby got to her feet. "Excuse me one moment," she said. "I've just seen someone I know."

She hurried out after him. Gabe had stepped into the marble foyer of the hotel as she reached the door after him. A footman sprang to open it for her. She saw Gabe's cape billow out as he crossed the foyer. She opened her mouth to call out to him, but before the word could come out, she watched a beautiful woman rise from a red leather bench. She watched the woman's face break into a smile. As if in slow motion, she watched Gabe offer his arm, the woman slip her delicate white hand through the proffered arm and look up at him. Then Gabe bent slightly to give the woman the most gentle of kisses and they swept out together into the night. Libby stood there, her hand on her cheek as if she had been slapped.

She had regained her composure as she sat down again opposite Mark.

"You said hello to your friend?" Mark asked.

"No," Libby said. "I made a mistake. It wasn't my friend at all." She picked up her knife and fork. "This chicken looks delicious," she said. "I hope I haven't caused yours to get too cold."

"To be truthful with you, I do not get too excited over meat," Mark Hopkins said sadly. "I much prefer vegetables, which are still of disgustingly poor quality in this city. I am hoping you and your gardens will soon remedy that. You'll be able to keep my new store supplied and become a very rich woman in the process, of course."

Libby managed a convincing smile, but it was as if she were a puppeteer, operating the strings that moved her mouth. At the end of the meal as Mark Hopkins escorted her back to her hotel he asked, "Have you given any more thought to buying land here? There are still some good bargains, but I doubt whether there will be much longer."

"Very well," Libby said decisively. "I'll take your advice. I'll have some money sent down to you and you can buy me land. I'm sure I can't go wrong if I rely on your guidance."

"You're a wise woman," Mark said. "And you won't be sorry. In fact, if I were the marrying kind, and I'd already made the fortune I intend to make, I'd ask you to marry me—although I'm sure you wouldn't want to be stuck with an old dodderer of almost forty."

Libby smiled, touched again by his kindness.

The next day she met with *Señor* Alfonso, the Chilean merchant. He was a little round man with a pencil-thin moustache and soulful eyes. His appearance was of a harmless puppy dog but a few words with him convinced Libby that he was very astute and probably very powerful.

"I have a very good trade going," he said suspiciously. "How I know you don't take my trade from me?"

"*Señor* Alfonso, I'm just one woman," Libby said demurely. "I am growing crops to support myself and feed my family. How could I possibly be a threat to you?"

*Señor* Alfonso shrugged expressively. "Very well," he said. "Alfonso will see what he can do for you. Just tell me what you need and Alfonso will get it for you."

When Libby left him she had put in an order for apple, peach, cherry, and lemon trees as well as grape seedlings and as many fruit and vegetable seeds as he could procure. Feeling well-satisfied, she took the girls shopping and let them choose toys and candies while she treated herself to luxuries like soap and perfume, hair ornaments and silk stockings. They met Ah Fong at the dock, looking very pleased with himself.

"I meet a man from my village," he said. "He will take letter home for me with money to look for bride. Also I tell him I will need men to work in the fields. Also," he said, grinning, "I get Chinese spices and noodles and now I eat proper Chinese food again. You wait till you taste, missee."

Later that day they sailed back up to Sacramento. By the time the first rains came in early November, Libby was installed in her snug little house with new furniture and real carpets on the floor. Potatoes and winter cabbage, turnips and beets were planted in newly dug ground. A shipment of fruit trees and grape vines was on its way from Chile and she enjoyed frequent visits from her Mexican neighbors, learning Spanish as she taught Conchita English. In fact, she would have been truly content for the first time in her life if it had not been for the empty void where her heart should have been.

# CHAPTER
# 31

THE RAINS BEGAN in earnest. When the creek came out of its banks and raced wildly down into the valley sweeping down tree trunks and other debris with it, Libby was glad she had taken Ah Fong's advice about positioning her house. She sat in front of the fire as the children played with new dolls or did their lessons in newly bought schoolbooks, and sewed clothes for the baby. She was glad she had something to do and something to look forward to, or the future would be impossibly bleak. So she put all her energy into the coming baby, sewing lace around delicate pillows and embroidering coverlets.

How surprised my mother and my governess would be now if they could see that I did finally learn my embroidery stitches, she thought with a smile. Then she was overcome with sadness that her mother would probably never see her new grandchild. For a moment she picked up a pen, intent on letting her mother at least know she was safe. Then she remembered her father's threats to take the chil-

dren and have her certified insane. It was better
that they not know where she was, at least not yet.
She thought of home with longing, especially now
that Christmas was approaching—good food, good
company, presents and parlor games—and suddenly
it wasn't enough that she was able to provide a warm
secure house for her children. She wanted more. She
wanted friends and family and a place where she
belonged.

With these memories foremost in her thoughts, she
put extra effort into preparations for Christmas as she
made pies and puddings. She decorated the house
with pine branches and red berries and at night after
the children were asleep she made doll cradles to
match the real cradle waiting for the baby. A box
under her bed was full of sugar mice and Chinese
teacups, oranges and nuts, hair ribbons and bright
beads which she had bought in San Francisco for the
children's Christmas stockings.

At least they will have a happy Christmas, she
thought wistfully.

On Christmas Eve she was shelling nuts in front of
the fire when a sudden spasm of pain swept over her.
She glanced at the little girls, sitting together cutting
out Christmas garlands from paper. The second jolt
of pain was so strong it made her gasp out loud.

"What's the matter, Mama?" Eden asked, glancing
up.

"Go out to the kitchen and get Ah Fong," she said,
trying not to convey any alarm. "Put on your cape, or
you'll get wet."

Ah Fong came over right away, his hands feathery
from the goose he was plucking. "Missee want?" he
asked.

"Ah Fong, go to the neighbors and get Dona Conchita," Libby said in a low voice.

"Now?" Ah Fong asked, looking out at the rain that was sheeting down. "I not finish goose yet."

"Now," Libby said firmly. "I think the baby's coming."

Ah Fong looked at her suspiciously. "Ahh!" he said. "I go now. Take mule, not horse—too much mud."

"Yes, take the mule," Libby said, trying to talk and breathe at the same time as the next pain shook her. She went through to her room and paced up and down, unwilling to go to bed while the pains came quicker and quicker. At last they were coming so fast and strong that she undressed herself and lay down, the sweat pouring down her face. She fought not to cry out and frighten the children.

Her first two deliveries had been a blur of pain and there had been a doctor and nurses hovering around her all the time. She was very conscious that both the girls had been small babies and this baby was in no way small. The pains came faster and faster until she scarcely had time to catch her breath between them. Her abdomen felt as if it was encircled by a steel girdle which was being squeezed tighter and tighter until breathing became impossible. When the pains got too bad she bit down on the bedsheet to stop herself from crying out and frightening the children.

The children, however, had never seen their mother in bed in the middle of the day and sensed that something strange was going on.

"Mama, can we bring you something?" Eden asked, her little face tight and pinched with alarm.

"Don't you feel good, Mama?" Bliss demanded. "You want me and Eden to come and sit with you?"

"Be good children and leave Mommy alone," she managed to gasp between pains. "Everything's going to be fine. Ah Fong will be back with Dona Conchita any moment."

But as the minutes turned to hours and no help arrived, she began to feel very frightened. The storm worsened, the rain drummed against the wooden roof and the wind screamed around the chimney. She felt hot, sticky blood running down her legs and still the baby did not come. She watched the light fade from the sky and told herself that no help would arrive once it got dark.

It got darker and darker.

"Mama, it's supper time," Eden whispered around the door. "Bliss is hungry."

"Can you be a big girl and light the lamp for me?" Libby asked in scarcely more than a whisper herself. "Then you can take sissy over to the kitchen and see what you can find to eat."

"I can do it, Mama," Eden said.

Soon soft light filled the room, but it was of little comfort. It occurred to her for the first time that she might die and she wept for the baby she would not see and for the children who would have no parents. She prayed that Conchita would bring them up as her own. She slipped in and out of consciousness, welcoming each brief respite when time was suspended and the world became unreal. It seemed to her that she was a ring of molten iron and was being forged in a furnace, stretched and molded into an impossible shape which must surely break her apart. Outside, the dark red glow of the furnace was the light of an open door and it would take only a small effort to fly toward it.

She was dimly conscious of a last great rending, then fireflies hovered around her face, disembodied heads floated in starlight, and she was suddenly cold.

"*Gracias a Dios. Est un nino*," she heard a distant voice saying and from very far away came the sound of a baby crying. A warm hand was holding hers. Someone was sponging her forehead.

They're laying me out for burial, she thought and was glad that she was not going to be buried unwashed. That's good, she told herself and slipped away.

When she heard noises again she opened her eyes very cautiously because the light was fierce and she was frightened to see whether she was in heaven or hell. She was very surprised, therefore, to find that it was ordinary daylight, a weak, wintry sun, shining in through her window. Someone was humming in the next room, a sweet, high voice that she couldn't quite identify.

"Mother?" she asked, because the voice reminded her of childhood.

Immediately, a face looked around the door and a small, round woman scurried to her side. "Ah, *querida*, you wake," she said, smoothing back the wet hair on Libby's forehead. "Miguel!"

Libby recognized Don Miguel's gray hair as he stood uneasily in the doorway. "My felicitations, *Señora* Libby," he said.

"Is it daytime?" Libby asked.

"*Si*. Is *Navidad*. Christmas," Miguel said, smiling broadly. "You have the Christmas baby."

"My baby?" Libby asked, cautiously bringing her hand down to her stomach. "I have my baby?"

"*Sí*. He sleeps. Beautiful boy," Conchita said, beaming at Libby.

"I have a son," Libby said, closing her eyes in contentment.

"Thanks to God," Conchita said. She wiped a tear.

"My wife fears last night that we come too late," Miguel said softly. "There was so much water. We could not cross. When we come we find you lying like dead and the baby just arrived. My wife sit with you all night and pray."

"Thank you," Libby said, reaching out to touch her hand.

"*De nada*," Conchita said. She moved across the room and bent to the cradle on the floor. Then she placed Libby's son in her arms. At the sudden movement he opened dark-blue eyes and seemed to look straight up at his mother, staring at her unblinking.

"He is a beautiful boy," Libby said.

"What name you give him?" Miguel asked.

Libby wanted to say Gabriel but she had a sudden inspiration. "He's a Christmas baby so he should have a Christmas name," she said.

"Jesus. Jesus good name," Conchita said reverently.

Libby smiled. "I can't call him Jesus," she said. "Imagine opening the door and shouting, "Jesus, lunch is ready."

"Is good name in Spanish," Conchita insisted. "Many men called Jesus."

"Not in English," Libby said. "He'd get teased in school. But I could call him Noel. That's a nice name, isn't it? And I'd like to call him Michael after Don Miguel."

"Not after his father?" Miguel asked, showing concern.

"His father is gone," Libby said. "I must forget the past and think of the future now."

# CHAPTER
# 32

THE WINTER RAINS ended, spring came with sweet-scented winds and new green grass, Libby's strength returned gradually, and Noel Michael continued to thrive. He lay on his blanket, watching his mother and sisters, his dark eyes seeming to be interested in everything around him, breaking into a body-wiggling smile when anyone paid him attention. To Libby he was still a miracle. She would watch him as she nursed him, marveling at the chubby hand clutching her finger, still amazed that she had produced anything so perfect. To the girls he was a large doll. He allowed himself to be carried and held, tucked in blankets and dressed in bonnets for long periods before finally putting up a howl of protest when Bliss squeezed him too tightly.

In the fields Ah Fong was watching over new shoots as if they were all his own new babies. When he wasn't pulling up any weed that dared to appear between his plants, he was prowling the Flores' land, coming home with a sack full of cow patties which he then

dug into his soil. He made the final arrangements
for four Chinese field workers to join him and Libby
had a construction crew build a line of one-room cabins behind the main house. The first winter cabbage
was harvested and sold. The first spring crops were
planted in their place and a procession of ox carts
bumped along the rutted track up from Sacramento
bearing fruit trees with roots in burlap, gnarled, dead-
seeming grape vine stock, and bags of seed corn, plus
packets of tomato, squash, melon, and pepper seeds.
Libby looked doubtfully at the peppers. "I'm not sure
about these," she said. "Will anyone want them?"

"Jalapeños, *si*!" Conchita said excitedly. "All miners
like jalapeños. Very hot! Make good chili beans."

So the peppers were planted and Ah Fong started
work on planting the fruit trees, looking out each day
for his expected helpers. The two lemon trees went
next to the house where Libby could admire them
and she started a grape arbor for shade. Don Miguel
also suggested she plant a cactus hedge around her
property to keep out wandering deer and cattle. He
gave her plants to start one around her fields but she
rejected the idea of one around her house.

"I chose this site for the view," she said. "I don't
want to look at a lot of prickly leaves."

"One day you might be glad of it," Don Miguel said.

She did, however, accept from him a fierce half-
grown puppy to train as a watch dog. He proved to be
afraid of nothing and tireless, chasing the two kittens
onto the roof when there was nothing else to do. He
also became completely devoted to Libby, not letting
her out of his sight for a moment.

Up in the mines the water slowly dropped in the
riverbeds and allowed more miners to go back to

work. It had been a hard winter for many of them. They had not made the profits of the year before and those newly arrived last fall had been near to starving. Rumors of highway robbery and marauding bands of outlaws filtered down from the mines, magnified with each telling. Libby, occupied with her family and her farm, was little worried about the rumors. They rarely saw strangers, not being on a main route up from Sacramento. She felt that her house was far enough removed to be safe and went unconcerned about her chores.

She was in the middle of hanging out a line full of washing when she heard the sound of hoofbeats. She looked up to see Don Miguel and his son riding up in great agitation.

"Thank God you are safe," Don Miguel said as she came to the door. "We feared the bandits had come to you too."

"Bandits?" Libby looked up in alarm.

"We were herding cattle for spring branding when a group of armed men rode up," Manuel said, glancing across at his father.

"They pointed guns at us. At first I think they kill us and I say my last prayers," Don Miguel said. "But they keep us there, with many guns pointed at us while their brothers drive off twenty of my cattle."

"That's terrible," Libby said.

"When they are done, they laugh and tell me that they will be back for more, whenever they want them," Don Miguel added.

"But they can't get away with it," Libby said. "Could you identify them? You must go to the sheriff in Sutter Creek."

Don Miguel shook his head with a bitter smile.

"What would he do? He is Yankee like these men. He is probably friend of these men. There is no justice for Californios in Yankee territory."

"We must get more men, as I have been saying, Papa," Manuel said. "We will hire our own guns to guard the cattle day and night."

"I do not like shooting and killing," Don Miguel said. "I do not wish to be responsible for bloodshed."

"Then what is the answer?" Manuel demanded angrily.

Don Miguel shrugged expressively. "I do not know, my son," he said. "God's will is the answer." He turned his deep-set eyes to Libby. "But more I am concerned for you, *Señora* Libby. Living alone with these animals around. Will you not bring the children to our house until these bad the men have gone?"

"Thank you, Don Miguel," Libby said, "but I can't leave my fields now. This is the most important time of year. I'll have four Chinese employees to supervise by next week and crops to be taken to market as soon as they are harvested. Besides, what could they steal from me? My money is in the bank and I have nothing of real value in the house."

Don Miguel looked at her with embarrassment. "These men are not just hungry for food," he said softly.

"I keep my rifle loaded at all times," Libby said, "and Buster barks when he hears anything suspicious."

"I think Buster needs to grow before he can defend you from *banditos*," Manuel said, smiling.

"I am saying you need a cactus fence," Don Miguel said. "Only a fool would try to come through prickly pear and you can defend one gate."

"I'll think about it," Libby said. "But I wish you would take your complaint to the sheriff. I'll come with you, if you like. I'll help you get justice."

Don Miguel shook his head. "No, *señora*. I cannot let you do this. If you speak for Mexicanos, whom these men think are so lowly, you may also find yourself with bullet in your back."

Libby watched them ride away, angry at her powerlessness. It seemed so unfair that Don Miguel and his son, who behaved in every way like gentlemen, should be victimized by any uncouth lout who could call himself a Yankee. When she got back to the house she did double-check the rifle and the ammunition supplies and she wondered if she should get guns for the new Chinese laborers.

The days passed with no unfriendly visitors and Libby relaxed her vigilance. Then, one evening she was bringing in washing from the line when Buster started barking. She scanned the horizon, listening for horses, but saw nobody. Buster continued barking, the hair on his neck erect as he looked down to the creek.

"What is it, boy?" Libby asked. She slowly put the washing into the basket at her feet. As she straightened she noticed a movement and two men came out of the willows, walking slowly up the slope toward her. They were unshaven and ragged, with shapeless hats pulled well down over their faces. Libby put her hand on Buster's collar.

"What do you want?" she called.

"Good day to you, ma'am," one of them said in a low, gravelly voice with a marked southern accent. "We was wondering if y'all had any odd jobs you needed done."

"Thank you, but I already have a helper who does my odd jobs," Libby said.

"We're mighty hungry, ma'am," the other man said, walking closer to Libby. "We could sure use a bite of food, if you can spare it."

"I'll see what I can find for you," Libby said. "Why don't you wait right there and I'll come out with it."

She hurried back to the house, taking Buster with her. She tried to tell herself that these were poor starving men and she owed them charity, but every instinct warned her not to trust them. She burst into the kitchen and grabbed the surprised Ah Fong. "Listen to me," she whispered. "Take both the horses. Lead them quietly away from the house and then ride as fast as you can to get Don Miguel. Tell him bandits."

"You be all right here alone?" he whispered back.

"I'm going to get the rifle," she whispered. "Go!" she added as he opened his mouth to protest.

As she came out of the kitchen she gasped to see the men right at the doorway. Buster was growling, showing his teeth.

"Cute puppy," one of the men said. "Might amount to something if he grows up." He aimed a kick in the dog's direction. "Shut up, dog," he said. Buster cringed and dodged but kept growling.

"I thought I told you to wait down there," Libby said angrily. "I don't want my children scared."

She still could not see their faces. "You live here all alone then?" one of them drawled. He was a tall, gangly man, like a daddy longlegs spider and his torn pants came up above his ankles.

"I have my field workers," she lied. "They live behind the house. They'll be coming up from my fields shortly. It's getting dark."

"We didn't see nobody in the fields, did we, Bo?" the tall man drawled.

"Sit down if you want food," Libby said. She started into the house.

"Kitchen's out here, ma'am, ain't it?" one of them called after her.

"But I keep my dishes in the house," she said short-ly. She ran up the steps, snatched the rifle from the wall, and threw her shawl over her, hiding the hand with the rifle in it. "Stay here and don't move," she whispered to the children, firmly shutting their bed-room door.

"Mighty cozy place you got here," came a voice behind her and the tall man stood leaning against the doorframe. "Seems a pity you ain't got no no man to share it with." He leaned in farther. "Specially that nice big feather bed through there." He grinned, showing a mouth of blackened teeth.

In the back bedroom Noel began to cry. The man looked at her with amusement. "Seems like you can find yourself a man when you need one," he said, "and you found yourself one not too long ago."

"I must ask you to leave my house," Libby said. "I was intending to be charitable and feed you, but I'll not be insulted. Get out and take your friend with you."

The man's grin widened. "Now who's going to make me get out, little lady?" he asked.

Libby threw back her shawl and levelled the rifle. "I killed a man with this once," she said. "I wouldn't hesitate to do it again."

"No sense in being hostile like," the man said. "I was only tryin' to make pleasant conversation. Didn't mean no harm, ma'am. Me and Willie could sure use some food and then we'll be on our way."

He started to back down the steps. Libby kept him covered all the way to the kitchen. Then she grabbed a lump of cold meat and a piece of bread, putting them together on a plate.

"Here," she said, putting the plate down without taking her eyes off the men. "Take this and go. Get off my property and don't come back."

She stood there, rifle still pointed at them as Bo slunk toward the plate and picked up the food. "Much obliged, ma'am," he muttered. He handed the food to his partner, then without warning, he rushed her. She shot and the bullet went wide as he grabbed the gun stock. Before he could snatch it from her, however, Buster sank his teeth into Bo's bare shin.

"Ow, get him off me," he yelled, hitting out at the dog and giving Libby a chance to regain the rifle.

"Get out while you're still alive," Libby said, calmly reloading the spent chamber. "I'm going to count to five and then I start shooting."

Before she could reach three the men began to move off. From over the hill came the sound of hoofbeats and yells. The men looked up in alarm as Don Miguel, his son, and Ah Fong all galloped into view.

"My workers returning," Libby called with satisfaction as the men scrambled to reach the creek.

"Are you all right?" Don Miguel asked, springing from his horse with gun drawn as Manuel wheeled after the men.

Libby nodded. "They were just leaving," she said, not wanting to tell him what a narrow escape she'd had.

Manuel stayed on guard all night, but the men did not return. "Those kind are like vultures," he said. "They only prey on those who cannot defend themselves. I do not think they will be back."

Libby hoped he was right. She couldn't help wondering how many more like them there were, roaming the countryside taking what they could, preying on the weak, beyond morals and beyond law. She was glad when the new Chinese helpers arrived. She decided it might be wise to arm them, and with Don Miguel's help taught them how to use rifles. She also gave in to Don Miguel's suggestion and had her workers plant a cactus hedge around the house as their first task. She now slept with her own rifle beside the bed and chained Buster outside the front door on guard.

She did not have the rifle with her, however, in the middle of the day when she was out in the kitchen baking bread. Buster cocked his head and sprang up barking. She came out of the kitchen, her apron and hands covered in flour, to see a dark figure riding up to the house. He also had his hat pulled down over his eyes and there was an air of menace about him. Libby thought of Ah Fong and the others out of reach in the fields, the little girls with them. Without waiting to hail the stranger, she raced to the house and got down the rifle, then she planted her feet squarely on the front porch as she watched the stranger dismount and come toward the house.

"That's far enough," she called and cocked the rifle. "State your business from there."

"I'm looking for a Mrs. Grenville," said a shocked voice. "I was told she lived around here. Would you happen to know where I might find her?"

He looked up so that Libby saw his face clearly for the first time. "Good God," she said, lowering the rifle. "It's Edward Percival Knotts!"

# CHAPTER 33

IF LIBBY WAS surprised to see her family's young lawyer friend riding up on a horse in the middle of the Californian wasteland, Edward Percival Knotts seemed even more surprised to see her.

"Libby? Is that really you?" he asked. "I can hardly recognize you. You look so different."

"Maybe it's the lack of velvet," Libby said with a smile. "I'm sure I used to look different in velvet but it's such an impractical fabric out here."

"I just can't believe it," Edward Knotts said, shaking his head. "Look at you—you look like a frontiers-woman with your dark skin and your wild hair and your trusty gun in your hand."

"That's because I am a frontiers-woman," Libby said. "I've no idea how you managed to find me, but you're very welcome. Please, come inside."

Edward Knotts got down stiffly from his horse and tied it to the porch rail. The way he walked up the steps told Libby that it was a long time since he'd sat in a saddle. She grinned and led the way into the house.

"What are you doing out here, anyway?" she asked, motioning to the sofa.

"Looking for you," Edward Knotts said, wiping his forehead with a silk handkerchief from his breast pocket. His face was very red and mottled yellow with dust. "Your father had been going down to the waterfront, trying to get news of you. Finally, he met a man who had seen a lady with two little girls and a Boston accent but no man with her. Your father asked me if I'd undertake the journey and I agreed, although if I'd known what lay ahead, I don't think I should have been so willing, even for your sake."

"You had a bad voyage?"

"*Bad* is not the word for it," Edward Knotts said, replacing his silk handkerchief, now streaked with dirt and sweat, delicately in his pocket. "It was pure torment. I had to share a cabin with three other men, all of whom snored and had the most appalling manners. The food was a disgrace—no fresh vegetables for weeks and the most awful, unidentifiable stews and puddings you've ever seen. We were all seasick around the Horn, and to cap it all, three horrible days in San Francisco. That place is a hellhole if ever there was one, and then I had to pay a completely ridiculous price for a horse in Sacramento."

"Poor Edward," Libby said, smiling to herself. "What an ordeal."

"I suppose you must have gone through pretty much the same sort of thing yourself," Edward said.

"Not exactly. I came overland," Libby said, still smiling. "We didn't have to worry about seasickness."

"Well, that's a blessing," he said, not hearing the sarcasm in her voice. He looked at her, shaking his head as if he could not believe she was real. "I think it's a miracle that you've survived so long. And you're looking well too. Your father was sure that you'd be destitute by now, if you were still alive."

"On the contrary," Libby said. "I'm doing rather well. I own this land and I also own land in San Francisco. I plan to make a small fortune in fruit and vegetables this summer and if all goes as I'm hoping it will, I'll build a house in San Francisco for the winters and spend just the summers out here."

Edward Knotts paled visibly. "You're planning to stay on out here—for the long term?"

"I think so," Libby said. "I like the climate. I like the country. I think it has a great future."

"But the lack of culture. The lack of civilization," Edward Knotts said.

"I have very agreeable neighbors," Libby said, "and I can go down to San Francisco when it seems too lonely up here."

Edward Knotts looked around the empty room. "You keep using the first person," he said. "Can I assume that you never managed to find poor Hugh?"

"I found him," Libby said, "but he's now dead. He was killed in an Indian uprising."

"I'm sorry to hear that," Edward said. "It must have been a great shock to you."

"I have learned to survive a great many shocks."

"And your daughters?"

"They're out in the fields down below the house with my Chinese workers. They think it is the greatest treat to plant seeds and pull weeds. They should all be up for lunch soon. I was in the middle of baking bread. Come and talk to me and I'll make you some coffee or tea."

Edward Knotts got to his feet. "This place is really cozy," he said, as if he had noticed it for the first time.

"It's fine for now," Libby said. "It only has two bedrooms and no guest quarters, so I'm afraid you'll have to sleep on the sofa, but I had to concentrate more on my fields than my house this year. When I have more time I plan to build an adobe home like my neighbors have."

"A what?"

"Mexican brick. It's so delightfully cool. Come on, the kitchen's out here—another trick one learns in a hot climate."

She led the way down the steps. Edward's horse stamped impatiently at the railing. "We'll have Ah Fong put it in the corral with the other horses and give it something to eat," Libby said. "He won't be long. It's almost noon."

"I can't believe you," Edward said, following her into the kitchen. "You're not only surviving on your own, but thriving on it."

"Maybe I was made for this sort of life," she said. "I never felt satisfied with my life at home." She took a pot from the stove and poured him coffee.

"You are not lonely?" he asked.

"Sometimes."

"You don't feel the need for a man in your life?"

"But I have a man in my life," Libby said.

"A new man?" Edward asked, shocked.

"Very new," Libby said. "Would you like to come and meet him?"

"He's here? Now?"

"He certainly is," Libby said. "Come on, he's in bed, but he'd love to get up and meet you."

"Libby, wait a minute . . . I can't, I mean, it's just

not. . . ." Edward babbled as she marched into the house ahead of him. A few seconds later she reappeared with Noel in her arms.

"Meet Noel Michael Grenville," she said.

Edward Knott's face was a picture of amazement. "You had a baby out here?" he demanded. Then more softly, "Was Hugh alive to see him?"

"Hugh died four months before he was born," Libby said.

"You poor thing," Edward said gently. "Fate has indeed dealt you some cruel blows."

"My father would no doubt say that it served me right," Libby said, nuzzling Noel up to her face so that he giggled in delight. "I'm surprised that he wanted you to search for me after so long."

"They say that absence makes the heart grow fonder," Edward said hesitantly. "And, of course, your mother missed you terribly."

"Poor Mother," Libby said. "It must have been an ordeal for her."

"For all of us," Edward said, "not knowing if you were alive or dead. Your father is a stubborn man, as you very well know, but I'm sure he has regretted a million times his parting words to you."

"Now you'll be able to go back and reassure them that their fragile little blossom has turned into a sturdy vine," Libby said, smiling at him. "I'll write them both a long letter."

Just then Buster started barking and there were squeals from the track below the house. The two girls came running up the path, yelling as they ran.

"Mama! We saw a snake and Ah Fong chopped off its head with the hoe and it went on wriggling and wriggling," Eden yelled.

"And Lee is going to make it into a soup," Bliss shouted.

They both stopped short when Libby and Edward appeared at the door. Edward took in the two tall, skinny girls, barefoot and both wearing old brown ginghams. "Merciful heavens," he said under his breath.

"Girls, we have a visitor," Libby said. "Do you remember Mr. Knotts. He often came to your grandfather's house in Boston."

"I don't remember my grandfather's house," Bliss said.

"I do," Eden said shyly. "And I think I remember you. You used to play croquet with us when we went visiting."

"That's right," Edward said, "and I remember that you always used to beat me. I don't suppose you play much croquet here."

"We don't have a lawn," Eden said. "It would be a waste of water."

"We might plant one later, when we see how this year has gone," Libby said. "Croquet might be rather nice, or how about a tennis court?"

"Who would we play with?" Eden asked, laughing. "Don Miguel's too old and Conchita's too fat. That leaves Manuel and the Chinese."

"Go and wash your hands for lunch," Libby said, "then you can help me carry the food through." She turned to Edward as the girls ran on ahead. "You see, they are thriving perfectly well, aren't they?"

"Yes, but Libby," Edward stammered, "not growing into the little ladies your parents would expect."

"There is not much call for little ladies out here," Libby said dryly. "I'm sure you too would welcome a wash before lunch. You can use the jug in my room. Come, I'll show you."

She led the way through to her room, noting how plain and simple it must appear after the overdone elegance of Boston. Then she ran across to the kitchen to check the meal with Ah Fong. The haunch of venison, steaming under thick brown gravy, would have graced any table and Edward Knott's eyes registered his surprise and anticipation when Ah Fong put the platter on the table.

"This was marvelous," Edward said when he had finished every scrap on his plate. "Everything tasted so good."

"You're lucky that my neighbors shot a deer," Libby said. "The beef from their cattle is very tough and stringy. We're used to it now, but you wouldn't be. But if only you'd come a month or two later, what a feast you could have had. I'll ask Ah Fong to see if any of the new potatoes are ready, but you're too early for tomatoes or fresh strawberries or grapes."

"You're growing all those things?"

"And plenty more. I aim to supply Sacramento and then even San Francisco."

"Good heavens," Edward said again. "Who would have believed it? Although I suppose I would. You always were in trouble for being too headstrong when we were children. Remember how we were forbidden to walk out on the rocks at the seashore and you did it and were swept off by that wave?"

"And you pulled me ashore?" Libby asked, laughing. "Dear Edward. You were always trying to keep me out of trouble."

"Maybe that is still my role," he said, blushing slightly.

After lunch, when Noel was put down for his afternoon nap, Libby took Edward down to the fields. Edward pretended to be politely interested as Libby showed him how she was training grapevines and how she planned to ship her fresh strawberries down to San Francisco before they spoiled. Their conversation deliberately steered clear of Boston.

They had tiny new potatoes for dinner that night and when the children were in bed, they sat together on the porch, talking.

"So tell me everything that has happened to you since you left home," he said.

Libby began to tell him, finding how difficult it was to leave Gabe out of the story and how melodramatic her adventures now sounded. In the end she glossed over almost everything except the last events: finding Hugh, his stupid, wasted death, and the cabin burning. Edward never took his eyes off her once, looking at her with such pity and understanding that she kept wanting to laugh. He reminded her of a spaniel her mother had once owned, who also sat with head on one side, gazing with big, devoted eyes.

"But you must tell me all the news from back home," she said. "Tell me what has been going on in the civilized world."

He began recounting everything he could think of; a second son for dear Katherine, a new house for this friend, a new carriage for another, a scandal in politics, a scandal in love life. "Of course, we've completely cut off the Bensons," he said. "You remember Ginnie Benson? It turns out she was carrying on an affair behind her husband's back for years and nobody knew about it. It was only when the child was born with dark hair and everyone in the family was so fair that people remembered the music teacher was dark. My dear, what an outrage it caused. It's completely ruined Toby Benson's chances of running for legislature, of course. What a tragedy."

Libby looked away, staring hard at a mockingbird sitting on a fence post, singing its heart out. How small the whole Bostonian world sounded, how narrow and petty. She remembered Ginnie Benson very well— a vivacious young girl who loved to dance—and Toby Benson, solid, middle-aged, and very boring. No wonder the music teacher had seemed so attractive. What would Edward think about me if he knew the truth? she wondered.

# CHAPTER
# 34

THE DAYS PASSED and Edward showed no signs of returning to San Francisco. They went riding together and she took him over to a meal with Don Miguel and Conchita. She showed him around the nearest mining sites and he tried his hand halfheartedly at panning.

"I believe you're hanging on here until the strawberries are ripe," she said, teasing him.

"I'm hanging on here because I'm enjoying your company so much," he said gently. "I had forgotten how much I always enjoyed myself with you. You are like a breath of fresh air, Libby."

Libby laughed, but she was touched.

When she was putting the children to bed that night Eden asked, "Is it true that I used to have a whole closet full of dresses back in Boston? And did we have ice cream all the time?"

"I suppose so," Libby said. "Has Mr. Knotts been talking to you about Boston?"

"Yes," Eden said, blushing.

"What did he say?"

"He asked us if we'd really like to go back one day."

"And what did you say?"

"I said maybe someday," Eden answered truthfully. "I'd like to go to dances and out skating in winter and picnics on the seashore. Do you miss all that stuff, Mama?"

"Sometimes," Libby said. "I miss having people around sometimes. I miss being able to be carefree. But after this summer we should have the money to do what we want."

"You mean take a trip back to Boston if we wanted to?"

"If we wanted to," Libby said.

"I want to see my grandfather," Bliss said stubbornly from her bed. "I want to show my new baby brother to my grandparents. Do you think they'll like Noel, Mama?"

"I should think anybody would like Noel," Libby said. "He's a delightful baby. But he's too young to take on a long trip yet."

When she lay in bed that night, hearing Edward's rhythmic breathing coming from the living room, she thought seriously about Boston. What would it be like to be back in a place where they were safe, where they would never have to worry again about hunger or bandits or lack of doctors or wildfires? A place where men treated you as if you were made of finest china and held out their hands to escort you up steps, opened doors for you, stood up when you came into the room and jumped to hand you your wrap, the way Edward was doing.

There are things that I miss, she thought, and having a charming man to wait on me is one of them!

Her thoughts went one stage further. Why, of all the men her father could have asked, did Edward Knotts volunteer to come?

The next day they strolled together along the creek, beneath the willows. Tiny fish darted through crystal-clear pools. Libby sat on a large rock, jutting out over the water.

"You look just like a mermaid," Edward said. "I shall expect you to start combing your long flowing hair and luring poor sailors to their death at any minute."

Libby looked down to him and smiled. "Dear Edward," she said. "You are the first man who has treated me like a woman in so very long. I can't tell you how much I've enjoyed seeing you again."

"And I you, Libby," he said. "When I heard that Hugh was dead, I should have felt sadness, but do you know what happened? My heart did a complete somersault. She's free! It shouted to me. And all this time I've been plucking up the courage to ask you." He came closer until he was standing beside her. "I know you don't love me the way you loved Hugh, Libby," he said, "but you're comfortable with me, aren't you? We laugh when we're together. I'd make you a good husband and be a good father to those poor children who need a father so badly." He reached out tentatively and took the fingers of her left hand. "Won't you marry me and come back to Boston? This is no life for a woman like you. You've survived wonderfully well, but the ordeal is over now. You can come home with pride and your head held high. What do you say, Libby?"

"I'm very touched, Edward," Libby said, "but I need time to think it over."

"That's wonderful, Libby," he said, his face flushing bright red. "That's much better than a straight no. I can keep on hoping."

"I want to make sure of one thing first," Libby said. "That you are not offering to marry me out of pity."

"Pity? Good God, no!" Edward said. "The very opposite, in fact. I want you to come home."

Home, Libby thought as they went back silently to the house. Just where was home? Did she really belong with someone like Edward Percival Knotts?

She glanced at him out of the corner of her eye. He was walking, pink and panting, back up the hill, pausing to mop his brow with his handkerchief. He was solid and reliable. He'd make the children a good father. Even if she could never love him, he'd always been devoted to her, which was better than nothing.

This was her chance to get back to a civilized world where food came from a store and her greatest worry would be over the color of her new hat. She didn't want to be alone forever. Who would she ever find to marry out here? Didn't she want to be safe?

The arguments were very compelling. The children did deserve more than this savage existence, she admitted. There was nobody to protect her here, and as for ever seeing Gabe again—she had to admit he was gone forever. He was now probably settled with somebody else, maybe even with that beautiful woman at the hotel. This might be her one chance of happiness.

"Are you still thinking it over, Libby?" he asked at dinner.

She nodded. "It's a big decision to make."

"Then don't make the decision right now. Come back to Boston with me and we can have the whole

voyage to decide whether marriage is right for us. I'll
respect your wishes, although I hope that all those
weeks on the ship will be enough to convince you
that you love me."

Libby laughed. "You are very sweet, Edward," she
said. "You've always been a good friend to me. I
am still touched that you made this terrible journey
for me."

"I'd do anything for you," he said. "If you marry
me, I'll be your slave forever, I promise you. What a
wonderful life we could have, Libby. We'll have the
finest house in town and maybe a little summer place
at the Cape. You'd like that, wouldn't you? Right where
you fell in the ocean! Maybe we could get a house at
the edge of town where you could have a big garden,
since you are now so interested in growing things."

"All this is going to cost a lot of money, Edward,"
Libby said. "Your law practice must be going very
well, or have you come into a fortune since I saw
you last?"

Edward turned very red. "I am not penniless,
Libby," he said, "and of course you are not without
money yourself. In fact your father has hinted . . ."
He broke off, then said hastily, "Of course I was
just speaking in the long term. Long-term plans and
dreams, Libby."

But Libby was sharp enough to notice his embarrassment. Was her money the big attraction after all,
she wondered. He must know that she stood to inherit
a large fortune if her father reinstated her in the will.
Had they made some sort of bargain between them,
her father and Edward? He was to bring her home
and in return was to get her hand and a settlement?
She could imagine them sitting on either side of the

fireplace in the big leather chairs, calmly making those plans, talking out her future as if she had no say in it at all.

Unable to sleep that night as she tried to get her jumbled thoughts in order, she went though to the children's room. She looked down at the three little angelic faces. She wanted to do what was right for them. And she supposed they would be better off with a father and a home in Boston.

Eden opened her eyes as her mother stood over her. "What's the matter, Mama?" she whispered.

"I just came to check that you're all right," Libby said.

"I thought we were getting ready to go to Boston," Eden said.

Libby smiled. "What gave you that idea?"

"Mr. Knotts said we'd be leaving soon," Eden said seriously. "He said we'd all be going to Boston together."

"Did he?" Libby said. "What else did he say?"

"He said our grandparents wanted to see us again and you'd have to agree."

"I see," Libby said quietly. "Mr. Knotts doesn't know me very well, does he?" she asked, bending to give Eden a kiss. "If he did, he'd know how very stubborn I am and how hard it is to make me do something I don't want to."

Eden wrapped her arms around her mother's neck. "So we're not going with him?"

"Do you want to?"

"Not if I have to wear shoes again," Eden said.

Libby laughed. "You'll have to wear shoes again one day, just as I'll have to wear corsets. But I guess it can wait a little while."

Next morning Libby faced Edward calmly. "I can't marry you," she said, "although I thank you for the kind offer. I'll always appreciate it, Edward, but it would be wrong to marry without love. If I married you, it would only be a way to escape from this terrible burden of responsibility I feel for my children. But I've grown strong out here. I'm brave enough to resist the temptation to escape. I'd like to see it through out here, to see if I have my father's ability with money after all."

Edward had turned very red again. "It's not right for you to waste your life out here, and think of those poor children. They are growing up, if you'll pardon my saying so, like savages, Libby."

"I plan to find them a governess soon," Libby said. "And I've been teaching them myself. Besides, they are my children and I'm the only one who can decide how I want them brought up."

"Not exactly true," Edward said, his face flushing once more.

"What are you trying to say?" Libby asked suspiciously.

Edward's face turned even darker red. "Your father has filed documents to make himself official guardian of the two girls."

"He has what?"

"Now, please calm yourself Libby and do try to see sense," Edward said. "I had my instructions to bring the girls home with me, whether you wanted to come or not. Your father is now their legal guardian."

"In the state of Massachusetts, maybe," Libby said, "but I am not in the state of Massachusetts."

"I think they would stand up in a court of law out here," Edward said.

"You'd really do that, Edward?" Libby asked, fighting to remain calm. "You'd really have my children taken away from me?"

Edward cleared his throat in embarrassment. "I had hoped it wouldn't come to this, Libby, but I do represent your father. As a lawyer, my responsibility is to my client. I'm afraid I'm going to have to present these documents at the nearest court, wherever that may be."

Libby got to her feet. "Do your damndest, Edward, but you'll not manage to take these children away from me. There's only one law here, and it is the gun. If you show up at this house again, you'll find my rifle waiting for you."

"Libby, this is so uncivilized," Edward said, the color draining from his face.

"So is trying to sneak a woman's children away from her on the pretense of coming to court her," Libby said.

"It wasn't a pretense. I really did want to marry you. I still do," Edward said. "I would not have undertaken the journey if I had no personal feelings for you."

"Naturally," Libby said coldly, "but I suspect the promise of a large settlement helped sway your feelings, didn't it, Edward?" She turned away from him. "If I ever marry again, believe me, it will be someone who is stronger than me and who can't be bought at any price."

"And where will you find him in these backwoods, Libby?" Edward asked.

"You'd be surprised at what there is to find in these backwoods, Edward," Libby said. "Now please pack your things and go. It's a long ride back to Sacramento."

# CHAPTER
# 35

FOR SEVERAL WEEKS after Edward Knotts' hasty departure on his rented horse, Libby did not let the children out of her sight. She would only allow them down to the fields when she was with them and she kept her rifle with her at all times. She also told Don Miguel and Manuel of the situation and they had instructions to ride up and disappear with the children if a large group of strangers was seen approaching. But as spring turned to summer and no posse made its way up from Sacramento, Libby began to believe that either Edward Knotts had not been able to prove his case in a California court, or else, which she rather suspected, that he was essentially a coward and afraid to face this new hostile frontiers-woman and her gun. She wondered if he would lie when he went home and claim not to have found her.

*April 28, 1851. I had a very narrow escape,* she wrote in her diary. *I cannot believe that I seriously considered marrying Edward Knotts. What a miserable life I would have condemned not only myself but the children to. He is*

*obviously weak enough to be swayed by the wind and clearly
did not love me at all.*

She had purchased a new, leatherbound book in
San Francisco and had begun to write in it again after
Noel's birth. It seemed right and proper to start a new
diary with the beginning of a new life. As for the time
between the loss of her old diary and the start of the
new, she felt no need to put it down on paper. It was
all indelibly written in her heart.

She did realize, of course, as she finished writing,
that she had now sealed her fate and was stuck in
California for good. There would now be no chance
of going home. Her father was now irrevocably her
enemy, but it didn't seem to matter anymore. She
was more angry than hurt that her own father had
tried to trick her out of her children. He obviously
didn't love me very much, she decided, or he would
not have tried to do such an underhanded and terrible thing.

She began to worry less. Everything began to blossom and produce fruit in great abundance. The
Chinese workers picked nonstop and Libby made
daily rounds of the nearest stores and weekly trips
down to Hopkins' store in Sacramento. She even
started sending the less perishable stuff by steamer
to San Francisco and received more orders from that
city than she could fill.

When she came back from Sacramento, her head
was full of plans for expansion. It seemed that there
was a market for as much as she could ever grow. Even
if she doubled or tripled the size of the fields, she'd still
be able to sell at the rate San Francisco was growing. If
she then bought her own fast-freight wagons, she'd be
able to get the perishable stuff down without spoiling.

Just think what they'd pay for fresh strawberries once a week, she thought. The big mansion on the hill where other mansions were already going up did not seem so far off.

"I think the time has come to hire more workers and prepare more land, Ah Fong," she said as they walked together between rows of head-high, feathery corn. "Can you arrange to come down to San Francisco with me and find more Chinese?"

Ah Fong didn't speak at once. Instead, he felt at a growing corn ear. "Missee, do you know when we last had rain?" he asked.

"Not for a while," Libby said.

Ah Fong nodded. "Not much since first of year. None for three months."

"But the stream has water in it year round," Libby said. "I thought that was one of the reasons we chose this site. And you've dug all these nice little channels."

"Stream has almost no water no more," Ah Fong said. "Not since last week. Come see."

They walked together down to the stream bank. Where a lively current usually swirled between rocks there was now the barest trickle of brown water. Small fish darted in isolated puddles.

"But it can't be dry already," Libby said. "It was flowing last year in October when we had had no rain for six months or more. Something must be wrong."

"Like what?"

"I don't know," Libby said, "but I aim to find out. Get the horses saddled up. You're coming with me."

Together they followed the course of the stream up into the hills. They passed moss-grown rocks that had

been hidden by waterfalls and saw a bridge spanning
water only a couple of inches deep.

"Something must have happened, Ah Fong," Libby
said. "This stretch of river was being mined last year.
Now there's nobody here."

The land was indeed surprisingly devoid of life.
Patches of bare earth and blackened stones showed
where miners' camps had been. There were even
deserted cabins with doors swinging open. Nothing
moved in the oak woodlands. It was as if a giant
hand had come down and plucked up every other
living thing except for the two riders. The valley narrowed and the path beside it began to climb, winding
around large rocks. At last Ah Fong looked up and
whistled through his teeth.

"There your water, missus," he said.

Libby looked too and sat staring, her mouth open
in disbelief. Across the valley now stretched a high
earthen dam.

"What have they done!" Libby exclaimed. "Come,
Ah Fong. Let's see what is going on."

The path was blocked off by the wall of dirt, so
they had to make their way up and around, coming
out onto a ridge above the dammed valley. From this
vantage position they could see an expanse of gleaming water, and a great booming, roaring noise echoed
up from the valley walls. Ah Fong looked at Libby with
frightened eyes. "In my country we would say demons
at work," he said.

Libby nodded with understanding. "I think we'd
probably say demons were at work here too," she
said. Her face set grimly, she spurred her horse forward, picking her way down the grassy slope. The
booming noise continued to echo from the canyon

walls and men could be seen, scurrying like ants as
they worked pieces of machinery. They came to the
edge of the lake. It looked blue and peaceful, as if it
had been in place for years. On the near shore a fine
house had been built, complete with turrets and gables.
As Libby started toward this a man came out.

"What do you want?" he asked rudely.

"Do you own this property?" Libby asked, eyeing
him as if he was the least of servants in her past life.
"In which case your wealth obviously exceeds your
breeding and manners."

"I don't own it, I just work here," the man said,
"and this is private property."

"And the master accepts no social calls?" Libby
asked. "Tell him a neighbor has come to visit."

"Huh," the man said. "You can go tell him yourself
if you want, although I think he's too busy for tea
parties right now."

Libby slid from her horse. "Hold this, Ah Fong,"
she said, handing him the reins, "and stay well out of
sight, just in case."

"I go with you, missee," Ah Fong said.

Libby shook her head. "Better not," she said. "I
don't like the sound of this place."

Mustering all her courage, she strode up the front
steps and in through the open front door of the house.
The hall was marble floored and the room leading off
it decorated with elegant furniture.

"Is anybody home?" Libby called.

A door at the rear of the hall opened and a
head poked around it. "What is it?" growled a
voice.

Libby took in the flabby, sagging jowls, the pig-
gy eyes, the cigar hanging from the corner of his

lip. "Oh, no," she said angrily. "I might have known. Sheldon Rival."

Rival's eyes narrowed when he saw her, then a grin spread across his face. "Well look who's here again. Our plucky little pioneer. Still managing to survive?"

"No thanks to you," Libby said. "I'm trying to grow vegetables down in the valley."

The grin spread so that his eyes almost disappeared into folds of skin. "Ah yes, so I heard."

"At least, I was trying to grow vegetables until somebody took away my water supply."

"Really? What a shame," Rival said.

"So you knew I was farming down below you," she stormed, "and you made this stupid lake quite intentionally."

"The dam didn't fall into place one night when I was sleeping," he said, still looking amused. "Of course I made it, woman, but it had nothing to do with you. In fact, I quite overlooked your existence until you just reminded me."

"I bet you did," Libby said. "You have that annoying habit. Well, Mr. Sheldon Rival, it's about time you realized that you are not the only man in this world. You're ruining my business just to give yourself a view with a lake in it."

"Not true," Rival said. "This lake isn't just for my view. It's pure business, lady. I told you the day of the little miner was over. I've got the equipment for hydraulic mining now. I'm using water cannon to blast tons of rock out of these hills every hour, crushing it in giant crushers and taking out gold by the pound—and to do this I need a lot of water, guaranteed and year-round. Hence the lake. The pretty view from my front window is just an added bonus."

"You can't just dam up a whole river," Libby said angrily.

"But I just did," Rival said sweetly.

"Then you're going to have to un-dam it," Libby snapped.

"And who's going to make me?"

"You'll have to tear it down again as soon as I go to court," Libby said icily.

"I think not," Rival said. "Check out what the law says. It says the highest property has first water rights."

"Rights, yes," Libby shouted, "but it doesn't mean you can keep all the water to yourself."

"It does until you can prove it otherwise," Rival said. "And I'd say you've got a long fight on your hands. There are few legal precedents in this state and most of the judges are my fellow lodge members." He raised an eyebrow at her angry face. "Oh, didn't you know that? We all belong to the same Odd Fellows Lodge. Brother help brother, you know."

"Then I'll take it to the highest court in the state. I'll appeal to the Supreme Court in Washington if I have to."

"Go ahead," Rival said. "Your little plants will be long shrivelled before you can get your case heard." He indicated his front door, as if ushering her out. "My advice to you, as before, is to go back where you came from and leave the pioneering to us men. Failing that, my advice would be to dig your gardens somewhere else."

"And my advice to you would be to go to hell, the sooner the better," Libby stormed. "Don't think you'll get the better of me, because you won't. And don't think you can make me quit. I'm not a quitter, Mr. Rival. I'll find a way to keep going and I'll find a way to get my water back."

She turned to sweep out of the door.

"And if you think of digging up my dam with your gardening fork, I do post armed guards," Rival yelled after her and laughed loudly at his joke.

Libby grabbed the reins of her horse from Ah Fong and swung into the saddle. As they rode away she related the entire conversation to him.

"You like I slink up to his house and cut his throat while he sleep?" Ah Fong asked.

"I'd like very much," Libby said, "but I wouldn't let you do it. Just because Sheldon Rival behaves like a skunk doesn't give us permission to act like him. We'll just have to fight him and win."

"But how? Who's going to listen to little woman when big man own hotels and gambling parlors and make plenty money?"

"I'll just have to find the best lawyer in the state and hire him to represent me," Libby said.

"That cost plenty money," Ah Fong commented.

"I don't care if it costs every penny I've got," Libby said. "I'm not going to be beaten by that man. I'd rather die than be beaten by him."

"But even if you get number-one lawyer, it still take plenty time," Ah Fong said.

"I know," Libby said with a sigh.

"What about plants growing now? What about new fruit trees? How we gonna get water for them?"

"I don't know, Ah Fong," Libby said angrily.

"Then no can do, missee," he said. "No other water

near enough to get to fields. Ah Fong can't dig canal for miles."

Libby's face suddenly brightened. "I know what we'll do," she said excitedly. "We'll have water brought up from the Sacramento River."

"How you do that?"

"In ox carts. I'll get big barrels made and have them brought up in ox carts."

"Are you plumb crazy?" Ah Fong asked. "How many ox carts you think we need to water all those plants?"

"A lot," Libby said, "but I'm prepared to spend what it takes to keep those plants alive until fall. Then, in the fall I'll have a pond dug on the property. Sheldon Rival's not going to make me move. What do you say to that?"

Ah Fong's face broke into a big grin. "I say you one crazy woman," he said.

# CHAPTER 36

LIBBY WASTED NO time at all. She went straight down to Sacramento and asked her friend Mark Hopkins for advice on selecting a lawyer. He thought he could recommend a man in San Francisco, but warned her that all public agencies closed during the summer.

"So we won't be able to get anything started until September," Libby said in annoyance.

Hopkins shook his head. "The aim of the new Land Act before the state assembly is to make sense of who owns what. All the old land grants will have to be proved. You might be able to prove that Rival has no claim on the land he has flooded and will have to un-flood it for that reason."

"I really hope so," Libby said. "It seems as if that man was put on this earth solely for the reason of thwarting me."

"Not just you," Hopkins said. "There are many men up in the mines who would wish him dead. Speaking off the cuff I'd say that maybe your best bet is to find yourself a hired gun."

403

Libby laughed; the remark was so uncharacteris-
tic of the neat, gentlemanly Hopkins. "You were joking, I hope," she said. "With my luck, it will transpire
that Rival has a horde of sons back home in Chicago,
or wherever it is, waiting to take over his property
and do even more damage." The smile faded and she
sighed. "I see there will be no quick solution. I had
better hire some ox teams and drivers and find the
easiest route to water."

"I wish you luck," Mark called after her.

All summer long a procession of ox carts, loaded
high with barrels, could be seen making its way down
to the nearest river in the early morning and returning late in the day, a distance of around twenty miles.
Each barrel would be transferred to a small handcart,
which Libby's workers would wheel down the rows of
plants, pausing to water each one.

As the water level dropped in the nearest river, they
had to look farther afield and then farther so that it
was necessary for the men to drive down one day,
camp on the bank overnight, and then return the next
day. By then, Libby's early crops, strawberries, and
peppers, melons, and corn, were all harvested and she
was able to concentrate the water on her fruit trees
and grapes. The early crops made her a large profit
and she looked angrily at the empty ground she did
not dare replant.

"Do it good to have a rest," Ah Fong said philo-
sophically.

"It's only just started working," Libby snapped. "It
really riles me to be held up like this and to have
so much of my money going on water carts when it
should be used for expansion."

"Only two more month and then we get rain maybe," Ah Fong said. "You hire men dig big pond then you be like Devil Rival."

Libby smiled. "A lake outside my front door might not be a bad idea," she said. "I could keep a pleasure boat moored."

"When you got time for pleasure?" Ah Fong asked scornfully. "You never stop working."

"One day," Libby said. "I had thought by the end of this year that I'd be safe and free from worries, but it seems I'm going to have to keep on fighting forever. Maybe I should have gone back to Boston with Edward Knotts. Maybe this is my punishment for disobeying the gods."

"Huh!" Ah Fong said. "What you do in big city? Drive everyone mad, that what you do."

"Quite possibly," she said. "Now let's go see if any of those tomatoes turned red today."

All through the blistering heat of September Libby managed to keep up her watering schedule. She also hired a steam shovel to start digging out a pond. Her neighbors came over to see the work.

"Now we'd better pray it rains this year," she said, looking at the gaping hole. "If we have a drought, we're finished."

"I pray God we get rain, for your sake," Don Miguel said. "I'm afraid rain will not help me and my family anymore."

"What do you mean?" Libby asked.

"You have not heard of this new Land Act they have passed in the state government?"

"I heard something of it," Libby said, "but I thought it was just a case of officially registering all Spanish land grants."

"I fear it is worse than that," Don Miguel said.

"Now the Mexican farmers will have to prove their land grants in an American court. If Yankees want their land, the claims will not be approved."

"Surely not," Libby said in horror. "Our courts are fair, Don Miguel. And you must have the title deeds?"

"All I have is a letter, handwritten, from the provincial governor of the time. Back in 1825, when I come here, it was enough. For a Yankee court, I don't know."

"I'll help you find a lawyer, if you like, Don Miguel," Libby said. "Since I'll be needing one of my own, maybe he can represent us both."

Don Miguel smiled sadly. "Let us hope there is justice in this land," he said.

"If there was any justice, Sheldon Rival would be blasted to kingdom come by his own water cannon," Libby said. "He has completely ruined all my plans for expansion and I certainly can't have water delivered for a second summer. I never thought I'd look forward to a nice rainy California winter, but now I can't wait for the first storm."

All through October the Indian summer continued, and Libby was glad to learn that her case would come up in the district court in Sacramento during the first week of November.

"Finally I'll get this matter sorted out," she said to Don Miguel, who was having water troubles of his own. The streams he used to water his cattle had dried. In the past he had also made use of Libby's river in such dry years. "The water carts have just about kept me going, but if we have a dry winter, my new fruit trees won't survive. It will give me great satisfaction to claim lost income from Mr. Rival. Let's see his face when he has to pay me for lost profits."

"And if you lose, *Señora* Libby?" Don Miguel asked softly.

"Lose?" Libby asked in surprise. "How can I lose? You and I both know that morally I am in the right. Water belongs to everyone. An individual cannot deprive a whole valley for his own selfish needs."

"I hope this is so, for both our sakes," Don Miguel said.

Libby gave him a convincing smile. "Don't worry, Don Miguel. If necessary I will turn my feminine charm on the judge and melt his hard old heart."

"Your lawyer, he is a good man?" Don Miguel asked.

"So they say," Libby said. "I have only corresponded with him so far, but I understand he is very clever, and honest, which are not a usual combination in the lawyers one finds out here."

"Then I would ask a big favor," Don Miguel said. He turned his hat over nervously in his hands. "I would ask you to speak to this lawyer for me."

"About your proof of ownership, you mean?"

Don Miguel nodded seriously.

"I have talked with my wife *Señora* Libby. We think you are right, we need Yankee lawyer to make Yankee judge listen."

"I'll be happy to speak to my lawyer about you," Libby said. "I hope he can help."

"I am very grateful," he said, bowing. "I know if you think he is honest man he will not try to cheat me."

The week before Libby was due to go to court, the rains began. One evening the sky was flecked with bars of cloud, hard dark lines among the pink of the setting sun. The wind sprang up, brisk and cooler. The next morning Libby woke to hear pattering on the roof. She ran outside in her nightdress, standing on the dry earth and letting the cold drops spatter all over her.

"It's rain, we've made it," she shouted, dancing around wildly. "Now all we need is enough of it."

As if in answer to her request, the skies suddenly opened and rain fell in a solid sheet. Libby gasped and scrambled back inside, her hair and garments sodden in that moment. The rain now drummed rather than pattered on the roof. Gusts of wind buffeted the house.

She had just finished dressing when Ah Fong appeared. "You don't think it will flatten the fruit trees?" Libby asked anxiously. "You did stake them well?"

"You know I did. You were there. You helped."

"I know," Libby said, "but it would be terrible if rain flattened all the things we've fought to keep alive all summer."

"I go inspect them now," Ah Fong said.

"I'll come too," Libby agreed. She pulled her cape over her clothing and they made their way, slithering and sliding through the new mud and rivulets, down to the fields. The wind and rain were so strong that they almost took her breath away. It was hard to see more than a few feet ahead of them and Libby's clothing was sodden and muddy. They went from tree to tree, tightening stakes and straightening saplings that had started to lean. By the time they got home they were both unrecognizable, caked and plastered in brown mud, their hair making rivers down their faces.

"Good job no man come courting missee right now," Ah Fong said. "He turn right around and go home again."

"You're right," Libby said. "And it's a good job your bride hasn't arrived from China yet, because she'd sail right home again too."

He and Libby looked at each other and burst out laughing.

"Ah Fong, I'm so glad you're here," she said at last. "I'd never have made it without you."

"I know," he said with his usual lack of modesty. "Now go get hot bath before you catch death of cold."

All day long the rain continued unabated. The new pond began to fill. It rained all night too and when they woke in the morning the water had risen significantly.

"If it keeps on like this, we'll have the pond filled in a few days," Libby said as she and Ah Fong went out to inspect it. "I've never seen it rain this hard for this long."

"In China it rain like this," Ah Fong said.

"It does?"

"And then we have big flood and many people get killed."

"Then I'm glad we decided to build above the valley floor," Libby said. "I wonder if the Sacramento River is flooding yet."

"Have to wait for rain to come down from mountains," Ah Fong said. "That's when water get real bad. In China river rise to banks and then water come rushing down from mountains and flood all over."

"At least we don't have a river to worry about anymore," Libby said. "I wonder if the rain's getting close to Mr. Rival's doorstep."

"Maybe it come right through his house," Ah Fong said.

The rain continued unabated for a second day,

blurring the horizon into a gray haze in all directions
and turning the ground around the house into mud,
so that the passage between house and kitchen was
very treacherous.

"If this keeps up, I don't know that I'll be able to
get down to Sacramento," Libby said to Don Miguel
as he rode by to check on her. "How ironic that my
case should come to court and I might be prevented
from appearing because of too much water."

"That is often the way of God," Don Miguel said.
"He mocks us sometimes, I fear."

"I don't think God is like that," Libby said seriously. "I can't believe that He is responsible for weather.
And if this is a heavenly warning that I shouldn't go
to Sacramento, then I'm ignoring it. If I can't get the
buckboard through, I'll take the mule."

Toward the end of the week the rain did ease to a
fine drizzle, interspersed with periods of watery sunshine and mild temperatures which brought out every
insect known to man. Inspecting the fields meant constant slapping at mosquitoes and swatting away flies.

"But at least I think I dare risk the buckboard,"
Libby said. "I'd hate to see that corn go moldy sitting
here."

"You like Chinese market woman," Ah Fong said,
grinning at her. "You go crazy if you can't make sale."

"It makes sense to take the wagon," Libby defended.
Hitch up the horse and the mule for me. "Maybe I can
pick up new plants to put in this winter."

"Take care, missee," Ah Fong said as she set off.

She kissed the children goodbye, adjusted the oil-
cloth over her clothes, and splashed away in the
buckboard. The going was tedious with large areas
so deeply flooded that it looked as if the buckboard

were travelling across a lake. Several times along the
way she had to get out and use old sacks to get the
wagon wheels through the thick mud. She looked
down at her mud-encrusted skirt. Her legs were a
most unfeminine brown to the knee and she was
glad that her case did not come to court until the
next day.

The fine light rain continued all the way down to
Sacramento. It was almost evening by the time Libby
arrived. By that time the rain had stopped and white
mist curled over the wet fields with a blood-red sun
setting above it. Over the city itself rose thick black
smoke, mingled with the mist and flattened into a
low cloud with clear blue evening sky above it. As she
approached she could see that bonfires were burning
on almost every city corner. The new levee had kept
the city from becoming another lake, but the streets
were still deep in foul-smelling mud and pools of
flood water dotted the surrounding area. Elegant
white egrets decorated the scene but insects rose in
clouds and Libby slapped at mosquitoes which whined
around her face.

Farther into the city, the air became so thick and
heavy with evil- smelling smoke that the horse became
alarmed and Libby was forced to get down from the
buckboard and lead it and the mule. She was glad to
see Mark Hopkins' new store ahead of her through
the murk and tried to scrape off the worst of the
mud as she tied the horses to the rail. The new
store, Hopkins and Hutchinson, Purveyors, looked
very impressive and civilized with its burning lamps
and brick frontage. Mark Hopkins came hurrying
through from a back room to greet her, a quill pen
stuck behind his ear.

"My dear, what a surprise to see you," he exclaimed. "I'm sorry I wasn't here to greet you. You caught me in the middle of accounts."

"A pleasant pastime, I hope?" Libby asked.

Mark smiled. "We have done well—very well indeed. I'll be looking at sites in San Francisco this winter. I aim to build myself a very fine house. But what brings you down here at this worst of times? It must be important, to take such a risk."

"What do you mean, worst of times?" Libby asked.

"My dear, haven't you heard? The city is riddled with disease. All this rain and the mild temperatures—every fever imaginable is raging through the town: typhus, cholera, smallpox. . . ."

"Is that what all the fires are about?" Libby asked.

"They are hoping that they will stop the sickness from spreading if they can eliminate some of the garbage in the streets," Hopkins said. "To my mind the fires are worse than the garbage ever was. Before, at least one could breathe. I wouldn't stay the night if I were you, unless you really have to."

"I'm afraid I do have to," Libby said. "My case comes up in court tomorrow. I'm on my way to meet my lawyer as soon as I've had a bath at the hotel."

"Could you not get it postponed?" Mark Hopkins asked with concern. "The situation here is very bad and a victory in court wouldn't mean much if you came down with cholera or smallpox."

"I can't postpone it now, Mark," she said. "Not after waiting too long and going through so much inconvenience. Besides, you chose to stay."

"I am a free man with no dependents," Mark Hopkins said, "and as you know, I am very particular in my habits. I do not eat or drink in public places anymore.

I have been burning mosquito coils in my rooms at all times and I think that helps. I can give you some for tonight."

"Thank you," Libby said.

"Take my advice and don't eat in public restaurants or go where people are," Mark said. "There is a new hotel just opened in town which seems to be a very high-class establishment.

"Oh, really?" Libby asked. "What's it called."

"It's the Orleans Hotel. I understand that they had it constructed in New Orleans and then taken apart to be shipped around the Horn. I don't know how they managed it, but the quality of the workmanship and the service is definitely superior—why, Libby, what's the matter? Are you sure you're feeling all right?"

"No, I'm perfectly fine, thank you," she managed to answer. How could she explain to an acquaintance like Mark Hopkins what memories his words evoked and the effect they had on her. Instantly, her mind swung back to the narrow back street full of puddles and a tall dark man stepping out of the shadows to rescue her.

"The weather is very unpleasant," Mark Hopkins went on. "So humid and this terrible smoke. I would go straight to the Orleans and rest if I were you, my dear. And have them send food up to your room. Avoid all public places—that's my motto."

"I can hardly have the court session held in my room," Libby said, smiling, "but I will take your advice and leave town as soon as possible."

After Libby left Mark Hopkins, she was of two minds whether to go to the Orleans Hotel. She knew it made sense to go to the place with the highest standards of cleanliness, and yet, to spend the night in a room built in New Orleans. . . . This is all nonsense, she said to herself. No good comes from brooding over the past. I'm a businesswoman and I've come here to win a court case. Nothing else matters.

It was already dark by the time Libby arrived at the hotel, well lit with polished brass lamps outside and equally polished marble steps leading to a panelled foyer. She looked around with approval. The counter was of rich mahogany. There were ferns in brass pots. Definitely a civilized establishment. She rang the counter bell and a pleasant-faced woman, dressed in black, came out of a back room.

"Not the best of times to be visiting the city, ma'am," she commented as she handed Libby the visitor's book. "Will you be staying long?"

"I plan to leave tomorrow," Libby said. "I understand that Sacramento is no place to linger in at the moment."

A look of concern crossed the woman's face. "Indeed it isn't, ma'am. We do our best in an establishment such as this, but one can never be too careful. I make the maids scrub everything daily and I'm boiling the sheets extra long in the copper, but these fevers don't seem to care whom they strike. There was a gentleman came in here earlier this week, as fine spoken a man as you could wish and obviously well-heeled too. He complained of feeling unwell and in the morning he was down with fever. I had to have him taken off to the hospital, poor man. I'd like to have kept him here, but it wouldn't be fair to the other guests, would it?"

Libby finished signing the book and her eye scanned the page as the landlady prattled on. Then she stood, transfixed, the cold creeping up her spine, as she saw at the top of the page the bold flourish of the signature: Gabriel Foster, arrived from San Francisco, November 3, 1851.

# CHAPTER
# 37

LIBBY CONTINUED TO stare down at the flourishes of Gabe's signature until she could regain her composure. She had almost perfect control of her voice as she turned back to the landlady.

"This gentleman," Libby said. "He wasn't, by any chance, the one who was stricken with fever?"

The woman leaned across the counter to read the name. "Why yes, that was him. Poor Mr. Foster. Such a nice man. Do you know him?"

"Yes," Libby said. "Was he here alone?"

"Quite alone, ma'am," the landlady said. "That was part of the trouble. I asked him if I could get in touch with anyone to come and take him away and he said there was nobody, so I had to have him sent to the fever hospital. It fair broke my heart. That hospital's no place for a gentleman, especially not now, the way they're crammed in."

"How do I get there?" Libby asked. "I have to see him right away."

"Mercy me. You're not thinking of going there

416

yourself?" the landlady stammered. "That's no place
for a lady to go, especially not after dark. The hospital's in the worst part of town. With all those drunks
coming out of the saloons! I'd wait until morning if
I were you. I hear the mud's terrible out that way. A
man fell down dead drunk and drowned in it only a
few days ago."

"Nevertheless, I still want to go," Libby said firmly.
"The directions please."

The hospital was one of the few two-story buildings
in town, built away from the prosperous merchants of
J Street, back toward the ramshackle immigrant quarter. The wooden sidewalks and street lamps ended
with the stores on J street and Libby had to pick her
way through the ooze in almost total darkness, past
open-fronted tents, low saloons, and gambling houses,
out of which spilled raucous singing and coarse laughter. She shrank into the shadows as two men staggered
out, one of them muttering curses. The scene brought
back a memory to her; the wet streets of New Orleans,
the singing in the piano bar, and the drunken men,
when Gabe had first materialized to rescue her.

"I'm not going to let you die, Gabe Foster," she muttered to give herself courage. "Not now. Not here."

She recognized the hospital right away, not by any
outward sign but by its smell. The odor of burning tar
could not mask the more overpowering sickly smell
of death. Libby put her handkerchief to her mouth
as she went up the steps and pushed open the front
door. Inside was cold and damp—a long unfinished
brick hallway lit by one feeble lamp. From the darkness came groans and the sound of someone retching.
As Libby stood shivering, one hand still on the front
door, as if this were her last link with reality, a large

man in a spattered apron came running down the hallway, carrying a pan. He started when he saw her.

"What are you doing here? No visitors," he snapped.

Libby decided he looked more like a butcher than
an orderly, adding to the nightmarish quality of the
place. "I understand you have a Mr. Gabriel Foster
here," she said.

"Lady, we have close on three hundred people here
right now," the man said, wiping off his forehead.
"They're bringing them in faster than we can find
them beds."

"This man was brought in several days ago," Libby
said. "Is there someone I can speak to to find out
where he is?"

"If he's still alive," the man said. "They don't often
last more than a few days."

"All the more reason to find him quickly," Libby
said angrily. "Where do I find the person in charge?"

"There's a doctor in the building somewhere, but
he'll be too busy to talk," the man said. "I can look
in the admitting book for you. They're supposed to
write in the names when they bring them in. What's
the name?"

"Foster," Libby said. "Gabriel Foster."

"You his wife?"

"A close relative," Libby said.

"Foster?" the man asked. He went over to a high
table and flicked through a dog-eared book, reading
through names so painfully slowly that Libby had to
quell her desire to hit him. At last he looked up, evi-
dently pleased with himself. "Ah yes, that's him."

"He's still here?" Libby asked.

The man grinned, showing a gap where two teeth
were missing. "Well, he ain't dead yet. His name ain't

crossed out," he said. "He's down in the smallpox ward."

"Smallpox?" Libby muttered in horror. "Can I see him?"

"I told you. No visitors."

"But I have to get him away from here," Libby said, her eyes pleading. "Couldn't I just see him for a second?"

"It'd be more than my job was worth," the man said. Libby caught his meaning. She opened her purse and took out a five-dollar piece. The man passed his tongue over his lips. "It's your own funeral," he said. "Every disease known to man running through this hospital at the moment."

"I'll risk it," Libby said. "Just take me to him."

"This way," the orderly said, and trotted off ahead of her down the darkened hallway. At the end of the hall a large sheet was hanging over a door, smelling strongly of carbolic. The orderly stopped. "Stay here," he said. "I'll go in and find him for you. What name was it?"

"Tell him Libby is here to see him."

The orderly disappeared behind the curtain. Libby waited, her heart hammering so loudly that she was sure she could hear it bounce back from the bare walls. After a while the orderly appeared, grinning more widely than ever. "He don't want to see you," he said, obviously enjoying her discomfort.

"He said that?" Libby demanded. "Are you sure?"

"Sure as you're standing here. I said there's a Libby wants to see you and he said don't let her come in here. I don't want to see her."

"Rubbish," Libby said, pushing past him. "I don't believe you. Where is he?"

The man made an ineffectual grab at her but Libby had already passed through the doorway into the ward. It was a long, bare room with an unglazed window at the far end, letting in the smoke and fumes from the street. The lamp on the table at the far end threw little light. Each wall was lined with iron cots and between them on the floor were straw mattresses, all occupied by tossing, moaning figures, wrapped, mummylike, in bandages. As Libby passed, one of them sat up, letting out a terrifying roar. "Let me get at 'em," he shouted, waving his bandaged hands. "They're driving me mad."

"It's the itching, see," the orderly whispered to Libby. "We have to bandage them and tie their hands so they can't scratch. It drives 'em crazy."

"Where's Mr. Foster?" Libby asked, shying away from the crazed patient.

"Third from the end over there," the man said, pointing at a bed covered completely in a sheet. Libby gasped and walked slowly toward it. The figure under the sheet did not move.

"He's not dead?" she asked in a tremulous voice.

"I'm not dead," came Gabe's voice from underneath, "and for God's sake, go away."

The man on the next bed thrashed, sending an arm flying into Libby's back. Across the room someone was vomiting into a bucket. A feeble voice was murmuring, "Mom? Where are you? Mom?"

Libby looked down at the sheet-covered figure. As he showed no signs of removing the sheet, she didn't quite know what to do. The orderly was grinning. "I reckon you'd better go, miss," he said, "before you catch something you don't want."

"All right, I'm going," Libby said loudly. "I came

to see if I could help an old friend and get him out of this terrible place. But he obviously doesn't need or want my help."

"Don't be a fool, Libby," Gabe's voice came, muffled through the sheet. "Get out of here while you still can. This is a place of death. Go away."

"Very well, I'm going," she said. "If you don't even want to look at me to say goodbye, that's up to you."

Libby stalked to the door. As she left she thought she detected the sheet being lifted, but she didn't look back. Once outside the door she reached into her purse and gave the orderly another five dollars. "Listen to me," she said. "I'll be back in the morning and I expect you to have Mr. Foster ready to leave. I'm taking him somewhere where he has a good chance of recovery, whether he likes it or not."

She hurried back to her hotel and met the landlady still at the front desk.

"Any news on your poor relative?" she asked.

"He's still alive but you were right. It's a terrible place. I've got to get him out of there as soon as possible," Libby said. "Where do you think I can find a room to rent where I can have him well looked after?"

The landlady shook her head firmly. "You'll not find anybody in this town willing to bring the smallpox into their houses," she said. "They come and take them away the moment the fever strikes whether the family wants it or no. I've seen some pitiful scenes myself these past days, mothers clinging on to the arms of their children as the poor wee one is carried out, and wives begging to go with their husbands. You'd best leave well enough alone, my dear. They say it's a terrible end."

That night Libby hardly slept, pacing the room impatiently, unable to wait for all the things she had to do next day. She was firm in her resolution that Gabe was not staying in that hospital a moment longer. If she couldn't find a place in Sacramento to take him, then she'd take him home with her and look after him herself. She wrote a note to Mark Hopkins, leaving him money and asking him to arrange her vegetable transactions for her as she was taking his advice and getting out of town again. She had almost forgotten the main reason for her journey. At nine o'clock she had to appear in court. Until that moment her number-one priority in life had been to beat Sheldon Rival and win back her water rights. Now it no longer seemed so overwhelmingly important. If Gabe died, then any victory over Sheldon Rival would be hollow indeed.

The fact that Gabe did not want to see her was her one consolation. It proved he was not about to die at any moment. If he had been, he would have made his peace with her, held her hand, and bid her tenderly farewell. Not wanting to see her showed that his pride and stubbornness were still working fully. Libby smiled to herself. How typically Gabe! How very much she had missed him!

At dawn she washed and dressed in clean clothes, ate a little toast, then walked over to the courthouse where she was to meet Jonah Fairbanks, her attorney. Mr. Fairbanks looked like the sort of man Mark Hopkins would recommend: tall, slim, somberly dressed with a neat little beard. He bowed when Libby introduced herself to him.

"This could not, unfortunately, have fallen at a worse time," he said. "You have heard of all the

terrible sickness in this city? I was loath to leave San
Francisco."

"How long do you think it will take?" Libby asked,
her thoughts still on rescuing Gabe. "It's all fairly simple, isn't it? It can't take a judge more than an hour
or so?"

Mr. Fairbanks stroked his beard meditatively, the
way Mark Hopkins did. "It depends, somewhat, on
the evidence produced by the defense," he said. "If
they have a lot of evidence which has to be examined
and sifted through. . . ."

"What evidence could they have?" Libby asked angrily. She had not counted on Sheldon Rival being
able to present his side fully in court.

The lawyer looked amused by her outburst. "This
being the justice system of the United States of
America, both sides are guaranteed equal access to
the law," he said. "I am sure that the opposing party
will not want to tear down his dam without a fight."

"But any judge would see that it's wrong, surely?"
Libby asked. "You can't just take a whole valley's water
away."

"That is what we hope to prove," Mr. Fairbanks
said.

"But we have to prove it," Libby exclaimed, "and
prove it quickly. That's why I hired you."

"Pray don't distress yourself, Mrs. Grenville," the
lawyer said. "I'll do my very best for you and you can
help your own case most by remaining calm throughout."

"How can I remain calm?" Libby snapped. "I'm not
sitting back and letting Sheldon Rival tell a pack of
lies."

"Then maybe it would be better if you stayed out

of the courtroom and let me present your case," Fairbanks said softly. "A hysterical woman would not influence the judge favorably."

"I am not a hysterical woman," Libby said, her eyes flashing dangerously.

"Of course not," Mr. Fairbanks soothed, "but you are very emotionally involved with this case— understandably so, of course. I beg you to keep your temper before the judge."

"Anything as long as you get this over quickly," she said with a sigh.

"I see you also desire to get away as quickly as possible," he said. "And I don't blame you one bit."

Libby realized he thought she was frightened for her own safety if she stayed in the city but didn't bother to correct him. Across the square a clock struck nine and Fairbanks ushered Libby through a large oak door into the courtroom. She expected to see Sheldon Rival himself sitting across the room from her, but instead there were only two dark men, both with beaked noses, their heads together as they talked, giving the impression of two vultures. Libby disliked both on sight. The judge, however, looked like a kindly old man, his round pink face surrounded by a fluff of white whiskers, and she smiled at him encouragingly as she took her seat.

The case was read and Mr. Fairbanks stood to present Libby's argument. Then one of the dark men was asked to reply. He did so in a southern drawl and with many gestures which Libby was sure would annoy the judge as much as it annoyed her. He spoke of the lack of definitive California laws on the subject of water rights, the only clear one being that upstream property had prior rights to it. He pointed out that

streams were being diverted and channelled all over
the mining area and that many streams no longer
flowed through their original beds.

"But this one doesn't flow at all any longer," Libby
blurted out, unable to sit quiet. "And prior rights
must mean that someone else gets subsequent rights
to it."

Her outburst only got her a caution from the judge
and a frown from Fairbanks. The southern attorney
was invited to proceed and placed several documents
in front of the judge to show registration of mining
claims. "It has been the precedent in California that
water may be used as needed to expedite the process
of mining," he said. "My client's process needs a large
volume of water available at all times."

"So do my vegetables," Libby said. This time the
judge wagged a finger at her. "One more outburst,
Mrs. Grenville, and I shall have to ask you to leave."

Libby glared at the southern lawyer and jammed
her lips together. The judge looked through the
papers he had been given. The clock on the wall ticked
monotonously and Libby felt as if she would explode
with impatience. At last the judge looked up. "At what
date do you say that you took up residence on your
present property, Mrs. Grenville?" he asked.

"October 1850, your honor," Mr. Fairbanks answered quickly for her. "My client has been in residence just over a year and during that time has
established a large, successful market garden business, dependent on a constant water supply."

"I see," the judge said. He glanced down at the
papers again.

"What made you choose this particular site, Mrs.
Grenville?"

"The constant water supply," Libby answered for herself before Fairbanks could speak.

The judge shifted the papers around. "You presumably did not have expert help in choosing this situation—no legal help, for example?"

"I didn't think I needed it," Libby said. "I bought the land from the man who held title to it."

"I'm only thinking," the judge said slowly, "that if you had conducted a thorough investigation into the pros and cons of your present situation, you might have discovered that your neighbor, Mr. Rival, was already in possession of the land directly above you and had already filed a claim with the mining commission of this state to begin hydraulic mining there."

Libby looked at him suspiciously. "He hadn't already built a dam when I moved in there," she said.

"But he had expressed his intention of doing so to several witnesses from whom these gentlemen have affidavits," the judge said. "Furthermore, I have before me a map of the gold mining area of our state. Your particular river, Mrs. Grenville, does not show up on it."

"That doesn't mean it doesn't exist," Libby said, not able to hold back her anger any longer.

"Of course not," the judge said, "but it does make my task a little easier, as it has not been officially recognized as a water source. I sympathize with you, Mrs. Grenville. You have obviously put a lot of work into this little project, but I feel you should have done your homework a little more thoroughly before starting on it. I have no alternative than to rule in favor of Mr. Rival. The dam is allowed to stand."

The hammer came down on the bench. Fairbanks put his hand on Libby's arm to steer her away. "Thank you very much, but I can do without your help," she said coldly. "A lot of help you were in there."

"I did what I could," Mr. Fairbanks said, "but I'm afraid we were up against insurmountable odds."

"Meaning what?"

"The laws governing the mining processes in this state are only being written," Fairbanks said. "And there are those in the mining commission who are not above putting signatures to documents for a fee."

"You're saying those documents were false?"

"I'm saying that there are those in this state who can be bought," he said. "I didn't like to tell you that we were fighting a losing battle before we went into court, but when I saw who we had as judge, I knew we were wasting our time. Sheldon Rival is already a powerful man and his hydraulic mining is making him richer by the minute. Only a fool would make an enemy of him at the moment."

"Then I must be a fool," Libby said, "Because I'm not going to give up. I'll go to the legislature and have them change the laws. I'll go to the Supreme Court if I have to. I'm not going to let Sheldon Rival win this time."

Mr. Fairbanks touched her arm lightly. "My dear, there is a whole big state waiting to be developed—more land than anyone dreamed of, waiting to be cultivated. Why give yourself such heartaches when they are not necessary? You could find somewhere even better to start afresh. Many of these Mexican land grants will be going begging. Help yourself to one—it would cost you nothing."

"Yes it would," Libby said. "It would cost me my pride."

# CHAPTER
# 38

BACK AT THE hotel, Libby loaded her bag into the wagon and drove straight to the hospital. It was hard going through the mud but eventually she tied up the horse and mule at the rail outside. The hospital looked even more desolate by daylight—a dark brick building around which black smoke still curled. She went in the front door and was greeted by a strange woman who told her very firmly that no visitors were allowed. It was only then that she realized she didn't know the orderly's name. She tried to describe him but the woman was in no mood to listen.

"Out!" she said, pointing at the front door. Then she stood with hands on hips while Libby went out again.

As she stood looking at the building, wondering how she could get access to Gabe, a heavy wagon rolled up and men came running down the steps to carry in three groaning figures, wrapped in blankets. They went to lift a fourth body, then yelled out breezily, "Don't bother about this one. He's already a stiff."

They turned to the carter. "Take him round back to the morgue."

Libby fought off her revulsion and seized her chance to slip in behind the stretcher bearers. The unfriendly woman was involved with admitting the patients, writing names in the book. One of the sick men started thrashing in his fever and threatened to fall off his stretcher. As the orderlies sprang to control him Libby fled down the corridor toward the smallpox ward. Inside all was quiet, except for some faint groans. Two beds next to Gabe's were empty but he lay there not moving, his eyes sunken, face alarmingly red and half obscured by bandages. An ugly boil poked out of the bandage at his chin. Libby swallowed with fear. She tiptoed over to him and stared at him for a long time until she saw that he was still breathing. Then she wasn't sure what to do next. Gabe was too heavy for her to drag out and she would certainly be stopped. She slipped out again and went around the building until she came to a door at the back which presumably led to the morgue. As she stood, undecided, two young men came out of it, carrying an empty stretcher between them, masks tied around their mouths making them look like bandits.

Libby ran up and grabbed one by the arm. "I need your help badly," she whispered. "My husband's in there and they won't let me take him home. He got sick when he came into town, you see, and I've just found him. Couldn't you bring him out to me? We live on a farm away from everybody. We wouldn't be doing any harm and I could nurse him back to health. If he's left here, he'll die."

"What do you want us to do?" one of the young men asked kindly.

"If you could just carry him out, pretend you were taking him to the morgue, I'll have my buckboard waiting," she said, "and I'll make it worth your while." She fumbled in her purse and brought out a handful of silver dollars. She watched the young men glance at each other.

"All right, ma'am," one of them said. "Which one is he?"

Libby hurried to her wagon and brought it round to the back of the hospital. A few minutes later the two young men appeared, carrying a white-shrouded figure between them. The white shrouded figure, however, was not acting the part of a body very well.

From under the sheet the figure was protesting loudly, "Will you put me down this instant? I'm not dead yet, I tell you."

"Quiet, your wife's come to take you away," one of the orderlies hissed.

"I don't have a wife. You're going to bury me," Gabe raved.

"He's delirious, poor thing, put him in here," Libby said quickly, motioning to the back of the wagon. The orderlies lifted him on top of the sacks.

"No, don't bury me. I'm still alive," Gabe moaned.

Libby slipped a handful of silver dollars to the men who nodded and slipped away. "Stop talking and lie back, Gabe," Libby whispered. "Nobody's going to bury you."

"Libby?" Gabe murmured as she pulled the sheet back from his face. "Are you dead too?"

"You're going to be fine," she said, trying to smile confidently as she looked down at his distorted features. "I'm taking you home with me. I'm going to get you well again."

Gabe closed his eyes and smiled. "That's good," he said, and passed into unconsciousness.

Libby drove away as fast as she could, terrified that she would be stopped and Gabe taken back. It was only when the smoke from the city hung low on the horizon behind her that she allowed the horse and mule to slow to a walk. Gabe still lay in the back among the sacks, being tossed back and forth like a doll as the wagon lurched over ruts and bumps. Libby stopped and tried to make him more comfortable. As she touched him she could feel his body burning with fever. He moaned but didn't open his eyes.

Libby pressed on as fast as she dared. Spray flew up as she whipped the team across the flooded pastures. The horse's side was flecked with foam but she didn't dare stop. She kept looking back at Gabe's scarlet face and sunken eyes and was terrified that he'd die before she could get him home. It was only as the gravel driveway and cactus fence appeared that she remembered she had lost her fight in court and maybe she would have to leave this place. A great lump rose in her throat and she wondered if fate could be so cruel that she could lose her home and Gabe all in one day.

Ah Fong came running out to greet her.

"Don't come any closer," she yelled. "I've got Mr. Foster sick with smallpox in the wagon."

"You brought smallpox back here?" Ah Fong asked, his face showing his alarm.

"I'm not bringing him in the house," she said. "Let's put him in the farthest cottage. We'll have the men sleep in the shed or with you until he's well again."

Ah Fong didn't say any more. He started yelling instructions in Chinese and soon his crew was hurrying to remove belongings and set up the little one-room shack as a sickroom.

"I'm going to need your help getting him out of the wagon," Libby said to Ah Fong. "He's too heavy for me to lift alone."

"That's all right, missee. I do it," Ah Fong said, his eyes still afraid as he bent to touch Gabe. Gabe moaned as he was moved, but he didn't regain consciousness. They helped Gabe to the bed.

"What he needs is good Chinese chicken soup," Ah Fong said.

"Good idea, Ah Fong," Libby agreed. "Why don't you go kill a chicken."

Libby sat beside Gabe all night while he burned with fever and raged in delirium. "Don't let them bury me, I'm not dead yet," he kept on moaning, every time she tried to touch him. She changed the dressings over his boils, sponged his face, and held his head to feed him sips of water. When she tried to feed him Ah Fong's chicken broth, he couldn't keep it down. As the night progressed, Libby fought to stay awake. She had had almost no sleep for the past two days and nodded off every time she sat down. She was frightened that Gabe would die while she was asleep, so she stood by the window and made herself walk up and down whenever her eyelids drooped.

Toward dawn Gabe woke and started moaning again. "They're digging, aren't they?" he asked with frightened eyes. "I can hear them digging outside." He grabbed Libby's arm frantically. "You won't let them bury me before I'm properly dead, will you?" he asked.

"You're not going to die, Gabe," she said soothingly, reaching for the cold towel to sponge his face. "Just lie back and rest. I'm going to take good care of you and you're going to get well."

His eyes seemed to focus on her for the first time. "Libby?" he asked. "Is it really you?"

"Really me," she said gently.

"I thought I heard your voice," he murmured. "Don't leave me, will you?"

"I won't leave you, Gabe," she said softly. "I'm right here beside you."

A smile spread over his face. "Libby," he muttered. His eyelids fluttered closed. His face became peaceful. Libby sprang up, afraid that he had just died. She put her ear to his chest. She felt the gentle rise and fall and realized that he had fallen into a real sleep.

With first light Ah Fong brought her food and hot water. "I watch for you," he said. "You go take bath."

Libby shook her head. "I don't want to come near the children until I know I haven't caught this," she said. "If you bring me some pillows, I'll sleep on the chair in here."

"Stubborn woman," Ah Fong said, but he didn't contradict her. "More rain today," he said, staring up at the sky. "Soon your pond get full and then you can thumb nose at Mr. Devil Rival."

"I wish I could," she said sadly. "That pond would be fine as an emergency water source, but it can't supply the farm for a whole dry summer."

"Then dig more ponds."

"How many ponds do you think it would take to water a farm the size I wanted it?" she asked angrily. "If I can't make him take down that dam, I'm going to have to move. I can never expand if we have to water plants from a pond."

Ah Fong nodded with understanding. He grinned

and looked up at the sky. "Good rain right now," he said. "Winter crops grow just fine. We make lots of money from winter crops then you buy fine house in San Francisco."

"I don't think I'd be content to live in a fine house in San Francisco all year. I need something to keep me occupied."

"You need man to keep you out of trouble," he said, peering into the room to where Gabe was sleeping. "He going to get well again?"

"I don't know yet, it's too early to say," Libby said. "Besides, he might have other plans."

"Wah!" Ah Fong said expressively and went back to the main house. Libby washed with the hot water and then cleaned up Gabe as well as she could. His shirt was black with sweat and stuck to his skin in many places, so that she didn't dare disturb it yet. He didn't wake as she ministered to him, but she thought his breathing seemed easier than the night before.

A long morning passed. The rain, which had begun as light drops, now drummed hard on the shake roof. Libby sat in the chair and stared out gloomily at the gray, drenched landscape. The willow trees, a few golden leaves still clinging to their delicate weeping branches, were only blurred images through the mist.

God, I love this place, Libby muttered to herself. Must everything I love be taken from me?

Around midday there was a loud rumble of thunder up in the hills. Libby looked up in surprise, as it seemed to her that the worst of the rain had already passed over and the sky was lightening. Almost immediately, a second deep rumble echoed back from the canyon walls above. Libby opened her cabin door

and went out, breathing in the fresh air, sweet with
new growth which follows rain. She was looking for
the direction of the storm when she saw Ah Fong,
rushing down the slope toward her like a madman,
his mouth open.

"Look, missee, Look!" he was yelling. He grabbed
her arm, gasping for breath as he motioned up the
valley. Libby looked in the direction he was pointing.
Through the wisps of cloud a dark line had been
drawn across the upper valley. It was growing as it
moved downward. It took Libby a moment to realize
that it was a wall of water.

"You take the baby!" Libby screamed. "Get everyone away from the river!"

"What about you?"

"Just do it!" Libby yelled. She had already turned
to run back to the little shack that housed Gabe, the
shack that was farthest from the house and closest to
the river. She slithered in the mud and turned to look
in fear at the advancing water. It was moving much
more quickly than she could have believed. She heard
the sound of trees snapping, of rocks tumbling, all
adding to the deep roar which grew and magnified
as the water approached.

She had just reached the steps to the cabin door
when it caught up with her. It swallowed the front
gate, the cactus hedge. The outer swirl of water struck
at the little building and knocked it off its founda-
tions like a child knocking over a block building. It
was thrown onto its side in the swirling water and its
walls split apart like matchsticks. Libby fell face down
in the icy water and struggled to get to her feet. As
she came up spluttering and choking she saw Gabe's
white body disappearing. With a cry she flung her-

self at him and grabbed at his leg. She could feel the force of icy water snatching at him but she clung on grimly as they were both dragged forward, scraped on rocks and tumbled like pebbles. Then the surge passed. They lay there, both coughing and gasping.

AS SOON AS Libby could raise her head she saw that her house was untouched. The water had taken the first two cottages, the fence, and driveway. It had flattened many of the willow trees but her house still stood. Black mud and tree limbs covered a wide swath of the valley. Among the debris was a grandfather clock, its face smashed beyond recognition. On the slope above she could see the figures of her children running toward her, Noel safe in Ah Fong's arms.

"Thank God," she murmured and staggered to her feet, her head swimming dizzily. Gabe lay motionless on the mud, sprawled like a rag doll. "Must get him inside . . . he'll die," she muttered.

As she attempted to drag him by one arm, he opened his eyes and glared at her. "I didn't want a bath," he said angrily. "The water was too cold."

"I didn't intend to give you one," Libby said. "I just saved you from drowning, but you don't have to thank me."

Gabe reacted to the sound of her voice. He seemed

to be trying hard to focus on her. "Libby?" he asked. "Where am I?"

"You're in the middle of a field," she said, wanting to laugh with relief. "We just escaped a flood."

"Whose field?" Gabe asked. "The last thing I remember I was at a hotel in Sacramento and my head was hurting like the devil. What are you doing here?"

"You got smallpox, Gabe," Libby said. "I found you at the fever hospital and I brought you home with me."

"You brought me home—with smallpox? Are you out of your mind?"

"You would have died," she said simply. "You nearly did die. You might still die if I don't get you warm and dry quickly."

"You should never have taken such a risk," Gabe said angrily. "What about your own family? What did your husband say when you brought me home?"

"Firstly, I've kept you apart from my family, in one of my worker's huts," she said, "and secondly, I don't have a husband."

His eyes focussed on her, puzzled but clear. "Hugh?" he asked.

"He died, a long time ago."

Ah Fong and two of the Chinese workers came running up to her, shouting with concern and joy at finding her alive.

"Water come right up to porch of house," Ah Fong yelled. "Now you happy you didn't build house where you wanted? You'd be floating down to Sacramento right now, just like I tell you."

Libby looked down to the shapeless area of devastation which had once been the willow-lined riverbank. "Yes, Ah Fong, I'm very glad," she said quietly. "Now

for goodness sake let's get Mr. Foster into one of
the huts quickly and bring him hot water and dry
clothes."

"You look like you could use hot water and dry
clothes too," Ah Fong said. "You look like drowned
rat."

"Did I ever mention you were very impertinent for
a hired hand?" Libby asked.

"You say Ah Fong not like hired hand. You say Ah
Fong manager."

"Then you're very impertinent for a manager," she
said, laughing.

Ah Fong grinned. "I go," he said. "I make hot tea
for you and I better bring brandy too."

Soon Gabe was installed in one of the remaining
worker's huts. With Ah Fong's help and Gabe's pro-
tests, she had taken off his wet clothes. He was now
wrapped in warm blankets, sipping hot tea with a
generous amount of brandy in it. She changed into
dry clothes in the hut next door and wrapped her
shawl around her shoulders, but found she was still
shivering from shock as much as from cold.

"I think we'll both try your chicken broth now, Ah
Fong," she said. "You better make enough for every-
one. We've all had a shock. And tell the children
Mama's just fine but can't come to visit them yet."
She poured brandy into her own hot tea, cradling
the cup in her hands as she sipped it.

After they were left alone, Gabe lay back among his
blankets and she sat beside him in silence, feeling the
warmth from the hot liquid gradually warming her
body.

"I think I'll try some more of that tea. I'm cold,"
Gabe said.

"At least the dowsing got your fever down," Libby said, helping him up and holding a cup to his lips. "You were burning up until this morning."

"I remember feeling I was on fire," Gabe said. "I thought it was all one long bad dream. You were in the dream too."

"I hope I wasn't a bad dream," Libby said dryly. She took the cup from him and put it down.

"Did you really come to see me in a big, dark room?" Gabe asked. "I didn't want you to see me, because I knew the room was a bad place. I remember thinking if I hid under the covers you'd go away. Was that a dream or was it real?"

"It was real," Libby said. "I came to get you out of the hospital and you wouldn't see me. You always were a stubborn man, Gabe Foster."

"And you always were an equally stubborn woman," he said. "I can't get over your bringing me here. The risk, Libby? Weren't you terrified of catching small-pox?"

"You don't think I was going to leave you there and let you die?" she demanded.

There was a long silence, then Gabe said, "So tell me about Hugh."

"We were only together a couple of months," Libby said quietly. "He died that same summer I brought him home."

"But I saw you with him last winter—you were dining at Browns in San Francisco," Gabe said in aston-ishment. "I didn't imagine it, did I? It was you?"

"It was I," Libby said, "but not my husband. I was dining with an old friend, Mark Hopkins."

"Mark Hopkins—you know him? I thought there was something familiar about him," Gabe said, "and I remember being surprised that Hugh looked so old."

"I'm surprised you noticed anything at all," Libby said dryly. "You were in a hurry to meet somebody, if I remember."

"I was?"

"A beautiful blond, or have you forgotten already?"

"Oh, Marcella," Gabe said with a smile. "Did you spy on me?"

"I just wanted to say hello to you, but apparently you were too busy to stop and talk."

"I didn't want to intrude. I thought I'd be an embarrassment if I greeted you and you had to explain me to a jealous husband."

"Oh, Gabe," Libby said, laughing hopelessly. "If you'd only known . . ."

"So what happened to Hugh?" Gabe asked.

"He was conscripted to put down an Indian uprising and he wasn't fit to go."

"Old Hugh went out to fight the Indians?" Gabe asked with amusement in his voice. Then, "I'm sorry. That was very undiplomatic of me. It must have been terrible for you."

"I survived," Libby said. "I've had to survive a lot of things since we last saw each other."

"But you seem to have survived well," Gabe said, "You've a string of workers at your beck and call and a property of your own."

"I've had to fight for that too," Libby said. Then it suddenly dawned on her that she had won her battle after all, at least for the time being. Nobody would be building a dam again in a hurry. "I'm supplying San Francisco with fruit and vegetables," she said proudly, "and I'm planning on doubling my acreage next spring."

"Who would have thought it when we first met in New Orleans and you wouldn't call me by my first name?" Gabe asked.

"I should have stuck to my principles a little harder," Libby said. "It would have caused fewer complications in my life."

Gabe laughed, then started coughing.

"You better rest until that chicken broth is ready," Libby said, "and I could do with a rest too. I've had no sleep for the past two nights and now an unexpected cold bath."

Gabe lay back and closed his eyes. "Thank you, Libby. You're an angel," he said. Libby smiled and tiptoed out, closing the door behind her.

After that, Gabe made a swift recovery. As news filtered down from the properties above, they heard the details of the tragedy. The continuous rain had been too much for Sheldon Rival's lake. It had overflowed its banks, sending flood waters swirling through his house. Rival had rounded up men to reinforce the dam with sandbags, but it was no use. The dam had suddenly collapsed, sweeping the men away with it. Pieces of furniture littered the whole length of the valley. Some of Rival's workers were never found. One or two lucky ones escaped death by grabbing passing trees or clinging desperately to floating timbers. Sheldon Rival's own body was not discovered for almost a week. It was wedged high in the fork of a tree and was bloated almost beyond recognition.

As Gabe regained his health Libby dared to hope that there was now nothing that could stop their reunion. Yet she sensed, as Gabe returned to his normal self, that there was a distance between them, a certain coldness that had not been there before.

Tentatively, she asked one day, "Gabe . . . is there someone in San Francisco who should be told you are here? Someone who'd worry about you?"

"Not that I can think of," Gabe said. "I was on my way up from San Francisco—a small matter of a duel. I had to make one of my hasty exits. Besides, San Francisco bored me after a while. I was going to pay another visit to the mines. A lot of miners idled by early rains with nothing to do all day. . . ." Libby smiled, but he went on seriously. "I ought to get on my way again as soon as possible. I wonder what happened to my horse?"

"I expect it's still in Sacramento," Libby said, "but I could lend you one if you really want to go?"

He sensed the unspoken meaning in her question. "You've already done enough for me, Libby," he said. "I can't impose on you any longer."

"Do you really think you are imposing on me?"

Gabe looked away. "I don't want your pity, Libby," he said.

"Pity?" she demanded. "Do you think I did this from pity? Do you really believe all I feel for you is pity?"

Gabe continued to look away. "I'm not a fool," he said. "I know what smallpox victims look like. Anyone who survives is horribly disfigured. You don't have to pretend any longer—I'm ugly as sin, aren't I?"

Libby sat down on the bed beside him. "You told me once that I didn't know what love was all about," she said quietly. "Now I'm telling you that you don't have much idea about love yourself. I love you, Gabe. Do you think I'd really care if you had half a face or one leg or no eyes? Do you think I'd love you any less?"

"But when a man has been blessed with good looks,

it's a sore blow to realize that he will be gazed upon with revulsion for the rest of his life," Gabe said, still staring at the wall. "I wouldn't want you to be put through that test again and again and eventually to find yourself wondering whether you shouldn't have deserved better. . . ."

"Gabriel Foster, you are, without doubt the vainest man alive," Libby said, laughing. "Stay there. I'll be back."

"Where are you going, Libby? Come back," he called after her. She ran to the main house and soon returned, carrying a little hand mirror. "Look," she said, handing it to him.

"I'd rather not."

"Coward."

"Very well," he said with resignation. Slowly, he brought the mirror to his face. Then he let out a great whoop of joy. "It's fine," he said incredulously. "My face is fine."

"Of course it is," Libby said, laughing.

"And all this time I've been lying here, imagining I looked like the ugliest man on God's earth," Gabe said, joining in her laughter. He reached out and took her hand. "I feel that I've been reborn, I've been given another chance. Do you believe in second chances, Libby?"

Libby looked into his eyes with longing. "I believe in miracles," she said. "After all that's kept us apart, Gabe, this is truly a miracle. Unless, of course, you still want that horse to ride away from here?"

His grip around her hand tightened. "You know what I've wanted from the moment I first saw you in that alleyway in New Orleans," he said. "I knew you were the woman for me right then. You've never been out of my thoughts or out of my dreams since. God knows I've tried hard enough to forget you."

"And I you," Libby said. She put her hand up to her cheek and brushed away a tear. "This is stupid," she said. "I've come through so much without crying and now I can't seem to stop."

Gabe put his finger to her cheek and brushed away the next tear himself. "There will be no more need for tears, my love," he said. "It's been a long hard road but it's all behind us now. We can make a fresh start together."

"Does that mean you're going to give up gambling and lead a good life this time around?" she asked, looking at him with a smile.

"Anything to make you happy," he said. "I'll become a missionary. I'll go around doing good works."

"Don't you dare change," she said, squeezing his hand. "I love you just the way you are, Gabe Foster."

"And I you, Libby Grenville," he said gently. "Do you think I am free enough from disease for you to risk giving me a kiss?"

"I'll risk it," she said and bent her head towards him.

Gently her lips met his, their eyes both open and gazing at each other with infinite tenderness. Then Gabe gave a choking sob, cupped Libby's head in his hands and crushed her mouth against his. Their lips remained locked together for what seemed like an eternity until Libby drew shakily away.

"I think that should be enough for now. Remember you've been very sick, Mr. Foster."

Gabe laughed. "You're the best tonic a man ever had, Mrs. Grenville." His face became serious. "I don't like that name, you know. I never have," he

said. "Do you think we could possibly change it to
Foster? A much nicer name—strong, reliable, American!"

"If you're asking me to marry you, Gabe Foster,"
she said, "I expect a better proposal than that."

"Very well." Gabe got up stiffly and dropped to his
knees. "I've never done this before," he said. "You'll
have to excuse me if I use the wrong words."

"There are no wrong words," Libby said, slipping
her hands into his.

"In which case, would you do me the honor, Libby
Grenville, of becoming my wife?"

Libby tried to answer but the words choked in her
throat. All she could do was nod solemnly, her eyes
bright with tears.

"So what do you think?" Gabe asked as she helped
him to his feet again. "This deserves a celebration. Am
I well enough to come out of my prison and meet my
favorite princesses again?"

"I think you are," she said. "They have been dying
to get in to see you all week. Ah Fong has had to
act as sheepdog and keep herding them back to
the house. I'll have him put a chair for you outside, so that you don't have to walk too far to begin
with."

Soon Gabe was installed in a wicker arm chair,
wrapped in blankets. "This is the first look I've had
of your house," he said. "It's very impressive. I was
expecting another shack like the one I've been in. I'd
no idea I was marrying a rich property owner, now
everyone will think I'm marrying you for your money
and they'll—" He broke off in mid sentence as the
girls came running from the main house, squealing
with delight.

"Mama wouldn't let us near you earlier," Bliss yelled. "Eden wanted to make stilts so we could peek in the window."

"Are you well again now?" Eden asked. "You're not still catching?"

"No, I'm not still catching." Gabe laughed. "And you have both grown so much that I wouldn't have recognized you. You've both turned into beautiful young ladies."

A loud cry echoed from the house.

"That's Noel. He wants to come outside too," Eden said. "Can I bring him?"

Libby nodded. Gabe looked up at her. "Noel?" he asked.

Eden appeared again with the squirming toddler. "He's just learned to walk," Bliss explained, "and now he hates to be carried anywhere."

"You'll get muddy feet, Noel," Eden told him.

"That's all right. Put him down," Libby said, laughing at the red-faced child.

"Oh, all right, walk to Mama," Eden said, dumping him at the bottom of the porch steps. Noel stood up cautiously and then began to stagger toward Libby, a look of triumph on his face. He came within a few feet, then stopped short when he saw Gabe, his mouth open, his large dark eyes wide with surprise.

"He doesn't see many strangers," Libby said, sweeping him up into her arms.

"Don't you like our brother?" Bliss asked. "He's a very nice baby."

Gabe was looking hard at Libby.

"He's not a baby anymore. He's going to be one year old," Eden corrected.

Libby felt her face flushing. Gabe's eyes lit up with amusement.

"Here," he said, "I think you'd better give Master Noel to me. The sooner we get to know each other, the better."

# CHAPTER
# 40

THE HOUSE WAS silent. Libby slipped on her robe and walked across to the window. The sun had not yet risen and the sky showed just a hint of red behind the dark rise of foothills. Between the house and the hills golden grass stretched unbroken, unfenced, as far as the eye could see. A giant landscape, Libby thought. A land of giants, no room for little people, like Hugh. Poor Hugh—this was definitely not the place for him. What had Mark Hopkins said? California ate people like Hugh for breakfast and spat out the bones. How lucky I'm so indigestible, she thought with a smile.

She looked back across the room, at the large oak bed where Gabe's dark head lay on the white lace pillow, still asleep. Am I doing the right thing, trying to tie you down? she wondered, looking at him with tenderness. I must make sure that the life we lead is right for both of us and not too narrow for you.

Gabe stirred. "Up so early?" he asked. "What time is it?"

"Close your eyes again, It's unlucky for the bride-

449

groom to see the bride on their wedding morning,"
Libby said.

Gabe chuckled. "If you expect me to go around
with my eyes closed until the judge arrives at two
o'clock, you can think again," he said. "Besides, we'll
have guests arriving all morning. I can hardly greet
them with closed eyes, can I?"

Libby came and sat beside him on the bed. "I hope
we're doing the right thing," she said.

"Getting married, you mean?" he asked. "Getting
cold feet at the last moment?"

She reached across and took his hand. "You know
I'm not," she said. "I'd follow you to the end of the
world and back. I meant having a big wedding party
when everyone knows you've been living here three
months already."

"It wasn't my fault the judge took so long to come
on his circuit," Gabe said. "Besides, they only have to
take one look at Noel to put two and two together.
He has my eyes and my hairline." He laughed and
grabbed her and pulled her to him, across the bed.
"This is California, Libby. It doesn't matter what anyone thinks. You're going to be a very rich and powerful lady—therefore everyone wants to be your friend.
They've all accepted, haven't they? They would have
turned you down if they were offended."

"You're right," she said, snuggling up against him.
"Now I've got you, nothing matters anymore."

He slipped his arm around her shoulders, holding
her close to him. "We'll have a good life, Libby," he
said. "I've certainly made my pile, as they say out here.
We can travel, go to Europe if we want to, build the
house you want. All things are possible."

Libby closed her eyes, forcing back the tears that

threatened to well up. Their peace was shattered as feet pattered down the hall and the girls burst in excitedly.

"Mama, guess what? There's a wagon outside with ice in it. It's all cold. The iceman gave me a piece."

"That's for the champagne," Libby said, sliding off the bed. "I'd no idea he'd be here so early. I'd better show him where to put it."

"Me see, Mama," Noel yelled, appearing in the doorway and lifting his arms to Libby.

"He's right, Libby," Gabe said, hastily pulling on a robe as he got out of bed. "Ice is a job for us men. Come on, son, we'll take care of it, won't we? These women can get on with their fancy hors d'oeuvres." He swept Noel up and deposited him on his shoulders. They ran off, Noel shrieking delightedly, down the hall.

"That's a dirty trick, Gabe Foster," Libby called after him. "If he weren't on your shoulders you know I'd have thrown something at you."

"Nonsense, from now on you've got to love, honor, and obey," Gabe yelled as he let the screen door slam behind him.

By midday a large crowd had assembled. The weather cooperated by being mild and sunny for January and Libby had had her Chinese workers, turned into waiters for the occasion, spread tables outside. Ah Fong, looking very distinguished in a new suit, had slipped easily into his role as maitre d'.

"Where did all these people come from?" Gabe muttered to Libby. "Did we invite this many?"

"I was surprised too," Libby whispered back. "I didn't realize we had that many friends. I suppose I must do business with more people than I thought."

Conchita bustled among the guests handing around plates until Libby grabbed her arm. "You're a guest too," she said. "Sit and enjoy yourself."

Conchita laughed nervously. "I happy when I do something," she said. "I not know how talk these peoples."

Don Miguel stepped up close to Libby. "When you have a moment, later, there is something I have to discuss with you," he said.

The judge arrived promptly at two. The ceremony was brief, the toasts were drunk, and then they sat down to eat in earnest. With Don Miguel's help they had rigged up a spit on which a whole young steer was roasting. There was hot spicy chili and potato salads from Libby's latest crop. Don Miguel sat beside Libby at one end of the long trestle table.

"What did you want to talk to me about?" she asked as the meal slowed to a conclusion.

"I am sorry to spoil a happy occasion with sad news," he said, "but today we are saying goodbye."

"You're leaving?" Libby asked in astonishment.

Don Miguel nodded sadly. "We are going back to Mexico, back to the village of my wife's parents."

"What happened?" Libby asked. "Is it the proof of ownership? Couldn't the lawyer help you?"

Don Miguel shrugged. "He tried," he said. "He was good man but . . ."

"He was a fool," Libby said. "We should have hired you a crooked lawyer, not a good man. I'll try and find one for you."

"Is too late," Don Miguel said. "This is now the land of the Yankee. We don't belong here anymore. They say my piece of paper no good. I must go to Mexico City and get documents to say this piece of paper is true land grant. This could take years and much money. If any Yankee want my land he just come and be squatter on it and it's his. This is no way to live. My wife is afraid. She wants to grow old and die at home."

"I'm very sorry, Don Miguel," Libby said. "You've been a very good friend to me. I'll miss you and your family very much. I am ashamed that it is my country's laws which have treated you so badly."

"It is always the way throughout history," Don Miguel said. "The powerful swallows up the weak. America is now powerful. Mexico is weak. My wife will be happy to go home and speak her own language with her own people."

"But what will happen to everything you've built here?" Libby asked.

"Ah, about this I wish to speak to you," Don Miguel said. "I wish to know if you want to buy my house and my land. I would rather it went to you than be taken by crooked Yankees."

"I'll have to talk to my husband, of course," Libby said, glancing down the table at Gabe, "but I think that we would be fools not to take your offer."

She didn't have a chance to mention anything to Gabe until early evening, when some guests took their leave and others were strolling down on the riverbank.

"If you want the house, buy it," he said, putting his arm around her shoulder. "I'm not going to interfere with any of your business decisions after you've shown such aptitude for making money. And anything that gets me out of making millions of adobe bricks myself sounds like a great idea."

Libby looked up at him and smiled. "As if you've ever done a day's labor in your life," she said.

"Ah, but I'm a reformed man now," Gabe said seriously. "I've given up all of my wanton ways. From now on I'm going to be a farmer and live by honest labor and the sweat of my brow. . . ."

"That will be the day, Gabe Foster," Libby said, turning to wrap her arms around his neck. "If I'd wanted to marry a boring, honest farmer, I'd have done so long ago. Just because you're not going to frequent any more gambling dens doesn't mean you can't put your considerable talents to good use."

"Meaning what?" he asked, his eyes teasing hers.

"You know very well what I mean. You've already got property in San Francisco. I've got those lots which we should start to build on. I can see you as a future property baron."

Gabe nodded. "Yes, I think that would suit me rather well. I think we should also make Don Miguel an offer for his cattle herd. I might enjoy playing cowboy too."

"I can see you doing that," Libby said, laughing. "At least it would keep you occupied when we're up here at the farm. You'd soon get bored pulling weeds."

"As if I could ever get bored with you," Gabe said, pulling her close to him and brushing his lips against her hair. "You might be a lot of things, Libby Grenville Foster, but you will never be boring."

Libby laughed, then straightened up as she saw a lone figure picking his way along the path. "There's Mr. Hopkins come to find us," she said. "We should ask his advice about those lots in San Francisco."

"A beautiful country," Mark said as he walked up to join them. "All that expanse waiting to be settled."

"And all those settlers waiting to buy their supplies from your store," Gabe added.

Mark nodded in agreement. "The store is just the

beginning. I've got so many plans."

"More stores?" Gabe asked.

"Communications," Mark said. "They will be the key. What happens in winter here? The roads become impassable and all commerce slows to a halt. The time is rapidly coming when California will need a railroad. And not just within the state, but to link it with the outside world."

"You think that's possible—a railroad across the mountains?" Libby asked, remembering their trip.

"Eventually," Mark Hopkins said. "It will be hard, but I have spoken to engineers and I think it will be possible. Just think how it would change the face of California. . . ."

"More settlers coming in," Libby said.

"And a way to send your produce back to the States," Mark added. "They could be eating your melons and peaches in New York."

"In the meantime," Libby said, "what about those lots you purchased for me. Have they appreciated at all?"

"Appreciated?" Mark Hopkins said. "They've gone up at least threefold."

"Then I should sell?"

"Absolutely not. Buy more, if you have the money to spare and in five years time they'll be worth ten times what you paid for them. And then," he said, stroking his beard meditatively, "then you can put the money in my new railroad and that alone will make you a millionaire."

"Then they'll all say I only married her for her money," Gabe said, squeezing Libby's hand.

"This is California," Libby said, laughing. "Who cares what they say?"

Janet Quin-Harkin is a best-selling author of over fifty young adult books and one adult novel. Historical accuracy is paramount, so a great deal of her time is spent researching her writing. She earned a degree in Modern Languages from the University of London and currently lives with her husband and four children in northern California, close to the gold country.

# ▤ HarperPaperbacks *By Mail*